BOY FROM THE

NORTH COUNTRY

BOY FROM THE NORTH COUNTRY

A Novel

SAM SUSSMAN

Penguin Press | New York | 2025

PENGUIN PRESS
An imprint of Penguin Random House LLC
1745 Broadway, New York, NY 10019
penguinrandomhouse.com

Copyright © 2025 by Sam Evan Sussman

Penguin Random House values and supports copyright. Copyright fuels creativity, encourages diverse voices, promotes free speech, and creates a vibrant culture. Thank you for buying an authorized edition of this book and for complying with copyright laws by not reproducing, scanning, or distributing any part of it in any form without permission. You are supporting writers and allowing Penguin Random House to continue to publish books for every reader. Please note that no part of this book may be used or reproduced in any manner for the purpose of training artificial intelligence technologies or systems.

PP colophon is a registered trademark of Penguin Random House LLC.

"Even when I am in Kyoto . . ." haiku by Bashō from *The Essential Haiku: Versions of Bashō, Buson & Issa*, edited and with verse translations by Robert Hass, translation copyright © 1994 by Robert Hass. Used by permission of HarperCollins Publishers.

Excerpt from "Footnote to Howl" from *Collected Poems 1947–1980* by Allen Ginsberg, copyright © 1984 by Allen Ginsberg. Used by permission of HarperCollins Publishers.

Excerpt from *The Narrow Road to the Deep North and Other Travel Sketches* by Matsuo Bashō, copyright © 1966 by Nobuyuki Yuasa. Reprinted by permission of Nobuyuki Yuasa and Penguin Books Limited.

Designed by Nerylsa Dijol

LIBRARY OF CONGRESS CATALOGING-IN-PUBLICATION DATA
Names: Sussman, Sam Evan, author.
Title: Boy from the North Country : a novel / Sam Sussman.
Description: New York : Penguin Press, 2025. | Summary: "An auto-fictional novel about the courage and resilience of motherhood as well as a window into the life of Bob Dylan at a peak moment of his creative output" —Provided by publisher.
Identifiers: LCCN 2024050167 (print) | LCCN 2024050168 (ebook) | ISBN 9780593835050 (hardcover) | ISBN 9780593835067 (ebook)
Subjects: LCSH: Sussman, Sam Evan, author. | Dylan, Bob, 1941- —Fiction. | Motherhood—Fiction. | LCGFT: Autobiographical fiction. | Novels.
Classification: LCC PS3619.U86 B69 2025 (print) | LCC PS3619.U86 (ebook) | DDC 813/.6—dc23/eng/20241112
LC record available at https://lccn.loc.gov/2024050167
LC ebook record available at https://lccn.loc.gov/2024050168

Printed in the United States of America
2nd Printing

This is a work of fiction. Apart from the well-known actual people, events, and locales that figure into the narrative, all names, characters, places, and incidents are the products of the author's imagination or are used fictitiously.

The authorized representative in the EU for product safety and compliance is Penguin Random House Ireland, Morrison Chambers, 32 Nassau Street, Dublin D02 YH68, Ireland, https://eu-contact.penguin.ie.

For my mother

It is good to thank Adonai,
and to sing of Your name, O Most High;
To tell of Your lovingkindness
in the morning and Your faithfulness by night;
With ten strings, with the lyre,
with a solemn sound upon the harp.
For You have made me
glad through Your works, Adonai;
I exult in the works of Your hands.

—Book of Psalms, Tehillim 92

We are here to take the pieces of the universe that we are given, burnish them with love, and return them in better condition than we received them.

—Fran Djuna Sussman

DAWN

One

My mother lived her own life. She was strong-willed and practiced in forging her own path. She had her private struggles and was used to enduring difficulty alone. Yet as I stood in the doorway of her home, one summer evening when I was twenty-six, nothing could have prepared me for what she had concealed.

A sea-blue dress hung from her gaunt shoulders. Her bare arms, usually lean with muscle, were flaccid and pale. Her hair, auburn the last time I had seen her, was graying and brittle. She smiled at me with the warmth she could always convey with ease.

I stumbled forward and hugged her. Her head to my chest, her arms around me, I listened to her steady breaths. She was my mother. She could not get cancer. If she did, she would tell me right away. But she did have cancer, and she had not told me until the phone call twenty-four hours before, midnight London time, her voice calm as she asked if I could fly home as soon as possible. Now, weary from the transatlantic flight and two-hour drive to her home in upstate New York, I held her closer to me.

We drew apart. Her hazel eyes settled in mine, joyful as she said,

"Did you see the peonies along the driveway, Evan? They're having their best year of the decade."

"Mom. Why haven't you told me you're sick?"

"Like I said on the phone," she said evenly, "the surgery is tomorrow morning."

"How long have you known?"

"I thought," she said, "we could have dinner outside. It's such a lovely evening."

She turned from me and passed through the sliding door. My mother, who made sure every leaf of salad she consumed was locally grown and every fish wild-caught, who could explain in charming detail the benefits of kale or coconut oil, who brewed her own kombucha, who practiced yoga each morning and meditated each evening, who jumped rope and lifted dumbbells, who wrote a health column for the regional newspaper, who as a holistic health practitioner spent her days with clients who came to her from across the Northeast, who at sixty-three was often mistaken for being in her forties—how had cancer infiltrated her body?

I followed her into the evening. The field between the farmhouse and woods had recently been mowed, and the smell of cut grass was rich in the August air. Pine trees swayed over the house. Paws tapped on the stone walkway. I turned to see Lucy prancing toward me, all nine pounds of toy fox terrier, her silken ears raised, her pupils as lively as any human eyes. "Are you a dog?" I asked, kneeling to accept her kisses.

The three of us walked silently up the hill behind the house. We were in my mother's landscape. White peonies swayed in flower beds. The crab apple tree held its twisted pose like an elegant dancer. Evening light fell on the maroon barn from which we had retrieved eggs from our hens on the mornings of my childhood. Five ash trees rose from the earth as if the fingers of an open hand. My mother had arranged the cedar table and wicker chairs on the hilltop, facing across the valley, toward the mountain. The only visible human structure in the valley was our house, its green siding blending into the hills.

I glanced at my mother, concerned that the walk might have caused her discomfort. She smiled, setting her hand gently on my shoulder. White clouds kissed in the sapphire sky.

Lucy scampered ahead of us, drawn to the smells rising from the table. My mother had spared no effort in preparing this feast. Rings of lemon lay atop seared tofu. Clay pans offered roasted eggplant, cauliflower, butternut squash, portobello mushroom. A ceramic bowl held blackberries, boysenberries, and Concord grapes, which she must have picked from the vines in our woods. My favorite white wine from the vineyard in town was wrapped in cloth to preserve its chill, thin beads of condensation dripping down the neck of the bottle.

"The berries have been wonderful this summer," my mother said, easing herself into the wicker chair. Lucy leapt onto her lap and tucked her little head over my mother's forearm. She reached for the blackberries, each berry leaving its delicate purple stain on her fingers, and I thought by instinct of childhood mornings I ran shirtless out of the house, sunlight on my naked skin as I hurried through the woods, eager to devour all the berries I could find.

"Try the cauliflower, it's so flavorful," she said, offering me the roasted vegetable in the clutches of a wooden server. "The butternut squash, too. It makes me think back to the first summer we were here, and every road seemed to lead to a farmstand. Oh! I forgot the peaches inside. You won't believe how sweet they are this year."

She made to rise, and I touched her arm, trying to fathom that, despite her tranquil expression, within my mother was a cancerous tumor that had withered her body and begun to gray her hair. Tomorrow morning, at sunrise, we would drive into Manhattan, where a medical team intended to drug her unconscious and cut open her body with technology so complex it had no rooting in ordinary parlance. The articles I had read while waiting to board the plane in London suggested that she could remain in bed as long as a week after surgery. Loved ones should be prepared to assist with walking and eating. She needed every possible moment of rest before the surgery. Over her shoulder I could see the barn, from which she must have hauled the wooden table and chairs at immense physical expense. She had driven to the farmer's market and spent hours preparing our dinner. She had made six or seven trips from the house up the hill, carrying the heavy clay pans to the table. Nothing could justify the effort she had exerted on my behalf.

"Mom, please sit. You need to rest."

"I need," she said firmly, "to enjoy dinner with my son."

She reached for the wine and poured the cool amber liquid into my glass. She nodded to the bowl of fruit, and I reached for grapes, biting into the sour skin, then the sweet pulp. I had been too anxious to eat in the twenty-four hours since I glanced at my phone in the boisterous London bar and saw eight missed calls from my mother. Now, exhausted from the rushed departure, I devoured moist tofu, zucchini, red cabbage.

My mother ate nothing. She reclined in her wooden chair, gazing at me.

The valley was ablaze with the last evening light. Dandelions lay in yellow patches across the lawn. A deer loped across the trail that led into the forest, and Lucy leapt from my mother's lap to give chase. My mother sighed contentedly. I reached for more squash, each bite ripe with the flavor of a vegetable grown less than a mile from where we sat.

Through the valley echoed the familiar clatter of the freight train. "Can you hear the cardinal?" my mother asked. "She always sings as the sun falls." And I could, the bird chirping as she flew over the woods.

She reached across the table to give me another slice of roasted cauliflower.

"It's nice," she smiled, "to have you home."

She looked at me with her bright hazel eyes, and I felt the guilt that lingered on my visits home. In my teenage years I had felt suffocated by the remoteness of the town and promised myself that I would leave Goshen to discover places where people lived and life happened. I had completed a literature degree at Oxford, then moved from city to city—Berlin, Jerusalem, London—working odd jobs and never staying long in one place. At eighteen, I had never left upstate New York; at twenty-six, I returned only occasionally to visit my mother.

We spoke by video every Sunday. We texted most days. But I had silently dictated the terms of our relationship. I was the son who lived abroad.

Pine trees swayed over the farmhouse. With each moment London seemed farther away. Last night's phone call had been so brief and, to me, so shocking that we had not discussed how long I would stay. My mother had cancer. I would have to tell friends I was home for the summer. Once the word was spoken it would accumulate an irreversible solidity, the disease within her body becoming a social fact, the explanation of my absence in London repeated by friends and acquaintances. I couldn't say when I might return. Looking at the wrinkles in her face, which seemed to have aged a decade in the two months since we had seen one another, I knew we were no longer living within the recognizable rhythm of time.

"I'll be here," I said abruptly, "as long as you need."

Lucy pranced back to us, leapt for a bite of tofu in my mother's palm, and trotted a celebratory circle around the table. My mother looked at me uncertainly. As if the elegant facade of the evening was giving way to what awaited in the morning. Or perhaps I was imagining this. I was projecting onto her what I felt, my discomfort with this increasingly apparent fact: she had known for some time that she was ill. She had asked to speak by phone rather than video the last two Sundays to conceal her appearance. I wanted an explanation. To argue, if necessary. My mother smiled, sunlight and shadow on her face. I could not bring myself to rupture the beauty of her evening.

Nor could I make ordinary conversation. I wanted to say something. To speak as we usually spoke. To tell or ask about a film or book. To listen to her talk about a patient who had come to see her with an unusual story. To share a memory. But I said nothing.

She withdrew the fraying, homemade pot holder from beneath the pan of cauliflower and said, "Do you remember your knitting craze?"

I laughed, with no idea what she meant.

"You don't remember? You were in second grade. You knit me a pot holder every holiday. On my birthday, you gave me a pot holder. Then Hanukkah, another pot holder. Christmas? A pot holder. Honey, you gave me a pot holder on New Year's Day. You were such a talented knitter. Look at how well this one has held up."

She handed me the pot holder, the aging crimson and white yarn soft to the touch. No memory came to mind.

My mother looked at me with that same hesitant expression, and I felt once more the urgency of the plane gathering speed on the London runway moments before cell service was lost to the clouds. I had reached for my phone and texted her: *Love you more than anything. I will be with you every step of the way.*

Now I was with her and didn't know what to say.

Dusk was falling over the hills. The mountain ridges had vanished into the night. The clay pans were nearly emptied, only the cauliflower stalks and squash skin uneaten. A coyote howled and Lucy barked in reply. My mother needed to rest before our early morning drive into the city.

"Thank you for such a lovely dinner, Mom. Why don't you rest, and I'll clean up."

"It's wonderful having you home, Evan," she said, looking into my eyes. "You might even say that time with you is my favorite part of being alive."

Two

I set the last dish on the drying rack, water dripping off the clean glass into the sink. Wind rustled in the trees beyond the kitchen window. The house was silent, my mother and Lucy asleep. Shadow fell across the stairs that led to my childhood bedroom, on the second floor, facing east onto the mountains. The room appeared smaller than in memory, as it often did when I returned home. Dim light fell onto the antique dresser and bookshelf arranged against the near wall. It felt inconceivable that the vastness of my childhood imagination and teenage disorientation had fit between these walls. That so much of my inner life had existed within the books and CDs on the shelf. That every dream I could recall from those years had been experienced in this narrow bed, which, I saw, my mother had made for my arrival. It was midnight at the house, five in the morning London time. I needed to crawl beneath the blankets and let my mind go blank.

Lying in bed, eyes closed, arms tossed limply overhead, all I could think of was the illness my mother had concealed from me. We were each supposed to be the person the other trusted most. The last weeks must have been terrifying for her. She had kept it from me.

Did she think a lie by omission was different from any other form of deception? Maybe I wasn't being understanding enough. She must have planned to tell me, then decided it wasn't yet time. She was still looking into treatments, reading medical literature as she staved off exhaustion after a day with clients, emailing speakers she met at a conference in the Berkshires, phoning friends of friends. I drew the covers overhead, trying to sleep. She had waited to tell me until the last possible moment, the surgery there was no practical way for her to manage alone.

But my mother always had her secrets. I stood out of bed, too anxious to sleep. The wooden floorboards creaked as I crossed the darkness. I raised the window and the cool night touched my tired eyes. Fireflies shone and died in the dark. The silhouette of mountains glimmered on the horizon. All families have subjects that are understood to be better not discussed and we were no different. My eyes shifted to the shelf of neatly ordered CDs, settling on the face of the man my mother and I had not discussed for more than ten years. His mess of brown curls and angled chin resembled mine. For years, I had done all I could not to think of that man. It was easier to refuse my thoughts about him when I was abroad, in the life I had made for myself. I had rarely spoken his name since leaving home.

On the shelf were the earmuff headphones and worn portable player I had carried everywhere as a teenager. I felt weary, my defenses weakened by the long day of travel and shock of my mother's illness. I could feel him in the room with me, where I had always felt closest to him. I reached for his CD and set the disc in the groove. Lifting the headphones to my ears, I was drifting back in memory to a spring night I was fifteen and stood sleepless at my bedroom window at four in the morning, headphones over my untamed hair.

I want you, Dylan sang, *I want you so bad.*

The moon glowed silver in the dark sky and possibility coursed through me. Beyond the window were black mountains and pine trees. Fifteen years old, gazing into the night, I wanted nothing more than to lift myself beyond those hills, climb onto the farmhouse roof and let the music carry me away from everything I knew too well. There was nothing for me in Goshen, just cows and church steeples. I knew that over the mountains and across the river was New York City. I could almost hear heartbroken actors feuding with destiny, music gathering like steam on a café window, a poet in a torn coat pleading with beauty on a street corner.

I glanced at my notebook. Half-formed stanzas scattered across the page, impulses that came to me in the night. I needed to write my way out of Goshen. At school I was ridiculed for being vegetarian, bookish, Jewish. I was a shy kid scribbling poetry into a marble composition book in the last row of class, hoping nobody looked my way. We hadn't had television or internet at the farmhouse most of my childhood, and I'd always been mocked for being unfamiliar with video games, sitcoms, popular films. I didn't fit in with the prevailing ethos in Goshen: masculine, rough-and-tumble. My mother had recently demanded to meet with the school principal after I'd been beaten badly by classmates, only for him to shrug off the incident, explaining that boys are boys. The implication was that I should fight back or stop complaining; the school certainly wasn't going to get involved in a matter as straightforward as three students punching another until he bled from the mouth.

Being bookish didn't help me with most teachers. One had failed me on every paper that year, accusing me of plagiarism because I had used words such as *apposite* and *macabre*. She asked how I could know words she didn't, then laughed at me when I said, "From reading."

There was one teacher who was kind to me. She had taken me aside after I handed in my first paper in her English class, and said, "Keep writing, Evan. It will take you somewhere."

Wind swept through the high grass. How strange to think that the written word could change my life, that the symbols I pressed onto the page could make me other than I was. I had never admitted to anyone that my ambition was to become a writer. I had never let anyone read my poetry. My mother had once found several pages in the printer and I'd wanted to die of embarrassment. She said the language was exceptional and I had a natural gift. Of course she said that. I was her son.

I want you, Dylan sang into my headphones, *I want you so bad.*

I'd been listening to his music since the year before, when my geology teacher told me I looked like him. Until that day I'd never heard of Dylan. After class the teacher sat at his desktop computer and typed Dylan's name into the search bar. I'd leaned over his shoulder and looked at the screen. I could see what he meant about our resemblance. It was uncanny looking at Dylan's image. I knew that face. We had the same smile, a youthful cocksure grin.

"He's a well-known musician," the geology teacher said, "some say a poet. You might like his songs."

That night I'd searched for Dylan's music on my mother's shelves of CDs and old records, well-kept in their original sleeves: jazz, classical, folk, complete operas on eight-track albums. She didn't have anything by Dylan. A few days later I rode my bike to the music store two towns away and bought *Blonde on Blonde* for fourteen dollars. I'd biked home over the hills with my earmuff headphones clamped over my brown curls, the CD player in my backpack, Dylan's lyrics taking me into another world. I'd never heard anything like his music. Standing at my bedroom window that night, looking at the mountain ridges, I could feel his every word moving through me like a diamond bullet fired straight through my heart. He didn't write anything concrete, just feelings and impressions of everything he lived. He sang about dreamy visions, historical events, something that happened to me yesterday in my own mind. He was unlike any writer I'd encountered. His language was a ladder between heaven and earth. With his folk-song voice and impressionistic lyrics he was singing to me from the Appalachian hills, from nineteenth-century Paris, from a train hurtling through the night. Soon I was biking back to the music store, imbibing more: *The Freewheelin' Bob Dylan, Highway 61 Revisited, Blood on the Tracks, Slow Train Coming, Infidels*. Every time I thought I understood Dylan he changed track, slipped into another artistic register. He sang torrid love songs, folk ballads, biblical mysticism, epic poems of intimate emotion, loyalty, betrayal, yearning, where the instrumentals and words came together into a language you'd never heard. I found a book of his lyrics and studied every mesmerizing page. He toyed with words so easily, just as he did with myth and character. The ragman drawing circles up and down the block—who the hell was that? It was me, of course. It was anyone listening to the song.

I wanted to know everything about this man. In the school library I found his memoir, *Chronicles: Volume One*, and read it in two nights. I was thrilled to learn that Dylan came from farmland of his own, a town in rural Minnesota that wasn't so different from Goshen. He'd been called east by the music, taken a freight train across the country to Manhattan and written his way into a life worth living. He was what it meant to be an artist, to transform yourself through song. He'd slept in dime stores and bus stations, written conclusions on the subway walls. He'd turned people against racism and war with his songs. He lived as I dreamt of living, like a bard from ancient times, traveling to distant lands and transforming his experiences into stories for the strangers he met along the way. He was a reclusive poet, an artistic outlaw, and, like me, a Jew. He was never less than an individual.

    Coyote howled in the night. The moon cast its silver glow over the hills. I had to flee Goshen as Dylan had fled Minnesota. I had to find that world of art and self-creation that Dylan had made his own. I'd never met an artist of any kind. My mother had taken me to see theater in New York City once a year when I was young. She had read to me when I was a child, passing on her love of literature. Beyond what she'd taught me, I'd had a sheltered life in our woods.

    There had to be people like me out there and I would write my way to them. Dylan had charged into New York when he wasn't much older than I was, arriving with nothing more than his guitar and pen. He'd devoted himself to something holy and come out the other side. When he sang that you've got to play your harp until your lips bleed, I knew he was telling me how to become a writer. Leaning through the open window, I could feel Dylan's lyrics and the luminous moon and my desire to describe the beauty of the hills all coming together inside me.

    That afternoon my history teacher had again said that I looked like Dylan's *spitting image*. He wasn't the first to use the phrase. As pure language the idiom didn't cohere for me. Dylan would never use it. The idea was that people spit out children, yet the imagery didn't work. The only thing close to parental spitting I could think of was God breathing into the earthy clay out of which he created Adam "in his image." I'd read that in the Torah my mother gave me on my thirteenth birthday, along with a note about how it wasn't necessary to take the theology literally, but any writer should know biblical allusion. I'd told her I was no more interested in religious allusion than I was in religious delusion. Then I started reading the Torah and had to admit to her that it made some interesting observations.

BOY FROM THE NORTH COUNTRY

The history teacher wasn't the only person to emphasize my resemblance to Dylan. Another teacher had recently emailed me in the middle of the night to say he was watching a documentary on Dylan and could not stop thinking about how much I looked like him. Strangers had stopped me in the gas station and health food store to tell me that I resembled him.

The clatter of the freight train echoed through the valley. Turning from the window I felt my way through the darkness for the book of Dylan lyrics near my pillow. His photograph shone through the room. I'd seen his expression in my eyes, that hint of sadness I knew all too well. My curls were growing off his head. Looking at his photographs across the years was like watching myself grow up. He was lean like me, my weight and height, slouching with the same shy confidence. He even talked like me, bouncing in his seat, nodding before he gave irreverence in place of an answer. We had the same baritone voice, sometimes tending toward a mumble or slur.

I had reason to believe my mother had once met him.

A few months before, Luke, my stepfather, had been driving me into town when "Like a Rolling Stone" came on the radio. I murmured the lyrics, looking out the window onto green hills and the russet barn at the turn in the road. Luke said, "There's a lyric in there about your mother."

I turned to him, unable to say anything. The idea was too outlandish for me to think straight.

"They used to know each other," he said. "In her early New York days."

Dylan's music meant nothing to Luke, but there was pride in his voice that his wife had once known a rock star, as if this raised her worth in his eyes. I didn't believe him. I loved my mother, but there was no chance someone as ordinary as her could have known Dylan. It was like claiming she had known King Arthur or Shakespeare. That was to say nothing of the suggestion in Luke's tone and glance: that my mother and Dylan once had an intimate relationship, one worthy of him writing a lyric for her. Luke often embellished. He'd once led me to believe he had played varsity basketball for the University of Texas at Austin, an NCAA powerhouse, only for it to emerge months later that he had played on the intramural team. Maybe my mother had met Dylan at a concert or for a moment on the street. Luke was wrong that any lyric in "Like a Rolling Stone" could have been about her. Dylan had released that song in the summer of 1965, when my mother was eleven years old.

Still, the idea was enthralling. My mother and Dylan.

Two nights later I made my voice as innocent as possible and asked my mother if she had ever known Dylan. She laughed warmly, as if the idea was too strange to consider. And it was. We lived in a modest farmhouse up a half-mile gravel drive in a remote town in rural New York. We didn't know anyone whose life was larger than ordinary. We certainly didn't know anyone in the cultured class—writers, professors, musicians. Even if she had a chance to meet someone like Dylan, my mother wasn't the sort of person who cared about celebrity or status. She wouldn't have gone out of her way to know someone because of their name. The suggestion that she could have had an intimate relationship with Dylan was even less believable. My mother had been falling in love for as long as I could remember, but never with anyone who had much artistic sensibility. She preferred men who had lived difficult lives, recovered alcoholics who talked earnestly about wanting to become a better man, as Luke did each Sunday as we drove home from church. I had come to love Luke since he married my mother when I was nine. He was intelligent, an engineer who could solve math problems in his head faster than I could with a calculator. He often said that if he'd managed his drinking earlier in life, he would have made a fortune in the tech boom rather than scrambling from job to job. Either way, his idea of great artistic heights was a Jim Carrey comedy. It wasn't plausible that a woman who had fallen in love with him could have had a relationship with the mythical musician whose songs came through my headphones. Not once in all the times she'd heard me listening to Dylan had my mother ever said anything about him. If she didn't appreciate the music, how could she have known the man?

More than this, the Dylan whose music I loved didn't seem like a living person anyone could have once known. He seemed more story than fact, more myth than man.

I didn't press the matter. My mother rarely discussed her past, like it was someone else's life and she had no right to share.

One evening, not long after Luke's remark, my mother and I stopped for gas at a station on the outskirts of town. I stood beside the car, holding the gas nozzle to the tank in the evening light. A man at the pump ahead glanced at me. He wore a blue dress shirt, faded jeans, and a curious expression. "Know who you look like?" he called out. "Uncanny, the way you look like him. Bob Dylan. You know his music?"

My mother leaned through the open car window, looking uneasily at the man.

"No," I told him, trying to end the conversation.

"Well, give a listen," the man said. "He's one of the best there is. And you're his image, dead to rights."

The trigger clicked on the gas nozzle. I nodded to the man and set the nozzle back on the pump. My mother looked through the windshield to the vanishing point where the highway met the deepening blue sky, lost in one of her meditative spells. I closed the passenger door behind me and handed back her few dollars of change. She started up the car and drove along the main street, past the post office and deli, the obsolete railroad station and redbrick bank. She halted at the traffic light in the center of town. We were silent a long moment.

"Luke says you used to know him," I said.

I glanced tentatively at her, waiting for her to laugh off the idea, as she had the first time I'd asked. Her eyes seemed far away. She said nothing.

That night, standing at my bedroom window, staring between Dylan's photograph in the book of lyrics and my reflection in the window, I thought of my mother's distant expression in the car. If she never knew Dylan, why had she not simply said so? I couldn't help but wonder: if my mother had known Dylan, could it be pure coincidence that I resembled him?

I glanced at the windowpane. In my reflection I saw my mother's features and Dylan's merging into mine. She seemed to have known him. Strangers who weren't aware of this insisted that I looked like him. My mother wouldn't talk about him. This couldn't all be happenstance. I could feel Dylan within me. We understood one another even if we had never met. His songs had given me a way to feel and live. He was the father I was meant to have. The idea was otherworldly. Everything that had been difficult in my life was insignificant in the light of this possibility: I could have a lineage straight from the most gifted poet of the age. If Dylan was my father, I was fated for something greater than I could imagine. With his blood in my veins nothing could stop me leaving Goshen and achieving my destiny.

It wasn't possible. Beyond the sheer implausibility of the idea, the timing didn't work. Luke had said my mother knew Dylan in her early New York days. That would mean the mid-1970s. She had given birth to me in January 1991. It wasn't as if she could have carried on a secret fifteen-year relationship with the most celebrated musician of his generation. I was telling myself a story to ease the pain left by the fathers I had lost. I never would have wondered this way about Dylan if my biological father, Simon, had not divorced my mother when I was two. She had always told me that he had fallen in love with another woman, with whom he had gone on to raise other children. I wouldn't have needed Dylan as an imagined father if Roger had not broken his engagement to my mother while I was in the hospital amid a medical emergency that nearly ended my life at six. Other men had come through our lives, winning my mother's trust just long enough for me to get ideas in my head about a new father. It was never long before that man left, too.

Of course I wanted a story larger than all that loss.

There was one memory that complicated everything. I tried not to trust the memory too much. I tried not to dwell on it. But this is what I remembered: One morning when I was four or five years old, my mother and I walked up the hill to the barn to collect our morning eggs. A man with scraggly hair stood by the barn, tossing feed to the chickens. My mother told me to go back inside the house. They talked behind the barn for what felt like hours. Later he came into the house, lifted me from the sofa, and held me a long moment, his eyes in mine.

In my memory the man looked like Dylan. But I couldn't be sure. I knew that I could be projecting onto that shadowy figure what I wanted to believe.

IF MY MOTHER'S SILENCE had never faltered, the story might have ended there. Better yet, there would have been no story. My mother's link to Dylan and my resemblance to him would have remained an inexplicable myth, one of those otherworldly elements of life that exist only for the purpose of remaining unexplained. Dylan would have been for me what he was for tens of millions of others: a fabled inspiration, a series of dreams.

But my mother chose to end her silence.

It was the week she ordered Luke to leave the farmhouse, that spring I was fifteen. We were driving a winding back road through the night to the therapist she insisted I see. I was sitting beside her in the passenger seat, my earmuff headphones clamped over my ears, Dylan's soothing voice asking if this could really be the end. It had to be. Everything I knew was falling apart and I had to flee the rubble. Luke had been the first man to overcome my skepticism that he would be one more father passing temporarily through my life, making promises he couldn't keep. Now he'd proven that I never should have trusted him. After what I'd witnessed Luke do to my mother I never wanted to see him again. I looked onto the darkness beyond the car window. There was nothing but fields and hills as far as I could see. I wasn't meant to live forever on this prairie. Through the headphones I could hear something more than the lyrics, a voice calling my own. I'd head to New York as Dylan had. I could change my name as he'd done. The voice was calling to me, louder now, there was no time to wait. I glanced at my mother and saw her lips moving. I took off my headphones.

"I'm not afraid to be a fool," she said. "Love makes fools of us all. But the greatest fool is the one so afraid of loss that she never lets herself love."

"Cool," I said. "Can the next guy be funny? Luke had a great jump shot, but his sense of humor was, on his best day, like a four out of ten."

"Keep your heart open to him," she said. "He can still find a place in your life."

Find a place in my life? Luke was an animal I never wanted to see again. What had been the purpose of six years of feeling like his son, playing basketball together in the driveway until dusk, surprising my mother with a curry tofu dinner as she walked upstairs after a long day with clients? God, who would come next? I couldn't take any more of the cycle: my mother's eyes kaleidoscopic as she described everything wonderful about a new man, my initial caution, then acting like a family, before the escalating difficulties and eventual teary conversation on the sofa about how, no matter what happened, my mother and I would always have each other.

"What are you listening to?" she asked. I held one of the earpieces toward her and Dylan's harmonica sounded tinnily between us.

She was silent a long moment.

Then she said, "I knew him."

I didn't dare look at her. I was certain that if I said one wrong word she would retreat into her silence.

"When I lived in the city. We met in a painting class. He started spending time at my place, playing me songs. It was wonderful, for a while."

She had known him. Not in passing, not for a moment. *He started spending time at my place.* The man whose image I had spent hours studying, tracing his similarities to me. The man who, more than any other, lived as I wanted to live. I needed to know every detail. I needed to know what mattered most.

"For a while?" I heard myself say.

"Well, a year was enough to know it wasn't right for me. He—"

"*You* ended things?"

"He wasn't right for me, and—"

"Like you've ever been a good judge of which men are right for you!"

"Excuse me?" She glared at me, indignation in her bright eyes. "I'm trying my best. I'm doing what I think is right for both of us. It's hard enough without your judgment!"

I clamped the headphones over my ears. My mother's eyes pierced the night.

Her lips formed the shape of my name. I lifted an earphone.

"Sorry I shouted," she said. "I know this is hard on you. All that matters to me is that you know how much I love you."

"I don't believe in love," I said. "If you weren't blinded by love, you wouldn't have married an abusive alcoholic, would you? Maybe all our problems start with you believing—"

"Evan, please—"

"Maybe there's a reason love has been difficult for you. Maybe you don't deserve it."

The car glided through the night. I hated my cruelty but I hated my mother more.

"Evan," she said. "You can despise me. You can resent me. You can question my choices. You can forget every word I've ever said. You can choose not to bury me when I die. But don't you ever forget that nothing in this life is holier than love."

"Did you ever see Dylan again?"

It was the only question that mattered.

"I did," she said, a quickness to her voice. She drove faster through the night, her eyes avoiding mine. "He called me years later. Showed up at my place and it was like no time had passed. That was the spring before you were born."

My mother's words lingered between us. I looked in the rearview mirror at my brown curls and angled face, measuring the time between her encounter with Dylan that spring and my birth the following January, thinking of the teachers and strangers who told me that I resembled him, feeling those nine months rearranging everything I knew about myself. I turned to my mother to clarify her story, and she stopped the car at a brick building on the desolate road, where a sign named the therapist I was supposed to meet that night. She said, "We're here."

"Mom?" She wouldn't meet my eye. "Is he—"

"I shouldn't have gotten caught in the past," she said, looking straight ahead. "What matters in life is whether people are there for you. When you suffer, when you thrive, who is there to love you as you deserve to be loved? I'm sorry Luke can't be the man I thought he could become. I'm sorry I keep getting it wrong. We're here because I don't know. Maybe talking to someone you don't know, maybe that person can offer you more than I can right now."

AFTER THAT NIGHT my mother wouldn't say another word about Dylan. She never became angry when I asked about him, but her eyes withdrew into a dark wound.

When she was asleep, the night so quiet I could hear coyote slinking in the high grass, I gazed at his photograph. Looking into his eyes, I knew that I had a future and a past.

I read all I could about his family. His private life was an optical illusion. Reporters had discovered a secret daughter whose mother had concealed her from public view. Dylan had set them up in a discreet location, it was said they lived normal lives. There were rumors of more women, more children. Nothing was more jarring than looking at photographs of his acknowledged sons. I more closely resembled Dylan than two of those three men. It wasn't even close. The third son looked roughly as much like Dylan as I did, maybe slightly more, depending on the photograph. Dylan's children were artists. His three sons were, in turn, a musician, a filmmaker, and a photographer. He had two daughters: a poet and a painter. These were the older siblings I needed, who could nurture my creativity, talk to me earnestly about meaning and beauty and truth.

I closed the tabs and promised myself to never again look at Dylan's children. Even if I could prove that he was my father, to his legitimate children I would only be a mistake their father made.

As much as I admired the artist, I was starting to feel less certain about the man. On the nights I had compared his image to my reflection, tempted to believe that our resemblance was more than coincidence, I had never considered the anguish of feeling that he was my father and had chosen to not be part of my life. I didn't want anyone telling me I resembled him. Lying sleepless in bed, I no longer dared listen to his music or look at his photograph. Every new thought was more distressing. If he was my father, did he ever think of me? Didn't he want to look at me, just once? Maybe he already had. If he was the man in my memory who had come to the farmhouse when I was four or five, that sparse encounter must have been enough for him. I burned with anger toward his indifference to me. Why was I marooned in Goshen, as if my life was a secret even I wasn't intended to discover? He had chosen to know nothing about me. Nobody could be that cruel toward their own child, even one conceived by mistake. In his absence I'd lived through his most scarred songs and it was his fault. Every time a stranger told me that I resembled Dylan it felt like a rusted scalpel dragged across an open wound. I cut my hair and the comparisons continued. I let it grow long and was told more than ever that I looked like him.

Maybe Dylan didn't know about me. My mother had not said that I was his child, only that she had seen him the spring before I was born. She had been married to Simon at that time. Was she unsure which man was my biological father? Maybe that was why she had not said that I was Dylan's son. If my mother was unsure whose child I was, she might never have told him about me. Even if she knew I was his child, she might have chosen not to say anything to protect her marriage to Simon. On the nights I considered that Dylan might not know about me, my impulse was to drive my mother's car the three thousand miles to Malibu, where he lived. I had a hundred dollars in cash saved from tutoring the son of one of my mother's clients, and that was enough to get me across the country. I could see myself driving into Dylan's compound in the dark, a porch light coming on and a man with shaggy hair crossing the damp grass. Dylan squinting at me with those eyes that looked like mine. I wouldn't need to say anything, one look and he'd know I was his child. My pain at not knowing my father would be healed by his joy in finding his son. I'd move in with him, escape my life in Goshen. I would never again have to feel vulnerable to the men with whom my mother fell in love. For the first time in my life I would be loved by my biological father. I'd sleep in his home and eat at his table. Dylan would teach me to be a writer and a man.

Even if I was old enough to drive, even if I dared steal my mother's car, I never would have arrived like that in Dylan's life. Because beneath my reverie of our father-son reunion lurked a more humiliating possibility: Dylan knew about me and had chosen not to be part of my life. Lying in bed with his music coming through my headphones, nothing could take away my connection to him. His lyrics couldn't reject me. Maybe the man already had. He had been married at the time of my conception and had every reason not to acknowledge another illicit child. After all, how many of us were there? It might change my life to be Dylan's child, but it wouldn't change his. I could be one of many accidental offspring, siblings I didn't know.

I was getting ahead of myself. What if my mother had given me Dylan as an imaginary father to compensate for losing my actual paternal relationships? It wasn't as if I looked nothing like Simon. I spent long nights studying photographs of Dylan and Simon, trying to decipher who I resembled more. My eyes and chin were closer to Dylan's. My hair was his. Certain of my facial movements were Simon's. In the school library I read everything I could about whether facial expression comes from genes or learned behavior. The science suggested that both biology and environment have a say. That made sense: sometimes my expression or laugh seemed most like Luke's.

After another sleepless night I would remember that no child looks precisely like either parent. I could see glimmers of myself in both Dylan and Simon. My similarities to one man were genetic and my similarities to the other were random. My mother had been with both men around the same time. It was all a matter of speculation, and the possibilities were exhausting and humiliating. By the time I left Goshen at eighteen I knew only one thing with certainty: I wouldn't be defined by any other man. I buzzed off all my hair. Dylan had never worn a crew cut, he wasn't the type. My plan was simple. I wasn't going to say his name, and if anyone told me I resembled him I would shrug off the idea and get along with my own story.

Three

"The more of the tumor Dr. Chen can surgically remove," my mother said, "the less chemotherapy I'll need afterward."

The formula's precision felt like a razor drawn across dry skin. I guided her Toyota Camry faster along the mountainous highway, toward Manhattan. My impulse was to get to the hospital as quickly as possible, that the odds of a successful surgery could be increased by beating the arrival time estimated by Google Maps. I'd already taken off six minutes.

She was leaning into a pillow pressed to the passenger window. A garnet-colored sweatshirt and blue jeans hung from her gaunt body. She knit from a ball of magenta yarn, her handiwork seamless and blind.

"At first I felt unusually tired," she said. "I know my body well enough to understand when something is wrong. I rested for a few days, but the exhaustion worsened. My blood work came back with concerns. Then the CT scan confirmed it was ovarian cancer."

Her eyes rested in the distant hills beyond the road. I sipped black coffee and angled past a dawdling Subaru, wishing I had slept rather than let myself be drawn into memory the night before.

"When I was diagnosed, I called every person I know who treats cancer.

Oncologists. Naturopathic MDs. Nutritionists. I wanted to learn how to support my body in as many ways as possible. And to find a doctor who doesn't think in binaries, who would proceed with chemotherapy and surgery while supporting holistic approaches. Dr. Chen has been wonderful. I just didn't expect the first round of chemo to be this grueling."

She looked with disbelief at the bony arm beneath her sweatshirt.

"You've already started chemo?" I felt simultaneous shocks of anger and protectiveness. I wanted to shout, argue, demand that she explain how she could have let me drift obliviously through my routines in London while an IV dripped chemotherapy into her veins.

"You have your own life," she said happily.

I exhaled my frustration. I was home now. She would have no more opportunity to convince herself that I shouldn't know about the most medically significant event of her life.

"So how's writing?" she said. "I could see all the work you put into that last draft."

For years, I had been writing a novel that, no matter how diligently I worked, always eluded my grasp. The story wove together memories of three of the fathers who had come through my early life with narratives of three women with whom I'd had romantic relationships after leaving home. The novel moved between time and place, the pastoral farmhouse to foreign cities, distinct events drawn together by the mysteries of love and disappointment, desire and estrangement. The last draft sprawled to more than nine hundred pages, a maze of memory from which I seemed unable to emerge with anything resembling a story. I wasn't ready for my mother to read the rawness with which I had written about Simon, Roger, and Luke. But she had read several hundred pages drawn from my time in Berlin. She was as insightful a reader as anyone I knew.

"I've been working on that story too long," I said. "I feel like I'm running out of time."

Her eyes withdrew into her knitting. She said, "You're twenty-six."

"Exactly."

"And how is Laurene?" she asked. "I'd still love to meet her."

"Right," I said. "We're not seeing each other anymore."

"Oh. I'm so sorry, Evan. When did that happen?" Her voice was wounded, as if it was her relationship that had ended.

"We were always on and off. I was never in love with her."

She looked at me carefully, as she always did when weighing what to say.

"I'm sorry things didn't work out," she said. "You will find the right person. You know nothing in life is holier than love."

I glanced at her, startled she could still say something like that aloud. I couldn't understand why she believed in love after all these years. I had never seen anyone fall in love the way my mother fell in love, her whole heart taken by whoever had aimed Cupid's arrow this time. Since leaving home I'd avoided committed relationships, insisted on an open sexual policy with most women I dated, and made good use of it. I felt satisfied with my romantic life, while my mother's search for love had caused more damage than love could ever remedy. At sixty-three, she lived alone. Of all the men who had passed through our life, temporary fathers to me and soul mates to her, none remained. I was home with her now because every one of her attempts at love had failed. I didn't want to hear her bromides about how love conquers all.

"Can you tell me the arrival time on Google Maps?" I asked.

I had saved another two minutes. I swerved past loitering cars, honking as I went. The forest highway emptied onto the George Washington Bridge. Glancing over the bridge and across the water, my eyes lingered on the skyscrapers in the distance. I thought of a description of the New York skyline I'd read in a novel years before: that it resembled wine bottles rising from the water. The description struck me as poignant and remained with me. Now as I looked at the skyline it seemed absurd that anyone could think it resembled a row of wine bottles. We descended onto the highway along the city's eastern flank.

Fifteen minutes later I turned onto a leafy street in the East 70s that seemed an advertisement for upscale urban living. Outside the hospital a uniformed man stood beside a valet parking sign. I looked at my mother and she nodded, the way we used to make decisions by a glance when we were in each other's daily lives.

She seemed unusually calm, with no hint in her expression of the significance of her impending surgery. We walked through glass revolving doors into a lobby studded with Roman pillars and Jerusalem stone. At the front desk a security officer asked for our identification. My mother offered her health insurance card. He glanced at it, then asked for her driver's license. He was bald, and heavy in the stomach, maybe a cop retired into a less demanding job. He looked between her license and what I presumed was a patient list, then informed us that no one with my mother's name was scheduled for surgery.

"Right," she sighed.

I had heard many times what she was going to say. The name on her driver's license, June Lore, came from her first marriage and for decades had not been her legal name, which was June Klausner, the name she had taken when she married Simon. To change the name on a driver's license, the Department of Motor Vehicles requires an original divorce certificate, which she no longer had, as her divorce from Ted Lore happened forty years before, when she was twenty-three. Receiving a new divorce certificate requires an original marriage license, and she didn't have that, either. It was a bureaucratic dead end, and, after many attempts to resolve it, she had given up. She explained this with a warm expression intended to appeal to the good nature of the security guard, because if you put together two Americans from any race, religion, or region, the one thing they will agree on is the unpleasantness of the Department of Motor Vehicles.

"And you've let this issue lag," the security officer said, "how long?"

"The name on your list," she said, in a voice that asked for his patience, "matches the name on my insurance card, which matches the first name and address on my driver's license."

"That may well be," the security officer said, "but you received a pre-appointment email instructing you to bring a government-issued identification to your—"

"What do you think," I cut in, "she's trying to break and enter?"

I'd slept too little and worried too much to indulge bureaucratic technicalities. I felt searing hatred for Ted Lore, this man I'd never met, a shadow from the years my mother lived in the city. Beyond his name I knew nothing about him. What they had wasn't even a marriage in anything more than name, a relationship of less than a year in their early twenties. Four decades later his name was on her driver's license, the security officer staring at my mother slack-jawed, her civic irresponsibility incomprehensible to him, because a woman who didn't make sure her driver's license reflected her legal name was surely the type to slink into a hospital and steal someone else's ovarian cancer surgery.

"As I said, you received a pre-appointment—"

"Is this a fucking joke?" I asked.

"Evan," my mother said.

"She," I said to the security guard, in a voice intended to convey that I was not a reasonable person and his best chance of defusing the situation I was about to cause was to wave us into the hospital, "has cancer. Are you going to be the asshole who doesn't let her get to her surgery on time?"

He scoffed at me as he gestured us past the security desk.

"Evan . . ." my mother said sadly. "You can't go through life treating people like that."

"'Is not the truth the truth?'" I laughed. *"Henry the Fourth, Part One."*

We entered a waiting room with floor-to-ceiling windows looking onto the river. An elderly man sat beside a coughing woman my age. The slickly dressed father of a bald preteen girl typed compulsively on his phone. One identical male twin slept on the shoulder of another. So this was the unspoken rule of the hospital: one sick person beside one healthy person. We sat in maroon plastic chairs, and my mother lifted her sweatshirt overhead, leaving her emaciated arms momentarily bare, and as I looked at the sallow skin loose on her shoulders and creased beneath her elbows, I thought instinctively and against my better judgment of the first photograph I ever saw of Holocaust survivors, cadaverous bodies standing in barracks they had barely survived, ribs protruding, a leg of the lone standing man almost entirely bereft of flesh. I was ten and sitting by the fireplace with Luke, tears in his eyes as he said, "It was the greatest mistake in the history of Christianity." My mother came into the den, saw the book, and shouted at Luke with anguish I had never heard in her voice. He shouted back, and as I fled the room I did not know that an entire line of my mother's father's family—his cousins Solomon, Benzion, and Rivka, aunt Feiga, and uncle Efraim—was extinguished at Chelmno in September 1942.

BOY FROM THE NORTH COUNTRY

For years I believed that, if my mother had let me stare at those tortured eyes and starved bodies, they never would have recurred in my dreams. It was not until Oxford that I encountered the image again. It was then I learned the photograph had been taken by an anonymous American soldier at Buchenwald, on April 16, 1945. It is among the most infamous visual portrayals of the Shoah not only because it depicts survivors at their moment of liberation, but also because, in the depths of the photograph, only his bald skull and tormented face visible to the lens, lies Elie Wiesel, whose account of the extermination camps in *Night* revealed more than any photograph could. Something else drew me to that photograph. On the twenty-three visible faces is the fullest range of human expression I have ever seen in one place: hope, resignation, thrill, humiliation, longing, and defiance.

The most anguished eyes belong to Wiesel. At Buchenwald, another captive tells Wiesel: "Here there are no fathers, no brothers, no friends. Everyone lives and dies for himself." Through the starvation, forced labor, beatings, and death march that Wiesel endures with his father, Shlomo, he regards this dissolution of human bonds, the subjection of each person to such horror that he or she loses the will to care for others, as the most defiling quality of the camps. Wiesel and his father struggle to remain alive for one another, until his father is beaten to death by a Nazi guard only a few months before the photograph was taken. Wiesel remains silent as his father is beaten, terrified that the guard's violent ire will be turned on him if he intervenes. In the photograph Wiesel's eyes reveal a piercing devastation unlike any I had ever seen on a human face.

I had recently chosen the photograph to appear beside a scathing review I wrote of a book that asked why Jews did not resist their extermination. The book dealt blithely with even the most daring acts of resistance, including the armed revolts by prisoners at Treblinka, in August 1943, and at Sobibor, in October 1943, each of which damaged those extermination centers sufficiently to end their operation. The author wrote that the revolts enabled only a few Jews to survive, while killing just twelve Nazis, and so, "regardless of what they chose, Jews came to the same end." Against this fatalism I argued that the achievement of the revolts was not the number of prison guards killed or inmates saved but rather the courage of resilience under circumstances designed to vanquish the very desire for life. My mother shared my essay on social media along with several sentences about the enduring will to live.

A male nurse in blue scrubs called my mother's name. I was allowing myself to wander into distraction. I wished I had something useful to say. She set her magenta ball of yarn and knitting needles into the cloth bag, and I asked what she was making.

"You'll see," she smiled, "when it's time."

The nurse led us down a corridor. Yellow curtains demarcated stalls. Aging men pushed walkers. A woman lay with IVs running from her arm into a beeping machine. Someone shouted, "Morphine!" This was the heart of the hospital, concealed by the grand architecture and river views. This was the place people were sent by words so assimilated into ordinary life they had lost their ability to shock: diagnosis, biopsy, transplant. These were the bodies struggling to stay alive, and we were among them.

The nurse led us behind a yellow curtain and nodded my mother into a medical chair. In a practiced voice the nurse asked yes-or-no questions. My mother gave each answer in her steady, warm voice, as if she was grateful to be asked. The nurse said, "You fasted the last twelve hours?" My mother nodded resolutely. The nurse said, "Then we just need you to change, and Dr. Chen will be ready for you."

The nurse handed my mother a moss-green medical gown, and I walked into the hall to give her privacy. A stall curtain fluttered and I saw a bald woman laboring to breathe. A hand pulled the curtain closed and the woman was gone.

My mother stepped into the hall in her medical gown.

"I'm ready," she said. The nurse gestured her into a wheelchair. This wasn't necessary. She had walked through the hospital with her own strength. Before I could say anything she settled into the wheelchair. The nurse wheeled her to an unmarked door and, turning to me, said, "You'll receive a call after the procedure."

The words struck me with destabilizing force. I knew that I wouldn't be beside my mother in the operating room. Still, it hadn't occurred to me that the fact of our eventual separation would entail a specific moment of separation. I kissed her forehead, trying not to think of the time she had spent alone at the house, frailer by the day, telling herself it was not time to call me.

"I love you," I told her. "The rest is commentary."

She smiled with amused tenderness.

"I love you, too, Evan," she said.

The nurse wheeled her through the unmarked door. I stood in the hall between pacing nurses and beeping IV machines and told myself it would be only four hours until I saw my mother again. In the brightly lit waiting room there were new pairs of the sick and healthy. A bald woman sat beside a blonde woman. An elderly man coughed onto the shoulder of a companion who was either his daughter or wife. I reclined in a plastic chair, trying to sleep. Against the darkness of my closed eyes, all I could see was my mother lying sedated on the operating table, doctors in blue scrubs arranging her beneath the surgical equipment, Dr. Chen opening her flesh, the more of the tumor she could remove the less chemotherapy my mother would have to endure, the sooner she would return to life as usual and I would kiss her goodbye and fly back to London. I withdrew my phone, navigating the hospital website and several social media pages until I found Dr. Chen. In her official photograph her head tilted forward, signifying her readiness for any task. She looked to be in her late thirties, with intent eyes and a smile unembarrassed by her crooked teeth. These details gave me the sense that she was concerned with the major events of life rather than its diversions. Her last post was a news article about a mother and son leaving their home in Iowa for Mexico, to reunite with the boy's father, who had been deported despite his son being a birthright citizen. Dr. Chen had written, "A brighter future for our children—isn't that what we all want?"

The post beneath showed a photograph of a crawling toddler with Dr. Chen's dark eyes. I felt calmed by these images. It was reassuring that Dr. Chen seemed so concerned with family bonds. She must understand the anxiety I felt as I stared through the hospital window onto the river. No, that was a uselessly sentimental thought. The only relevant consideration was Dr. Chen's precision with surgical equipment. I was happy for her daughter that she seemed to be a loving mother and for the country that she was a caring citizen. These virtues had no bearing on the procedure she was carrying out on my mother's body. The more of the tumor she was able to remove, the less chemotherapy my mother had to endure. This was all that mattered.

My phone pinged and I reached anxiously into my pocket for any news. Of course I wouldn't hear from the medical staff for hours. The text was from Linda, a patient of my mother's who hosted a dog day care in her home, where we had left Lucy. She had sent a photo of Lucy prancing on the lawn with her orange ball held proudly in her mouth. I sent back a heart emoji.

BOY FROM THE NORTH COUNTRY

Across the waiting room a boy with ginger hair sat beside a middle-aged man, the parallel slope of their forehead and slouch marking them unmistakably as father and son. I touched the birthmark on the rear of my shoulder that was the same raspberry color as the mark on my mother's shoulder. I should have slept the night before rather than remaining restlessly awake. I felt guilty for thinking of Dylan. That story was not my life. It bore no relevance to the urgent matter at hand. She had raised me. I was the adult my mother was relying on to help her through her illness, not a child looking for his father. My fingers moved over my birthmark, and I felt myself drawn back in memory, before any of the men arrived, before I knew Dylan's name, to the time it was only my mother and me at the farmhouse, and I woke each morning to light glowing through the window as she stood in the doorway, auburn hair on her shoulders, eyes bright as she smiled, "Good morning, my sunshine boy." On those mornings we walked through the woods with Bessie, our beagle, who barked at deer from a distance but whimpered when they came nearby. We walked in the summer when my bare feet sank into lush mud and in the winter when the trees were barren and the ground was hard with frost. We walked through the forest to a barn with crates of pears and apple cider and vegetables still dirty with the earth. On winter evenings, as snow fell through the sky beyond the farmhouse windows, my mother heated that cider on our stove. The coyote howled and the freight train echoed through the valley and the pine trees swayed over the farmhouse. When the hot cider touched my lips winter lost its chill.

Cider was not my mother's only method of tempering winter. On frigid afternoons, we walked into the snow in our warmest coats, my mother carrying her wooden ax. Standing over maple trunks that fell in that year's storms, she lifted the ax high overhead and swung it into the fallen trees. The rhythmic thudding echoed as I wandered the forest, searching for kindling. Sometimes the sound paused, and I turned to see my mother struggling with the ax overhead, its blade stuck in the round cut of wood, a woman in a green winter jacket with auburn hair about her shoulders and a fierce glare in her eyes. She heaved the ax and cut of wood to the ground, pressed her black boot to the heart of the wood, and withdrew the ax with a sharp breath.

We carried the wood to the iron grate beside the fireplace. My mother set our burnt offering in the stove. She lit a match and set the flame beneath the kindling and stoked the fire with a rusted steel poker. The flames blazed and warmth spread through the den and my mother said, "Where shall we go tonight?"

I walked to the bookshelf and, like an adventurer surveying the globe, grandly pointed to our destination. On the sofa by the fire we visited Robin Hood in Sherwood Forest and King Arthur in Camelot. My mother's eyes moved across the pages, her voice changing tone and temperament as she conjured the Arthurian knights into the room. I have no memory earlier than this, my mother's words creating the world. "'Whoever draws this sword from the stone,'" she proclaimed as the boy Arthur eyed the sword, "'has been rightfully born King of England.'" I had never felt anything like the thrill of Arthur drawing Excalibur from that stone. King Arthur and his knights galloped through our den, drawing blood from dragons and wicked kings, pursuing love and justice and truth, and so, too, did I. This was exhausting work and I often fell asleep as my mother read.

Other nights I recruited her into my own stories, written at the same time they were performed.

"Suppose," I might say, five years old, "you are the king of Spain and

I am Columbus and must convince Your Highness to grant me all the Royal Navy to set sail for the New World!"

Or some other plot I plagiarized straight out of a book on the shelf.

My mother put on an expression of regal skepticism and said, "Why does Columbus require *all* the Royal Navy to set sail for the New World?"

"I said *suppose!*" I cried, to which she might say, "I am supposing! Isn't Columbus supposed to convince me?"

At which point I would make a lengthy list of arguments for my rights to the Royal Navy, until I fell asleep on the sofa, mid-sentence, my mouth open. My mother carried me to bed, a woman alone in the woods with a child convinced he was Christopher Columbus.

My favorite of all the stories my mother read to me, the book whose arrival I awaited all year, counting the days until the release of the next volume, was *Harry Potter*. We lounged in the hammock on summer afternoons, living within the words she read aloud. When Harry discovered he was a wizard, so did I. When Voldemort came for Harry's life, he came for mine. When my mother read the last page of the book we had savored all summer, it felt inconceivable that I would be deprived of reading the next book in the series until the following year. One evening, as we walked across the field at dusk, I asked my mother why we had to wait an entire year for the following book.

"Because the author needs time to write the story," she said. And that is my first memory of understanding that a book is not part of the natural landscape, as are other sources of beauty, such as the mountains or sky, but rather is made by the human hand.

If the knights of my Round Table were the characters in the books my mother read to me, the knights of her Round Table were the animals who lived in our barn. She was never more at ease than with our horse, Misty, our several sheep, and our dozen stouthearted chickens. Each morning we walked up the hill to the barn, and my mother asked, "How generous do you think our hens have been today?"

She opened the barn door and I ran inside to rummage in the straw, eager to discover if our hens had left us two eggs or a complete dozen. "Thank you," my mother said, stroking the hens' feathered necks.

She taught me to give Misty a carrot with my palm held flat. "You can trust her," she said. "A horse can sense what's true in any soul." She taught me to tighten Misty's girth and guide the bit into her mouth. "Just remember," she said, "she feels as much as you or me." We rode through the forest, my mother holding me around the belly as Misty broke into her gallop.

On warm afternoons I lay in the mud beside our sheep, my mouth open to digest the book I was reading. Our chickens squawked encouragement as I neared the end of a book. When the last page was read I squawked beside them, elongating my neck in imitation of my feathered friends. Misty was also interested in literature: she once devoured all of *Charlotte's Web*.

Strangers visited my mother. From my bedroom window I observed aging women and young children walking the stone path to the sunroom at the rear of our house. Crouching behind the closed door to her office, I listened for their voices. People came to my mother to tell her their stories, and I wanted to know every one. I invented those I could not hear. That woman in the black sweater was telling my mother she had sailed the Seven Seas. She had seen storms at sea and lightning in the pale blue sky. She had chased pirates around the Horn of Africa. I could smell the ocean.

I asked my mother why a man cried as he left her office.

"Because it can be upsetting to realize," she answered, "that no matter what has happened to us in life, we can always heal."

When I needed to heal I lay on the olive massage table in my mother's sunroom, looking upside down at shelves of health bars, homeopathic remedies, nutritional supplements, kinesiology magnets, books. She sat beside me at her cherry desk beneath the bay window. "What are you feeling, Evan?" she would ask. Lying on the massage table, sunlight radiant on my skin, I could tell my mother about pain in my body or disturbing feelings in my mind. If I was reluctant to describe my discomfort, she would say, "Whatever it is, we can work on it together."

She made careful notes as I spoke. She reached for a book or bottled supplement, saying, "If your stomach aches, let's try a break from dairy for a few days. In the meantime, I'll make you ginger tea."

Skin irritation was soothed by caladium cream. Arnica was never far out of reach. Earaches met their end with herbal ointments.

On days I felt a strange sorrow, within a part of myself to which I did not want to travel and could not describe, my mother asked me to think of a particular word.

Perilous. Love. Together.

"Try to focus on the word," she said. "Can you tell me what it makes you feel?"

With my eyes shut I could see the word against the blank interior of my mind. I was stunned by the force of four or five letters strung together. If I thought of *fear* I could feel the emotion itself within my body. I feared that I would wake in the night and find my mother dead on the floor, her eyes staring dully at me in the dark. I feared that the sun would vanish from the sky and we would live in endless darkness. My mother listened to these fears, nodding as I spoke. Then she would ask me to think of *love*, and I felt the warmth that seeped through my heart when, during a thunderstorm, I crawled beneath my bed to lie with Bessie, stroking her sleek ears as she panted and whined. Love meant the soft touch of our hens' feathers, and coming into consciousness each morning to my mother in the bedroom doorway, smiling as she said, "Good morning, my sunshine boy." Repeating the word *love* to myself, I could feel the fear and sorrow in that darker part of myself giving way to the comfort of my more contented self, a child who lived in the woods with his dog, horse, sheep, chickens, and mother.

This overwhelming charge of feeling moved most powerfully through my body when she asked me to repeat a particular phrase.

"I am loved," I would say three times, the sentence more true with each repetition. "I am protected. I am free."

"Do you want to end with a fun one?" she always asked.

I would nod, and she might say *adventure*, and I was running up the hill to the barn and saddling Misty and riding across the Sahara. I could feel the hot sand on my face.

I knew I should fear this strange power of a single word. Instead, I was enchanted.

If we needed more tulip bulbs, or to replace a garden hose, or mail a letter, she drove our rusted station wagon past sloping farmland and grazing cows. The same man always wandered over the hills. He wore a dark suit and fur hat with a lock of hair curled over each ear. I never understood how his body changed. Sometimes he was lanky, other times plump. He was often short and occasionally tall. He never took off his suit and fur hat, even in the summer when he must have been unbearably hot and through the winter when he must have been miserably cold.

"What is he looking for?" I asked my mother.

"A way to be alive," she said.

One day, two men in dark suits and fur hats wandered over the hills and through the valley. "Look!" I said. "Now there are two people searching for a way to be alive."

My mother laughed. I was her sunshine boy. She turned the car around and drove through the hills to a village of narrow streets bustling with hundreds of men in dark suits and fur hats and curly earlocks. Women in black dresses pushed strollers past signs written in a language I did not know. Boys my age ran happily among themselves, dressed in miniature black suits, locks of hair dangling over their ears. Looking through the car window, long before I understood that the Hasidic community in Kiryas Joel was a remnant of the extinguished world of religious European Jews, I felt as if we were as far from home as Sherwood Forest or Camelot. The clothing reminded me of the costumes of a play, and I asked, "Are they actors?"

"In a way," my mother said, "but they believe in these roles with all their heart and their only audience is God."

In our one-street town was a post office, bank, garden supply store, and church with a towering steeple. Walking along the main street, on our visits into town, I noticed men noticing my mother. By five, I understood that those parts of my mother that were ordinary to me—her hazel eyes, radiant auburn hair, knowing smile—stirred in male strangers feelings of desire and bravado, so that, striding toward us, one might proclaim, "I'm Jim." Or, folding his arms across his chest to emphasize the brawn beneath his shirt, he might say, "What's your name?" After a few pleasantries, he might add, "Why don't you come with me to the diner—and of course the boy is welcome to join."

My mother always nodded politely and said we were about to be on our way.

She received the same desirous stares from men who came to repair a leaking faucet or broken door hinge. A man with gray side chops took off his shirt to better inspect the electrical outlet. When was my mother's husband coming home? The repair job was simple, the man wanted my mother to know, and he was more than happy to do it at no cost. And what plans did she have for the weekend?

"Thank you," my mother said firmly, "I'll be handling this myself."

One morning, as we walked up the hill to retrieve our eggs, a man stood beside the barn, tossing feed to the hens. He wore ragged blue jeans and muddy boots and did not seem to notice us walking up the hill. My mother went still. The man reached into his burlap sack, each handful of feed dissolving into countless grains as it arced through the blue sky into the grass, where our chickens pecked and squawked. The man turned and I had seen his face before, his expression so much my own. For an infinite moment his eyes marked mine. I looked at the cheekbones angled like mine, the scraggly brown curls, the eyes that in my teenage years I would spend countless nights comparing to my own, and before I knew his name, before I tried to learn all I could about this man, I understood that we knew one another.

My mother knelt beside me and whispered, "Evan, can you please read inside?"

They sat together on the wooden bench beneath the crab apple tree. I lay on the sofa beside the fireplace, traveling through Sherwood Forest with Robin Hood and his merry men. Several times I crept to the window and, raising my eyes just over the window frame so that I might see without being seen, looked for my mother and the man. They were walking in the pasture beyond the barn. They were sitting beside one another on the hill. They were nowhere in sight. I curled on the sofa and fell asleep within my book. I woke to the man staring down at me. His eyes were wide and strange as if he had never seen a blue-eyed boy. He smelled of chicken feed and I wanted to smell that way, too. He bent near to me, and his arms settled beneath my little body, and he lifted me from the sofa and held me to his chest. In his embrace was the warmth of the fire. With a longing I could not explain I wanted him to stay with my mother and me.

No more than a moment passed before he set me back on the sofa, drew the quilt to my chin, and, looking resolutely at my mother, rasped, "Glad you're doing well, June."

He never visited again.

Around that time other men began to arrive at the house. From my bedroom window I could see my mother's suitor walk the stone pathway to our door, flowers in hand, adjusting his collar or nervously checking the time. My mother came into my room, and kissed me good night, and told me she had placed wood on the fire that would burn through the time she was away. She turned from my doorway, and a moment later the front door opened beneath my window. An expression of feigned confidence appeared on the man's face, and my mother and her date walked the stone steps in the uncertain way any two strangers walk a narrow path, and I wondered if this would be the knight to win her heart.

I could always tell when my mother was falling in love. When my mother fell in love sunlight shone more brightly in the mountains and the pine trees swayed more passionately over the farmhouse. She walked freely and sang easily. "I can feel my heart opening," she said one morning as we walked up the hill to the barn. "Oh, nothing is holier than love!"

If I asked about the man who had arrived at our door each of the last four weeks, she would only say, "You'll meet him when the time is right."

And the time rarely was. A day or week or month later I would wake to sobs in the night. I crawled from bed, sliding across the hardwood floor in the wool socks my mother knit me. At her door I paused, unsure what to do. If I returned to bed she might fall asleep, as she had on other nights. She inhaled a sharp sob, and I crossed the black landscape into her bed, and she held me to her and kissed my forehead, and neither spoke nor cried as we drifted into sleep.

Other times I woke to my mother's murmurs. I followed her voice through the dark house to the slightly ajar sunroom door. My mother stood before an easel, brush in hand, paint-stained newspapers on the floor. One night as she painted I heard her say, "What about you, June—can you love? Can you heal?" I was startled to think that my mother, who could in an instant transform herself into the Sheriff of Nottingham, who spent her days with strangers who came to seek her guidance, had ever suffered anything from which she might need to heal.

I remember a night in those years when we sat in darkness at the kitchen table. My mother struck a match, her hand carrying the flame to a white candle. She said, "Hashem may not be above us, the Mashiach may never come, the Temple may never be rebuilt, but tonight we tell a story."

Once each year we ventured to the city. We rose early in the morning, shoveled snow from the driveway, and glided in the station wagon down the forest highway. At the bridge with views of the city we met a stream of cars, and I began to worry if we were all going to fit into the theater. Then with relief I remembered there was more than one theater in New York. Curious about the destination of our fellow theatergoers, I stared through car windows, wondering if that mustached man might seek a stern lecture by Arthur Miller or a heartwarming romance such as *Beauty and the Beast*. Perhaps he would surprise us by walking straight into *Cats*.

We parked near the water. Strolling along the river, beneath maple and cherry trees, felt like walking the woods behind our house, as if there was not, just above us, the throbbing metropolitan center of the world. As we sat on a park bench, eating whole wheat tofu sandwiches and watching sailboats on the river, I could not have known that on these sparse visits to New York I was barely glimpsing the city that had consumed my mother's life until shortly before my birth.

At the theater she gave her name and received two tickets, an exchange in which she seemed to gain the better bargain. We sat in enchanted anticipation as the audience took their seats and the actors came onstage. Then the figures began to enact the Ibsen or Chekhov drama we had traveled this great distance to enjoy, and I was mesmerized to see my mother, who the day before had split a fallen maple tree into firewood with an ax, reciting to herself the actors' every line.

When we returned to the farmhouse the coyote were no longer howling and the freight train was silent for the night and the pine trees swayed protectively over the house, and my mother said to me, "Now please wash up, a full bath before bed, and don't argue, the city is a filthy place."

STANDING AT THE HOSPITAL window I observed light reflecting off the river. I should have received a call from the medical staff by now. Did that mean Dr. Chen had been able to remove more of the tumor than she thought possible and was still operating? Or had there been complications? I stared at my phone, demanding that it ring. I thought again of the fireplace with which my mother heated the house when I was a child. I had never described it to anyone. Not because I was ashamed that my mother had found it more economical to cut firewood than pay for oil heat. Rather, in the eight years since I'd left home, I had never mentioned my mother's fireplace and wooden ax because they never occurred to me as relevant. I had learned to describe myself in the ways other people wanted to hear. The literature degree from Oxford, the years in Berlin, Jerusalem, and London. I'd found university grants and paid internships to justify summers in Beijing, Bangalore, Santiago. I felt like a winner of the rigged meritocracy, a shining beacon of overconcentrated opportunity. When I looked over my shoulder, Goshen seemed the dark mouth of a tunnel I had improbably escaped. If asked where I was from, I said New York. These two words led invariably to other people describing their favorite restaurants and neighborhoods in the city, happily diverting the question of my origins.

I had left Goshen as I intended. I had traveled farther from the farmhouse than I could have imagined those nights I gazed onto the hills beyond my window. I had almost never spoken about Dylan. This was a private matter, a parallel life detached from the one I sought to make for myself.

I had never found what I left home to seek. For years I had told myself that nothing returns us to ourselves like a story rightly told. I had spent long hours at my desk, devoting myself to the novel I was determined to write. Yet despite the relentless attempts, endless drafts, and taunting embers of creative hope, I had never known how to tell my story, not even to myself. Now, looking at the light reflecting off the river, waiting for a call from the hospital, I felt like what I was: a man wading toward thirty without making anything of his life but a single continuous flight. I was failing to become myself.

I paced the hospital halls, no destination in mind, the transatlantic flight and sleepless night dragging my weary legs past blank-eyed nurses and murmuring doctors. Bach began to play, one of the cello suites, simultaneously soothing and urgent, the music promising to awaken its listener to the precariousness of life and at the same time guide him through it. Right, it was my ringtone. A voice asked to speak to someone with my name.

"Here I am," I said.

"Your mother is in her recovery room," the voice said.

"How was the procedure? How much of the tumor was removed? How's she feeling?"

"I'll let Dr. Chen walk you through those details in the morning," the voice said.

I hurried into the elevator, striking the number to my mother's floor, rushing past exhausted nurses to her room.

She was asleep beneath white covers in her medical bed. Her eyes were closed and her expression peaceful. The dim outline of her body beneath the covers could not tell me what mattered most, the volume of the cancerous tumor that remained within her, how much pain the surgery had spared or caused, and what it meant for the time ahead. I drew a chair beside her and held her hand as night fell over the city, the lit apartment units becoming fewer, their glare more conspicuous in the night. Before I relinquished consciousness for sleep, my mother's eyes fluttered open and she knew we were together.

Four

I woke in the chair beside her hospital bed. My mother was curled on her side in the morning light, her hands folded beneath her auburn hair, most of which had escaped the teal hairnet while she slept. I wondered how long she had stood in the doorway of my bedroom those childhood mornings, taking a protective pleasure in observing my sleep before waking me by saying, "Good morning, my sunshine boy." She stirred in bed, her eyes dazed and bloodshot. She recognized me and murmured for water. I reached for the bottle on her nightstand, removed the cap, and handed it to her. She lifted the bottle and the water trickled along her parched lips.

"Evan," she said faintly, returning the bottle to me.

"Good morning, Mom. How did you sleep?"

She looked at me as if through a fog.

"These painkillers . . . cloud out everything."

"We'll be home soon," I said. "You'll be able to sleep in your own bed."

Even as I spoke I understood that the comfort I was suggesting was adjacent to the complaint she had made. If the painkillers were fogging her mind in the hospital they would do the same at the farmhouse. Still, my obligation was to project optimism. We had to move from one unpleasant condition to the next, advancing, however slowly, toward recovery. I had no control over how much of the tumor Dr. Chen had been able to remove or how disoriented the painkillers made my mother feel. But I could do everything possible to keep her spirits high.

She pressed the help button on the bed controller. I asked what she needed and she nodded to the toilet in the corner of the room. Right, she couldn't walk on her own. The nurses should be in soon. My mother winced. There was no reason I couldn't help her from bed to the bathroom. Except that I would have to stand nearby as she sat on the toilet, ready to intervene if she slipped or the pain suddenly intensified. I couldn't listen to the trickle of her urine or her release of excrement. I told her I'd be back in a moment and walked into the hall. Behind what appeared to be an intake desk sat a woman in teal scrubs.

"Hi," I said. "My mother rang the help button a few times. She needs the toilet."

"Someone will be there as soon as possible," the nurse said, without looking up.

"She's just had ovarian cancer surgery," I insisted. "She can't walk on her own."

How could this woman not understand that my mother was subject to an overwhelming array of discomforts, that any matter within our control had to be attended to immediately? The phone rang and two nurses wheeled by an elderly man on a stretcher, his arm dangling near the floor, and I understood that in every room were people in medical conditions as undesirable as my mother's. She needed help and I was the only person in the hospital who loved her. I had to overcome my childishness. Soon we would be in the farmhouse with no help button to press.

In our room a male nurse my age was easing my mother out of bed. She took hobbled steps to the bathroom, leaning on his shoulder as I watched, feeling useless.

She slept through the remainder of the morning and the afternoon, waking only to ask for more of the painkiller, oxycodone. I sat beside her bed, trying to read a novel I had taken from my flat in London, the second in an absorbing series written by a Scandinavian epicist with a notoriety for detail. My eyes moved across the pages, unable to retain the words I read. In the evening she was able to sit up in bed. She asked for her cloth bag and withdrew her knitting and a worn paperback.

"Read to me?" she said, handing me the book. On the cover a boy with a lightning-bolt scar across his forehead flew his broomstick over a castle. I was on that broom beside him, alive with the thrill of my mother reading *Harry Potter* to me as we lounged in the fields behind the farmhouse so many summer afternoons.

"Chapter One," I began, "'The Boy Who Lived . . .'"

I read through the evening as she drifted in and out of sleep.

"More moving," she said, "every time I read."

"You've reread this since I was a kid?"

"Can't tell you how many times," she said.

She laughed in the moment Harry Potter learns he is a wizard. "When I read that page," she said, "you ran through the field, shouting, 'I'm a wizard! I'm going to be a wizard!'"

By the time she fell asleep that night Harry had been saved from the Dursleys and would soon be leaving for Hogwarts. I looked at my mother, her eyes closed, her auburn hair falling on the shoulder of her moss-green medical gown. I felt grateful that we were together. I didn't know anyone who had experienced cancer. I didn't know what to expect in the time ahead. What mattered most, I told myself, was that we remain together.

Her phone buzzed on the bedside table. On the screen was a familiar photograph, my grandmother holding me on her lap in the pizzeria to which she had taken me every Friday evening after she moved to Goshen, when I was four. She read to me those nights, looking up from *Charlie and the Chocolate Factory* to say, "Why is Augustus Gloop such a schmuck? That child was not raised right!" If my baked ziti did not arrive promptly my grandmother would declare, "You must be hungry. Your dinner will come if you go to the bathroom." I would get up from the table and do as she said, walking to the bathroom whether I needed to use it or not. I could hear her shouts through the wall: "Where is that boy's dinner? He's a *growing* boy! You bring his baked ziti this minute, or you'll have something else coming to you!" When I returned to the table, the baked ziti would be waiting for me, and my grandmother would grin and say, "Always trust your Bubbe."

I took the phone into the hospital hallway, closing the door to our room behind me. Two nurses in scrubs conferred down the hall.

"Bubbe," I said into the phone, registering my hoarse voice.

"How is my daughter?" she asked sharply.

"Sleeping," I said. "The surgery went well."

I didn't know if it was true, but it felt like the right thing to say.

"Is she getting everything she needs?" she asked.

"Absolutely," I said. "She's well. Talking, laughing."

"If one damn thing goes wrong, that hospital is going to be hearing from me."

In the background I could hear the lawn mower that perpetually cut grass in her retirement complex in Key West. She had moved there when I was eighteen, for warmer weather and younger grandchildren.

I visited her twice a year, my mother always helping me with the cost of the flight. We spent days drinking coffee on her sunlit balcony, my grandmother telling me stories from her life. I had recently begun asking her more about her upbringing in Depression-era Brooklyn, and the cataclysmic events that had brought her parents from eastern Europe to America. Our favorite ritual was to drive to the vineyards on the southern tip of Florida, where my grandmother got tipsy off the tasters, then insisted the sommelier was checking me out, shouting loudly enough for the woman to hear, "Go talk to her! She can't take her eyes off you!"

Nurses hurried along the hall. Exhausted by their brisk walk I eased into a windowsill.

"I wish I was there," she said. "Tell that to my damn hip replacement..."

"Don't worry," I said. "She's doing well. You'll see when she calls you. First thing when she wakes in the morning, OK?"

"Not a minute later," she said. "By the way, I have something important to tell you."

"What's that, Bubbe?"

"I want you to meet Belinda's granddaughter."

"Bubbe..."

"Evan, listen to your Bubbe. You are going to meet this young woman. Belinda just moved into my building. I went over to her apartment to say hello, and on her wall was a photograph of a gorgeous young woman. She's your age. She lives in New York. She's Jewish. So I went back to my room and took your photo off my wall to show Belinda. Don't worry, I made sure she knows that you're more than your handsome looks. You see, I'm your—what do they call it? I'm your wingwoman."

"Thank you, Bubbe. That's very thoughtful of you."

"Of course I'm thoughtful. What should I be—thoughtless?"

"I'll make sure Mom calls you when she's up."

"If anyone in that hospital needs to be put in line, you know who to call."

We said our *I love you*s and hung up.

MY MOTHER WOKE on Sunday morning feeling less woozy. A nurse brought a breakfast tray of mashed potatoes and Jell-O, and my mother stared glumly at the food.

"Mass-produced, microwaved, no nutrients," she said to me after the nurse left the room. "Any patient here needs nutrition to recover, and the hospital serves this?" She sighed in exasperation, reached into her wallet, and withdrew a credit card. "There's a place called Matter of Health a few blocks away. Can you see if they have plain chicken breast and veggies?"

I walked through the hospital's revolving doors, almost surprised to find myself in Manhattan. There were the numbered streets and yellow cabs speeding up the avenues, young professionals walking dogs as they spoke into cell phones, women laughing over Thai lunch. It was a Sunday in August and you could feel it in the humid air. For as long as I'd been visiting New York, these streets meant plans, which friends to text and galleries to see. Walking east on 77th Street, it was strange to consider that the life of the city was ongoing, art exhibits and plays and film premieres as indifferent to me as I was to them. I hadn't told anyone I was home. I had several friends in the city who I'd usually never miss the chance to see. But I was exhausted by two nights on the hospital chair and in no mood for the obligatory reportage and consolation.

In the health food store I wandered past organic shampoo and teas, remembering the warm feeling of walking beside my mother through our health food store as a child, filling cloth bags with tofu, avocados, walnuts. "The foods we eat," she said as we walked the aisles, "become who we are." Once I stared at a frozen food that looked suspiciously like the leg of one of our hens. The name for this food, *chicken*, was even the same as the name of the friends who gave us their daily eggs. I asked my mother who had made this mistake. She explained to me the unpleasant facts. I listened, feeling outraged and fearful that the assassinated chicken was a relative of the hens I squawked with in the dirt.

"I don't want," I announced, "to eat anything with a face."

"No faces," my mother nodded. She never again asked me to eat meat or fish.

She was reading *Harry Potter* when I returned to our hospital room.

"Mmm," she said as she bit into the chicken breast. "Now that's food."

SHE ASKED ME NOT to join her meeting with Dr. Chen on Monday morning. My instinct was to insist that I listen in and make note of every word spoken about her treatment. "Wouldn't that be useful—to have me take notes?" I said, standing by the window. She was sitting upright in the hospital bed, legs crossed beneath her. I didn't want to say what I feared: that she would minimize the severity of what Dr. Chen told her.

"I'll tell you everything she tells me," my mother said, replying to what I had thought rather than what I had said.

"Everything," I said, looking her hard in the eye.

"Everything," she nodded.

She had a professional knowledge of health and would likely discuss her medical condition with Dr. Chen in terms that would have to be translated for me. The only role I could play in the meeting was anxious son. However nervous I was to know the result of the surgery, however wary I was of her wanting to protect me from what Dr. Chen might say, I knew that she had a right to a private conversation about an operation on her reproductive organs.

Dr. Chen appeared in the doorway of our room as she had in her official photograph, a woman in her late thirties exuding kindness and professional attention to detail. She said hello without any hint that the last time they saw one another Dr. Chen had been dressed in sanitized medical garb as my mother lay naked on her operating table.

I nodded to my mother, trying to release my anxiety with a deep breath. The door closed behind me. Pacing the hospital corridors, I knew all that mattered could be compressed into a simple formula: the more of the tumor Dr. Chen had been able to remove, the less chemotherapy my mother needed. Rounding the corner, I glanced at a wall plaque engraved with the names of the hospital's benefactors. Irving, Teitelbaum, Lerner, Weinstein—what were we trying to prove? That Jews are the model minority, or that we aren't a minority at all? I felt uncomfortable with the ostentatious public display. In Goshen, I had never wanted anyone to know I was Jewish. A few miles away was Kiryas Joel, the village of Hasidic Jews. Sometimes, when my school bus passed the village, other boys shoved my face to the window, pointed to the Hasidic men on the street, and asked which kike was my father.

I had tried to laugh at the irony that the Hasidim wouldn't even think of me as Jewish. We had never gone to synagogue. I hadn't yet discovered that twentieth-century American literature had been significantly influenced by Jewish writers: Roth, Bellow, Ozick, Malamud, Paley, Gornick, Mailer, Salinger, Potok. I wasn't even circumcised.

The day we read Anne Frank's *Diary*, Terry Murphy chased me down the hall, shouting that he was going to run me out of Goshen like Hitler chased my ancestors out of Europe. I barricaded myself in a bathroom stall, pleading with the lock to hold as Terry roundhouse-kicked the door. My face was marked with bruises and dried blood when I came home that afternoon. My mother insisted that we drive to the school, then refused to leave until the principal met her. She was angrier than I had ever seen her, and when the principal at last met with us she told him in unapologetic terms that the school had a legal responsibility to protect me and was failing so abysmally that a court would consider the principal an accomplice to the violence against me. Even her threat of a lawsuit didn't change anything. None of my attackers were ever disciplined.

Wandering the hospital halls, I knew I had to forget the boys who beat me at school. They were probably working unenviable jobs in the trades, while my life had been made rich with opportunities they were never given. Maybe that was the wrong way to think of class. If those men were police officers or construction contractors, they had higher and more reliable income than I cobbled together by tutoring, editing college admissions essays, and teaching summer writing classes to high school students. The uncomfortable thought reminded me to check my bank balance. The cab across London, flight, and rental car had not been cheap, especially at the last moment. I tapped my phone and my balance stared back at me: £323.07.

My mother hadn't said anything about money, but I knew she must be concerned. She wasn't healthy enough to work. Like all self-employed people in New York State, she was required to pay tax for unemployment insurance even though she wasn't eligible to receive it. She'd be on her own until she could work again. I didn't know the details of her health insurance, but even with a good policy the deductible and uncovered bills would be substantial. She had always been cautious with money. Her relationship to her work was rooted in the meaning she found in helping people live healthier lives, not the amount of money she made. She had always emphasized to me how lucky we were. To eat healthy food grown only a few miles away. To live in our own home in a beautiful part of the world.

I had taken after her. I'd arranged my life to pursue the writing that gave my life meaning. I knew how many hours I needed to tutor and how many admissions essays I needed to write to cover my modest monthly expenses. When I traveled, I short-let my apartment, often making more money from the rental than I spent on the trip. By these means I found the freedom to pursue what gave me meaning. But meaning could not pay for her cancer treatment or compensate for the income she was losing every day. It would have been easy for me to launder the prestige of my Oxford degree into lucrative work, as so many of my classmates had done. Instead, I had taken my own path and achieved nothing. I'd lived within my delusional artistic reverie, writing a novel that, at nine hundred winding pages, had neither artistic nor commercial merit. Now the person I loved most needed support and I was in no position to give it. I had forgotten the governing fact of the country in which I'd been raised: this was America, where you lunged into the brutality of the market, seizing enough money for you and your loved ones, or risked shortened life spans, medical bankruptcy, unforgiving financial ruin.

There was no prospect now of reversing my choices. The least I could do was activate the short-let listing for my London flat. I'd ask a friend to clean the room and lock my valuables in the closet. I tapped the app on my phone and a moment later the listing was live.

My phone pinged and I lunged a hand back into my pocket. The text was from my mother. *We're all done. I'm here.*

I hurried through the halls, up staircases, past grim-faced nurses. I glanced down the hallway for any familiar landmark, scolding myself for not having paid attention to where I was walking. I was supposed to be the adult caring for my mother and I couldn't even wander ten minutes in the hospital without getting lost.

In her bed she sat upright in her lotus pose, eyes closed. She drew slow, meditative breaths. Her auburn hair fell over the shoulders of her moss-green medical gown. She opened her eyes into mine and her pupils were steeled with calm.

"Dr. Chen removed most of the tumor," she said, her voice careful over each word, "but not as much as we hoped. I'm in for significant chemotherapy."

I hugged her. Her arms around my shoulders. Mine around hers. The warmth of her face touching mine.

"I could need your help for months, Evan."

"I'll be here. However long it takes."

It required no effort to make my voice firm. I didn't know what lay ahead, but I would have to transform myself into the person my mother needed me to be.

"I'm going to lose my hair," she said, glancing hesitantly at me.

Sunlight glowed on the white bedsheet. I wasn't sure what to say.

"My skin will turn gray."

"Mom . . ."

"I won't have strength to talk."

"Mom, please."

She looked into my eyes and there was no fear in her expression.

"Whatever happens," she said, "I'll still be myself. Can you remember that?"

Five

She did not leave her bed through our first day at the house. She lay beside Lucy, the two of them inseparable, my mother stroking her ears and feeding her bites of the scrambled eggs she had no appetite to eat herself. She readjusted herself constantly, the strewn sheets an archive of her futile search for comfort. She asked for the painkiller, oxycodone, and complained about the wooziness it caused. She did without and complained about the pain. She closed her eyes and meditated, her palms held open at her sides. She explained that meditation can reduce the mental fog caused by painkillers. She listened to neuro-acoustically modified classical music designed to combat cognitive fatigue. I sat in the antique wooden chair beside her bed and tried to distract her from the pain by reading *Harry Potter* aloud. She gazed beyond her window to the pine trees swaying in the summer breeze.

"Is the marijuana here yet?" she asked that first evening.

She had ordered medical marijuana that was supposed to dull her pain without fogging her mind. The California supplier had promised it would be waiting by the time we returned from the surgery, but it hadn't arrived.

"I don't see any packages, but I can find pot. I'll walk into Goshen High waving a twenty and come out with the best weed in town."

"Please check again," she murmured, easing herself onto her side. "California shipping address. Medically engineered. This fog . . ."

It was not until our second day at home, when she had the strength to rise from bed, that I realized how completely my mother had transformed the house into a stronghold against the cancer. We limped downstairs, her hand gripping my shoulder. The guest bedroom was lined with medical equipment. She eased herself onto a vibrating black plate and explained that it had been developed to prevent astronauts from suffering muscle atrophy in space. Research showed it could also help chemotherapy patients retain weight. She had installed a cedar infrared sauna, which research linked to increased immune function in chemotherapy patients. She lay in a device that looked like a lawn chair, called a BEMER, that pulsed electromagnetic waves through her body, increasing blood and oxygen flow, a shadow war on the cancer cells.

"The human body," she said, reclining on the BEMER, "is designed to heal. With the right support, our bodies can recover from far more than we think."

Lucy pranced around her. My mother lifted her carefully onto her lap.

"There are so many ways to support the body through cancer," she said, caressing Lucy's glossy ears. "Most women are never educated about this," she continued, a hint of frustration in her voice. "The diagnosis comes, and the pressure is for an immediate, maximalist procedure: surgery, chemo, radiation. Women are made to feel that if we just do everything the doctors say, we'll be fine. But surgery and chemo aren't complete strategies. Rather than research all the ways to help our bodies through cancer, people tend to displace their anxiety onto one rigid plan."

My back creaked as I stretched over a rubber medicine ball, readjusting after the three nights on the hospital chair.

"Last year," she went on, "I watched two colleagues die from cancer. One refused any conventional treatment and the other refused any holistic treatment. These were savvy women, health professionals. It broke my heart to see these women so crippled by anxiety that neither could draw on her own best judgment. When I was diagnosed, I promised myself I wouldn't be led by fear."

She looked at me intently. I felt pride that she was managing the density of medical information alongside the physical and emotional burdens of her diagnosis. The CT scan had revealed that Dr. Chen had removed sixty percent of the tumor: more than the average debulking, less than she had hoped. The approach now was to eliminate the remainder of the tumor with chemotherapy, while my mother did everything she could to strengthen her body against the debilitating side effects.

The refrigerator was lined with kale, chicory, chard, each selected for its biochemical virtues. She unscrewed a bottle marked Huel, releasing a putrid stench. "Each scoop has five hundred calories," she said, "it's helping me slow weight loss. Too bad it tastes like steamed rodent." She reached for a raw burger from the refrigerator, and I felt the usual repulsion of seeing murdered animals transformed into conveniently shaped meals.

"After the first chemo," she said, dashing coconut oil into a stainless steel pan, "I hardly had the strength to chew. These burgers are grass-fed, the meat is so high quality I can eat it practically rare. Don't worry, I'll cook these myself."

The meat hissed in the pan, the awful stench wafting through the kitchen. I felt relieved that I didn't have to touch the meat. My mother yawned. Her body had dwindled from its healthy weight of one hundred and thirty-seven pounds to one hundred and eighteen. She had arranged everything in her life against the cancer, and I had to arrange myself that way, too. It didn't matter that dead animal repulsed me. There was no time to indulge any emotion besides my desire for her to heal. I reached for the spatula in her hand.

"Really?" she said, looking at me uncertainly. "I understand why you're not comfortable cooking meat."

"You should rest, Mom," I said.

"All right," she said, letting go of the spatula with some reluctance. "But you can tell me if you change your mind." She glanced at the meat. "If you are able to cook the burger, try to leave it pink at the center, OK? It should look almost raw. It's easiest for me to chew that way."

We climbed the stairs to her bedroom, my mother gripping my arm for balance.

Back in the kitchen I stared at the maimed remnant of cow sizzling in coconut oil, trying not to think about the animal grazing on a summer day. The only relevant concern was preventing my mother's weight loss. This cow had died so that she could live. I prodded at the meat, trying to sense how quickly it cooked. Our struggle rested now in detail. My mother's health depended on the precision with which the burger was cooked, the changes to her cancer cell count induced by the sauna and BEMER, the struggle for her weight fought by the Huel's addition and the chemotherapy's subtraction. After a few minutes the meat was lightly browned around the edges and pink at its center, as she had said it should be.

She sat up in bed, inhaling the scent of the meat. "Too well-cooked," she said, spitting out her first bite. "The meat is so tough, I don't have the energy. Can you try again? I'm sorry, honey."

She gave the burger to Lucy, who licked tentatively at the greasy surface, glancing at my mother as if asking for permission to eat.

"Yes, that's right, Lucy," she said. "It's all yours. That's how good you are!"

Lucy nodded politely, then devoured the meat.

On my fourth try the burger was rare enough for my mother to chew slowly. I sat beside her on the bed and tried not to cry with satisfaction.

THAT EVENING the medical marijuana arrived. Relief eased my mother's face as I handed her the package. She was reclining on the sofa, responding to emails from clients, Lucy's head tucked over her ankles. Inside the bubble wrap was a white vape pen, a dozen cartridges of oil cannabis, and twelve dropper bottles of tincture. The tinctures would have to wait. We were vaping tonight, like any responsible mother and son.

"You know how to use this?" she asked, looking skeptically at the vape pen.

"I have never," I said, "done drugs."

I slid one of the oil cartridges into the vape pen. There was a silver button on the barrel of the pen, and I held it down as I inhaled from the mouthpiece. The soothing force of the vape was far more immediate than the rolled joints I usually smoked.

"Oh, it's nice," I said. "You try. Just press that button as you breathe in."

She put the vape pen to her mouth and took a hesitant whiff.

"Come on, Mom, not some Clintonian non-inhalation."

She inhaled more deeply, coughing over the hit. Lucy looked up with concern.

"There we go! Just breathe, like you're meditating. That will prevent coughing."

She took another hit, this time calmly inhaling the drug.

"Oh, it's strong," she said. "Strange to think I used to do this all the time."

"Strange to think we've never lit up together," I said.

She reclined on the sofa, the drug already setting her at ease.

"When did you first smoke?" she asked.

"Second year at Oxford. This guy on my hall, Yonatan Emontovic, knew all about German lyric poetry, Japanese literature, Russian rock music. First time I smoked was from his water bong. Before the hit I was talking about Dostoevsky and afterward I felt like a kitten."

My mother laughed, the way she did on our video calls, even at my bad jokes.

"How about you?" I said, taking another drag. Gosh, that felt good. Just to breathe. That was the secret of marijuana, it was a breathing meditation as much as anything.

"I was fifteen. Some park in Great Neck. It was '68, you weren't invited to the revolution if you didn't have a joint in hand."

"A revolution in Great Neck?"

"A revolution in our minds."

"What did you want out of it?"

"To make love not war, haven't you heard?"

I was starting to feel the weed, could sense the room turning soft. Lucy wagged her tail. That's right, she was a dog. We held one another's gaze. *You are a dog*, I told her telepathically. I scooped her onto my lap, her eyes staring meaningfully into mine. Her ears were so soft. Oh,

I wanted to sauté them. Yes, that would be superb. To take off those doggie ears, so sleek and rare, and sizzle them in coconut oil. Those ears would go wonderfully with portobello mushrooms or eggplant. Maybe a little sliced onion and garlic. A Manhattan restaurant would charge a hundred dollars for that meal. I could have those ears here in the house for free. Lucy nuzzled her head into the crook of my arm. She needed her ears, I supposed. Through her ears she sensed predators in the woods, knew when to bark at coyote and dart away from a falling fork. No matter how tasty her ears might be, the sauté would be only a singular experience for me. Meanwhile, she would be condemned for all her days to a diminished life. No, it could not be justified.

"—much as anyone," my mother said.

"Sorry?" Smoke lingered between us. Lucy licked my face. What was she trying to tell me? Maybe she wanted me to have just one bite of her scrumptious little ears.

"I was saying how lovely it is to see you two admiring each other," my mother said, lowering her phone. Had she photographed me considering whether to sauté Lucy's ears? I would have to destroy the evidence. She slouched on the sofa, holding the vape pen like a teenager with a prized spliff. Gosh, it was good to see her smiling.

"Lucy," she said, "has taught me as much about life as anyone. She was so scared when she came to me. She barked and bit. The rescue shelter misled me. I told them I could only have a dog who was comfortable with people, six or seven patients come to my office every day. The first day Lucy snarled at a little boy. I didn't know what to do. If I sent Lucy back to the shelter, she might die. Still, I couldn't ask my patients to let a dog nip and bark through their sessions."

Lucy wagged her tongue at these past troubles.

"You know what Lucy taught me? There was more grace in my life than I knew. I could tell my patients Lucy is a rescue, has a traumatic past, and might bark or snarl. Some people let Lucy stay in the office. Others asked Lucy to stay in my bedroom. With enough love, she stopped snarling. She cuddled. She kissed. Lucy had never been loved before. Once she learned about love, her world opened."

Lucy stared at me, taking measure of my reaction to her biography.

"It's amazing to watch her live," my mother went on. "Every moment is joyful for her. A snuggle, a romp outside, a good meal. The same squeaky toy thrown the same way is always an adventure. We walk the same trail in the woods three or four times every day, and for Lucy it never has less than infinite potential. Every smell is divine. Life is magical because she sees it that way."

I took the vape from my mother and inhaled, the drug moving seamlessly through me.

"Do you remember," she asked, "when I used to read you Martin Buber's Hasidic tales?"

I didn't. I was certain I had discovered Buber in college.

"Buber was interested in this idea," she said, "first expressed by the Baal Shem Tov, the founder of Hasidism. The idea is that divinity is in every moment. The Baal Shem Tov lived in the eighteenth century, when Jewish knowledge was hoarded by the rabbinical class. He was a democrat, the Jewish version of Martin Luther. He believed ordinary people have access to the divine through every moment of our lives. Buber thinks Hasidism has forgotten this. Hasidism tries to find divinity in the preordained: ritual, prayer, clothing. Buber doesn't think that's how God works. God is in this world rather than outside this world. Every blade of grass is holy. In a way he's more Hasidic than the Hasidim. So is Lucy."

My mother took another hit on the vape pen.

"Because I have never," she said, "met anyone who finds more divinity in every moment of life than her. Lucy is my Baal Shem Tov."

Lucy lay serenely in my lap. Lucy, the last in the line of animals who lived at the farmhouse, the knights of our Round Table.

My mother reached to the shelf over her shoulder, withdrawing a book I recognized, a Ginsberg collection. "I," she said, "am in the mood for poetry."

She circled the room, glancing at the page before declaring, "'Holy! Holy! Holy! The world is holy! The soul is holy! The skin is holy! . . . The typewriter is holy the poem is holy!'"

I remembered the day I was thirteen and discovered that Ginsberg collection, read all I could, and then, embarrassed by its sexual explicitness, hid the book out of fear that my mother would discover it, forgetting that it was hers.

"'Holy forgiveness!'" she recited. "'Mercy! charity! faith! Holy! Ours! bodies! suffering! magnanimity! Holy the supernatural extra brilliant intelligent kindness of the soul!'"

"Holy!" I called.

"Holy!" said my mother.

Lucy stared anxiously between us. She need not worry, her ears were safe for now.

"I've always loved that poem," my mother said. "After 'Howl,' people thought Ginsberg had only criticisms to make. He didn't hate the world. He wanted to tell us what he loves."

"The typewriter is holy!" I called out.

"Your turn to read me something," she said.

"Did you ever meet Ginsberg?" I asked.

She looked quizzically at me.

"Why would I have met Ginsberg?"

"Because he was friends with Dylan."

My mother's fingers tensed on the vape. I sensed her lifting herself beyond the reach of the drug, as if she did not trust what she might say under its influence.

"I didn't meet his friends," she said. "If that's what you want to know. It wasn't that sort of relationship."

"What sort of relationship was it?"

"Let's discuss this another time."

"What other time, Mom?"

"Evan, please."

In the years since I'd left home I had almost never spoken about Dylan. I'd done all I could to keep the painful story pressed below the surface of my life. I had sought to become my own person on my own terms. But the question was always there, present even when absent. Blazed in the den, I wanted to know everything my mother had concealed from me. Every detail of their time together. What he was like as a person. If there were ways we were similar. Or if there was no reason we would be similar. Because above all I wanted clarity on a singular biological fact.

"You never talk about that period in your life," I said. "I hardly know anything about who you were at my age."

She breathed slowly, closed her eyes, and said, "My beloved son. Will you please share with me a poem you love?"

I didn't need to press the matter tonight. This was the first time since her surgery that she was at ease and I didn't want to take that from her. We had time ahead. This was the best chance I'd had in my adult life to speak with her directly about him and I wasn't going to waste it.

"From Bashō," I said, running my hand over Lucy's ears as I recited:

"'Coming with a light heart / to pick violets / I found it difficult to leave / and slept overnight / in this spring field.'"

"I've always loved Bashō's love of nature," my mother said, her voice calm once more.

"Then you'll like this one: 'Light, fancifully / sprinkled upon this world / tiny rains of spring.'"

She sighed contentedly, her eyes in mine.

"Even when I am a dog," I recited, "when I howl at the coyote / I miss being a dog."

"That's Bashō?" she laughed.

"With edits," I said. "You want the original?"

"Yes, please."

"'Even when I am in Kyoto / when the cuckoo sings / I miss Kyoto.'"

"It's beautiful that you committed all this to memory," she said.

"I don't know about commitment. The words just stayed with me."

She inhaled on the vape pen. Since we'd been smoking she hadn't said anything about the pain.

"One more Ginsberg," she said, holding up the book.

"Three more," I said.

She read. The words gathered around us. I could see the poem in the space between us.

"I saw the greatest minds of my generation," I intoned, "ruined by smokin' weed with their mothers."

"I've seen some of the dullest minds of my generation lately," my mother laughed.

"Dating again?"

"This last one charges into the diner fifteen minutes late, clutching a bouquet of roses. He says he's sorry to be late but he *had* to find the perfect roses because *I am the one*. He knew from the moment he clicked on my match.com profile. Didn't I feel it, too?"

I took another hit, sending the smoke through the open window.

"He starts rambling about his work in boat sales and all I can think is, *How soon am I allowed to leave?* On he goes: no breath, no questions, no distraction, except when the waitress comes he orders for both of us ('You have to try the broccoli omelet here!'). The first question he asks is whether I mind if he goes to the bathroom. As soon as he was out of sight I left the diner."

"Bravo!" I cheered. "I've been telling you for years to bail on these dunces."

"So much to unlearn. *Men!*" She tossed her arms overhead.

"Remember that time," I said, "you called me frantic from the car because you couldn't remember your date's name? You asked me to go into your office and find his dating profile. On your desk were all these photos of men, and I found the one you described, Hank. But I told you his name was Humbert. You kept repeating the name: Humbert Humbert Humbert. I was laughing so hard I had to hang up."

My mother gripped her abdomen as tears of laughter shone in her hazel eyes.

"But then I felt bad and called you back to tell you that his name was Hank. You were almost in the restaurant. I could tell you were stressed, you were going on so many dates at that point. Sorry I made things harder for you."

"I remember thinking," she said, still laughing, "that Hank/Humbert was so boring I'd rather have gotten his name wrong."

"I think part of me wanted you to know it was a prank. I mean, *Humbert?*"

She turned earnestly to me and said, "Thank you for being here."

"Mom?"

"Evan?"

"Where else would I be?"

She looked at me a long moment.

"We can talk," she said, "about New York. You should know it wasn't the easiest time in my life."

"Whatever happened," I said, "I want to know."

She nodded, and her expression relaxed into a smile, and she said, "Oh, you know what would be wonderful? Raspberry chocolates!"

She stood woozily from the sofa and wandered into the kitchen. I followed her, calling out, "Mom, you have the munchies?"

She reached into the cabinets and withdrew bar after bar of chocolate.

"And a sweet tooth? Who are you and what have you done with my mother?"

"They're all at least seventy percent cocoa," she laughed. "Did you know pure chocolate has anti-cancer properties? Chocolate is a natural insulin resistant *and* anti-inflammatory! Chocolate gets a bad rap because the commercial brands use so much sugar, but it's actually a health food. Antioxidants, endorphin boosters, dopamine support, oh my!"

"Mom, you are *blazed*."

She pointed the chocolate bar like a dagger at my heart.

"Mine eyes have seen the glory!"

From the cabinet she withdrew almond butter, stevia, and cacao, and heated the ingredients in a pan. She dripped the molten chocolate into the twelve penguin shapes on an ice cube tray. Then she set a raspberry atop each of the chocolate penguins and placed the tray in the freezer.

"I love," she said, "healthy sweets!"

This was the next best thing to sautéing Lucy's ears.

"Isn't it lovely," she said, "the way cancer gives as well as takes?"

At the word she was gaunt again, her hair gray beneath the kitchen light.

"Gives?" I said.

"We wouldn't have this time without it," she said. She was right. I would never have returned home just to read poetry and eat chocolate raspberries with my mother.

We sat on the sofa eating the raspberry chocolates as the coyote howled and the freight train echoed through the valley and the pine trees swayed over the farmhouse.

DAY

Six

That Friday morning at the hospital the security guard did not ask for our identification. On the second floor a woman behind the check-in desk asked my mother's name and how she would like to pay. My mother reached into her wallet, her expression uneasy as she handed her credit card to the hospital employee. She signed the receipt for the day's treatment, which, I saw over her shoulder, cost more than three thousand dollars.

A nurse in blue scrubs and a hairnet led us to a secluded room. My mother sat in the padded medical chair, and I took the chair near her. The nurse knelt beside her, searching her arm for a vein into which to insert the IV that would slowly drip the chemotherapeutic mixture into my mother's bloodstream. The drip began and the nurse said, "You'll be all set in eight hours."

My mother withdrew her magenta yarn and knitting needles from her cloth bag. "It's so strange being back here," she said. I imagined her in the same chair through the chemotherapy treatment she had taken alone, knitting as she told herself that it was not yet time for me to come home. "Yorkville has hardly changed," she said. "It feels like stepping back in time."

She looked through the window, and the street number and avenue came together in my mind, and I realized that we were in the neighborhood in which she had lived at my age. She was responding to my plea. She was bringing me into her memory. I studied her, imagining the young woman she must have been, as she appeared in the only photograph I had seen from that period of her life, a girl with yearning eyes, her auburn hair falling over shoulders left bare by a floral dress.

New York, my mother said, in the steady voice with which she read me stories when I was a child, was on fire when I arrived. This was the summer of 1973. Every night I'd climb through my bedroom window and up the fire escape onto the roof. From my building, near York and 78th Street, I could look north onto the fires in the Bronx and south onto the fires in the Lower East Side. It was Sodom and Gomorrah. The destruction of the Temple. The Triangle Factory fire on every block of New York.

Everything had burnt to the ground in my life as well. I was nineteen, alone in the city, too ashamed to tell anyone why I'd dropped out of college. My parents weren't speaking to me.

You know enough about my parents' lives to understand what it meant for them to send me to Bennington. They were children of the Depression, children of immigrants. When I was a child we used to go every Friday night to my grandparents' apartment in Bensonhurst, where my mother's parents lit the shabbes candles and whispered to one another in Yiddish. My mother never stopped seeing her life as one long escape from the shtetl her parents transplanted to Brooklyn. She was so proud of spurning the rabbi her father demanded she marry; you've probably heard her tell that story. My parents' instincts were for jazz, rock and roll, everything American. They danced to Louis Armstrong on their first date. My mother sang and my father played piano; they were a music act in the years between when they first fell in love and when I was born. I was their first child, the daughter who was supposed to make good on their choice to sacrifice their artistic ambitions, move to Long Island, strive for the white picket fence. My parents struggled to adjust to that life. When I was young my father moved from job to job, eventually working at a paper supply company. My mother studied to become a teacher. So what greater feeling of success could there be than sending me to Bennington to be educated alongside people whose families walked off the *Mayflower*? These were the real Americans my parents always wanted to be.

Of course we couldn't afford Bennington. I said it was fine, I'd go to Hunter. I liked the idea of being in New York, and I knew how many brilliant people went to CUNY. Vivian Gornick, the iconic feminist writer. Grace Paley, whose poetry I idolized in high school. Herbert Zuckerman, my parents' most valued friend. Herbert directed theater on Long Island, and I first fell in love with theater as a child going to his productions of Arthur Miller and Eugene O'Neill. Herbert was unlike anyone we knew. He could quote almost anything from the American stage. He knew people in the New York theater world, or at least said he did. My parents trusted Herbert far too much. He had dated my mother and been best friends with my father until my parents married. He would come to our house whenever he pleased, laughing at some joke he claimed Elia Kazan had told him at a party. Herbert taught a summer theater class for girls, and when I turned twelve he insisted I join, flattering my parents with the idea that I had a natural gift for theater. By the time I was thirteen he was taking me alone to Broadway shows.

My parents were furious that I'd even consider turning down Bennington. My father told me, "If you need to take two jobs on campus, you take two jobs. If you need to take three, you take three." He was a warm man, I wish you had known him. He was sensitive, introverted, artistic. Rarely domineering. He must have felt that he had worked so hard, and now I had a chance to cross the bridge from our semi-middle-class life into genuine American possibility, if I'd only stop complaining about how hard the walk was.

Bennington is surrounded by woods and mountains. The buildings blend into the landscape, the way Shakespeare's pastoral plays unfold entirely within nature. I remember discussing *A Midsummer Night's Dream* in the forest, six students sitting cross-legged on branches and moss as we listened to Ralph Summers, whose plays my father had given me in high school. Summers was ruddy and handsome, at the peak of his talents in his mid-forties, always dressed in linen suits.

Every night I read on the wicker chair outside my dorm. Homer, Virgil, Dante, Marlowe, Ibsen. Nights of earth and sky and feelings. I sat alone with my notebook and felt—you must know this from your own experience—that life could make sense through the written word in a way it never otherwise does. When the sun rose over the hills, and figures wandered out of the dorms, I was always surprised to remember there were other people on campus.

I worked fifteen hours a week in the library and another fifteen in the cafeteria. I stacked books and cleared dishes. It wasn't easy making friends. I wasn't part of the world everyone else seemed to come from. Boys who drove Mustang convertibles to New York on weekends. Girls who knew each other from boarding school, their fathers were partners in the same law firms. I didn't care that prep schools had armed my classmates with witty lines about *Hamlet*. I had my own observations to make. Through those nights on the wicker chair that autumn my thoughts and feelings came together into a first play.

One night a few weeks before Thanksgiving my mother called. She told me the paper supply company my father worked for had lost a major client and demoted him to part-time. My parents couldn't help with tuition any longer. I felt bad for my father, that company worked him so hard and didn't seem to have the slightest loyalty to him. He'd been there eight or nine years. The least of my frustration was that I'd have to leave Bennington. I didn't fit in on campus anyway. I'd had this notion that my ideas could make up for not having the same background as most other students. That just wasn't true. No matter how hard-earned or sincere my ideas might be, I was never going to speak in the right way, know the references that mattered, wear the right clothes. More than that, I didn't care about those norms. I didn't come from money and had no interest in pretending otherwise. I resented the idea that culture and class are synonymous. I told my mother it was fine, I'd transfer to Hunter. She wouldn't hear a word about me leaving Bennington. She kept insisting that I could find more work on campus, yelling that this wasn't an excuse to give up, that nobody in our family had ever had an opportunity like this and I wasn't to throw it away. I wanted to make her proud.

She was right that I could find more work on campus. I started doing odd jobs: typing classmates' papers, washing their laundry, even changing the oil in the boys' muscle cars. I never minded the work. But the comments—being a woman and more guarded in my sexual life, because, well. A few of the boys let me know that changing oil wasn't the only thing they'd pay me for. Bennington is a small campus, and I could feel people starting to see me a certain way.

It was worthwhile for the nights I wrote in the wicker chair and the Shakespeare seminar with Ralph Summers. By spring I had finished a draft of my play. One day, after class, I gathered my courage and asked Ralph Summers if he might read the opening pages. He flashed his white toothy grin and said to give him the entire play. Every time I walked into the forest that semester I wondered if this was the day Summers would say something about my play. He never did. Then, on the last day of the spring term, the class sat on fallen tree trunks and Summers passed around champagne and lectured on *The Comedy of Errors*. When he finished, the mood was buoyant and congratulatory, everyone talking about where in Europe they were off to for the summer. We all wandered across the campus lawn, and Summers smiled at me, as if just realizing I was there, and said too quietly for the others to hear, "June, your play—why don't you come to my office."

There were well wishes for the summer, and promises to write, and Summers and I walked alone into a barn converted to faculty studios. He led me up the stairs into a loft with books piled against every wall. There at the center of his desk was my play. Summers gestured me into a chair, and circled me in his cream linen suit, saying my writing was simply spectacular. Then he went silent as his hand slipped inside the front of my dress.

I don't remember standing. Or running across the lawn. I remember turning the lock on my bedroom door and knowing I had to leave campus that night. I couldn't risk the humiliation of seeing Ralph Summers again. What was I supposed to say if he asked to speak with me alone? If he tried to convince me I had misunderstood? I could still feel his hand on my skin. I wanted to report what he had done but didn't know who to tell. It would be my word against his. He was a famous playwright. A star of the English department. Who was going to believe me? Anyway, he had been the adult I felt closest to on campus.

I called my mother and told her I needed to leave Bennington that night, could she meet me at the bus station in New York?

After a few questions I admitted to her that my final exams were the following week, and if I left campus before the exams I wouldn't receive credit for the term. She shrieked at me. I held the phone to my ear, tears streaming down my face, thinking of Herbert Zuckerman. I wanted to call him. He would let me stay with him. He would drive to Bennington in the middle of the night. I told myself: don't you dare call that man.

In the morning I lugged my suitcase into town and took the bus to New York. I didn't say goodbye to anyone at Bennington. I would have had to say goodbye as myself, and I didn't want to be myself. I wanted to go somewhere nobody knew me. Staring through the bus window, farmland and hills passing by, I didn't care that Summers had the only copy of my play. I never wanted to write again.

It wasn't hard to find waitressing work in New York. Within a day I was working at a diner on Madison and 76th. The uniforms were tight leggings and low-cut shirts. Men whistled or did worse. I dissociated. Told myself: I am an actress, cast as a waitress sexualized by male patrons. Sometimes I played this role as Chekhov's Yelena, beautiful and bored. Other times I was Nora from Ibsen's *A Doll's House*: naive to the outside eye, plotting within. I'm not sure if this will make sense to you, but it helped that I was always standing and the men were sitting.

For the first weeks I was on the move, sleeping on different sofas or floors. Eventually another waitress told me about an open apartment in Yorkville, a third-floor walk-up on 78th Street, in an old rent-stabilized building. The moment I walked into that apartment I loved every bit of its dilapidated charm. Paint cracked across the ceiling. There was a gaping hole where the heat pipes met the floor. The window looked onto a courtyard garden with a cherry tree. Gazing through that window felt like opening the pages of *The Secret Garden*, the book I loved most as a child. When I signed the lease and paid my deposit I felt this tremendous sense of freedom: The city is mine. Nobody knows me. I can become anyone I want.

So those evenings I climbed the roof and watched the fires burn across New York, I felt kinship with the flames. Everything in my life was being destroyed and reborn.

One morning, while waitressing in the diner, I heard two girls my age talking about how anyone could walk into Stella Adler's acting studio. I was taken aback. My mother had been talking about the Adlers since I was a child. They were the most celebrated family of the New York Yiddish theater. Stella's father came from Russia in the late nineteenth century and did as much as anyone to establish Yiddish theater in New York. He was known for starring in Shakespeare plays adapted to the Russian shtetl, he once played a Yiddish King Lear. Stella was practically born onstage. She grew up to become the first Adler to make it from the Yiddish theater to Broadway. Then she went to Hollywood and changed her name to Ardler. She was six feet tall, blonde, and could easily be mistaken for Ingrid Bergman. Stella was everything my mother wanted to be, the child of Jews who fled decaying European empires and became someone in America. My mother loved telling me how she snuck into the theater as a teenager to see Stella in *He Who Gets Slapped*.

It seemed inconceivable that anyone could walk into Stella's studio. She was the most influential acting teacher in the country. You're probably familiar with method acting, the idea that, rather than drawing from her own life, an actress should abandon her experience and imagine her way into the character. Marlon Brando made it famous. Later there was Warren Beatty, Robert De Niro, Harvey Keitel. Every one of those men learned method acting from Stella Adler.

I didn't understand why Stella would waste a moment on someone like me. Still, I had nothing to lose. I didn't want to write anymore but was thrilled by the idea of transforming myself into someone else. The promise of no longer having to be myself. I walked into Stella's studio because it was a portal into a different life and every other door seemed closed.

That first morning at her studio I followed voices down the corridor into a theater at the rear of the building. Onstage a dozen pairs of students were repeating lines to one another. Standing with her arms folded, dressed in an elegant black blouse, was a gracefully aged woman who radiated the authority of a military commander. Stella strode toward a lanky blond boy who was anxiously circling his partner, shouting his monologue at her.

"Stop," Stella ordered. In her accent there was no trace of her father's Yiddish or my grandparents' Russian.

"Where is the feeling?" She glared at the boy. "You are all motion and no emotion. You are repeating the words without understanding their meaning. Alma has no idea why you're furious with her because you don't know yourself. Now begin again."

Stella circled the room, hands clasped behind her back, pausing to inspect each rehearsing pair. She delivered her corrections with dignified outrage. After several minutes she looked across the theater at me and snapped, "You came here to stand or act?"

I paired with the blond boy. The scene was an argument between Alma and John in Tennessee Williams's *Summer and Smoke*. Stella circled us, her eyes penetrating each student. Midway through my second line of dialogue I sensed her standing behind me. I tried to imagine what my mother would say if she knew Stella Adler was looking at me. If she would forgive me for leaving Bennington. I felt all the loneliness of my first weeks in New York. My confusion about what I was doing with my life. My shame that I had invited Ralph Summers's attention by asking him to read my play. What a fool I'd been, hanging on to his every word all semester, making clear just how much I admired him.

What had I thought I was getting myself into by going alone to his office when he'd had that much champagne? Now I couldn't go back to Bennington. I had wasted everything my parents worked to give me. I'd been sensitive and let my feelings get the best of me. I'd given up one of the best educations in the country and instead become a waitress. No wonder my parents weren't speaking to me. I turned to the blond boy and delivered my lines, feeling Alma's despair for John through the despair I felt for myself.

"Stop," Stella commanded. Her brutal blue eyes fixed on mine. "What are you concentrating on?"

I told her: "I am thinking about my mother's disdain for my decisions, and experiencing Alma's loneliness through my own."

"That's the last time you'll do that," Stella snapped. "Acting isn't about you, young lady. It's about imagining things you haven't experienced. And I've got news for you: there's far more you haven't experienced than you have. You're not going to be a very interesting actress if you interpret every character through your own viewpoint, are you? You're here to turn yourself into other people, not turn other people into you. Now begin again."

I went to the studio every day. We trained in Eugene O'Neill and Clifford Odets and William Saroyan. The blond boy, Kenny, became my scene partner. He had hitchhiked to New York from Indiana ten days before. Stella's class was filled with people who had snuck onto Greyhound buses or walked across a dozen states to New York, fleeing small towns and narrow destinies. Everyone you met was draped in their own mythology. They were lovely stories.

There wasn't one day Stella didn't reprimand me. When I sensed her behind me, I knew it was only a moment before she would begin to shout at me.

"Thinking about your mother again?" she'd yell. "Well, nobody pays five dollars to see you think about your mother. They want Alma wounded by John. Understand?"

I'd wake on my bedroom floor to Stella shouting, "Don't you dare think about your mother!" But in the dream Stella was my mother.

I flinched when Stella shouted at me in class. It also felt liberating. When Stella told me everything I'd done wrong I felt tremendous possibility, that if I listened to what she taught me, it didn't matter that I'd dropped out of college and was alone in New York. The greatest drama teacher of her generation cared enough to raise her voice at me. Every day after class I watched the fires from my roof and tried to deliver the lines the way Stella instructed me.

The only time Stella became genuinely angry was when she felt a student wanted to succeed overnight rather than learn the fundamentals of acting.

"Don't you dare try to be discovered," she'd shout. "Try to discover yourself."

One day, as class dispersed, Stella called my name. She handed me a page clipped out of *Backstage*, with a casting call circled. I stammered my thanks. Stella looked hard at me and said, "Straighten your hair, young lady. You're auditioning for the American theater, not the Yiddish theater."

The audition was for the first ghost in *Macbeth*. The ghost has two lines of dialogue, and I spent weeks perfecting my delivery. At the audition, the director nearly laughed when I finished my lines. He dismissed me with a flick of his wrist.

I was embarrassed to tell Stella. Still, it was better that she heard it from me than someone else.

"Did you think you had a chance at that role?" she said. "There are reasons to try out besides getting the part. You needed the experience, young lady."

I started going to every audition I could. Kenny and I watched the fires from my roof and looked together through *Backstage*. Once, I auditioned for Ibsen's Hedda Gabler the same week Kenny auditioned for Biff from *Death of a Salesman*. For two weeks we only spoke to each other in character. We'd go to the pizzeria on 78th and First, and I'd conduct myself as a bored Norwegian housewife and he as an aging high school football star. Neither of us were satisfied with life, but we couldn't understand one another's disappointments. Hedda was unsympathetic to Biff's obsession with middle-class stability, while Biff didn't understand why Hedda wanted more than the comfortable life she already had.

By the time the audition came I'd been speaking as Hedda for so long that when my name was called I didn't walk onstage.

After my audition, as I was leaving the building, the director found me in the hallway and said, "You're Hedda Gabler."

My first thought was *Yes, I know*. Then I realized he was offering me the role.

The production was in an unknown theater downtown. There were seats missing all through the theater, like broken teeth in an open mouth. Half the stage lights didn't work. Gordon, the director, paced the rehearsal stage in a torn black coat, shouting at me to repeat every line. I couldn't understand why he'd cast me. Where I was reserved, Gordon wanted turbulence. Where I was turbulent, he wanted aloofness. He was only a few years older than me, but he shouted at me as if he were Ibsen and I were illiterate. I hated when he raised his voice. It was humiliating to feel unable to give what he expected. I'd only been in Stella's studio several months and wasn't ready to play Hedda. I should have known better than to try.

One day, after class, I asked Stella the most respectable way to withdraw from a role.

"Excuse me?" she said. "If you relinquish your role, you won't be welcome in this studio ever again. Now, if you'd like to tell me why this role feels beyond you, we can work together on the difficulty."

We began meeting every evening after class.

"Before we begin," Stella said that first night, "I want you to know that your insecurity is selfish. Acting is not about you. It is about the relationship between the character and the audience. The actress is a medium, nothing more. It is a great privilege to serve as that medium. You are part of a tradition that has existed for twenty-five hundred years. It will continue to exist whether you are arrogant, insecure, celebrated, or ignored. None of that should concern you. All that should concern you is achieving your character to the greatest possible extent."

If Stella told me that my own name shouldn't concern me, I would have agreed. Having time with her in the studio after the other students left felt like being invited home by God.

She divided our hour into two halves: studying the text and rehearsing scenes. I don't know if you're familiar with *Hedda Gabler*. It's about a woman who encounters a lost lover, cannot endure the contrast of that former passion with her loveless marriage, and reacts by telling her lover to commit suicide, then killing herself.

Stella told me she once heard a man describe the play as a critique of Hedda's nihilism. "The man who told me this," Stella said, "either slept through the play or slept through life. Nihilism is what Hedda objects to. All around her is a society in which people endure marriage without love and conversation without sincerity. That is what Hedda seeks to escape by suicide."

She never covered more than a page in our hour together. She dwelled on each stage direction and line of dialogue.

"There is no throwaway word," she'd say. "Every line is laid like train track."

In the evenings I rehearsed my lines on the rooftop and the fires burned the city and with each hour I was less myself and more Hedda Gabler. Her resentments coursed through me. I was sick of mindless men who saw me as a body. I was repulsed by their empty witticisms and unconvincing advances. Gordon was as repulsive as any of them, storming the stage in his ludicrous torn blazer to lambast me for departing from his vision. When he shouted at me, I replied not in my voice but Hedda's. As she explained her rationale for the way she held her body or used her voice, Gordon quit shouting.

No matter how intently I rehearsed, there were two moments that always left my mind blank, the dialogue simply refusing to surface in my mind.

The first is when Hedda is visited by Judge Brack, a cunning gossip whose sexual interest in her is leering and unrequited. Judge Brack circles Hedda on her sofa, threatening her against reuniting with her lover. Hedda is supposed to respond, "I am glad you have no hold over me."

Any time Judge Brack stood outside my line of vision I couldn't remember the line.

The second moment is Hedda's final conversation with her lover, before his death. He says to her, "To kill his child is not the worst thing a father can do."

Hedda's reply is simple but I could never remember it.

"June!" Gordon would shout after a humiliating silence. "Get your goddamn lines down!"

The line should have been easy for me to recall.

Hedda's lover: "To kill his child is not the worst thing a father can do."

Hedda: "Not the worst?"

On opening night there wasn't one empty seat. I strode onstage and was shocked to see my parents in the fourth row. I couldn't think of how they knew about the play. I was thrilled to show them everything I was working toward in New York. To prove that I was making something of myself, despite my mistakes at Bennington. Still, for the sake of acting, I had to remind myself: I don't know those people. I am Hedda Gabler. That woman is not my mother. My father is the deceased General Gabler.

When Judge Brack circled me, I silently pleaded that he stood in my line of vision. In the moment he threatened me, I glimpsed his judge's robes and shouted, "'I am glad you have no hold over me!'"

I looked into the audience for my parents but saw Stella. She hadn't told me she was coming to the play. I reminded myself that I didn't know her. She was any ordinary woman. The rest of the performance I couldn't rid my mind of the image of Stella finding me after the show and saying that I'd assimilated everything she taught me into the role. In the closing scene, as I lay dead on the floor, the pistol that ended my life still in my hand, I imagined emerging from the dressing room to find Stella and my mother discussing my performance.

The curtain fell, and I stood from the floor and hurried into the dressing room, changed clothes, and came out to find my parents. They weren't there. I stood in the theater lobby as the crowd thinned, realizing I'd imagined my parents in the audience.

After class the following day I thanked Stella for all she had taught me.

"I don't compliment myself," she replied curtly, "and I'm certainly not going to compliment you. So go fishing in some other lake, my dear."

Then she listed everything I'd done inadequately, culminating with my greatest sin: "I saw you looking at me no less than four times. If you ever do that again, I'll stand up and walk right out of the theater."

The show only ran for a week.

THE CITY BECAME my university. New York teemed with people like me who didn't know where we belonged and decided it must be with one another. We crowded into each other's apartments, reading poetry, playing music, acting impromptu scenes. Alph, one of the regulars in Stella's class, gave violin lessons at his apartment in the East Village, six of us passing around two instruments. We held quirkily themed poetry readings—you could only read a poet whose last name began with a vowel—and blindfolded dance parties.

That winter Stella told me to visit a studio on the eleventh floor of Carnegie Hall. I didn't dare ask where she was sending me. Carnegie was a haunted house, with burst pipes hanging out of the walls and parts of the ceiling caved in. When I arrived that morning, fragments of music drifted down the stairs. I walked the corridors, glimpsing rehearsing actors and dancing children behind closed doors.

In the studio to which Stella had sent me, twelve people sat on the floor. Sunlight washed over easels and piles of paint-stained rags. Every eye followed a gray-haired man who was circling a smoked mackerel set on a silver tray, his gnarled fingers stained with silver paint.

"None of your paintings are even interesting failures," the man said in a heavy Yiddish accent. "None of you have told me anything I do not already know. All I have learned from your paintings is that this is a fish. Have I learned to desire this fish? No. Have I learned the succulent, seductive, irresistible taste of this fish? No. Rembrandt makes you hungry for his peaches, yes? Peeters make you desperate for her cheese. I feel neither hunger nor desperation for your fish."

I sat cross-legged at the outskirts of the group. Nobody looked at me.

"In your paintings," the man went on, "I see mere description. Nothing more than information. Any idiot on Seventh Avenue knows the information you have painted. Fish have scales. Fish have eyes. Fish have gills. A painting must tell me something I don't know. Tell me I desire this fish more than I dare admit to myself. Tell me I would walk across the tundra for this fish. Like Doctor Zhivago for Lara, nu?"

There was a cot in a nook of the studio. Beside the cot was a table with a jar of Nescafé. *This man*, I thought to myself, *lives entirely within his painting.*

"Do not despair that you have failed," he went on. "Every painting is a failure. Anything worthwhile, that is. I'm not talking about what passes for painting today, what the clever fools have managed to convince the world is art. I'm not talking about soup cans. Genuine art is incomplete. It is a failure. You must create the worthiest failure possible. Now enough talk, everyone get back to failing."

That first day I did not paint. I sat on the radiator and observed the other students and listened to every word spoken by the gray-haired man.

Soon I was attending Norman Raeben's class several times a week. His studio operated by the same rule as Stella Adler's: anyone who wanted to learn could walk in. There were gruff guys who maybe worked construction. Wealthy women in pearls. Young painters who dropped out of art school. People like me who were actors or poets but understood Raeben was teaching more than painting. Some days there were thirty students, others five. Raeben never appeared to notice. He paced and painted and talked in a rolling monologue that seemed to have begun in the Russian shtetl where he was born. He spoke about

Dostoevsky's relationship to God and Steve Reich's mastery of silence. He spoke in Yiddish, English, French, Russian, and cursed God in biblical Hebrew. I'd only ever heard Yiddish when my grandparents didn't want me to know they were talking about the ovens. Raeben spoke with such confidence that I wasn't embarrassed to hear the language. One of the other students told me that Raeben was the son of Sholem Aleichem, the best-known writer of nineteenth-century Jewish literature, whose Yiddish short stories were adapted into *Fiddler on the Roof*. Raeben had been born in Russia as Nochum Rabinovich and come to New York at thirteen, in 1914.

Most mornings Raeben described what he had seen on his walk to Carnegie Hall from his apartment, on Central Park West and 100th. The expression on a squirrel's face as it fled a bicycle. Sweat on a jogger's throat. Shadow and light on lovers' clasped hands. He spoke about the feelings and memories each observation evoked in him. He would say, "Only paint if it is holy. This is what the Hasidim understand. Your painting must be a prayer to life. Your painting must be a way of life."

Raeben had an intensely physical relationship to his canvas. He stood before his easel with his feet firm on the hardwood, weight held back. Then he seemed to lunge forward, moving his brush across the canvas with impassioned sweeps. It was easy to mistake this method as impulsive, to miss how meticulously he studied the canvas before he began.

His style itself was otherworldly. Looking at his canvas was like seeing life and a dream at the same time. His painting was more romantic yet more brutal than life. Raeben believed a painter was a kind of journalist, but he should report the truth rather than the facts. He should report expressions on the street. His paintings were mirages, quotidian scenes glossed with a feeling of transcendence, the way detail in Proust is ordinary and spectacular. A man smoking a cigarette, a car on the open road. Raeben said every grain of sand was divine. He had been influenced by the Ashcan School, especially Robert Henri, who rebelled against both impressionism and figurative realism. For Henri, impressionism had no appreciation for life as it is experienced. Impressionism could only paint beauty, but not every moment in life is beautiful. At the same time, Henri felt that figurative realism was too removed, analytic, unfeeling. That style, too, had no love for ordinary life. Henri's project, which Raeben made his own, was to paint the glory of ordinary life in all its rough mundanity.

He'd look up from his canvas, wet paint on his arms, and scowl: "If you are imitating me, leave now. You will become an embarrassment to the very idea of painting. You will be like a chicken clucking after another chicken. You need to become your own chicken, nu?"

If something angered him on a student's easel, he painted over it, scolding as he went. "What is this? Now you're a conceptualist? Then please go make non-paintings with the other riffraff. If you don't know by now what is the problem of conceptualism I won't begin to explain. God forbid I ever again have to say the name Warhol."

He could be brutal. Once, he flicked paint off a brush into the eyes of one of the younger boys. "You enjoy being blind?" Raeben shouted. "Everything you've done is worthless. Completely worthless!" The boy never came back.

Another time Raeben shoved a canvas off a woman's easel. The painting clattered to the floor, and Raeben shouted, "You are proud to know nothing? If you want even the slightest chance of ever creating anything worthwhile, then start at the very beginning."

He gave her a Torah and told her to sit on the floor and read.

On the canvas I painted the first month in Raeben's studio, a seated woman came alive in gold and white. I couldn't say what I was painting.

Maybe it was me at the diner, enjoying rather than serving a meal. Or *Hedda Gabler* on the sofa. Or the wicker chair at Bennington where I read so many nights. I asked Raeben if it was wrong that I didn't know what I was painting.

"Wrong?" he laughed. "None of you should rush into any so-called understanding of what you are painting. In Stalinism, there are five-year plans. In art, there are no five-year plans. An artist must learn to react in every moment. You must feel in each moment what you feel in each moment. That is what you paint. When you are old and limping you can ask me about so-called understanding. In my own case, I am just beginning to understand. With luck, I will know what I have spent my life painting before I meet my creator."

In the evenings we critiqued each other's work. Raeben always had the last word.

"Why are your colors so sweet?" he shouted at an older woman one evening. He snatched the brush from her and began painting over her work in brooding brown. "You want to be Renoir? Go into the candy business. Buy yourself a little store on Seventh Avenue and sell sweets to the children. Nu? Now, if you want to be a painter, please paint something true rather than something sweet."

Nothing angered Raeben more than the question of talent. "Yes, you all have talent," he'd bark. "The man touching himself on Seventh Avenue has talent. But who among you has rags?"

Around this time Gordon called to say he wanted to stage *Hedda Gabler* again. He wasn't going through the gatekeepers, men in two-hundred-dollar coats drinking whiskey at noon. We didn't need their permission: he was going to stage the play in a friend's loft.

The loft was in the Manheimer building on 23rd and Seventh. Almost all of *Hedda Gabler* is set in her living room, and as we walked through the loft I saw how natural this setting would feel. The loft could fit fifteen folding chairs and we'd cap the audience there, which would give the performance an intimacy missing on the professionalized stage.

By the third night there was a line outside the building an hour before curtain time. We didn't charge for tickets, but before the play began Gordon stalked the loft in his torn blazer, speaking about how theater has been the most democratic art form since the time of the Greeks, today's gatekeepers care more about making profit than art so it's up to us to create an alternative, please give what you can. We split what came in and I made more money than any week I waitressed.

We performed every Friday and Saturday evening that spring. One night I saw Stella in the rear of the loft. When I looked for her after the play she was gone.

A few days later I was in Raeben's studio. He was painting a still life of a smoked mackerel, pacing intently around the fish, pointing with his brush at its silver skin. "The relationship of the painter to the painting," he said, kneeling beside the fish, "should be like love in Proust, madly desirous and just beyond reach. When Swann loves Odette, he does not understand her. When Swann understands Odette, he no longer loves her. Why? Because to understand a lover is to deny the most sublime experiences of intimacy, nu? So it is between Swann and Odette, and so it is between you and any worthwhile painting. Try to feel what you paint, not to understand it."

The door opened and an unshaven man with shaggy hair wandered into the studio. He wore dirty jeans and a rumpled shirt and looked like he'd slept the night in Central Park. I couldn't say where I knew him from. Maybe we had gone to high school together in Great Neck, or once auditioned for the same role. I was wondering if he was one of the men who played cards at the pizzeria on 78th and First Avenue when I realized he was Bob Dylan.

The unshaven man in the doorway didn't align with any of the Dylans of my mind. There was the Dylan of my childhood, the baby-faced folk hero singing "A Hard Rain's A-Gonna Fall" on my parents' record player. The Dylan whose songs I heard as a teenager, people singing "Masters of War" at high school protests against the war in Vietnam. By then Dylan had vanished. He was out somewhere in the north country, upstate New York. Biding his time, refusing to be the prophet everyone wanted him to be. There were stories of people tracking him down in his small town, climbing through his bedroom window and demanding he lead the country toward the promises in his songs. Rumor was that the attention had driven him mad. People said he'd fabricated a motorcycle accident to get away from it all. I'd heard people claim that if you listened closely to his last records, you could hear it wasn't Dylan singing but a hired imitator. Dylan seemed more lost Byronic poet than living artist. It was startling to think all that myth had been built around the man slouching in Raeben's doorway, an anxious hand in his unkempt curls, taking in the paint-stained rags on the floor.

"If you're here to paint," Raeben said, "your first task is to go to the drugstore across Seventh Avenue and retrieve for us two jars of Nescafé. And take the elevator rather than the stairs, we don't have all day."

Dylan nodded earnestly and turned out of the doorway. Whispers drifted through the studio. Raeben knelt beside the smoked mackerel. One of the art school dropouts, Henry, leaned beside him. His words were reincarnated as agitated wrinkles on Raeben's face.

"He is who? So you are telling me he wrote some nice songs? Good for all of you who like pretty songs. Perhaps he will sing you a lullaby."

It seemed unthinkable that he didn't recognize Dylan's name. But

Raeben never made a contemporary reference. The closest he came were dismissive comments about "what the fools count as art these days." Lichtenstein and Warhol were "those foolish boys." Raeben considered himself part of a tradition that reached back to the Torah, to the days when God created heaven and earth. He was unimpressed with commercial success, didn't have much himself. He believed we were living through a time plagued by foolishness, he liked to say there was an idiot wind blinding our age. He seemed to believe that, until this passed, the only thing to do was paint and teach anyone who cared to learn. Perhaps Raeben really was unaware of anything remotely new.

Or maybe he knew Dylan's music and was making clear that this was his studio and nobody was going to fawn over another artist.

"I have made a mistake with this amber," Raeben said, looking disgustedly at his canvas. The class gathered behind Raeben's easel. Dylan came through the door with a Nescafé jar in each hand. His expression was quietly focused, as if he had completed the mundane task with the conviction that it was the first step toward wisdom.

"I have applied the amber too thoughtfully," Raeben said, "and thought is the death of the artist. Look at these symmetrical amber lines. What is truthful about this? Nothing. What is symmetrical in life? Nothing. Truthful painting is asymmetrical. And here I have painted symmetry. The artist must be intelligent enough to leave his intelligence behind. What matters is sight, yes? And this amber sees nothing."

Raeben painted over the amber with thick brown strokes. "Now everyone get back to your own problems," he said, glowering at the smoked mackerel.

Dylan carried an easel to the corner of the studio overlooking 57th Street. He glanced between the easel and the rest of us, deciding whether to arrange himself such that his canvas was concealed and his face visible or his canvas visible and his face concealed. Whispers flitted through the room. He positioned himself behind the easel, his shaggy hair and aloof expression on view to the class for the moment before he withdrew sunglasses from his front shirt pocket. Dylan still hadn't said a word. There was an aura about him, and I wondered if it would shatter the moment he spoke. It was hard to describe his magnetism, the way everything oriented itself around him, the air and silence. He was handsome, even if I'd seen better-looking men. No, it was that I could hear the music when I looked at him. One glance at him and "Just Like a Woman" was playing in my mind. Everyone else must have been feeling this, too, different songs playing in every heart. We'd all kissed and smoked and cursed the war to his words and rhythms. He didn't have to say anything; just standing there he was a silent repository of other people's memories. I felt the awe and fear of what that could do to a life.

I turned back to my canvas. Still life was always a struggle for me. When we painted a nude model I felt intimate with the human body in a way I never did with my own. When we painted landscapes I felt the freedom I've always loved in nature. Still life felt like some stiff task set by a Dutch master. I was moved by everything that came after that: light and movement and color in Monet, Pissarro, Renoir. I never dared voice this to Raeben. He insisted that still life was where an artist came to meet himself. It was easy, Raeben said, to transform a landscape by color, imagination, emotion. That was the bread and butter of the impressionists. What about transforming the object that by itself evokes no magnificent feeling? Can you paint grapes or a glass of wine with such vibrancy that the paint transcends the canvas and becomes the object itself? Remember, Raeben said, the hunger Rembrandt makes you feel for his peaches. Remember Cézanne, who said, "With an apple I will astonish Paris." Across the studio Dylan stared between his canvas and the smoked mackerel, as if the intensity of his gaze could vanish the distance between the object and his painting.

In the early evening Raeben gestured us into a circle. He examined each of our canvases, describing their flaws and stunted successes. Dylan knelt outside our circle, drawing no attention to himself. I sensed he'd learned to live behind those sunglasses, that he was so used to being removed from other people that it didn't occur to him to speak to us. When his turn came Dylan took off his sunglasses and angled his easel toward us. Even without the glasses I couldn't see him. There was a stoic gloss over his eyes, a shield he lived behind.

He had painted something like the fish and porcelain plate. The elongated fish arched over the canvas, eyes desperate with the last moments of life. The silver plate waited below. The fish, plate, and background were all shades of blue that bled into one another, a tale from the borderland of the figurative and abstract.

An older woman with golden earrings said, "Your brushstrokes speak like your lyrics."

Dylan looked like a cold-eyed killer. He didn't even bother glancing at her.

"If I close my eyes," said Henry, and he closed his eyes, "I hear 'Mr. Tambourine Man.'"

One of the other art school students said, "You calling this *Blue on Blue*?"

Everybody laughed, except Dylan. He looked bored. Nobody was telling him what his painting might be. He wasn't being treated as a beginner who wanted to learn but rather a genius to be revered. He must be treated like this all the time, I thought to myself. I could think of nothing that would make a person more lonely or withdrawn. Staring into Dylan's canvas I saw that alienation. The shades of blue were so remote from one another it was hard to feel any intimacy. When it was my turn to speak I told him so.

"If the blues were differentiated more subtly," I said, "the darker shades would dominate the canvas less, and offer a more natural way into the painting."

The room went silent. Dylan glared at me, as if I had no right to tell him what was wrong with his work. No one else had dared criticize his canvas. I had miscalculated. Dylan must be as protective of his status as he was resentful toward it. But the longer Dylan's eyes lingered in mine, the more he seemed to be looking at me as if I knew something he wanted.

Raeben lumbered toward the painting, gesturing with his stained hands.

"You are imagining without seeing," he declared. "You want to transform a fish into a feeling? Fine. We are all here to transform objects into feelings. First you must see the object. Here I do not see a fish but only your imagination of a fish. Where are the scales? You have forgotten them. I see an idea detached from anything in this world. Now it is clear where to begin with this one." He said this to the canvas rather than Dylan, as if he planned to teach the paints how to rearrange themselves.

Every time I went to Raeben's studio that week Dylan was there. He never said a word to anyone. Just took his easel as far from the rest of us as he could and worked in silence. Sometimes he drew instead of painting. A few times I glanced up from my canvas and saw him looking at me.

One evening I was working on the painting of the seated woman. I brushed thick sienna paint across the canvas, and caught sight of Dylan, his eyes hidden behind sunglasses, standing before his easel in working jeans and a flannel shirt, and I recalled almost involuntarily the evening of my thirteenth birthday, when I came home from a Broadway show with Herbert Zuckerman to discover my parents dancing in the living room to "Absolutely Sweet Marie." Herbert began describing our evening to my parents, and my mother released my father's hand and beckoned Herbert to dance. He put his hand on her lower back and guided her through the room, talking about how much we enjoyed dinner and *Yerma*, the Lorca play that had opened that night. My mother interjected every few sentences to say, "How wonderful!" I sat in the rocking chair, and as the song ended Herbert stood behind me. I rose immediately and hurried upstairs to my room.

The paintbrush trembled in my hand. I shook myself from memory. The seated woman on my canvas stared at me.

I thrust the brush into the shallow red pool on my palette and with Raeben's urgent jabs began to paint a man leering over me. My brush conjured not the arrogant pupils and pale linen suit of Ralph Summers but rather the fleshy face and beetle eyes of Herbert Zuckerman. I painted Herbert's eyes as they had marked me for as long as I could remember. The greed and lust in those eyes as he touched me in the dark theater or the front seat of his car, those eyes holding me in place as his hand or mouth moved along my skin, eyes that told me not to say a word, you're just a little girl, nobody will believe you. I remembered an evening I lay despondent in bed, fourteen years old, Herbert on his way to retrieve me for a Broadway show. My mother walked past my door, and, surprised to see me in bed, snapped that Herbert was on his way. I didn't move. She came into my room, repeating herself in a louder voice. I stared blankly at the ceiling. Gathering all my courage, I whispered, "I don't want to go, Mom." She told me to dress. "There's nothing wrong with Herbert," she kept repeating. "There's nothing wrong with Herbert." I hadn't said his name. Herbert arrived and we went together to the play. Every time after that I even considered telling my parents what Herbert was doing to me, I thought of my mother saying those words: "There's nothing wrong with Herbert." The brush swept across the canvas. Herbert had been my mother's lover until she married my father. He had reached for her simulacrum in me. Was my father blinded to Herbert's transgressions by his own guilt at marrying his best friend's lover? Had I been sacrificed to ease my parents' guilt at betraying Herbert? Or had they chosen the friend they admired over their own daughter? Why else had my parents never listened to me all the times I said I didn't want to go to the theater alone with him? How could they not have known something was wrong simply by the way he looked at me? Had my parents' determination to give me more than they could manage—that *Mayflower* education at Bennington—been an apology for their failure to protect me? And why had I obeyed Herbert's demand for silence? It all poured out in crimson on the canvas.

The sky was black by the time I walked out onto Seventh Avenue. Yellow cabs sped downtown. I wanted to flee the painting of Herbert and me, and I wanted to show it to everyone I knew. Someone called out, "Scuse me!"

I turned to see Dylan nearing me in a trench coat, his hands covered with streaks of paint. He stared at me without saying hello. Then he asked what I thought about hosting a party for the class. The way he asked—it felt like being panhandled. That's apart from the fact that the request made no sense. I hardly knew anyone in class. My apartment was a cramped walk-up. Dylan could have rented any hotel or restaurant in New York. There was also the fact that we'd never spoken. Everything about the request was inverted. So when I went to say no I heard myself saying yes.

Seven

My mother sat in shadow. I gazed at her, seeing not only the woman I knew, the mother who had raised me, but also the young woman she had been in the city of her youth. She smiled warmly as the nurse knelt to remove the IV from her arm. I wanted to ask what happened after Dylan suggested the party at her apartment. My chest felt tight with her revelations about Herbert Zuckerman and Ralph Summers. She had never spoken either name to me. She had never told me a family friend sexually abused her. The sky was dark beyond the hospital window. She rose from her chair, and leaned on my shoulder, and we moved haltingly down the hall. She was asleep almost as soon as she settled in the passenger seat.

I drove east on 78th Street, past the avenues in descending order, Third, Second, First. Youthful faces shone in bar windows, handsome heads thrown back in laughter. I glanced at my mother, thinking of all the ways these wounds must have formed her. She had been a girl afraid to tell her parents the most shameful fact of her life. She had learned to live with secrets. Her parents had failed to protect her in the most fundamental way a parent can fail a child. I couldn't recognize the domineering mother in her story, the grandmother who, after my mother, had been the most loving adult in my life. I thought of her voice coming through the phone in the hospital, the day after my mother's surgery: "Is she getting everything she needs? If one damn thing goes wrong, that hospital is going to be hearing from me."

We crossed the bridge, the skyline momentarily illuminated in the rearview mirror. Then we turned onto the forest highway and the city vanished.

My mother had never told me the reason she dropped out of college was that a professor sexually assaulted her. She had never told me that she had wanted to become a writer until a professor she admired had taken advantage of her. Through all the years she had encouraged me to pursue my own writing, she had never told me that this had once been her dream, too. Looking at my mother as she slept, her white pillow pressed against the window, I felt a strange protectiveness for this girl I could never have known, the thirteen-year-old in Great Neck, the eighteen-year-old who arrived at Bennington eager to create herself. The last several summers I had taught writing seminars to high school students, and I had come to know the shy expression with which a student might ask me to read a few pages of a novel or the first scenes of a play. I felt violent repulsion that Ralph Summers had exploited that vulnerability in my mother.

She turned into her pillow, exhaling labored breaths. I reached into her cloth bag on the floor, rummaging for her marijuana tincture.

She had spoken Dylan's name to me tonight, without my provocation, for the first time in our lives. She was telling me their story. She was bringing me toward him.

"Oxycodone," she said through lidded eyes. That meant she was in too much pain for the marijuana alone. I handed her the cloth bag. She opened her eyes and hastily withdrew the knitting needles and kombucha thermos. Anxiously she said, "Seen painkillers?"

I hadn't. She fumbled in her pockets, then the glove compartment, panic intensifying in her weary eyes. "Evan? Could you have moved the oxycodone by mistake?"

I had kept my eyes on the road while reaching into the bag for the marijuana tincture. It was possible that I accidentally knocked the tablets to the car floor. I punched the interior lights.

"Mom, can you look around?"

She drew her knees to her chest and murmured in discomfort. I could pull over and search the floor, but there was hardly any terrain between the highway and forest. On the cement shoulder we would be exposed to any car rounding the bend. If I was going to search thoroughly my mother would have to stand out of her seat, which would intensify her pain. Any search would delay returning home, and the odds were that the oxycodone was there or in the hospital.

She sat upright and the magenta ball of yarn rolled from her lap to the car floor. I had to call the hospital and ask the nurses to look for the oxycodone. We were closer to the hospital than the house and my mother needed the drug as soon as possible. Someone else must now be sitting in my mother's medical chair, an IV dripping chemotherapy into their veins. The nurses couldn't walk in and form a search party for the oxycodone. Even if they found the pills, it was thirty minutes back to the hospital. My mother let out an anguished breath, shifting backward in the seat. She needed the oxycodone now.

Why hadn't I gone over everything she needed that morning? I could have staved off her pain by simply asking if she had everything she needed for the day. So much was beyond our control: the effectiveness of the chemotherapy, the severity of its side effects, the accumulated benefit of the Huel, BEMER, infrared sauna, and vibration plate. It was all speculative, a matter of playing the margins amid incalculable medical uncertainty. But the location of those white pills should have been in my control.

"Mom?"

"Found painkillers?" she gasped.

Since her surgery she had avoided the oxycodone when possible, cursing the mental fog it brought her. Now her eyes were wide with the desperation of any chemical dependent.

I described the options. The first was to call the hospital and ask the nurses to look for the pills. While they searched, we would have to decide whether to return to the hospital or continue to the house. The second option was to drive home and hope the pills were there. If they weren't, I'd drive to the CVS in Goshen. The third option was to drive directly to the CVS. This meant the longest drive, but it was our only guarantee that she would have oxycodone within an hour.

"Nearby drugstore?" she said. "Call hospital, change pickup location."

My mother sighed a pained breath and I reached for my phone and searched for the hospital number and realized there was no service on the forest highway. I told her.

"Home," she said. "Evan, the pain . . ."

She needed the comfort of her bed as soon as possible. The road wound into darkness. There were no cars within sight and I trusted myself to talk down any police officer who saw my mother's condition. I accelerated to the highest speed I could comfortably drive. The car careened around a curve, the wheel steady in my hand but the angle sharper than anticipated. My mother yelped as she slid against the window.

"Evan! Slow, please . . ."

Right. She was in pain just sitting still. I could not add the uncertainty of a car moving ninety miles an hour. If I drove faster, we would be home sooner but the drive would be less comfortable. If I drove slower, she would be in the car longer but the drive would be more comfortable. There was no optimal solution. We couldn't drive our way out of this situation. We had to live within it. That was why my mother was taking concentrated breaths, calming her nervous system, relaxing her pained muscles. I needed to do the same.

I couldn't breathe past the knot in my sternum. I tried harder and the knot tightened. I had always imagined a time, far in the future, when I would be a more complete version of myself, able to more easily maneuver through life. I would meditate in the morning and confront anxiety with grace. There was no imagined future. This was life. This was the time I needed to be the sturdiest version of myself. She was relying on me.

"Pull over," she said abruptly.

I veered to the side of the highway and she pushed open the door. She leaned out of the car and vomit splattered on the pavement. There were no cars in sight. Why hadn't I taken the simple measures to avoid this situation? I had seen she was in pain when we left the hospital. There were an infinite number of places in the city to refill her oxycodone prescription. The thought hadn't occurred to me. Now every mile would cause her pain. She vomited again, her emaciated body keeled over in the dark. I looked for water in the car but couldn't see any. Was there a gas station nearby? She couldn't be asked to endure fifty minutes with the taste of vomit in her mouth. Oh, the kombucha. I shook the thermos, registering with relief that there was liquid inside. My mother heaved the passenger door shut and nodded wearily. I handed her the kombucha and sped into the night.

The car gained momentum and she lowered her seat until it was nearly flat. She gazed at me, breathing slowly, holding the air in her lungs, and I began to breathe as well, my shoulders loosening, hands relaxing on the steering wheel, breathing her breaths, inhaling the air she exhaled, the knot in my chest dissolving.

"That's right, Evan," she said. "You're doing so well."

We descended the mountain highway onto a winding back road. Houses stood atop distant hills, prized views of the valley. I could feel my mother's eyes on me, her breaths calm. I glanced at her phone; there was service. I called the CVS and confirmed the store was open until ten and the prescription would be ready by the time I arrived. I tried to calculate whether it was worth looking for the oxycodone when we returned home. If the tablets weren't there, every moment I searched would prolong my mother's pain. If they were, she would not have to wait the twenty minutes it would take me to drive into Goshen for the new prescription.

I turned onto our road, easing the tires over the train tracks to spare my mother the usual jolt. The farmhouse emerged on the hill. "We're almost home," I said, trying to draw from this announcement all the comfort it implied.

She clutched her abdomen as I steered around the driveway potholes. High grass rose tunnel-like on either side of the gravel drive. I guided the car into the garage, turned off the engine, and hurried up the stairs to find the oxycodone. At the door into the house I looked over my shoulder. The passenger door was open but she hadn't moved from the seat. I walked to her side of the car. She looked at me with tender fear. I understood. I knelt on the cement floor. She draped her arms around my neck. I set one hand beneath her back and the other beneath her sweaty knees. Slowly I lifted her from the car. She settled in my arms.

BOY FROM THE NORTH COUNTRY

It was terrifying how little she weighed. We took a tentative step forward and she winced. My view was partial over her shoulder. I stepped forward and she slipped slightly and tightened her arms around my neck. I clasped her nearer to me. All our effort was trained on crossing the dark garage. I could not speak and she could not hear but I knew she felt me telling her, *The worst of the discomfort is almost over, a few more moments and you can sleep in your own bed.* And I could hear her telling me, silently, without needing words, *You're doing so well, honey. Keep breathing. We're almost there.*

I took the first step up the stairs and she winced again. Holding her frail body in the dim light, listening to her breaths, I thought of the night I was six years old and lay in bed with unbearable stomach pain. She had carried me to the car, driving me from doctor to doctor, insisting I was suffering more than the stomachache with which each doctor diagnosed me, until she at last brought me to the emergency room with a bursting appendix that, I did not understand until years later, nearly ended my life. Is this what she had felt that night, the urgent responsibility of loving someone who is so vulnerable to you?

We took another step up the stairs. She exhaled. The sixth and final step brought us to the closed door. I rested her legs on my bent knee and freed my hand to turn the doorknob. We came onto the landing, and I saw our reflection in the mirror, my mother Pietà-like in my arms. Lucy scampered into the room, her little doggie head knocking into my ankles, unaware of the precarious balance of two bodies moving as one. My mother whispered and Lucy lay flat. We ascended the stairs toward her bedroom, cautious with each step. We were almost there. I could feel the fragile bones of her back in my palm. We moved through the dark hall, my mother's breaths all I could hear. The silhouette of her bed gleamed through the open door. We walked the last remaining steps. I eased her atop the bedsheets, and she exhaled, tears in the wrinkled corners of her eyes. We were home.

FOR TWO DAYS AFTER her treatment my mother was so weakened by the chemotherapy that she needed help on the stairs between her bedroom and the lower floors of the house. Despite her discomfort, she was intent on following the regimen she had set for herself. She began each day on the BEMER, electromagnetic waves pulsing blood and oxygen through her vessels. She sipped her calorie-heavy drink of Huel, yogurt, and berries. She spent a twenty-minute interval on the vibration plate. She took a binder of medical studies into the infrared sauna. She was determined to give her body every advantage against the cancer. No detail was too small, no footnote in a medical study too insignificant.

While she read in the sauna, I scrambled eggs and sautéed cruciferous vegetables known to reduce inflammation. I sliced avocado for healthy fat and brewed turmeric tea, which has a naturally occurring compound, curcumin, that preliminary studies linked to slowing the growth of cancer cells. Lucy, who did not understand why she could not enter the sauna with my mother, circled me as I cooked, leaping for the egg I offered her, licking my hand as I asked, "Are you a dog? Would you like to help make breakfast?"

"There's new research from Columbia University," my mother said as she came out of the sauna on Sunday morning, sweat dripping along her neck, "that modified citrus pectins have cancer-resistant effects. I've just ordered a crate."

She walked gingerly up the hill each morning, leaning on my arm, determined to spend time outside. We ate breakfast at the cedar table with the view of the mountains.

"I just don't have any appetite," she said on Monday morning, staring at her plate of eggs, cauliflower, bok choy, and avocado. She ate anyway.

She needed rest and nutrition and we organized our days for these purposes. We sat in the wicker chairs on the hill and sipped the iced tea she made from the red clovers that grew in the fields around the house. Deer grazed in the high grass. Crab apples fell from the gnarled tree. Lucy set several world records for chasing squirrels. My mother closed her eyes, reclining in the wicker chair as I read her *Harry Potter*. Harry walked through Platform Nine and Three-Quarters, onto the Hogwarts Express, where he was lucky to sit next to Ron Weasley. Harry was surprised to remember that he was already famous in the wizarding world for defeating a dark wizard who could not be named. My mother knit, the ball of yarn resting on her lap. Her magenta fabric was growing into a circular shape, perhaps a pot holder.

"What are you making?" I asked.

"You'll see," she smiled, "when it's time."

She looked longingly at the trail into the woods, without the strength to walk.

For lunch each day I cooked her a grass-fed burger, holding my breath against the smell of burnt flesh. I cooked her fish and yams, miso soup, roasted broccoli and cauliflower. She chewed slowly, eyeing her gradually dwindling plate as if wishing away the food.

One afternoon, I recognized the paperback she was reading. She had given me that worn book when I was seven, saying, "I think you're going to like this one." I'd lain in the chicken pen with the book held to the sky, absorbed in the story of a boy who lives on a forest island with wild horses. The fiercest of these horses will let no rider near her, but the boy approaches patiently and wins her heart. The evening I finished reading I found my mother in her sunroom and told her about the magical island. "Would you like to go there?" she had asked. I was mesmerized by the idea that the island was real. We arrived by ferry to Chincoteague. We spent the week biking the pine forest, swimming at the beach, and glimpsing wild horses galloping through the woods. From then on, we returned to Chincoteague one week each summer, until I left home.

"Mom," I said. She glanced up from the book. It had been more than half an hour since she'd said anything about the pain. "Did you learn about Chincoteague from that novel, or did you learn about that novel by visiting Chincoteague?"

"First I read the novel," she said happily. "Imagine my wonder when I realized Chincoteague was a real place."

"Let's drive there after this is all over. There's no reason I have to rush back to London. It will be nice to have time together without the cancer."

"Oh, I can already feel the ocean breeze," she said, closing her eyes.

The pain came without warning. Later that afternoon she was reading a medical study in the lawn chair when she suddenly grimaced and asked for help returning to her room. We walked slowly down the hill, her arm on my shoulder, each step its own difficulty. She lay in bed, breeze drifting through the open window, her eyes closed. Lucy leapt onto the bed, kissing her face. She streamed marijuana tincture onto her tongue and tried to sleep. After twenty minutes she reached reluctantly for the oxycodone. She was asleep by six that evening.

The following morning as I set ground coffee into the Moka pot, a sharp cry sounded from my mother's bedroom. I walked upstairs, hesitated a moment at her door, then knocked.

"I'm fine," she said in a wounded voice.

She opened the door. A bald spot gleamed on the left side of her head. She held a clump of hair in her palm. "I knew it would happen," she said, trying to hold back tears.

"I'm so sorry, Mom," I said, hugging her close to me, conscious not to hold her so tight that it hurt her frail body.

We drew apart, and she inhaled a steadying breath.

"I know it's hard," I said. "It's also temporary, right? After chemo, your hair will grow back more beautiful than ever."

"That's right," she said. "Everything is temporary."

She looked through the window at a sparrow fluttering toward the birdhouse.

"It's just always been a part of me, you know? People come and go. Work changes. Trees fall. I've always been a woman with auburn hair."

"Always? You were born that way? Like one of those medieval portraits of Mary and Child where Jesus looks like a little man-baby?"

She laughed, and I saw new wrinkles in her cheeks.

"I have to be stronger than this," she said.

"No," I said, "you don't."

IN THE EVENINGS she was too weakened to do anything but lie on the sofa. We watched her favorite films. Julie Andrews sang joyfully through the mountains in *The Sound of Music*. We rooted for John Cusack and Diane Lane to fall in love in *Must Love Dogs*. My mother sighed with wonder as Dorothy walked the yellow brick road in *The Wizard of Oz*. The young grew old, the powerful became powerless, Doctor Zhivago walked the tundra, and my mother gave in to the pain and swallowed two oxycodone pills. Lucy tucked her head onto my shin. My mother cried as Elizabeth Taylor fell in love with her horse in *National Velvet*.

"I remember that feeling," she said, looking longingly at the horse and girl on the paused screen. "Falling in love with a horse for the first time. I was six. Every time we drove past her farm I would crane my neck out of the car window for a glimpse of her. I can still remember her galloping through the fields. Oh, that freedom! She made my heart soar. We never met. We never touched. But she was my first love."

"That's beautiful, Mom."

"I miss that silent intimacy. With every horse I've ever loved. Leaning over her tender neck, feeling the lengthening of her stride. Our bodies in sync. That is its own love."

We watched *Fiddler on the Roof*. A man in ragged clothes walked through a shtetl in the Russian countryside in 1905. Tevye declared, "Here in our little village every one of us is a fiddler on the roof. Why do we stay up there if it's so dangerous? Because this is our home. How do we keep our balance? One word: tradition!"

Tevye prayed each day and God rewarded him by having his eldest daughter reject an arranged marriage to a wealthy man for a marriage of love to a poor man. Tevye observed shabbes each week and God rewarded him by having his second daughter marry a man who rejected Judaism for communism. Tevye marked the holidays each year and God rewarded him by having his third daughter marry a man from the Russian village that coveted the land held by Tevye's community.

A Russian mob charged on horseback through the wedding of Tevye's first daughter, overturning tables and hurling bodies to the ground. Tevye stood amid the ruins of the pogrom, persecuted by a hostile government, mocked by God, abandoned by his daughters, a stranger in his own land. He looked to the fiddler on the roof, and I heard my mother sniffling.

"It always makes me think," she said, stroking Lucy's silken ears, "that you can tell the story of any life two ways. You can tell the story of Tevye's life as one of abandonment, loss, futility. Or you can tell the story of Tevye's life as one of resilience, strength, hope. I've spent so much of my life coming through the first story and into the second."

SHE WOKE ON WEDNESDAY with renewed strength. She rose from bed without my help, and walked with ease up the hill to the cedar table, and ate more than on previous days. Even her skin tone seemed healthier. After breakfast she said, "Would you like to walk with me in the woods? I have the strength today."

Her steps were tentative on the path into the woods, but she could walk without balancing on my shoulder. Lucy romped ahead of us, impatient for the glories of the day. Her ears fell flat against her neck, her body elongating and compressing, accordion-like, with each leap forward. Wild mushrooms grew on weathered stones. The trail turned and the horizon opened, revealing the jagged mountains reigning over the valley, an Escher print of peaks concealing peaks.

"I've heard people say chemo is a cycle," my mother said. "I didn't understand until the last few days. I can't believe how all my energy vanished this weekend. It will be nice to feel more myself these next days, even if I'll feel depleted again after the treatment on Friday."

"We'll have another quiet few days," I said. "However slowly you need to take it."

Lucy leapt over a fallen log, wagging her pink tongue like Michael Jordan taking off from the free-throw line.

"I'm not happy that my weight is down," my mother said, looking to the horizon. "That's part of the cycle, too. I've lost six pounds since Friday. I'm down to one-twelve. That means I have to adjust my nutritional strategy. I can double the Huel dosage," she said, thinking aloud, "and can you start using a whole avocado with the burger rather than half? I need to increase healthy fats. Let's see if I can gain back three or four pounds before the treatment on Friday."

Light fell across the sloping trail. Mountains rose into clear blue sky. Lucy stared impatiently over her shoulder, stunned we were not bounding like her through the woods. I wanted to give myself to the trees but couldn't tame my restlessness. My mother smiled, as if unfazed by all she was enduring. I tried to find her calm within me. She had lost nearly a fifth of her body mass. Trees closed in around us. Sun shone on the bald spot on her head. I turned instinctively away. Her hair was thinning; the baldness had nearly taken over the left side of her head. I felt repulsion at her baldness and guilt for my repulsion. It was only a matter of time before her hair fell out entirely. I couldn't let her sense my discomfort. I had to help her feel at ease with however the cancer transformed her body. My mother was my mother. Nothing could matter less than whether she had hair. I looked directly onto the bare portion of her skull.

Birds flew through blue sky. My mother sighed contentedly.

She gestured toward a gnarled oak tree and said, "Do you remember when this was your favorite tree? There was one summer you spent nearly every day trying to climb this tree."

I looked at the oak tree, its branches falling toward the earth and rising toward the sky. No memory came to mind.

"I've lived so much of my life beside these trees," she said, continuing along the path. "I can't imagine being without them. One of the best decisions I ever made was to let nature heal me. Do you know spending time in nature is linked to lower blood pressure, a stronger immune system, reduced anxiety and depression?"

Clouds drifted in the open sky. Lucy darted back to us, stared bewildered at our tardiness, then darted ahead. The trail opened into the field behind the house.

I said, "Do you have a favorite tree?"

"Oh yes," she said, nodding to the maple tree nearest to the house. "Sometimes I'm overwhelmed by how much I love that maple. It's given me so much. Blossoms in spring. Shade in summer. Foliage in autumn. Syrup in winter. I've wondered if I'm mad to love this tree so deeply. Then I remind myself: The question isn't *How much can you love a tree?* The question is *How much can you love?* How much can you open yourself to the glory of life? The way it's always changing. Always giving. The way life breaks and mends your heart."

I followed her through the sliding door into the house, Lucy trotting behind me. My mother stood near the sofa in the den, glancing down at her phone. She murmured that she had a missed call from Dr. Chen. She hardly made eye contact as she walked past me, through the sliding door and into the field behind the house. She raised the phone to her ear and I saw her lips move but could not hear her words. She nodded hopefully, her eyes on the distant mountains. Then she smiled as I had not seen her smile since I returned home. She closed the phone and hurried across the field toward me, joyful disbelief in her hazel eyes.

"The results of the last CT scan are back," she said. "The tumor decreased by another ten percent. Between the surgery and chemotherapy, we've removed seventy percent of the tumor."

We embraced, her arms warm around my shoulders.

"Mom," I said. "Oh, Mom. Everything you're doing is working."

"I want to celebrate!" she said. She went into the house and a moment later returned with her yoga mat. She walked into the field and stood with her arms raised to the sky, her breaths seeming to synchronize with the wind. She knelt on the mat, her head to the ground, her back arched. Then she lifted her legs into a perfectly vertical headstand, and for the moment she held the pose it was inconceivable that a cancerous tumor remained within her.

Eight

We drove the highway into the city that Friday morning, my mother gazing through the window onto green hills in the distance. She had regained four pounds in the second half of the week. The treatment was working, and faster than she had expected. Seventy percent of the tumor had been eliminated. If each round of chemotherapy continued to eliminate ten percent of the tumor, my mother would need only three more weeks of treatment, perhaps a fourth to make completely sure. Even if each of the following chemotherapy treatments was half as successful, she would need only six or eight weeks of treatment. We would be free by October.

"I can't wait," I said, turning to her as we came onto the George Washington Bridge, "to drive to Chincoteague with you. After this is all over."

"Oh, that will be wonderful," she smiled.

I could feel us coming through her cancer. She stood easily from the car when we arrived at the hospital. We walked through the revolving doors, into the lobby, along fluorescent hallways to the sanitized room. The anticipation of my mother's recovery came together in my mind with the longing to be led back into the story she had begun last time in the hospital. In the same treatment room a high-rise blocked our view of the street on which she had lived forty years before. She settled in the padded chair. The nurse appeared in the doorway, said good morning, and knelt matter-of-factly beside my mother to find a vein in her arm into which she could insert the IV. My mother breathed deeply, the chemotherapy flowing into her bloodstream.

She reached into her cloth bag and withdrew her knitting and ball of yarn. She looked at me a long moment. She knit as she began to speak, the woman in the medical chair morphing once more into the girl I never met, whose auburn hair fell onto shoulders left bare by a summer dress as the first guest rang the buzzer of her 78th Street apartment.

There were already two dozen people in the apartment, my mother said, by the time Dylan arrived. He wore a stained flannel shirt, blue jeans, and red cowboy boots. He stood in the center of my tiny walk-up as people tried and failed to make conversation with him. He nodded, murmured, looked straight at one person while he spoke a fragment of a sentence, then turned to someone else and said nothing in particular. He didn't seem to know what he wanted. He'd spent half his adult life accumulating fame and half running away from it, and all the contradiction was right there in his face. After forty minutes he still hadn't said hello to me.

Things eased up once the joints were passed around. Someone read Ginsberg's "America," and Dylan thumbed through my record collection. I didn't have his music and was embarrassed for him if he was looking. I didn't know what he was after, why any of us were there. He looked up from the records with this mischievous smile and said, the room going quiet, "Let's listen to the greatest poet of the age." He held a record so it covered his face. It was Leonard Cohen's *Songs of Love and Hate*.

After we were feeling the pot, a few of us went out to the fire escape. Dylan's joint glowed beside me in the darkness. Neither of us looked at the other, you know that feeling when you're first getting to know someone, and your body is beside theirs, and you can feel the tension of unspoken attraction, so even the slightest motion—their body leaning toward yours, the briefest touch of your shoulders—feels significant? That pleasure and tension, along with the doubt that everything you are feeling is in your head, that for the other person it is only an ordinary night smoking a joint beside a stranger on a fire escape. Dylan handed me the joint, his fingers brushing mine. I inhaled, wanting to draw out the drug, to drift into whatever was happening between us. I also wanted to pass the joint back to him so our fingers touched again. I took a drag, and the smoke lingered in the night, and I held the joint toward him, and as he took it I felt his calloused fingers, the roughness of skin that came from a lifetime of playing guitar. I was not beside some lost boy from Stella's studio. Dylan's fingers were touching mine not because of unspoken attraction but rather a misunderstanding that he would soon recognize, and, when he did, leave my apartment.

He leaned over the railing and looked onto the night and spoke in a low voice about Raeben. He was, Dylan said, a gift from the other world. He could see things the rest of us didn't. Even if we spent our lives at Raeben's feet, Dylan said, we would never understand how different the world appeared to him. We were trying to recreate life with paint and light and texture. That was how life simply appeared to Raeben. His work seemed visually transcendent but in fact he was the canniest realist to ever live. After a moment, Henry, the art school dropout, said Dylan didn't understand realism, he was abusing the term. Henry went on with these technical terms and Dylan stared at him skeptically over his cigarette. After the monologue ended, he nodded, mumbled, "Indeed, indeed," and climbed through the window back into my apartment.

Every time I looked at him that night his eyes were wandering over the aged wooden floorboards, the poetry and plays on the shelves, the cracked paint across the ceiling, the records stacked against the wall, the gaping hole where the heat pipes ran into the floor, as if the most banal detail of the dilapidated apartment was more intriguing than the people trying to speak with him. Maybe nobody was speaking to him. They were speaking to his songs. Speaking to the memory of how his songs made them feel some night they kissed their high school love. Of course he didn't want any of them wanting him. How could he talk back to any of that? People began to leave around two in the morning. He closed the door behind the last guest with a sweep of his red cowboy boot. Then he turned to me, a hand in his mess of brown curls and that mischievous smile in his eyes as he said, "Well, that was boring."

I woke on the mattress to sunlight. He was gone. I lay there furious with myself. What a stupid thing I'd done. Of course I'd wanted him, that wild hair all down his neck. I felt burning fury for having reduced myself to an object of his sexual desire. Now I couldn't go back to Raeben's studio. If word spread to Stella she'd lose any respect for me. I'd never thought of myself as the sort of girl who slept with famous men. Lying there naked with the imprint of his body on the bedsheet, I felt repulsed by what I'd done. I was in New York to become myself, not sleep with celebrity musicians. I was alone in the city and had to be more protective of myself. I could also still feel the thrill of his touch on my skin.

I got out of bed and pushed back the blinds. I walked through the bedroom door and there was Dylan perched on the windowsill, his legs dangling over the ledge. For a moment he went on writing in his little red notebook. Then he looked up and said, "You slept through Leonard. He just gave a sermon on having an emotion."

Dylan nodded to the record player, where the needle lay on the inner groove of *Songs of Love and Hate*.

"By the way," Dylan said, "how'd you find him?"

"Huh?"

"Our man from the world to come."

It took me a moment to realize he meant Raeben.

"Oh, Stella Adler sent me to him. Been acting at her studio."

Dylan's eyes lit up.

"Stella Adler? One of the greats of the stage. What does she have you studying? You have a favorite Chekhov? So you're one of these young theater people shaking things up in New York? You should have said as much."

I told him about playing Hedda Gabler in Gordon's apartment theater. That we were skirting the gatekeepers, making theater democratic like Athenian times.

"You don't charge nothing?" he asked. "That's how it ought to be."

The conversation wandered from Ibsen to Aeschylus. It was like reading on the porch at Bennington all those nights, except instead of being alone with Dante and Marlowe I was talking to someone who seemed to have spent as much time with those books in his head. He quoted Virgil and Thucydides, said Pericles had been like Kennedy, every man who sent another to war should read his "Funeral Oration."

No matter where our conversation meandered, Dylan kept bringing everything back to Raeben. He wanted to know if my life was the same since I started studying with him. Could I talk to the same people the same way? Because he couldn't.

"Raeben's changing me so much," Dylan said, tapping out his cigarette on the windowsill. "Nowadays I can't recognize some people and some people can't recognize me."

Dylan lit another cigarette and said he'd been struggling to see for longer than he cared to remember. He hadn't been satisfied with anything he'd written in years. He'd toured for the first two months of that year, '74, and didn't have a good word to say about it. It'd been his first tour since his motorcycle accident in '66, after which he sequestered himself away, believed he needed silence to make anything worthwhile. He'd written plenty, put out seven albums in eight years. He toured none of them, wasn't satisfied with the work. He'd spent years off the grid and hadn't made the music to prove it. He was thirty-three and his best work had been written, he said, before he was twenty-five. He kept saying if he didn't find his way back to something worthwhile soon he didn't know if he ever would.

He spoke more like a Village straggler than the most celebrated musician of his generation. He inhaled his cigarette, his leg still dangling out of the windowsill, and the veneer fell away. I wasn't looking at a rich and famous man, all that was as ephemeral to him as the smoke wafting into the courtyard garden. He wasn't different from any artist separated from his way of feeling and desperate to get back. He dragged on the cigarette and I felt almost protective over him.

He kept saying Raeben was changing everything for him. Teaching him how to dig up the parts of himself that he'd forgotten where he buried. I only went to Raeben's studio once or twice a week and hadn't realized Dylan was there every day. He kept saying Raeben was curing his blindness. He talked about Raeben like he was a biblical prophet, even used that word. He said Raeben lived simultaneously between different centuries and continents and that was why he could see what nobody else did.

We talked all morning. Dylan sat on the windowsill, and I lounged on the sofa and every now and then lit another cigarette. The more he spoke the more I understood that everything he did was driven by this desperation to see again, as he put it. He'd heard a few people describing Raeben's ideas, and the following morning he'd driven to New York. He'd been studying with Raeben every day since. Listening to him speak, I got the sense Dylan would go anywhere or do anything to regain his sight. If smoking a cigarette on my windowsill and talking Chekhov helped him feel what he needed to feel, he didn't have any other concern in the world. If he heard there was a guru on an Indonesian island who knew something about truth or beauty, he'd be on the first boat there.

At some point we found ourselves on the floor, Dylan's head in my lap, my hand running through his curls. He glanced sidelong at my record player and I told him to play something. He played Seeger and I played Guthrie. He played Son House and I played Muddy Waters. He played Lou Reed and I played Cohen, I wanted to see him experience what he described that morning, "a sermon on having an emotion." Several chords into "Love Calls You by Your Name," Dylan leapt up from my lap and said, "That reminds me." He tugged on his jeans and cowboy boots and ran out the door.

I assumed it was a one-night event. I wasn't sure if I should go back to Raeben's studio, I didn't want to embarrass myself. But if the last time the others saw me was alone in my apartment with Dylan at the end of the party, their impression would be that I cared more about sleeping with him than painting. I wasn't going to let that impression stand.

When I arrived at Raeben's studio the following evening, Dylan didn't look at me and I didn't look at him. I felt foolish for thinking our conversation meant anything to him, he probably spoke that way all the time. Of course I knew better than to think that sleeping together was personal to him. He must have been with hundreds of women. I did my best to focus on my canvas.

In the late afternoon Raeben seized the brush from a young woman and painted over her canvas in brown strokes. Turning to the class he shouted, "You have all lost your eyes today. Have you never seen color? You are painting in black and white."

Raeben strode angrily to a cabinet and rummaged out of sight. A moment later he returned with a print. "Look at these colors," he said, holding up the print. "Let Chagall's sensual blue welcome you into the painting. Let yourself become a child looking into the sky."

The painting showed a young boy with a sheep at his side. Dylan wandered toward Raeben, took off his sunglasses, and stood directly in front of the print, as if there was nobody else in the room. I could see the outline of his naked body beneath his jeans and flannel shirt. He leaned nearer to the painting and I wanted him with a completeness that frightened me.

"Allow yourself," Raeben said, "to look into this boy's eyes. You are looking at Joseph from Genesis, shortly before he is sold into slavery by his brothers. Do you feel his innocence? Look at the blue sky and olive hills and his ivory skin. Chagall chose each color to emphasize Joseph's innocence. For those of you who are illiterate, Chagall also put these emotions in Joseph's expression and posture. Color makes this a painting. If even looking at Chagall you cannot understand that color seduces, then please let yourself onto Seventh Avenue at this moment."

Dylan paced around Raeben, staring at the boy and his sheep from every angle. I wanted to lie with him in my bed and know his every thought and impulse.

"Observe," Raeben continued, "Joseph's naked ivory chest. Look at the carob color of his coat. With color like that Chagall turns Joseph into a hooker in Times Square. Do you see how appealing Joseph's body is made by that cerulean sky? Look at this painting long enough and you begin to see Joseph as one of Caravaggio's naked boys. Even Joseph's sheep cannot resist directing his head you-know-where. You consider this an accident? In the Hasidism of Chagall's childhood, the relationship between man and animal is holy. Look at the angelic white of that sheep. With color Chagall is telling you about the love between man and animal. With color Chagall is recreating the feelings of his childhood."

Dylan stared at me and his eyes were bloodshot and I wondered if he felt in that painting the majesty that I did.

"So we are seduced into this painting by color," Raeben went on. "Once he has our attention, Chagall tells a story none of you expect. Do you notice something about Joseph? He is the spitting image of Chagall. Why does Chagall choose to portray himself through Joseph? You know the story of Joseph: He is sold into slavery by his brothers, then rises to power in Egypt by interpreting Pharaoh's dreams. When famine comes to Canaan, Joseph's brothers journey to Egypt. They are petrified to learn that Joseph wields great power in Egypt. Rather than punish his brothers, Joseph gives them the most fertile terrain in Egypt, the land of Goshen. There the Hebrew people thrive. Goshen is paradise divine. Life rises from the soil. The Hebrew population grows. The Egyptians become envious and fearful and force the Hebrew people into slavery. This is the great turning point in Jewish history. For if the Hebrews had been left to flourish in Goshen, if they had not been enslaved, there would have been no Exodus, no parting of the Red Sea, no revelation at Sinai, no land of milk and honey, and no Jerusalem. Joseph lives to see none of this. He dies a rich and powerful man in the land of Egypt. Yet on his deathbed, he asks that his bones be buried in the home to which he never returned, Canaan."

Dylan murmured and the class murmured with him. There were rumors that he'd had a religious conversion, he'd been photographed at the Western Wall in Jerusalem. I wondered what Dylan was seeing in the story that I wasn't.

"Moishe Segal," Raeben went on, "grew up in a shtetl in the tundra of Belarus. At the age Joseph traveled to Egypt, Segal travels to Paris. There Moishe Segal transforms himself into Marc Chagall. How? By interpreting Pharaoh's dreams with color and canvas. Chagall wins this future by painting his past. He paints the huts and dancing fiddlers and bearded Hasidic men of Vitebsk, the childhood home he lost as Joseph lost Canaan. His style carries him into Parisian modernism while his subject bears him back into the Jewish past. With this self-portrait Chagall is reclaiming his origins. He is saying, *I am not only the acclaimed artist but also the shepherd Joseph. I have been a stranger in a strange land. I have come a long way from home, yet I would still allow the sheep of that shtetl to put their noses you-know-where.*"

Raeben stared into the canvas. People glanced at Dylan, who seemed too taken by the painting to care about all those eyes on him.

"This is only one interpretation. What is important is not that my ideas are right. What is important is that I can interpret these ideas through Chagall's color. Do not try to paint something that allows only one interpretation. Then you will become a true illiterate. Any art must resist simplistic understanding. Anything worthwhile, that is. I'm not talking about soup cans, nu? Genuine art is a failure. Why is Chagall's

Joseph, a Shepherd so successful a failure? Because of color. If there was only metaphor between Chagall and Joseph this would be a soup can. Now, enough talking, everyone back to failing, and this time please fail in color rather than in black and white."

Dylan set sunglasses back over his eyes. The rest of the afternoon he painted in silence.

After class I was walking east on 57th Street when I heard my name shouted over traffic. I turned to see Dylan hurrying toward me, guitar slung over his shoulder. He started talking in a breathless voice about the Chagall painting. Had I seen those colors? Really seen them? Because he felt that boy's innocence as richly as any true love. Dylan talked all the way from 57th and Seventh to my place off 78th and York, walking faster than I could follow, scanning the street, his pace quickening whenever strangers stared at him. He seemed relieved when we came to my building. He kept talking as we went up the three flights of stairs and he settled on the windowsill overlooking the courtyard garden, into which the smoke of his cigarette drifted as he reached for his guitar.

He began playing one of his early ballads, a song of yearning and lost love. He played the song a way I'd never heard. Rather than the steady rhythm of the recording he'd released, he slowly drew out every phrase and chord progression, as if each moment he sang carried him farther away from the lost love he was remembering through the song. He altered the lyrics as well, replacing *her* with *him*, singing with wounded emotion about the boy from the north country. He sang with his eyes closed and scrunched face taking on each of the ballad's emotions, like he was part of the song, it was a story he was living inside. He'd become a different person when he entered the song, the way Stella said the best actors entered a character, the way Chagall became Joseph, and as he pleaded another stanza it occurred to me that Bob Dylan himself was a character of his own creation, a work of fiction. Nobody by that name had ever been born. The man on my windowsill had been Robert Zimmerman until he sang himself into somebody else. He'd come to New York just as I had, a kid from nowhere, thirteen years before. Maybe that was why he didn't care that I had nothing to my name. Dylan went on singing, and I was standing on the shores of the Red Sea, the whole world opening to me. It didn't matter that I'd dropped out of college and hadn't yet found myself as an actress and even my own parents didn't believe in me. All that mattered was the world to come.

Dylan finished the song and gazed into my eyes.

"Play it again," I said, "and draw out that third stanza. I want to feel more of that sorrow."

He played the ballad six or seven times, tinkering with pace and emphasis. Music and sunlight eased across the apartment. He set down the guitar and lit a cigarette and said Raeben was teaching him that all his problems came down to perspective. He had become too satisfied in seeing things from one point of view. Raeben, Dylan said, didn't see the totality of anything but glimpsed slivers of truth from different times and places. Raeben saw into the old world his father had chronicled, he'd broken bread in the Russian Empire, grown up under Nicholas II, seen the czar shoot workers and socialists in the streets. Raeben was also a man of the modern world, he'd lived in Manhattan sixty years, knew every wine bar and jazz club in town. He could slip between languages, colors, thinking and feeling, different eras in time.

"What's been troubling me these past years," Dylan said, "was trying to see the totality of things. There ain't no such thing."

Now he was just after slivers of truth, he said, like Raeben.

BOY FROM THE NORTH COUNTRY

Darkness was falling and I liked the look of his shadow on my wall. On the bookshelf a rosewood pipe lay atop a book of Italian poetry. I lit a burner on the stove and offered him the pipe. Dylan closed his eyes as he inhaled.

"Do you know *Il Canzoniere*?" I asked, opening the book of Italian poetry. "It translates as *The Songbook*. Three hundred and sixty-six poems Petrarch wrote for a woman named Laura, who he met only once. Some people say they never spoke, others claim she never existed."

Dylan closed his eyes. I read aloud. Petrarch's words gathered around us.

When I had spoken the poem's last word he reached for his guitar and played that same early ballad. His voice broke over every word and the music rose out of him, and he looked at me as if the two of us understood something nobody else knew.

Later that week the door buzzer woke me in the night. I lay sleepy in bed, figuring the buzzing was an accident. The noise went on, not a moment between rings. I stumbled out of bed for the talk button. Dylan's voice boomed into my apartment: "You there, June?"

A moment later he was marching into my room with a cigarette on his lips, talking about how Petrarch stood between everything significant, touching God with one hand and man with the other, the past with one hand and the future with the other. He said Petrarch was a chronicler of antiquity and progenitor of the Renaissance. Petrarch had reached back to the Romans and Greeks and used their wisdom to refashion his own notion of humanism. The idea of the humanities, of a society that valued language and philosophy and poetry, Dylan said, could be traced to Petrarch's devotion to the ancient world and his influence on what became the Renaissance. "We're all living," Dylan said, tapping his cigarette ash out on the windowsill, "in the world Petrarch made. We're all his sons."

He paced the room and smoked another cigarette and went on talking. He'd spent the last days reading Petrarch's poetry and everything he could find about his life. He knew that from an early age Petrarch had an intimate relationship with Dante. Dylan kept repeating this—"He knew *Dante*"—as if, through Petrarch, Dylan could trace his own lineage to the author of *The Divine Comedy*. Dylan sat on the windowsill and repeated one of the lines of the poem I had read to him, and it occurred to me that this was how he went through life, someone read him a poem or mentioned a song, and if he was intrigued he learned all he could, and that led to something else. He was constantly moving through time, place, language. He was so erudite but hadn't lasted a year in college. He'd dropped out, was self-taught, needed to understand the world on his own terms. He was relentless in pursuit of anything that could help him get there, whether it was a Leonard Cohen song or the lifework of an Italian poet.

He started coming by all the time. He'd show up at my apartment mid-conversation, as if he'd carried on our last discussion in his mind and was surprised I wasn't up to speed. He'd ring my buzzer at three in the morning and come through the door saying, "Can you believe what Rimbaud does in *A Season in Hell*?" Or he'd arrive with his guitar and start playing before I closed the door behind him. After five minutes or two hours he'd glance up and say, "What d'you think?" One day he arrived with canvases, paints, and two French easels. He kept running up and down the stairs in his sunglasses, hauling the materials from a double-parked white truck. We smoked and painted and read aloud and lay in bed. Dylan never remembered anything about time. I'd say, "Don't come by Friday night, I'm performing *Hedda Gabler*." At three that morning I'd wake to the phone and he'd be rambling about Petrarch's *Seniles*, then pause to say he came by 78th Street earlier to tell me all this, he'd rather speak in person, "See you in a few minutes."

He'd come into something new and I could see it in his eyes. He spent hours sitting on my windowsill, tapping his foot on the hardwood floor and playing fragments of new work. He'd sing a verse, sometimes with the guitar and sometimes without, pause mid-word and bang his fist on the window and go silent. Then he'd sing the same verse with different words. "What do you think?" he'd ask.

"Not any better," I said one night he'd been playing the same verse for hours, "than the last eighteen times. You're wandering the desert, Bob. You're worshipping a golden calf. That song's no good, you've got to let it go."

He'd get up and walk the apartment and talk about what it meant to write like Raeben painted, to react in every moment. For years, Dylan said, he'd been trying to recreate the spirit of his early work. That was madness. He felt then what he felt then and he felt now what he felt now. He'd been trapped in the fires of time and Raeben was setting him free. He played the same songs different ways, chords and melodies and lyrics constantly rearranged. He said he needed to write a song where you could see the different parts of everything and you could also see the whole. The way Raeben stood between centuries and continents and the divine and quotidian. When he wrote a song like that, Dylan said, he'd have learned what Raeben was trying to teach.

There were days we woke late and he sang and played and we talked into the early evening, then he'd suddenly look at me and say, "Should we eat?" and I'd realize we hadn't all day. I'd run to the pizzeria on 78th and First. He never came with me, he didn't want to be seen.

"Every time you recollect," he said one night, sitting on the windowsill and looking at me over his guitar, "the memory is different in your head. Every time you read a book it changes because you've changed. You have to keep seeking or everything goes flat. All those years I was trying to close the book but I've got to keep it open."

That night he said there was nothing final and no foundations and he was plunging to the depths of the earth because that's where heaven was. He had an energy now that couldn't be contained. He put it all into his notebook. I'd fall asleep as Hedda Gabler while Dylan wrote on the windowsill, tapping his foot absentmindedly on the floor as he tried to get a line right. In the morning he'd be where I left him, leaning against the window frame in the same clothes, the same distant expression. One morning as I came out of the bedroom he glanced up, exhaustion shadowing his eyes, and said he was calling his new album *Blood on the Tracks*.

Other nights I'd wake to the heat of his body beside me, coming to bed at who knew what hour, whispering something I couldn't make out. One night, with the warmth of his chest pressed to mine, he said, "You're one of the mad ones, June. You want to burn the night away." I kissed him, half asleep. Only later did I realize he took the line from Kerouac.

I was performing *Hedda Gabler* two nights a week with Gordon in the Chelsea loft and auditioning for whatever else I could find. I went to Stella's and Norman's studios as often as I could. Most nights he was over I walked around the apartment as Hedda, and Dylan wrote or played guitar. No matter how hard I worked there were still those two moments I couldn't master.

"Goddamnit!" I shouted one night after stumbling over the lines.

"What's that?" Dylan said, sitting cross-legged on the floor with his guitar.

I told him about the two moments that always outdid me: when Hedda rejects Judge Brack's sexual advance, and when she replies to her lost lover's claim that killing his child is not the worst thing a father can do. Dylan looked at me, perplexed.

"What you got to do is become your own father. Then this won't be a concern."

"I'll tell that to Gordon," I said, "next time I forget my lines."

"Don't be sore," he said. "Let's act out the scene."

Dylan took the playbook out of my hand and scanned the page. I could almost feel the lines burning into his mind. He circled the room, face concealed from me. Then he turned and his eyes were manic and his gait bent, and he roared, "'I have destroyed it nonetheless—utterly destroyed it, Hedda!'"

"'I don't understand,'" I replied coolly, sitting upright on the sofa.

"'Thea said that what I did seemed like a child-murder,'" he hissed.

"'Yes, so she said,'" I observed.

"'But to kill his child—that is not the worst thing a father can do.'"

"'Not the worst?'" I asked skeptically.

"'Suppose now, Hedda,'" Dylan said, coming very close to me, eyes gone mad, "'that a man came home to his child's mother in the small hours of the morning, after a night of debauchery, and said, "Listen, I have been here and there, and I have taken our child to this place and to that, and I have lost the child. The devil knows into what hands it may have fallen!"'"

Dylan's was a menacing glare. I never again forgot that line.

Other times he searched the disorderly piles of plays and poetry, picking out Chekhov as he said, "This'll help me think, act it out with me. You be Irina and I'll be Fedotik." He handed me *Three Sisters*, and I drew myself into Irina, and a moment later said with unbearable anticipation, "'The game is working out right. So we shall go to Moscow!'"

"'No!'" Dylan howled, bitterness in the very movement of his jaw. "'It's not working out. You see, the eight is over the two of spades. So that means you won't go to Moscow.'"

After we finished the scene Dylan said, "Nobody ever makes it to Moscow in Chekhov. We're always heading there and never arriving. Like the Mashiach on his way."

"We can go to Moscow," I said, reaching for a Tchaikovsky vinyl and taking him in my arms as we began to dance.

It was uncanny how he could intuit his way into a character. He'd take Chekhov off the shelves and be Trigorin in a moment. Shakespeare in his hands and he was Lear. His expression transforming, he'd look a way I'd never seen him. He'd come into his own in folk ballads, stories passed down on the idea that when you sing someone's story you become who they are.

The morning after we acted out *Three Sisters* he was up before me, making coffee in the kitchenette. I kissed him as he handed me a mug. When I drew back his face was contorted into an expression I'd only seen in his most desperate moments with his notebook.

"Gonna make a film," he said in a strained voice. "Need someone to play my wife. You want the role?"

He stared at me innocently, as if there was nothing to the comment.

"What the fuck does that mean, Bob? People have feelings beyond acting and painting and singing, don't you know?"

"All right!" he said, storming out of the kitchenette. "So you won't take the role."

He put on his shoes and walked out the door.

I knew he was married. Some of the time he must have been with Sara, although I was never sure if she was in New York. Other times he went to his farm in Minnesota. Sometimes he'd say, "Yesterday when I was in San Francisco," and I hadn't realized he'd left New York. I never asked what else he was up to in the city and he never said. Was he going out on the town with other celebrities? Or holed up in some hotel alone with his guitar and ideas, trying to write himself out of his blindness? Maybe both. Usually he'd stay the night with me. Other times he'd pack his guitar at dawn and say, "Best be on my way."

I loved the evenings with him, the poetry and plays and painting and music. But there was a space between us and nothing could close it. He didn't want it closed.

One night he read me a Verlaine poem, holding the fraying volume between us in the dim light. He read the last word, and his eyes lingered in mine, and he kissed me. His hand was warm on my cheek and he slipped off my dress and I lifted his black undershirt from his thin, angular body, and we were borne across the room by the emotion of the poem. He held me to the bookshelf and our breaths were rapid and my hands were in his curls, the books falling from the shelves to the floor, Ibsen, Chekhov, Petrarch, Dante.

Later we lay naked on the hardwood floor in the summer heat. Dylan drew me nearer and whispered, "June, if I had the stars from the darkest night I'd forsake them all for your sweet kiss." I lay in his arms and he kissed me and we fell asleep.

A few days later I was sitting on the fire escape and the words played again in my mind. I heard the sentence in its familiar rhythm, as Dylan sang it in "Boots of Spanish Leather." He'd taken that sentence right from his own song and tried to place it in my heart. It wasn't for me. It was from him to himself.

My instinct was to vaporize all that, Dylan as Dylan. I wanted the man rather than the myth. One night, after a particularly intense orgasm, he was lying blissfully in bed, his head on my chest as he breathed slowly. I ran my hands along his naked back and whispered, "You're a beautiful man, Robert Zimmerman." He leapt up from bed, didn't say a word as he hurried into his clothes and ran out the door.

He showed up at my place two nights later like nothing happened, and we never discussed Zimmerman. Dylan played guitar as usual and we talked about the songs he was writing. Late that night he went out for cigarettes and left his notebook on the windowsill. I knew it was wrong to look, but I wanted all of him. The music and conversation and sex weren't enough. I opened the notebook. The pages were filled with half-formed sketches, fragments of stanzas jotted at odd angles, lines of poetry written over one another, every bit of handwriting illegible. Staring into his notebook didn't tell me anything more about the man than looking into his sleeping eyes. I heard footsteps on the stairs and put the notebook back on the sill.

"Just think about the Talmud," Dylan said, coming through the door with a cigarette on his lips. "Hundreds of years of commentary all on the same page. Nothing fixed in time. How we have lived and how we should live and how we will live. Endless meaning on a single page. Playing the same song the same way is like asking the Torah to mean the same thing to everyone who ever read it. No color there, nothing worthwhile. Got to keep that page open."

He handed me a cigarette and I gestured us onto the fire escape, away from the guilty charge of the notebook.

"When you react to every moment," Dylan said, clambering after me through the window, "that's when you're alive. Art as a way of life, like Raeben says. You must feel that onstage. I thought I'd never have that feeling again, making something that doesn't just imitate life but goes right beyond life. Tells you something truer than life ever can."

"I've had moments when Hedda feels more real than I do," I said, putting my cigarette in his lips and his cigarette in mine, just for fun.

Dylan looked hard at me. "And she teaches you something about how to live?"

"I think so," I said.

"It's all real," Dylan said, the tip of his cigarette burning in the night. "Don't ever let anyone tell you otherwise."

When we were together in the 78th Street apartment there was no other world. When we weren't, everything between us seemed detached from my life. It's strange to say this, but it was partly because of the apartment. My room was in the rear of the building, which put it halfway between 78th and 79th Streets. The building was halfway between First and York Avenues. So if you drew a rectangle along those four streets my apartment was at the precise center. You couldn't hear a thing from the street, it felt like being outside time. Everything slowed. On the street it was different. Dylan was all motion, eyes restless behind his sunglasses, anxious about being recognized, glancing over his shoulder for the photographers or would-be acolytes who had tracked him to Woodstock and searched the garbage on his curb for existential truth.

We never talked in Raeben's class. I couldn't tell if Dylan was being protective of me, or if I should be offended that he was ignoring me in front of people we both knew. I was grateful and hurt at the same time. There wasn't anyone in my life I felt close enough to tell what was happening between us. What was I supposed to do, call my mother and tell her I was seeing Bob Dylan? She would have laughed at me. And it wasn't as if I could bring him home or share him with anyone. Once, my younger brother called while Dylan was in the apartment, and the words just slipped out of my mouth, I said: "I'm here with Bob Dylan." My brother asked to speak to him, and of course I said no. He laughed and said, "Well, I'm here with David Bowie. He says hi!"

The fact that I didn't speak about the relationship contributed to my sense that it wasn't quite real. Maybe that's also why I never felt vulnerable. I should have. He was thirty-three and I was twenty. He was a celebrity and I was nobody. He was married and I wasn't close to my family. He'd been with a thousand women and I hadn't been with many men.

The closest we came to discussing anything directly was an evening he lay naked on the floor, his head in my lap. We'd been smoking that rosewood pipe and his eyes were closed, and as I looked down at him I felt as if my life was enclosed by unreality. I was twenty years old, waiting tables and living off my dreams. I wasn't sure why Dylan had spent so much of the last months in my run-down apartment. I heard myself asking if he didn't have anyone better with whom to spend his time.

"What the hell kind of question is that?" he grumbled, staring up at me. "One look at you and I knew right away."

At some point late that summer Dylan said he'd be traveling. He didn't say where and I didn't ask. Every night I was at Denise's or Alph's or Kenny's apartment, acting scenes or reading poetry to each other. Sometimes Dylan called at three in the morning from the road and started playing, that was his hello. I'd imagine him in some hotel room, the phone propped on the bed, extension cord tangled on the floor, guitar on his knee, eyes closed as he sang.

One night the phone woke me at what must have been four in the morning.

"Early one morning," Dylan sang, "I was laying in bed."

BOY FROM THE NORTH COUNTRY

He sang a roaming ballad about a man in search of lost love. It wasn't clear if the man was after one woman or every woman he ever loved or only love itself. Some elements were the same between stanzas and some were contradictory, so the man and woman were always the same and always different. The way that in love we know ourselves most deeply and we know ourselves the least. We know everything about the other person and we know nothing. Dylan roved between first person and third, the story was from the perspective of the man in search of lost love, and also from an outside observer who both was and was not the man. Every stanza described the present while imagining the future and recalling the past. The man is journeying toward his lost lover, but his notion of a future with her is rooted in the past. Even as she walks away he hears her say they'll meet again someday.

Dylan went on singing, and I thought of a visit to the Museum of Modern Art with my parents. I was twelve and stood alone beneath Braque's *Man with a Guitar*. I was terrified by the way Braque tore the man open, showing me more than I wanted. I glanced over my shoulder, expecting to see Herbert, who had taken me to the theater two nights before. When I was certain he wasn't in the gallery—there was no reason he would be—I looked back at the Braque. The man's angled forms opened to me on the canvas and I felt I'd never seen a person so completely. Listening to Dylan's voice on the phone, I felt as if I was standing once again before that Braque.

He began singing about a woman who read to him from a book of Italian poetry, and every word rang true, it was written in his soul from me to you. My breath vanished. I could see him across the room, eyes closed as I read him Petrarch. I couldn't say whether Dylan was singing to me or to the song, if I was the "you" in his stanza, if he felt for me what he was singing, or if he had been looking at me and thinking of someone else—his wife, or another woman, or no one at all? Was he lending this intimate moment between us to a love story that had nothing to do with me? Or had he merely seen an opportunity to fictionalize from the silhouette of fact? Perhaps as he scrawled in that red notebook the moment between us was transformed from life into literature. Maybe Dylan's "you" was as elusive as Petrarch's Laura, the woman he met only once, who might never have existed.

"We always did feel the same," Dylan sang into the phone, "we just saw it from a different point of view."

He paused over a long breath, then started the song again. After a few stanzas I realized what he was doing with the chord progression. Each stanza was structured by two chords, and the second always retained the root of the first. So even as the music moved forward it repeated itself. That's what Dylan admired about Petrarch, right? He was moving forward by recreating the past. That's the concept of Renaissance.

After he finished a song he usually asked what I thought. This time he started talking in a rushed voice, saying this was the first song where he was making sense of what Raeben taught him. He was finally reaching into every moment. He could see the parts and the whole. He smelled the layers of paint coming off every word.

"It isn't even one song," Dylan said, "it's a living thing. Nobody has ever finished writing a poem, you know that. Whitman was rewriting *Leaves of Grass* the hour after he died."

He said no poem is ever finished because it's a way of life, there's never anything on the other side of struggle but more struggle. Dylan said his hands were deep in the dirt of this song and that's what the word *poem* means in the original Greek, "constructed by hand." He said that as he wrote the song he felt tangled in Raeben's colors and as a tribute he was calling it "Tangled Up in Blue."

Before we hung up I said, "By the way, Petrarch lived in the fourteenth century."

"Oh right!" he said.

A FEW DAYS LATER, Gordon told the cast of *Hedda Gabler* that an acquaintance had agreed to let us stage the play at her townhouse on Fifth Avenue. The location meant we could draw an upscale audience, and if word caught on maybe be reviewed in the mainstream theater press. Rehearsal was relentless. The cast arrived at eight each morning and often didn't leave until midnight. I no longer had the hours in the week to study with Raeben.

Dylan returned to New York that September. One night he came by the apartment around three a.m., hair matted and unwashed, shadows beneath his eyes, nervous like he was on the run. He lit a cigarette and blew the smoke through the window into the night and began speaking about Rosh Hashanah.

"People say it's a celebration of the new year, they don't know nothing. It's more than the new year. The world is reborn every Rosh Hashanah, don't you know? One more year of human life and the first year of human life. The world is timeless and the world is new. I'll die just as I'm reborn. That's what will happen on Rosh Hashanah, mark the date. September 16, 1974. Tishrei 1, 5735. Spread the news, darling. Sing it from a mountain. The levees have broken. The flood's coming. I was blind but now I see. Raeben heard my pleas and set me free. I've been—"

"Take a smoke, Bob, you'll sound less mad."

"Mad? Who said mad? You'd seem mad, too, if you were living in the past, present, and future all at the same time."

He sat on the windowsill and played a few songs with his longing eyes cast in shadow.

Dylan began in the recording studio soon after that. Through that autumn he came by in the night and sat up rewriting lyrics in his red notebook. He stayed one hour or twelve. We slept together or he hardly said hello. We painted, and I rehearsed my lines, and he wrote. He talked to himself. He lay in my lap on the hardwood floor as he had so often that spring and summer. He'd stand suddenly, saying to himself, "Oh, that reminds me!" and he'd speak only to his guitar the rest of the night. A week would pass with no word from him, then he'd be at my apartment six nights in a row.

Hedda Gabler premiered the week after Thanksgiving, and we sold out every night. In a performance the second week I saw Stella Adler in the audience. I looked for her after the show but she was gone. Three city papers ran unusually strong reviews of the show. We knew this meant people from the more established theater world would want to see the show. Gordon extended the performance two weeks, which required a shouting match with the apartment owner, who was planning to return for Christmas. Gordon threatened to squat if she didn't keep out of our way.

One night around this time I woke to the phone at three or four in the morning.

"No need to worry about me," Dylan said. "I'm used to the Minnesota cold."

"When did you fly out, Bob?"

"Tracks weren't working. We're rerecording. It's Rosh Hashanah all over again."

"Thought you liked those tracks?"

"Too much blood, too little tracks. Every word is too damn raw. Nobody wants to listen to that kind of anguish. You can't make art out of seppuku."

"Isn't that a samurai tradition? Death poems? The rawness works, Bob. It's honest."

"Honesty don't sell. Nobody wants my tears, honey. David's taking care of me. Brothers always do. He's setting me straight, making me smile. Gonna sing that song a way people can hear. Hold on, I'll play it for you."

I could hear him reaching for his guitar on the other end of the line. He was silent a moment, then started playing a more upbeat version of the song he was calling "Tangled Up in Blue." I thought about telling him that he'd lost the verve of the song, he was taming the rhythm against its own interests. But he seemed in a bad way, so I didn't say anything.

Our last performance of *Hedda Gabler* was on New Year's Eve. That morning a city weekly called the show "the theatrical surprise of 1974" and Gordon "the most creative thinker working the off-Broadway stage." The review included the history of Gordon's apartment theater, how he organized a theatrical experience independent from the conventional gatekeepers. Gordon wouldn't stop reading his own quotes aloud, the same things he'd been saying all along, "Theater is the most democratic art form and we can't leave it to the profiteers." The review was generous to my performance, even called me "an actress whose name is well-known to the underground theater community," which was an exaggeration.

The thrill in the townhouse that night felt palpable. We all knew that on the strength of the review we could continue staging the production, maybe even at one of the more well-known off-Broadway theaters. Suddenly everything seemed possible.

Minutes before the show started Gordon found me in the dressing room, a bedroom with Central Park views and Thomas Cole landscapes in gold frames. In a voice almost incoherent with excitement, Gordon said the review made it impossible to meet the audience's expectations. We had to escalate the tension of the play. He reached into his torn jacket and withdrew the silver antique pistol we used as a prop.

"That pistol," Gordon said, "is loaded with two bullets. When Judge Brack nears you, fire the first bullet into the ceiling. When you step offstage to commit suicide, fire the second bullet into the wall." He pressed the pistol into my hand and turned out of the room.

I gripped the pistol and felt Hedda's fearlessness. Her daring desire to live on her own terms. I stared into the mirror and the woman looking back at me with straightened hair and a black lace dress was not me but Hedda Gabler.

That night I didn't once think about a line of dialogue. I simply spoke as Hedda. When Judge Brack neared me, I pointed the gun at his mouth. "'Don't stand aiming at me!'" he shouted, and by the tremor in his voice I understood that he knew the pistol was loaded.

I fired overhead. The audience gasped. Plaster dust fell from the ceiling onto the stage.

Every time I reached for the pistol the audience went silent. When the final scene came, I let the weapon dangle a moment in my hand, then aimed into the front row. There were screams in the crowd. I strode off the stage into the bedroom with Central Park views, burning with disdain for the falsity of this world, clutching the pistol in my hand, aiming the weapon at the neatly arranged white pillows on the bed, ready to fire at the men who treated me as nothing more than a body without mind or soul, and I saw lounging there on the linen bedsheet Ralph Summers, Herbert Zuckerman, and, with rage I had never let myself feel, I saw my father. Because he had known. He looked at me from the bed, as he had one summer morning when I was fifteen and he drove me to Herbert's home for a private acting lesson, responding to my insistence that I didn't want to be left alone with Herbert by sternly repeating, "Herbert's been a fine mentor to you."

The shot rang out. The pistol trembled in my hand. The image of my father vanished from the bed.

Applause thundered from the main room. Dust rose off the pillow, and I remembered that first evening when Stella told me that whether the actress is arrogant or insecure or celebrated means nothing. She can only care whether she achieves her character to the greatest possible extent. I stood with the pistol trembling in my hand and understood why Stella vanished after my shows and why she never complimented me, and I felt a gratitude to her unlike anything I ever felt for another person. She was standing behind me, and I felt Raeben and Dylan, too, heard him saying art could become more real than life, and I understood.

Gordon led the cast on a charge through the streets. The Upper East Side was deserted, everyone had left the city for the New Year or was in Times Square to see the ball drop. Gordon waved the pistol overhead, shouting, "I'm a Bolshevik! I'm a Bolshevik in the Winter Palace!"

We came into my apartment and Kenny put on a Keith Jarrett record, and Alph and Denise danced through the smoke, and Gordon shouted his quotes from the review. People passed around joints and wine. Looking through the smoke at all these people in my life, I thought to myself, *This all happened in my first year in New York. I can't wait for the years to come.*

The phone rang. I waded through the smoke and put the phone to my ear, and Dylan said, "We finished recording, it's all over now, baby!" Victory broke through his hoarse voice. He'd struggled so hard and at any point could have given up and settled for everything he already had. He'd come through the other side after all those years of blindness. For the first time everything between us felt real. I'd never let myself love him until that moment. People were shouting and laughing and smoking and I said it into the phone. Dylan didn't miss a beat. He said, "I love you, too, June. See you soon!"

Nine

She fell asleep almost as soon as she curled into her pillow in the passenger seat. I drove west through Central Park, pencil skyscrapers casting artificial light on the trees. We couldn't be far from the Fifth Avenue townhouse where she once fired Hedda Gabler's pistol. I glanced at her, thinking of all she had never said. Stars lit the sky above the farmhouse by the time we returned. We walked up the garage stairs with her weight on my shoulder. Lucy greeted us on the dark landing. She bent, lifted Lucy to her chest, and carried her through the sliding door into the night. We stood silently on the porch as Lucy peed beneath my mother's favorite maple tree. She scampered back toward us, and my mother carried her to bed. They lay together atop the covers and within moments were asleep.

I stood at my window, looking onto the night. Pine trees rustled against the house. I heard a voice joining mine as it said, "I love you, June." In all the years I had wondered about my mother and Dylan I had never considered that they ever loved one another.

My reflection glanced back at me from the window. For years I'd kept my hair closely cropped in a crew cut, the style that made me look least like him. I hadn't had time for a haircut since returning home, and the first suggestion of his curls were beginning to grow off my scalp. I opened my laptop and let myself look at him. He stared at me from the screen with an expression I'd seen on my face. When I was younger it had been early photographs that struck me most, shots taken not long after he'd arrived in New York. Now I was growing into his late twenties look, the years after he'd vanished into the woods in upstate New York under the cover of his motorcycle accident. He still had that knowing look in his eye but it was harder-won; our cheekbones had the same angle.

Into the search bar I typed keywords I had avoided for years. I leaned closer to the screen, reading about Dylan's secret child. Her mother had done everything she could to keep their daughter from public view. Dylan had set them up in an unknown place, they lived normal lives.

I searched for his concert schedule, just to know where he was. I knew he was still touring constantly, playing concert halls, theaters, outdoor stadiums, the Never Ending Tour he started a few years before my birth, nearly three thousand concerts in all. He had never stopped living within his music. He didn't speak to the audience from the stage or comment on his lyrics. Those were distractions, lies, masks. In his rare interviews he was elusive as his songs. He was devoted to nothing more than the music. But if he saw me in the audience, standing above the crowd, would his trance falter? Would his eyes meet mine? If he saw my mother beside me, he would know.

Dylan's concert schedule materialized on the screen.

He'd been touring out west, the overlooked states, cities mistaken for towns. He'd come east last week. I stared at the screen. He'd played New York City tonight, the Beacon Theatre, a twelve-minute cab ride from the hospital, according to Google Maps. He had been performing onstage as my mother conjured him from memory in the hospital on the other side of Central Park. On impulse I clicked the set list. He'd played "Tangled Up in Blue" for nearly the 1,600th time in concert, more than any other song. He'd never stopped tinkering with the lyrics and perspective. Glancing at his schedule, I saw that he was resting now as she rested. He was playing in five days at Bethel Woods, the farmland venue an hour west of Goshen, built on the original site of Woodstock. Coyote howled in the high grass beyond the window. He was coming to Bethel. To get to that venue from the city he would be driven along the interstate highway we had driven tonight. He would exit onto Route 17, five miles from the farmhouse. His eyes would look onto my hills. I had to be at Bethel. The worst of last week's chemotherapy cycle had been the three days after the treatment. Saturday, Sunday, Monday. The concert was Wednesday. The heat of the night drew sweat down my chest. Dylan was coming to the north country and there was no choice but to meet him here. I reached for my credit card and bought two tickets, at exorbitant expense, that would place my mother and me at the foot of the stage.

THAT NIGHT I startled awake to the sound of vomiting. Moonlight glowed in the dark sky. I hurried into her room. My mother knelt on her bedroom floor, wiping paper towels over a puddle of yellow vomit. "Mom!" I shouted, snatching the paper towels and cleaner from her and spraying the floor as if it was the cancer itself I could wipe away. I knew I had to rid myself of the impulse to yell. Strands of her auburn hair lay amid the vomit. Lucy looked anxiously between us. "Sorry I yelled," I said, my hand on her shoulder, helping her to bed. "Just call for me next time you vomit, OK?"

"It's fine," she rasped, drawing the bedcovers over her. It wasn't fine. She needed to rest as much as possible.

"Marijuana . . ." she whispered. "Oh, the pain . . ."

"You want to smoke together?"

She shook her head. She wanted the tincture, the simplest way to flood the drug into her bloodstream. I reached for the dropper bottle on her bedside table and she opened her mouth and greedily swallowed the stream of drops.

She asked me to read *Harry Potter* as she lay beneath the covers, trying to sleep. Harry sailed on a broomstick through the sky above Hogwarts Castle, in desperate pursuit of the Snitch. "Damn Snape," I said as Harry's nemesis muttered a spell to knock Harry off his broom.

"Remember, he redeems himself in the end," she said, her words groggy in the dark.

"Did you know that Snape was secretly on the right side all those years you read to me?"

"No, I despised him. How cruel he was to his most vulnerable students. The end of the seventh book completely surprised me. Reminded me, you never know the change people are capable of."

She turned beneath the covers, groaning in discomfort. She asked for the oxycodone and took an unusually strong dose. Each time I thought she was sleeping, and closed the book, her voice came through the darkness: "Keep reading, Evan. Oh, I love this story . . ."

I woke in the chair beside her bed, sunlight filtering through the window. My mother lay facing me, sleeping peacefully. Lucy stretched on her hind legs, eager for the day. I scooped her from the bed, her fur soft on my skin. I walked downstairs with Lucy's head tucked over my wrist, her tongue licking my hand. Morning light shone through the fields behind the house. I set Lucy in the grass and she pranced toward the forest.

Trees swayed in the breeze. She darted into the woods, pausing to sniff, her ears perked for chipmunks and deer. On either side of the trail blackberries grew on prickly vines. I felt returned to those childhood mornings I had run into the forest with only the lush berries in mind. I knew every patch in these woods, and after collecting all the berries from one bush I would run to the next, my bare feet tripping over roots and stones, trying not to spill the berries in my palm, desperate for the sweet taste of a new grove. So much within me had changed since those days. The blackberry bushes remained as they were. I reached through the vines, the tips of my fingers stained as I collected the fruit. It didn't seem likely that my mother would walk the woods today. How happy she would be with the luscious taste of berries.

She slept most of the day. She asked for turmeric tea, marijuana tincture, oxycodone. She meditated in bed, back slightly arched, palms up, her rib cage rising and falling with each breath. I had been selfish to think she would be able to travel to Bethel on Wednesday.

"You can meditate from anywhere," she whispered, lying atop her bedsheets. "At any moment of your day."

"Mom, can you eat more burger?" I asked, looking at her mostly uneaten plate.

"Not hungry now," she said in a withdrawn voice, gazing onto the woods.

"How about the Huel?"

"So awful . . ."

She weighed a hundred and eleven pounds, as of that morning. She needed to eat. She had told me to insist if she said no.

"Mom, I'm cooking you another burger," I announced.

She opened her eyes and looked wearily at me.

"You have to gain back the weight," I insisted. "Let's give you more marijuana if we need to stimulate your appetite. We're at the low point of the cycle, like you said last week. We've been here before. We know how to get you out of this. We just need to stick to your regimen."

She couldn't bring herself to eat the burger. I blended Huel with coconut milk, yogurt, and frozen berries to dull the rancid taste. She eyed the glass skeptically.

"Don't worry," I said, "I brought you a chaser."

I handed her a bar of dark chocolate.

"You know my weaknesses too well," she smiled, sipping the drink.

BY THE FOLLOWING MORNING, Sunday, she had the strength to begin her regimen again. She lay on the BEMER. She took a binder of medical studies into the infrared sauna. She ate two poached eggs and drank the Huel blend.

"Every bite matters," she said, staring down the last half egg. "Every pound matters."

"There we go, Mom. You're doing so well."

I did not dare mention the Dylan concert in three days.

In the evening she showered. I was cooking her burger, Lucy circling my ankles and sniffing at the meat, when I heard my mother scream. I ran upstairs, Lucy bounding after me.

"I'm fine," she said in a controlled voice as we came into her bedroom.

"Mom!" I shouted through the closed bathroom door. "What's going on?"

I could hear the shower water rhythmically echoing off the bath floor.

"I'm fine," she repeated.

She came downstairs thirty minutes later in a white summer dress.

Her long auburn hair was nearly all gone. The last strands lay atop her bald head like the first hair on a newborn. She smiled resolutely. I looked onto her baldness and returned her smile. Gesturing to the burger and sautéed cauliflower, I said, "Would you like to have dinner?"

That night she ate more than she had in the last weeks: two grass-fed burgers, an avocado, a plate of roasted vegetables, and a blended Huel drink.

SHE WAS ABLE to sleep through Sunday night. Early Monday morning I came downstairs to see that she had already scrambled herself eggs for breakfast, the iron skillet lying in the sink and the pleasant scent of cooked olive oil in the kitchen. I was surprised to hear her voice in the sunroom office, in the gentle cadences she used with clients: "Any time you want to talk, all right?"

She was sitting at her cherry desk, beneath the bay window, my mother in her place, where she had sat for twenty-five years, listening to the struggles of people who came to her for guidance in strengthening their mind, body, and spirit. In her bare arms I could see the weight she had regained in the last days. There was more color in her face than at any point since her last chemotherapy. She had once again come through the lowest point in the cycle. She was drawing on everything she knew as a holistic health practitioner to guide her body through illness, and it was working.

"You look amazing!" I said. Lucy emerged from the tossed blankets on the massage table, as if surprised to find herself there.

"It was rejuvenating to speak with Susan," my mother said. "I miss my patients. I'm used to asking how I can help other people. It feels strange only helping myself."

"You'll be able to work again soon," I said.

"I had such a lovely conversation with Susan," she said. She reached for her kombucha, and I sat on the sofa across from her, settling in for her story. "It always amazes me," she said, "how difficult it is for us to see ourselves. Susan is thirty-four. The mother of two young girls. A wonderful music teacher. Stunningly beautiful. All she sees are her flaws. She's ten pounds heavier than she wants. She doesn't always find the right words with her girls. It's difficult to express her needs to her husband."

Two walls of her office were lined with shelves of supplements, protein powders, homeopathic remedies. The third wall was taken up by the bay window and a framed photograph of an article about my mother in the regional newspaper. The headline, in large print above her photograph, read: "Much More Is Possible Than You Think, According to Local Health Practitioner." On the fourth wall was a painting of a white horse galloping through clouds.

"I told Susan," she went on, "you can change whatever you want about yourself. What is life if not a series of transformations? But your foundation has to be love for who you are now. I started thinking about this hairdresser on 78th Street, maybe because we've been talking about the city. He had a shabby place on my street, and we struck up a friendship. Over the years, I followed him as he upgraded to nicer places. Eventually, he opened the first hair salon at Barneys. By then, he mostly cut celebrities, plus a few old regulars. One day, in his chair, I listed everything that bothered me about my appearance. 'Stop!' he said. He reeled off a list of film stars. 'Not one,' he said, 'can sit in that chair and like what they see in the mirror.'"

Lucy stretched her hind legs on the massage table, a perfect downward dog posture.

"It took a long time," she continued, "for me to understand that it doesn't matter how beautiful the rest of the world finds you. It's about making peace with our own reflection. How can we unlearn harshness, and replace it with the kindness we would offer a child? So we'll talk about the ten pounds later, I told Susan. For now: Can you give yourself that kindness? Can you look at your reflection and know you are beautiful? Susan said, 'Do you always feel beautiful, June?' She doesn't know about the cancer. I've been telling patients I'm taking personal time. I looked in the mirror at my bald head and flabby arms, and told Susan, 'Yes, I feel beautiful.'"

Lucy leapt off the massage table and barked at the window.

"Shall we let Lucy walk us?" my mother said.

The three of us stepped into the summer morning. Birdsong echoed in the woods. My mother inhaled the warm air. We followed the path into the woods. I said, "You haven't told your patients about the cancer?"

"I'm here to support them, not the other way around."

She smiled, and I knew there was no object in arguing.

"What about friends?" I said. "Do Audrey and Virginia know?"

"Audrey drove me to chemotherapy before you were here," she said, and with relief I felt the image of my mother alone in the hospital for her first chemotherapy session vanish from my mind. "Virginia helped me find the medical marijuana," she went on. "They've each been supportive in their own way. And each offered to stay with me if you need a break."

"That's not what I'm saying. But it's nice to know you have their love."

WE SAT ON THE HILL that afternoon as Lucy chased squirrels across the field. My mother knit her magenta yarn, the ball noticeably smaller with the passing days. We were drifting through time toward the concert but my mother didn't yet know this. I wanted her to understand that we were going without me having to say anything, for us to walk silently to her car and drive to Bethel Woods and sit at the foot of the stage as Dylan strode toward us. For us to look at him together. My mother glanced up from her knitting and her eyes settled in the distant mountains. I had to say something. Her phone rang, and I heard my grandmother anxiously ask how my mother was feeling. She looked at Lucy pawing the earth, and me sipping her iced red clover tea, and she spoke in a hopeful tone, reporting that the treatment was going well and she was enjoying time with me. Our eyes met, and I was grateful to the cancer. I was grateful to be with her.

"Here he is," she said, handing me the phone.

"Evan!" my grandmother said in the upbeat voice with which she always greeted me. I imagined her sitting on her sunny balcony in Key West with a mug of coffee. I couldn't sense any continuity between the grandmother I loved and the woman in my mother's story. My grandmother had always been fiercely protective of me. Once, after I was beaten in high school, she had proclaimed that she, who was in her late seventies and weighed a hundred and ten pounds, was going to give my attackers "a Brooklyn boxing lesson." The hilarity of this image was worth more than the promised retribution. I tried not to think of the woman in my mother's story as I said, "Hi, Bubbe."

"I have an answer for you," she said, "about why my father wasn't resentful about being left behind in Russia."

We had discussed the question at length on my last visit to Key West. She had told me the story since I was a child, but lately she had dwelled on it with new urgency.

The story went like this: Her father, David, had been born in Russia in 1906. When David was seven, his parents decided to sell their modest belongings and buy steerage tickets to America. Before they left, David's grandfather asked that one child remain behind to care for him in old age. It was decided that David should stay in Russia while his family made a new life in Manhattan. Grandfather and grandson struggled to remain alive by tilling a rocky strip of farmland, while the country was laid to waste by the First World War, the Bolshevik Revolution, and the Russian Civil War. David and his grandfather survived two pogroms, three bloody raids by the Red Army, and the potato famine that killed five million Russian peasants in 1921 and 1922. This was life in Russia as it was lived and lost, not the bright colors and floating lovers of Chagall's shtetl paintings, not the stylized production of *Fiddler on the Roof*—rather, the tireless labor, poverty, hunger, and violence that led two million Jews to flee Russia between 1880 and 1920. My grandmother had told me that her father was so hungry one winter that he and his grandfather had eaten dirt. They survived the famine, only for the older man to die in 1923.

By the time David arrived in the United States, his younger siblings had become American. They had forgotten their lives in Russia and did not care to be reminded of their early immigrant days. They mocked their brother's accent. They taunted him for his provincial ways. All his life he remained an immigrant in his own family. He struggled to find consistent work, even after his siblings owned modest businesses in the garment district and homes in Bensonhurst. His first child, my grandmother, was born in July 1929, only months before the onset of the Great Depression. Throughout her childhood the family struggled for necessities: food, rent, heat. But my grandmother always emphasized to me that her father was never bitter. He never resented that his life would have been easier had he immigrated to America with his family.

The story had taken on new forms and colors over the years. In my childhood it seemed a mythic tale, my great-grandfather a silent hero, bearing his burden as King Arthur bore responsibility for his realm. With time, I saw my great-grandfather as a terrified boy, lying awake in the night, abandoned in a town his parents had fled. He had been formed by starvation and violence and fear. He had survived, only for his family to ridicule him. I had never believed my grandmother that he carried not the slightest resentment.

"What's the answer?" I said.

"I've been thinking about this story for eighty years," my grandmother said pensively, "and this thought is only coming to me now. Here it is: my father must have loved his grandfather very much. The love he felt in the years they lived together must have made all his later hardship worthwhile."

I wanted to accept my grandmother's story. I imagined the boy observing the man as he aged and died. The man observing the boy as he grew into an adult. They had lived together from the time my great-grandfather was seven until he was seventeen. They must have formed a universe of two, with rituals, references, and intimacy that no outsider understood. I thought of the embarrassment my great-grandfather's siblings felt toward him. Even his parents seemed to have shown no interest in what their son had experienced after they left him behind in Russia.

"I love thinking of the story that way," I said. "But wouldn't that have left your father even angrier? That nobody else cared about this man he loved? I don't understand why he wasn't angry."

"Because," my grandmother said, "he wasn't angry."

My mother knit her magenta yarn. She had never spoken to me about the difficulties in her relationship with her mother. She had never said a word against my grandmother. She had never given even the slightest hint that she had felt her mother did not do all she could to protect her from a family friend who had sexually abused her. She had welcomed my grandmother into our lives. Perhaps it was not impossible to imagine my great-grandfather living without bitterness toward his family.

"Well," I said into the phone, "that makes sense: being a loving grandparent certainly runs in our family."

"Oh, what a mensch you are," she said. I thought I heard her sniffling back a tear. "Love you, Evan."

"Love you more, Bubbe."

I handed the phone to my mother.

"I'm lucky to have my mother," she said to me after she hung up. "I'm lucky to have you. I'm lucky to have Lucy. So many people go through something like this alone."

I nodded, trying to think of how to tell her about the Dylan concert in two nights.

Ten

Late on Tuesday morning I found her sitting in her lotus position beneath the crab apple tree. Her eyes were closed, her back erect, her palms open to the sky. I took my own lotus pose beside her. The sounds of nature took on a heightened quality, each bird chirp and gust of wind a distinct note. I could sense my mother sensing my presence. All the world was still.

"May I be filled," she said, "with loving-kindness. May I be well in body, mind, and spirit. May I be peaceful and at ease. May I be happy."

I repeated the prayer to myself. I could feel the love of the meditation ritual within me, as I had in the childhood days I lay on the massage table in my mother's sunroom and she asked me to think of a particular word or repeat a phrase to myself. *I am loved. I am protected. I am free.* She had taught me to draw quiet strength from the feeling of a single word. I wondered when I had lost that grace. The peacefulness of childhood could be regained here in the grass.

"Now we say the prayer for someone about whom you feel neutral," my mother said.

I said the prayer for the cab driver who had driven me from my flat to Heathrow, his weary eyes and balding head vaguely cohering in memory.

"Now we say the prayer for someone who has harmed us," she said.

I thought instinctively of Luke standing over my mother as she grimaced on the floor. I tensed in the grass. My mother and I had rarely spoken about Luke since she divorced him.

In the years Luke lived with us, from the time I was nine until I was fifteen, he listened to me describe every book I read, helped me with algebra when I struggled in seventh grade, and spent countless evenings playing basketball with me in the driveway. These memories were blurred by the image of Luke standing over my mother on the den floor.

She had taught him breathing exercises to tame his anger. She had taught him yoga. She had given him the respect he needed to go to therapy. She had gone with him to Alcoholics Anonymous. She had brought him to seminars for spiritual searchers and recovering addicts, adults who had been physically abused as children. She had spent Sunday mornings with him in the Evangelical church in town. Most of all, she had forgiven him.

She had drawn on all she knew as a healer to help Luke transform himself. She imposed on Luke only one unbreakable condition: if he was ever violent toward her, she would end their marriage.

I often came into the kitchen to find him meditating in his lotus pose. "Just trying to become a better man each day," he'd say as he opened his eyes. Luke had overcome his addiction to alcohol in the first years he lived with us. But he couldn't overcome his dry anger. Anything might set him off. I'd seen him hurl an antique chair down the stairs. Kick a hole through the barn wall with his bare foot. Speed at ninety miles an hour down the highway, swerving at another driver as he screamed, "Why the fuck shouldn't I? Give me one reason!"

It was terrifying to know he was sober. This was not alcohol speaking through my stepfather, but rather Luke as Luke.

In these moments my mother would look him in the eye and say, "Breathe, Luke. You can breathe away anything in life."

Her shout woke me one night the spring I was fifteen. The sky was black beyond my window. I hurried out of bed. Their silhouettes emerged in the den. Luke pacing around my mother. Her palms raised. Then his hands on her shoulders. Luke held my mother by the shoulders with all the strength of his six-two, two-hundred-and-twenty-pound body. Her eyes were wild. He shook her and she flailed doll-like. Then with the force he used to cast off men his own size who dared compete with him for a rebound on the basketball court, Luke hurled my mother to the floor. She crumpled on the hardwood. The house was silent. She lay prone on the ground, turned from me. I wanted a gun. I wanted the wooden ax in the garage. I wanted to strike Luke's face with a steel mallet. My mother's head turned and her eyes found mine. She gazed at me with an expression that was almost calm. Then she turned to Luke and her eyes were as fierce as I have ever seen human eyes appear, and I knew it was over, that the father turning to me, horrified to see me in the room, was leaving our lives. My mother groaned as she reached for her lower back, and it was only then I realized that I had stood still the entire time.

I hated no one as I hated the father in that memory.

No. I hated more my fifteen-year-old self who had stood passively on the stairs.

"Where the fuck did that come from?" I said, standing out of my lotus pose and glaring down at my mother's balding head, her few short strands of auburn hair lifted in the wind. "Why would I pray for someone who harmed us?"

"Because anger is a poison," she said, her eyes closed and body at ease, "that harms the one who drinks it. Or if you prefer Shakespeare: 'Heat not a furnace for your foe so hot that it do singe yourself.'"

"If you prefer Shakespeare," I snapped, "'There is a time to kill and a time to heal. A time to love and a time to hate.'"

"That's Ecclesiastes, honey, not Shakespeare," she said.

"Whatever, Mom. I'm not praying for my enemies."

"There are no enemies in life," she said, "only people who wish they could love more than they know how."

She inhaled. I tried to focus on my own breath.

"Let's just breathe together," she said.

Tension quickened in my chest. I had no interest in the meditation. Exhaling exasperation, I settled back into the lotus pose. I knew she was right: anger is a poison that harms the one who drinks it. How could I not be angry? Luke had been my father. I had been his son. We had not spoken since I was a teenager. His life could only have become more bitter after my mother told him to leave. But that was wrong. I didn't know what had become of his life. That thought came from the pain I felt toward Luke rather than my love for him. No matter the condition in which Luke found himself today, wherever he was, however he felt, he still had the power to make each day better than the day before. He had proved himself capable of profound transformations. He was capable of that again. No matter what had happened between us, that was what I wanted for him.

"Let's close," my mother said, "by repeating the prayer for a loved one."

I repeated the prayer for her. My mother. The woman in the grass beside me.

May you be filled with loving-kindness. May you be well in body, mind, and spirit. May you be peaceful and at ease. May you be happy.

Luke strode into my memory, rage glowing in his eyes. I inhaled, asking him to take his own lotus pose and meditate away his anger. I was thinking of my mother. This time was hers.

There was so much she had never told me about her life. I had known she spent her twenties trying to become an actress in New York. This was shadow knowledge, the vague contours of her life before she was my mother. I had never understood how similar the experiences of her early adult life had been to mine. All the years I had been traveling away from her I had been traveling toward her. I could recognize myself in her memories of reading through the nights at Bennington. I, too, had arrived at college in pursuit of something I could not name, speeding out of Goshen as fast as I could drive, heading three hours west on the highway to the state university at Binghamton, exhilarated to be leaving home at long last. I was unleashed from Goshen and determined to make the most of my freedom. Those first weeks on campus I could hardly sleep. Every night I stayed up reading Socratic dialogues. Murmuring the most mystifying portions aloud, I could feel everything known and solid coming apart. Every assumption about the world could be questioned and nothing known for sure. I had to get to the foundations of everything, answer questions I'd never heard. In the morning I charged into class with a thousand questions in my palm. What did Socrates mean by the soul? What does it mean for the truth to already be inside of us? After class I'd knock on the door of the professor, a Scottish woman. We sat facing one another in high-back wooden chairs, my eyes lingering on the bookcases against her wall. The knowledge contained in those books felt infinite and I wanted it all. The Scottish professor listened carefully to my questions and suggested reading. "I think you would be interested in what Nietzsche has to say about that," she might say. "Have you read *On the Genealogy of Morals*?"

This was the opposite of high school, where I could be accused of plagiarism any time I used a three-syllable word. Now I saw that other people had been talking about everything worthwhile for thousands of years. I was eighteen and knew hardly anything, but I was part of that conversation and there was no going back.

My favorite conversationalist was Sartre. I was stunned by his idea that each person is his or her own creator. I walked everywhere on campus with his collected essays, rereading his conviction that "existence precedes essence." Sartre means that we come into the world naked and only then decide who we are. "Man is free," I read, "man *is* freedom." Sartre made me feel that my life was bound neither by biological fate nor by the designs of other people. It didn't matter that I'd felt lonely and worthless in high school. It didn't matter that, of the two men who might be my biological father, Simon had abandoned our relationship before it started and Dylan didn't seem to know or care that I existed. Sartre told me that no decision made by another man could determine who I was. Only I could choose my essence and my freedom.

Reading Sartre made me want to live all I could, then describe my experience with words truer than life itself. I didn't know how to write, but I could learn. Sartre hadn't known either. I reread his account of the moment the Holy Ghost told him he would become a writer.

"What is there, Lord, that you should choose me?" Sartre asks.

"Nothing special," says the Holy Ghost.

"Then why me?" Sartre asks.

"No reason," says the Holy Ghost.

"Have I at least some facility with the pen?" Sartre wonders.

"No," says the Holy Ghost.

"Then how shall I write?" Sartre pleads.

The Holy Ghost tells him: "Through diligence."

Diligence, I could work with that. Each night in the library I tried to learn all I could from anyone who'd ever told a story. Reading Stendhal's *The Red and the Black* or Rousseau's *Confessions*, I took comfort in discovering people like me, young men who came hungry from the country for a different life. Jotting the beginnings of my own story in a blue notebook, I knew I wouldn't get it right the first hundred times. Diligence would lead me nearer to truth.

The more I read, the more I felt there was a world out there and I didn't know a thing about it. I had to get out of upstate New York. The Scottish professor had studied English literature at Oxford and I wanted to know about that. Oxford's program was the oldest in the world, reaching back to the origins of the language, classes in *Beowulf*, Chaucer, medieval myths. Oxford's castles and grand halls looked like the gathering places from which Arthurian knights set out to pursue beauty and truth. I knew my destiny was across the ocean and there was nothing I wouldn't do to get there.

The day the letter came in the mail, offering me a full academic scholarship for the three-year undergraduate degree in English literature, I felt seven years old again, Harry Potter learning he is a wizard.

"I'll miss you," my mother said, kissing me on the forehead as I headed to my gate at the airport. I hardly looked over my shoulder. She'd be there when I got back, all that mattered was heading into the great unknown.

I had never left upstate New York. I could never have known what I did not know.

Each evening, in a dining hall of ancient stone and stained glass windows, I met people from another world. Children of Yorkshire gentry who'd been sending sons to Oxford since the time of King James. English women who could recite Hamlet's nunnery soliloquy. People from countries I didn't know existed, Namibia and Suriname. Americans, too: children of executives at the banks that went under a few years before, promised leaders with their speeches down straight, they could tell you how they were going to return to their landlocked states and make things better for the common man. First-timers from the great rural north, ready to explain how the Thatcherites robbed their coal towns blind. Even the portraits on the wall conjured other worlds: John Locke, William Penn, W. H. Auden. Every one of those men had left behind unconventional thoughts and I couldn't wait to immerse myself in their ideas.

I read every night. Thucydides, Pinter, Aeschylus, Chekhov, Sophocles, Dostoevsky, Emily Brontë—there was blood in my eyes and nothing could stop me turning the pages. Lectures at Oxford were open to every student, and there was no limit to how many I was allowed to attend. Undergraduates were expected to attend three or four a week but I went to sixteen or twenty, biking recklessly across the cobblestone streets to absorb everything I could. Lectures on Greek tragedy, Kafka, Hegel's dialectics, the revolutions of 1848. Kant and Mill dueling over whether people are moral ends or means, firing wooden muskets at one another across the barricades of a wood-paneled lecture hall. In a lecture on Kierkegaard, a professor with white hair said, "Read until you understand this: We can only become ourselves by renouncing ourselves. We can only act independently when we give ourselves to the divine."

Divinity was in the books piled on my desk. Divinity was in the conversation that flowed into common rooms, dining halls, debating societies, pubs. What is beauty? What is truth? What is the purpose of art? I knew the answers were in the night air and we could talk our way to them. Every idea was ripe with meaning. By discussing purpose we could create it.

Early one morning I lay in bed, sun shining on a willow tree in the garden beneath my dorm window. The room was on the south side of the college quad, looking onto the neatly mannered lawn. I couldn't say how long I'd slept. The novel open on my naked chest had again transported me from its dream world into my own dreams. Images moved through my mind: a child lying in bed, a mother's goodnight kiss, walks through the countryside. I tried to distinguish the images of the dream novel from my own memories. Did the novel happen to be similar to the motifs and feelings of my early life, or was I remembering my life through the style of the novel?

I needed something stable to grasp on to, a reminder of the distinction between fact and memory, literature and life. I looked around my dorm room, at the uneven stacks of books, handwritten pages on my desk, clothes strewn on the floor. Nothing felt as solid as the dream novel. The words were not black letters on white pages, but rather love and yearning and memory itself. Proust's four thousand pages, seven volumes, a million and a quarter words were as vivid as Oxford's intimately tended lawns and flower beds. The novel was itself a life. Every page radiated human touch, sight, sound, tastes. The narrator was always in all the places he had ever been. Time bent and blurred: hundreds of pages were spent on a few hours, then years were covered in several sentences. Proust's narrator was mesmerized by life as it is remembered. For it is only memory that makes each of us a self. Memory, the narrator suggests, is hidden in the stray objects of our lives, and only chance may bring us across the tree or mug or person who will return to us a lost piece of our self. We can never hope to collect all the pieces of our self, so none of us are ever more than a series of fractured recollections, incomplete, contingent, subject to infinite revision, and, to that extent, fictional. We are all fasteners of the fiction of the self, the narrator proposes, each of us an artist from an unknown country, always in search of that first land from which we set sail, which can only ever be found in memory. The dream novel moved between spacious settings: gardens, parlors, carriages, sparsely populated vacation towns, as if the narrator believed that it was only open space into which epiphany could arrive. In the vastness of the novel I could feel my own realization taking form: I needed to learn to write this way, even if it took decades to write one sentence of this beauty.

That spring I went to Paris to see a woman with dark eyes. One afternoon, as I wandered the Centre Pompidou, I caught sight of a canvas painted in earthy green and snow white. There was something in that color I had never felt before. I neared the painting. The colors cohered into a man taking flight from a wood-thatched roof. Beneath him was a remote town, a church steeple and farmhouse, smoke rising from a chimney. I could feel the warmth of the fireplace in that distant time and place. I could feel the figure's desire to fly away, carried to freedom by the fiddle on his shoulder. I stared at the canvas, shaken by the emotion it was conjuring within me. I had felt nothing like this since the dream novel. How had Chagall used physical materials, paint and canvas, to create within me such intensity of longing and desire? I opened my notebook, trying to replicate in words what I felt in light and color.

By the time I came home on break that April, I was spending most nights trying to create in my notebook the sensation I felt looking into the Chagall canvas and reading the dream novel. Between sessions with her clients, my mother came into my bedroom, sitting cross-legged on the floor, asking me what I was reading. I was surprised to find she was familiar with everything that interested me: Joyce, Kafka, Rilke. I shared my work with her, too. Vignettes, half stories, first attempts. She read carefully, asked questions, and suggested writers I could learn from: Toni Morrison, Carson McCullers, Virginia Woolf.

"Your story comes more into focus in this draft," she said one night as we ate dinner on the hill. "But it's so dark. Where's the redemption at the end? Don't you want to leave us with what's beautiful in life?"

I EXHALED, releasing tension from my chest. Wind moved over my neck. An insect crawled along my thigh. I could sense my mother beside me in her lotus pose. She had told me years ago how to resolve the struggle I was experiencing in my futile attempts to write a novel. I had not understood. Through the years I had devoted myself to writing and rewriting the novel that always seemed beyond my grasp, I had let myself be led by resentment rather than redemption. There were elements of that work I was proud of, particularly the several-hundred-page description of a six-day raft trip in Myanmar, when the allure of nature rose above all else and every ripple of sunlight on the water took on a heightened feeling, because in those days on the river I had not spoken a single word. But the remainder of the novel was blackened by disappointment in the fathers who had come through my childhood and the women with whom I'd had my own failed relationships since leaving home. In my nine hundred pages there was not the beauty of a single Chagall brushstroke. The work was unfinishable because it was unworthy. I had not sought to redeem my experiences, as my mother had said, but rather justify my bitterness. The diligence with which I had committed myself to writing the novel did not matter. I had pursued a misguided path.

"One last, slow breath," my mother said. "Feel the breath move through your body."

I inhaled as calmly as I could, feeling the swell of life in my heart. I had to learn to write toward the love my mother had tried to teach me. I was capable of that transformation. I thought of Nochum Rabinovich becoming Norman Raeben, and Moishe Segal becoming Marc Chagall, and Joseph of Canaan becoming Joseph of Egypt. My mother, too, had gone by many names. She had been June Katz, June Lore, June Klausner, June Klausner-Rivers, then again June Klausner. Maybe we were both working toward a new name. She wouldn't be the same after cancer. Nor would I. The days were changing us, I could feel that in the humid air. By the time I returned to London, I thought, I would have a different name.

"We finish by saying the prayer one more time," my mother said.

Our voices rose together as one: "May I be filled with loving-kindness. May I be well in body, mind, and spirit. May I be peaceful and at ease. May I be happy."

She opened her eyes into mine. My mother, balding, withered, and as peaceful and at ease as I had ever seen her.

"Thanks for meditating with me," she said. "I admire that you stayed with the meditation even when it brought up difficult feelings."

"Thanks for encouraging me to stay," I said.

"By the way, Dr. Chen called this morning," she said. "The tumor has shrunk by another twelve percent. We've eliminated eighty-two percent now, between the surgery and chemotherapy. We're making so much progress, honey."

Joy shone in her hazel eyes.

"I'll be ready for the chemo on Friday. I wouldn't have the strength without you, Evan."

"It's your resilience, Mom. Everything you're doing is working."

"Let's walk in the woods," she said, rising from the grass. "Oh, I feel wonderful."

"Do you feel well enough," I heard myself say, standing out of the lotus pose, "to drive to Bethel with me? He's playing there tomorrow evening."

Her smile vanished and concern shadowed her eyes.

"Evan . . ."

"Mom. He's going to be an hour from here. I want to see him. That's all I'm asking."

We held one another's eyes.

"Did you know," she said, "that women who have suffered a major life trauma are nearly twice as likely to develop cancer? You can move on from anything in life, except the past."

Eleven

We drove west on Wednesday afternoon. Wind rushed through the lowered windows. My mother inhaled the summer air. She wore green linen pants, a loose white shirt, and a pale blue beanie on her balding head. She hadn't taken any painkillers since we left home; she was having a good day. Her weight was up to one-fourteen, as of that morning. I drove at an even seventy miles an hour, tempering my instinct for speed, making sure she was comfortable in the passenger seat.

The road led at an incline into blue sky. She smiled at me, and I remembered driving the six hours together from Chincoteague to Goshen, homebound and exhausted after our yearly week at the beach. We never said much on those drives. Rather, we remained content to gaze through the windows at foliage and ocean. My visits home in the last years often felt pressured by the need to talk every moment, to make the most of our limited time together. Now I felt the pleasure of drifting into our silent intimacy. She sipped her thermos of iced clover tea.

We passed signs for Monticello and Kauneonga, Americana and Native claims coming to a head. Lush green hills rolled as far as we could see. It seemed unfathomable that Dylan was coming to this farmland.

I tried to imagine him on this road the night before, in the rear of a black car. Hiding out in a quiet lakeside hotel, thinking about what he was going to play tonight. In less than an hour I would be at the foot of his stage.

My mother looked to the distant hills, and I wanted to gaze through her eyes into the memories she had yet to share with me. To know what happened after she and Dylan said they loved one another in the last minutes of 1974. To know when she had last spoken to him.

Grain silos rose out of the landscape. We passed billboards for lumber, farm stands, diners. She must have known we had always been heading toward Bethel. That one day she would have to tell me this story.

A road sign pointed us toward our destination, and I turned off the highway. Bungalows and cottages rose on the shores of an expansive lake. Hasidic men gossiped on deli porches. A modest town, not so different from Goshen. I'd read about Bethel in the Torah my mother gave me on my thirteenth birthday. Bethel was where Abraham pitched his tent when he fled famine, traveling south to Egypt for sustenance. Where Jacob slept the night he dreamt of a ladder between heaven and earth. The word was Bet-el in biblical Hebrew, translated as the House of God. A mythic meeting place of yearning and possibility.

"Have you ever seen," I said, turning to my mother and speaking over the wind, "Chagall's painting *Jacob's Ladder*?"

"Not that I remember," she said, raising her window so we could hear one another. I raised mine in turn. She said, "Tell me about it."

"When I first saw it," I said, driving past the last storefront onto a road cut through farmland, "it seemed unusually ordinary for a Chagall painting of a Torah story. It has far less emotion than, say, Chagall's *The Sacrifice of Isaac*. Then I noticed something intriguing: Chagall chose not to include God in the painting, but the angels resemble Bella, his wife."

She nodded, thinking this over. We rounded a curve, the road leading us toward a line of cars idling in concert traffic. Ahead of us were an antique convertible, two rusted pickup trucks, and a station wagon with children pressing their faces to the rear window.

"Bella," my mother said as we sat in the traffic, "was the only person he allowed to know Moishe Segal and Marc Chagall. The boy from the shtetl and the world-renowned artist. He stopped painting after her death."

A state trooper directed us down a country lane. We passed a stone house that might have been built in colonial times. Dust rose off the gravel road.

"Did you know he lived not far from here?" my mother said.

"Chagall? When was this?"

"He fled to New York after the Nazis invaded France. He lived on 74th Street, close to my old apartment. It was the darkest time in his life. The Third Reich killed thousands of Jews in his hometown, Vitebsk; the city was burnt to the ground. Then Bella died suddenly of a virus that should have been simple to treat, if not for wartime medical shortages."

A parking attendant in a reflective vest pointed traffic into a field. Rows of parked cars gleamed beneath the evening sun. I held my phone toward him, showing the parking pass I'd purchased to reduce the distance my mother had to walk. The attendant nodded us onward.

"Bella," I said, driving up the hill. "The floating lover beside Chagall in his early works."

"Painted when he missed her most. When he was in Paris and she was in Vitebsk."

We turned into a paved lot and I parked as close to the entrance gate as possible. My mother stood easily from the car.

"It's strange to think of Chagall in New York," I said as we walked toward the venue entrance, a wooden building with two rusted turnstiles. "I imagine him in another dimension, like those floating lovers. Someone whose feet never quite touch the ground."

"He felt out of place in Manhattan," she said. "He stayed because Bella loved it. After she died he drove into the Hudson Valley and found a cabin in the woods."

We came to the turnstiles, and I showed our tickets. Ahead of us stretched a footpath lined with white tents from which vendors hawked beer and merchandise.

"Chagall alone in our woods," I said, walking the footpath. "I'd have never guessed."

"He wasn't alone," she said. "He fell in love, had a son, and began to paint again. He must have felt after Bella died that life couldn't go on. But he found a way. He found love."

My mother paused on the path, smiling warmly at me. I should have known that she was telling me a story about love rather than art.

"Maybe," she said, continuing our walk, "if things had gone differently, Chagall would have lived out his days not far from us, painting our landscape, the patron saint of the Hudson Valley. Instead, the war ended, France was freed from Nazi occupation, Chagall's American visa was denied, and he returned to the South of France."

The concert pavilion wasn't in sight. I hadn't realized how much she would have to walk. She was moving well, but the pain could come at any moment.

"Are you feeling all right, Mom?" I asked.

"Oh, yes," she said. "I'm enjoying an evening with someone I love. How about you?"

"That's interesting," I said. "I've been having the same experience."

She laughed. We were in the midst of the crowd, walking beside men with beer bellies, polo shirts, tank tops, blue jeans. Bikers, barefoot women in cowboy hats, muscled gay couples, aging hippies smoking a spliff that'd been burning since Woodstock. I couldn't remember the last time I'd seen so many different people in one place. Fathers carrying sunburnt children, Parisian types in worn berets, teenage girls in tie-dye shirts. Anticipation on every face. Dylan cut across every social difference. He was a Jew from the Midwest who understood something everyone wanted to know. These were people who had grown up on Dylan and people who had discovered Dylan three months before and people who had listened to Dylan in the most joyous and painful moments of their lives, through love, heartbreak, death, renewal.

The path opened onto a hill flooded with thousands of people laughing, drinking beer, reclining on lawn blankets. At the foot of the hill was the concert pavilion, its imposing roof jutting high over the stage. There were five thousand seats beneath that pavilion and another ten thousand people on the lawn. Looking onto the crowd, I felt myself emerging out of my own private drama into a destabilizing collective truth: it was a summer night and the audience had arrived for nothing more than music. No one else was thinking of unspoken origins and cancerous tumors.

I marked the distance we had walked from the venue gate to the pavilion as roughly three times the length of the path that looped through the woods behind our house. That was more than my mother had walked in weeks. She was managing, moving cautiously down the hill toward the pavilion. I showed our tickets to the attendant, and she gestured us toward our seats, three rows back from the stage. The shade of the pavilion was a pleasant release from the strong evening sun. We took our seats. We were at the foot of the stage and I wasn't ready for Dylan to appear. I glanced at my mother but didn't dare say anything. We were past the point of the evening when we might talk about Chagall. She sipped her thermos of iced clover tea.

The stage lights went bright. Silence descended over the crowd. My mother looked patiently to the stage.

Shouts broke out, people whistling and hollering his name and standing to get a look. Dylan was walking toward us in a black suit and white cowboy hat. His head was bent, eyes hidden. He paid no heed to the crowd. He didn't glance at his band, the two guitarists, bassist, and drummer in the shadows. He walked straight to the grand piano at center stage and began to play, raising his eyes as he murmured, "Go away from my window, leave at your own chosen speed."

His voice reverberated through the sound system, that folk-song drawl I knew so well. The crowd went silent, enraptured not by the usual joviality of a rock concert but near solemnness, as if every person here tonight was determined not to miss a single word he sang. He was frail beneath his fitted suit, and the hair that showed beneath his cowboy hat was thinning. But there was an aura around him. He leaned over the piano, eyes closed, communing with the music, nodding rhythmically as he struck the keys. The brass buttons on his suit shone beneath the stage lights. He was seventy-six and still had the magnetism of a rock star. The crowd was hushed, sensitive to every lyric he sang and each note rising off the piano. He was playing at his own uneven tempo, beyond the reach of his band, the way he'd hidden behind his canvas in Raeben's studio. He drew the microphone nearer, singing the lyrics he sang differently every night, the words so muffled you could hardly tell what he'd changed, refusing to enunciate the poetry he'd spent his life revising. He was playing three-four, he was playing four-four; he was a born-again Christian, he was an orthodox Jew. The folk ballad he recorded fifty years ago was a blues hit now. Behind the song he was playing were all the other ways he'd played it through half a century, ten thousand variations between this rendition and the recorded track. He was hunched over the keyboard, playing for himself, playing because he knew how to play, because that was what it meant for him to be alive. Nothing was fixed for him, there was no such thing as stone. Since he'd come east from Minnesota at nineteen he had never ceased transforming himself into the artist he wanted to be. Fifty-seven years later he was still becoming himself.

I looked into the ragged lines of his face. The stage lights glared on his sweating brow. This was the man I'd thought of all those nights at my bedroom window. Since I'd left home at eighteen I'd told myself that I didn't need to dwell on him. But no matter how far I fled he'd never been far behind. He had followed me through Oxford, Berlin, Jerusalem, London. All those nights at my writing desk, seven years of devotion to the novel I'd tried and failed to write, he had been the shadow in the room. In every sentence, in every word, in every futile search for truth and beauty, it was him I had in mind, even when I didn't admit it to myself. He was the person I wanted to tell me that my effort was worthwhile, my diligence would pay off, I would make something of myself. He was the writer and man who mattered most to me.

He stood with his feet wide behind the piano, playing with an emphatic determination that lived somewhere between obligation and joy. His harmonica rested in the harness around his neck. We were nearer to one another than we'd ever been. If I stood out of my seat, above the crowd, his eyes would find me. He would see my mother. He would know.

She smiled at me, her balding head moving with the music. She had chemotherapy in thirty-six hours and needed every possible hour of rest. Dylan sang a lyric that cost his aging larynx everything he had, and I looked at my mother and tried to understand what could justify her coming here tonight at my request. Dylan's voice resounded in my chest. I thought of him saying he loved her in the last minutes of 1974, and their reunion nine months before my birth, and his secret children, and our uncanny resemblance, and the day I was four years old and a man who resembled him came to the farmhouse, and I wondered if, for only the second time in my life, I was in the presence of my parents.

He was leaning over the keyboard into the rhythm of the song, murmuring another lyric, his white cowboy boots tapping the score beneath the piano. He had chosen not to know me. I felt fury at myself for insisting that we come to see him tonight. For pursuing a father who did not want me as a son. Why was I tormenting myself this way, offering myself to a man who either had no reason to know me or had chosen not to?

I needed to transport myself back to those days before I learned my mother had known him, when he was only the music coming through my headphones. To see Dylan as nothing more than an artist I admired. To enjoy the music the way my mother seemed to be in this moment, her foot tapping to the rhythm of the song, looking at me with a smile that suggested no hint of their past together. I inhaled, trying to free myself.

Dylan sang the last lines of the song and the concert lights went dark. The final piano notes rose into the night. Then the lights shone on him once more and he was a new person because he was playing a new song, his outward intensity transformed into a melancholy gaze. He was slow dancing behind the piano and his rhythm moved through me. I was fifteen years old, looking onto the black hills beyond the farmhouse with his music coming through my earmuff headphones.

BOY FROM THE NORTH COUNTRY

He was singing lyrics that spoke to Homer, Shakespeare, Whitman, Ginsberg. He could transform himself into whatever he wanted to be. He came straight out of American folk, a boy on a freight train moving through the night, a student of Guthrie, Seeger, Hank Williams. He was a Roman king descended from Ovid, Virgil, Horace. He was a Greek satyr, half man and half beast. He was the child of Robert Johnson, mystery man of the Mississippi Delta. He was brother to the Beatles. He could sing about thunder on the mountain and the changing of the guards. He knew Blind Willie McTell just as well as T. S. Eliot. He'd written tribute ballads to John Lennon and John Brown. He sang chapter and verse on the beatniks just as easily as the Bible. It was all language to him and he was alive to make more of it. There was nothing beyond his line of vision. There was nothing he couldn't become. He refused interviews, turned away from celebrity, gossip, nonsense, commentary. The art was deep inside himself and only that was worth pursuing. He'd chased it across decades and continents, and here he was telling us what he'd found, the lights dim and the silver moon glowing as his voice consumed the night.

Who else could range like this from the country to the city, Greek antiquity to modern pop, the Bible to the blues?

He hardly paused as he moved on to another song, adjusting his microphone and ignoring the applause. He was here to work, not for fanfare. He'd sung until his voice went hoarse and played guitar until his wrists went limp, the tendonitis in his forearms so severe that he'd long ago given up his guitar for the piano, which he was playing now to a new rhythm, conjuring an early folk hit, a portrait of a woman he once knew. I could see the song gathering between us like paint on canvas, a landscape in the style Raeben painted: mirages, quotidian scenes, glossed with transcendence, the beauty of ordinary life in all its rough mundanity. That's what Dylan's songs did, painted coal towns and the open road. He liked portraiture, too: false lovers, empty-handed saints, a man who danced at county fairs across the South. Everything he touched turned into song. All his life he'd been reacting in every moment for the purposes of art, like Raeben taught. Talent alone couldn't explain the constant reinvention, the way he never stopped reaching into the American songbook, Italian poetry, Roman lore, creating himself in the image of the past. Then there were the received stories he made his own, his fourteen-minute ballad about the sinking of the *Titanic*, replete with Shakespearean references and the poetry of ordinary scenes on board the death ship. Life and death coming together on the same page. He leaned over the piano, playing to a swifter tempo, singing for the woman in the portrait to come nearer to him. He looked up longingly from the piano and I could see her moving through the night toward him. He'd been singing that song for more than half a century and he was still beckoning her nearer, asking her to come with him into new music and new language, fusing folk with classical literature. Inventing folk rock, hardly waiting for the door to close behind him before he wrote himself into another genre, call it country rock. He hadn't cared when his own devotees shouted him down, calling him Judas for playing the electric guitar. He knew they were the ones bought with thirty pieces of silver, not him. They wanted to fix him on the cross of time but he was already on to the next verse.

Dylan turned abruptly from the piano at center stage, touching his lips to the harmonica in the harness around his neck. The moon vanished behind drifting clouds. The sky was dark, I'd lost track of time. Dylan was talking to his harmonica and the rest of us were eavesdropping. He'd first made his name on that instrument and he was telling us why. The long wave of each note seemed to bear all the emotion of a wounded love affair. The rhythm of the harmonica was its own story and his lyrics were only commentary. I'd rarely felt music move me this way. I glanced at my mother, and she smiled knowingly. There was no hint in her expression of the emotion she must be feeling. The vulnerability of choosing to be with me in his presence. I wondered if she could see and hear more than I could, through his musical act into the man himself. He played another anguished harmonica stanza. I thought of her staring into his notebook in her apartment, trying to understand this man who always seemed beyond reach. I knew he'd lived his life like a specter of a self, under the cover of night, rarely visible to others. He had few friends. Journalists could never find him, he'd made that mistake before. When he wasn't touring he hid out in Malibu, Minnesota, the Scottish Highlands. I'd read that a reporter once arrived at the gate of a home on a bluff over the Pacific rumored to belong to Dylan, only to be told by a man in a pinstriped suit: "This entrance belongs to you and only you, and now I close it for all time."

He strode back to the piano at center stage, and I looked into his closed eyes and wondered if I came from him. Every moment he sang was one less until he walked off the stage and out of my sight. This was his fourth song and I knew he usually played twelve or fourteen. The moment to stand was now. I hadn't come here for his music but for him.

Dylan freed his lips from the harmonica and his voice rose into the night. People were shouting and swaying and singing as he sang. He stood still a long moment, taking in the crowd, as if aware for the first time that there were other people there with him. I looked at him and felt beside me a version of myself I had never known, the son raised by my mother and Dylan. The child of the poetry and music and painting he and my mother shared in the 78th Street apartment. The child of the life he and my mother made at the farmhouse in Goshen, where, on those evenings the coyote howled and the freight train echoed through the valley and the pine trees swayed over the house, there would have been three of us in the den by the fireplace, acting out stories of adventure and imagination. This child would have been raised not only with my mother's love but also the warmth I felt in the moment he lifted me from the sofa that day I was four years old. I could see the three of us dancing through the living room to the music we loved best. My father reading to me as I fell asleep. I woke in the night and wandered through the dark house to the sound of him tapping his foot on the hardwood floor. He sat at the kitchen table trying to get the lyric right. In the morning light we drank black coffee, my day beginning and his ending, his eyes bleary with the song he had written through the night. We would have laughed at jokes neither of us needed to finish and lived within silence we did not feel compelled to break, bound together by the ordinary moments of which intimacy is made. I saw the three of us eating dinner on the hill with the view onto the mountains, talking theater and music and literature as the sun set. I would have learned so much from him. I would have become a different person, a more talented and loved version of myself. It was he to whom I would have brought my first poems. I could see him sitting beside me on the sofa near the fireplace, a hand in his mess of hair as he spoke in his rasping way about my first attempts. It would have been his eyes holding mine when a day went wrong.

I glanced at my mother, wondering if she had ever let herself think this way. I wanted to see the memories moving through her mind. She reached into her pocketbook, withdrew the marijuana tincture, and streamed the liquid onto her tongue. I imagined her joyful and in love, as she had been when I was a child and she described everything wonderful about a new man. In this variation of our lives my mother did not endure one heartbreak after another, but received the love of a man as sensitive and sophisticated as she was. Her life would not be shaped by the pursuit of love but rather love itself. This version of myself would never have had to contend with the men who came and left. I never would have woken in the night to Luke's shouts, rushing into the darkness in my boxers. If Dylan had raised me, he would have taught me how to become myself. He would have nurtured me. I would not be struggling through the disfigured book I had been writing for seven years, fleeing from city to city with no notion of how to become the artist I wanted to be. I would have made something of myself.

Dylan leaned over the piano keys and I could hardly look at him. The crowd vanished, it was only him and me. I looked into his eyes. All the world was in the taut air between us.

I said to myself, just to feel the word, *Dad*.

Tears welled in my eyes. He might never have been given a chance to be part of my life. I could change that now by standing above the seated crowd and drawing his gaze. I wouldn't have to say anything. I only had to let him see me. What I was experiencing was not intimacy but proximity, bought online with a credit card and shared with fifteen thousand strangers. If I wanted a chance for anything more than this, I had to act.

My mother smiled at me. There were three possible endings to the story she was telling me. He had decided not to be part of my life. She had decided that he shouldn't be part of my life. Or I wasn't his child. Her smile refused to acknowledge that she could end the ambiguity at any moment. She could set me free. She owed me the truth.

Dylan reached once more for his harmonica and I remembered my mother saying nobody ever spoke to him but rather to his songs, to the memory and feeling his music evoked within people he did not know, the power of his art overwhelming the man who made it, every room he stepped into a story someone else had already written about him. Dylan's harmonica rose into the night and the crowd shouted and cried out. These were fifteen thousand of the tens of millions of people who for half a century had flocked to concert halls and stadiums to hear him sing, who bought his records and lay in the dark listening to his voice, people for whom the man onstage evoked the most intimate emotion. I looked again at my mother, and for the first time understood the magnitude of what she had chosen to protect me from. Nothing could mutilate my life more than being revealed as Dylan's son. Other people would cease to see me as myself and instead be blinded by their own idea of me as his child. I would be unable to give strangers what they wanted from me. I would be burdened with expectations no person could survive. I would be condemned to be a detail of another person's life rather than achieving my own. Had my mother agreed to come tonight so that I could feel the fear she had always felt for me? So she could show me everything she was protecting me from, and I could choose as she had chosen?

I thought of the childhood days I had laid on her olive massage table, my eyes closed as I focused on the words she asked me to repeat.

I am loved. I am protected. I am free.

I closed my eyes and listened to the music and tried to carry myself back to the time before I knew my mother had known him, when he was only the music coming through my headphones. Dylan sang that you can't lose with a winning hand, and I knew that I wasn't going to stand and draw his attention. I would let my mother finish telling her story. When she had told me all she wanted to tell me, I would ask what I had every right to demand: that she tell Dylan about me. The pretenses had to end. She would ask him to meet me. The man now onstage would call me to Malibu, or come up our driveway as he had so many years ago, and we would sit and talk and know each other. We didn't have to become father and son, to talk every day, to know everything in one another's lives. But we had to end the silence.

My mother reached into her pocketbook, withdrew two oxycodone tablets, and swallowed the pills with a gulp from her thermos.

"Early one morning," Dylan rasped, "the sun was shining and he was laying in bed."

The melody came for me and I was singing with him, Dylan changing *I* into *he* and roaming from one lover to the next. He'd been seeing now for years, and here were the fruits: the melodies and turns of phrase that only he could give. He was taking me somewhere I'd hardly ever been, I felt nothing short of destiny surging through me. I'd struggled and failed, but there was a world to come and I'd do anything to get there. My mother had seen Dylan through his darkness and she'd see me through mine. I was in the 78th Street apartment with Dylan and my mother, and he was leaning back on the windowsill, singing his way to the truth. He'd finally made a painting worthy of Raeben. The levees had broken. The flood was here. He'd been blind but now could see. God had heard his pleas and set him free. He was living simultaneously in the past and present and future. Dylan stood behind the piano, playing the second chord of the stanza, the root of the first chord repeating even as the song moved forward. Night, dawn, and day all coming together. He sang about a woman who lit a burner on the stove and offered him a pipe, and my mother began to laugh, she was not a cancer patient who weighed a hundred and fourteen pounds, she was not losing her hair, bone, and muscle, she was a woman whose heart was in every breath of laughter coming from the purest place in her soul. Dylan sang that all the people he used to know were illusions to him now. He didn't know what they were doing with their lives. My mother's arm came around me and her laughter turned to tears. She was crying and I was crying with her; we were weeping and holding each other, and people were gawking at us, mother and son gone mad. Dylan sang his infamously mutating lyrics and my mother's hand pressed into mine, and I understood that in the intervening decades those words must have become about almost anything other than the young actress in the East 70s walk-up. It didn't matter if the *you* in Dylan's song had been my mother or Sara or any of the other women or a muse as elusive as Petrarch's Laura or no person at all. Dylan didn't need to know that the woman whose words once glowed like burning coal was sitting at the foot of the stage. My mother's tears were not for the young lovers in the 78th Street apartment but rather for the life she had made her own, in her house in the woods, with the son who held her as we cried together.

There was no parallel life. There was no other version of myself. There was only my mother and me holding one another as we wept beneath the stars.

We had come through so much that could have undone us, but we were together in the moment that mattered most. Everything we had experienced had bound my mother and me to one another. All she had suffered was the source of her perseverance. This was what gave her the strength to resist and survive the cancer. I would remain with her through the summer and autumn and winter, if necessary, until sunlight gathered once more in her auburn hair as we walked through the woods with Lucy. For all the years ahead, we would remember this as the time we endured her cancer together.

Dylan strode across the stage gasping that truths are lies and lies are truths.

My mother touched my arm. I could see the pain in her eyes. She didn't need to say anything.

We stood. She steadied herself on my shoulder. We moved step by step down our row, my mother apologizing to the strangers standing to let us pass. She moved slowly up the inclined aisle toward the pavilion exit, pausing every few steps to breathe deliberately. We passed two sisters dancing with their eyes closed, a bearded man singing to himself. Shouts and applause rang from the pavilion. We came into the night, the concert finally behind us, my mother taking slow steps toward the footpath. I could hear Dylan singing an early folk hit, his aging voice cradling the emotion of the song. My mother reached into her pocket for the marijuana tincture and streamed a significant dose onto her tongue. We were at least ten minutes by foot from the car. I had asked too much of her. I hated my selfish need to know the truth. The dark path was lined with pine trees. Stars shone in the night sky.

My mother gasped, "Pain came so suddenly..."

We walked slowly, her hand on my shoulder, her eyes straight ahead. We passed through the exit gate and I pressed the car key. The headlights flashed at a mercifully close distance. A moment later she opened the door and lowered herself into the passenger seat. She propped the pillow against the window and closed her eyes. I started the car and drove the gravel road, past the yellow flare of a lit window. Trees swayed in the headlights. A man pumping gas in my memory asked if anyone ever told me I looked like Bob Dylan. My mother turned to me on that dark road the evening I was fifteen. I tried to leave these memories behind, to focus on my mother and her discomfort, her eyes closed as she inhaled meditative breaths. But I couldn't wait until the end of her story.

The car swept through the night, and I heard myself ask what happened the time she saw Dylan that spring before my birth. Whether my resemblance to him was not coincidence.

She rested her head against the window. Her eyes opened but she would not look at me.

"Mom," I pleaded. "I am twenty-six. I have every right to know."

She gripped the pillow. Tears glistened on her cheeks. We drove home in silence.

Twelve

Gagging woke me that night. In her bedroom she was kneeling in the dark over a pool of yellow slime. "Mom," I whispered, reaching for the glass of water on her bedside table. She drank, handed me back the glass, and said, "Marijuana." I found the dropper bottle on her nightstand. She tilted her head back and streamed the liquid onto her tongue. Lucy's eyes glistened in the dark. My mother wobbled upright, the marijuana she must have taken through the night setting her off-kilter. Her shoulder was clammy to the touch. She eased beneath the blankets, closing her eyes. I went into the bathroom closet for paper towels and cleaner. Wiping at the putrid yellow puddle, I knew that my insistence on bringing her to the concert had led us here, my mother groaning as she lay in bed, only thirty-six hours before her next chemotherapy treatment. I had failed to observe the most rudimentary facts of her situation. I had put myself first.

"Can't sleep," she said. "Read to me?"

I sat beside her in bed and read *Harry Potter* aloud. Harry stood before the Mirror of Erised, gazing at his mother and father, whose lives had been lost when he was one year old. His parents had never appeared more real to him than in that mirror. "It shows us," Dumbledore explained to Harry, "nothing more or less than the deepest, most desperate desires of our hearts."

"Couldn't have written the story," my mother murmured, "without everything she went through. J. K. Rowling. Single mother. Abusive husband. Mother's death."

She lay with her eyes closed and seemed to speak to herself as much as to me.

The following morning she slept late. I brought her scrambled eggs, sautéed broccoli, and a whole avocado sliced in two. She shook her head.

"Can't," she said. "Not hungry."

"You can do it, Mom."

"No . . ." she said quietly, looking through the window onto the woods. Lucy kissed her face.

"Mom, remember what you said, chemo is a cycle. You're at a low moment. We'll get past this point in the cycle."

I didn't say what we both knew: she had already recovered from the lowest point in this week's cycle. The exertion of traveling to the concert had cost her nearly as much as another round of chemotherapy.

It was evening by the time she had the strength to rise from bed. She eased down the stairs with her hand on my shoulder. She lay with her eyes closed on the BEMER, her phone playing the neuro-acoustically modified music designed to counter cognitive fatigue. She sat cross-legged on the vibrating plate, murmuring a meditation to herself. She was gathering all her strength against exhaustion and pain. In the sauna she read a new medical study on the optimal hydration levels for chemotherapy patients. She stood on the Tanita scale in her office, gripping the handles designed to measure body composition. "I've lost another three pounds," she said despondently. "I'm back down to one-eleven."

"I'm sorry, Mom. Can we make any nutritional adjustments?"

"I'll increase the Huel dosage," she said, determination once again in her voice.

That evening she carried her yoga mat into the field behind the house. "I need to do something," she said, "that makes my body feel alive."

She stood on the mat with her feet set wide and arms reaching skyward. Her eyes rose to the distant mountains. She reached toward the earth, her emaciated body arching gracefully into the downward dog posture, her palms flat on the mat. Then she winced and her right hand slipped and she crumpled to the mat. I came up beside her in the grass. Sweat trickled along her sunken cheeks. We lay silently beneath the clouds, my mother inhaling pained breaths.

THAT NIGHT she told me a story.

I sat beside her bed, and she reclined on her pillow and spoke in the voice with which she had told me stories for as long as I could remember. Lucy lay beside her, resting her head on my mother's bare ankle.

"Once," she said, "a young woman unsure of her place in the world begins to wander the land. She speaks to old people and young people, rich people and poor people, happy people and unhappy people. She takes pleasure in listening to the story of each life.

"One day, this woman meets another wandering woman. The second woman says she is listening to the story of each person she meets because she is the Mashiach, the Messiah, the Holy One. The first woman walks ahead, distrustful of anyone who would think of herself in such grandiose terms. She hopes not to see the second woman again.

"That night, the two women rest at the same inn. The first woman watches the second woman speak to an elderly man. She hears the questions she asks. She sees the same smiles and laughs. She realizes the man does not know which of the women believes she is the Mashiach and which is merely a wandering woman. Both are lost. Both are trying to make sense of the world's infinite complexities. With this realization, the first woman approaches the second. They share their stories. They embrace. They journey on together."

She smiled knowingly.

"Mom?"

"Evan?"

"I don't understand the story."

"I know, honey. But you will."

ON FRIDAY MORNING we drove toward the city for her chemotherapy treatment. She rested on two pillows in the passenger seat. Loose navy sweatpants and a garnet sweatshirt hung off her gaunt body. A mile into the drive the front tire struck a pothole and my mother yelped. I stamped the brakes and she shrieked louder.

"What's happening?" I said, staring bewildered at her.

I didn't dare drive forward. Twenty feet behind us the road disappeared, placing us in the path of any car speeding around the curve. She reached into her pocketbook, rushed marijuana tincture onto her tongue, and swallowed three pills of oxycodone. Her face was pale and her rib cage visible through her loose shirt.

The grotesque fact struck me. The chemotherapy had eroded so much of her protective flesh that her joints and bones were exposed to the anguish of her every movement.

It was inconceivable that we could drive ninety minutes to the hospital in New York.

"Keep going, Evan," she said, biting her lower lip.

I'd driven these back roads since I was sixteen and knew that with the potholes and sharp turns it would be impossible to spare my mother the anguish of her bones rubbing against bones. I was sick even thinking about it.

A car sped around the bend, honking as it swerved past us. We had to get off the road.

She inhaled, her eyes resolute. She said, "Drive."

I released the brake. The car moved forward on the winding road. I breathed to the rhythm of my mother's breaths, the steering wheel tight in my grip, trying to circumnavigate every pothole and rough patch of pavement, my mother wincing each time the car struck uneven road. We drove this way along the back roads, onto the highway, never more than forty miles an hour. My mother looking calmly at me, cars speeding past us, each minute an hour, each mile we crossed one less that could cause her pain that morning and one more that would cause her pain on the drive home that evening. In the two hours and thirty minutes of that drive we did not speak. As if we were two silent monks crossing the desert. As if we were afraid of what we might say to one another.

Tears stained the loose skin beneath her eyes by the time I parked outside the hospital. She grimaced with each step on the sidewalk and through the revolving door. We crossed the lobby, and I felt conscious of strangers staring at us, mother and son limping beneath the fluorescent lights, as if we had walked across the tundra, the last survivors of an unspeakable catastrophe. We took the elevator to our sanitized room on the second floor. My mother eased into her padded chair, releasing an anguished breath. She needed to rest for as many of the hours as possible before we had to drive home. I knew it was out of the question that she would continue telling me her story. By insisting on the concert I had not only caused her unimaginable pain, but also interfered with her telling the story it had taken her years to share. She reclined in the padded medical chair, as weary as I had ever seen her. A nurse greeted us, kneeling beside my mother as he searched her arm for a vein into which he could insert the IV. We sat in silence, the chemotherapy beginning its drip into my mother's bloodstream.

"Can you bring me water, Evan?" she asked, nodding to the sleek black dispenser across the room. I filled two plastic cups.

"Would you like me to read to you?" I asked.

"Need rest," she said, raising the plastic cup to her lips.

She slept through the morning, reclining in the medical chair, her mostly bald head gracefully relaxed into her white pillow. I looked at her, thinking of Harry Potter and Dumbledore standing before the Mirror of Erised. Dumbledore had told Harry that, when he looked into the mirror, he saw only his reflection holding a pair of woolen socks. Eleven years old, in awe of Dumbledore's wisdom, Harry knows no better than to believe that his teacher is so content that these socks are his greatest desire. Only with time does he come to understand that Dumbledore's life has been shaped by suffering that he has carefully concealed from Harry. Later, we come to know that Dumbledore has looked into the mirror twice. The first time he saw his lost lover, who betrayed him in pursuit of power. The second time he saw his mother, father, brother, and sister, the family happy and unified, in the years before their relationships were decimated by a series of jarring acts of violence that left Dumbledore's sister and mother dead, his father imprisoned for a revenge killing, and his brother estranged from him. Looking at my sleeping mother, I wondered what she would see if she looked into the Mirror of Erised. Perhaps a happy marriage. Perhaps loving relationships with her parents in her younger years, untainted by her fear that they would take Herbert Zuckerman's side if she told them he had sexually abused her. Perhaps, I thought, only a pair of socks. For my mother understood what Dumbledore tells Harry the night he forbids him from looking into the mirror: it reveals neither truth nor knowledge. People have wasted away before the mirror, driven mad by taunting hopes, unsure if the dreams reflected in the mirror are real or imagined. Dumbledore tells Harry that he must not dwell on dreams but rather live his own life. That had always been my mother's way. She never expressed anger or regret at the past, preferring to reach forward to what felt meaningful in her life. That is why she had never dwelled on the story she had chosen to tell me in the last weeks.

It was early afternoon by the time she woke. She seemed less pained, her eyes and body at ease. The marijuana and oxycodone she had taken in the car were quieting her pain. Sleep, I had heard her say many times, is when the body heals.

"How did you sleep, Mom?" I asked.

"Wonderfully," she smiled. "I had such a nice dream."

She reached for her cup of water, draining the liquid with a few gulps.

"I dreamt that I was a girl, riding the horse who was my first love. We were galloping through the woods. I had no saddle or reins. We understood one another. We leapt over a fallen tree, and I realized, we are one another. I am the horse and the horse is me."

There was no trace of pain in her voice. I felt like crying at how much strength she had regained since the terror of the car ride.

"I want to tell you," she said, her voice suddenly determined, "the rest of the story. What happened with Dylan."

"Mom, you don't have to talk about that anymore."

I meant it, even if the words were difficult to say. She needed every moment of rest. I had to break my gaze from the Mirror of Erised. Staring at Dylan's reflection had led us to Bethel, causing the pain my mother had suffered the last two days. For years I had pleaded with her to speak to me about him. I had felt certain that the truth would transform me. Only now that she was carrying me deeper into the story could I understand how dependent I had become on the ambiguity. To know with certainty that I was or was not Dylan's son would make me other than I was. I wasn't sure that I wanted to be transformed.

"I want to tell you, Evan. You need to understand."

She looked into my eyes. I had to trust her. I nodded, and she began to speak, and the frail woman in the hospital chair gave way in my mind to the girl with long auburn hair and a floral dress who lived in the third-floor walk-up on 78th Street.

After the New Year, my mother said, Dylan came back to New York. He had come through his blindness with his recording of *Blood on the Tracks*. I had come into myself with that last performance as Hedda Gabler. I was looking forward to quieter time together, reading poetry aloud, his head in my lap as we talked.

One afternoon I was walking against snow and wind toward my building. I glanced up and saw Dylan on the stoop, hunched over in a winter coat, the smoke of his cigarette rising into the cold air. He saw me coming toward him and hurried up from the stoop and kissed me a long moment. In my apartment I made us tea and Dylan paced through the room, speaking in a rushed voice about how well he was writing. He said he'd crossed the Rubicon of his own making. He was working at a pace unlike anything since his earliest days in New York, before anyone knew his name. He was writing songs of love and yearning, portraits of mythic figures, landscape paintings. He wanted to play me every song. He looked frantically around the apartment, as if just realizing he hadn't brought his guitar. He seemed to be struggling more than usual to keep the thread of our conversation. He kept interrupting himself to scribble in his red notebook. His absentmindedness wasn't the same as in the spring and summer. He'd been searching then, contemplative. Now he was in the place he'd tried so hard to find, and all he could think about was putting words on the page.

"Just sit, Bob," I said. "Tell me about the songs. You can play for me another time."

"Gotta run," he said, hardly looking at me.

I didn't hear from him for a few days. That was fine, it was a demanding time for me. After the reviews of *Hedda Gabler* in the Fifth Avenue townhouse, Gordon had talked us into the Cherry Orchard Theater, one of the best off-Broadway theaters in the city. The rehearsals crowded out everything. I wasn't going to Stella's studio or Raeben's classes. I was waitressing less. I knew that if I could play Hedda as I had on New Year's Eve, a new horizon would open for me. Everything I could have dreamt of felt within reach.

I couldn't find Hedda inside of me. It was as if she left me the moment I'd fired the pistol in the townhouse bedroom.

The rehearsals were humiliating. Gordon shouted every time I lost a line. I just wasn't Hedda anymore. I had come through her and was myself again.

Each evening before rehearsal, I'd remind myself of everything Stella taught me: The character is not you. The actress must imagine the character apart from herself. No matter what I tried, I couldn't conjure Hedda. She suffers so much. Her father's death, a loveless marriage, failed love. Hedda weaponizes that grief against her lover, telling him to commit suicide. She weaponizes that grief against herself through her own suicide. Hedda helped me find the strength to confront what Herbert did to me. But she couldn't help me heal. She didn't know how.

Gordon was all highs and lows. One day, he'd howl that I was hopeless. The next, he'd say I'd played the best Hedda he had ever seen, and I'd regain my sense soon enough.

One night, as I was nearing my building after rehearsal, a man appeared out of the darkness. He flashed a knife and nodded me down the stairs into the garbage storage beside my building. It was an animalistic transaction. He took what he wanted. I stayed alive. Neither of us said anything. I remember thinking, as I limped up the stairs into the building, that I hoped nobody could see me. I ran the shower and closed my eyes. Felt the scalding water wash his sweat and smell off my skin.

I lay on the floor and tried to cry. I was too humiliated to call my mother. I thought of the evening I lay despondent in bed, waiting for Herbert to arrive at our house, my mother demanding that I dress, telling me nothing was wrong with him. My instinct was to reach for the phone and shout the truth about Herbert at my mother. But I couldn't risk that she wouldn't believe me. Herbert and Ralph Summers and the stranger who had raped me crowded into the room. I tried to think of who to call. Stella. But she was so tough. She would find a way for this to be my fault. I crawled into bed and let the world go dark.

I don't know how long I slept. If I missed rehearsal. Or if it was even the same night. At some point the phone woke me.

I said hello and Dylan began playing a harmonica ballad. He sang in a melancholic voice, wailing his wife's name and remembering their life together. It was the most wounded human voice I have ever heard. I lay in bed with the phone to my ear and wondered if he felt the irony of singing me a love song about his wife. He went on singing about his children playing on the beach and his longing for this woman who no longer loved him. His voice was a shattered emotion. The more he sang the less sense the song made. He described his wife as a sweet virgin angel and radiant jewel and glamorous nymph. He sang that she was easy to look at but hard to define. He went on singing, and it struck me that the emotional charge in his voice concealed the absence of emotion in the descriptions of his wife. Sweet virgin angel? If he was desperate to make things right with her, why wasn't he saying that to her rather than singing to me? He sang a stanza about staying up through the night writing one of his famous early ballads for her in the Chelsea Hotel, and I remembered him telling me he'd written that song in Nashville. He was gifting his wife the song he was playing for me, along with one of his treasured early pieces, while the gift she needed was not his music but rather the love he was struggling so desperately to express. Dylan sang another stanza, and I couldn't resist feeling that the song was devoted to the Sara for whom it was named and not the Sara to whom he was married, the character in his mind rather than the woman in his life. Rather than giving the song to Sara, he was giving Sara to the song.

I felt moved by his voice, against my will. He was singing to me about another woman. He was admitting he was more capable of singing about love than loving. He sang another stanza about his children, and I realized he had never mentioned them. Every moment he spent with me he had been the father of five children younger than ten. I imagined their confusion at his absence all the nights we spent together, and felt flaring anger at my own parents.

Dylan sang another line and I thought of all the times he'd said art was a way of life. He meant it. My idea of quiet time to ourselves after his triumph with *Blood on the Tracks* was a dream. He'd been on the run since he left Minnesota at nineteen. He moved from song to song and woman to woman and wasn't going to stop for me. It was unthinkable to ask him to stop singing so I could tell him I'd been raped.

When the song was over Dylan said, "What d'you think?"

I understood things were over between us. I needed love, not love songs. I needed to live my own life, not be a lyric in his.

"It's wonderful, Bob," I told him. After several more niceties I hung up.

I'm not proud that I never told Dylan we were through. He deserved to hear it from me, even if I was one of many women in his life. The buzzer would ring in the middle of the night and I wouldn't answer. I changed my phone number so he couldn't reach me, trying to make it look like I'd left town. A few times I saw him waiting on my stoop, smoking a cigarette. I'd just turn around and walk down First Avenue. He wrote me love letters, I never replied.

"But he was still trying to reach you?" I asked.

"He didn't love me, Evan," my mother said, once more the woman in a garnet sweatshirt and pale blue beanie. I stared at her, taken aback by the abrupt ending of her story.

"Mom, did he come to the house when I was four or five?"

"When you were a little boy," she said, looking at me carefully, "I saw a photograph of a woman named Ellen Bernstein, taken in 1974. I was mesmerized by our physical resemblance. The photograph showed a Jewish woman my age with curly hair and shoulders that sloped at almost the precise angle as mine. She was involved with Dylan at the same time I was. I learned later that Dylan often visited her in Berkeley, and she visited his farmhouse in Minnesota. Maybe she was there the evenings he called me. Or maybe he called the nights she left. Maybe he was with her before or after any of the nights we spent together in New York. I don't know. Looking at Ellen's photograph, it occurred to me that Dylan's occasional inability to follow the line of a conversation, the way he spoke as if he had continued our conversation in his head and expected me to know what had been said—perhaps this was not because he was having a running conversation between him and me but rather because the boundaries blurred in his mind between Ellen, Sara, myself, and the other women in his life. I don't know what that is. But it's not love."

"Mom? I have a memory of him at the house."

She looked at me, her eyes bright.

"Evan, please listen to what I'm telling you. Please."

After I was raped, my mother said, I couldn't control when I cried. I would be having what felt like a normal day, and then realize I had been lying on my bedroom floor for hours. One day I realized I was crying not only for myself. I was also crying for the man who raped me. I was crying for the idea that a person could be so bereft of love, so bare of all emotional sustenance, so detached from and indifferent to other people, that he would put a knife to a stranger's throat and force himself inside her. I needed an antidote to a world that permitted such loneliness. Stella Adler wasn't that antidote. Hedda Gabler wasn't that antidote. Norman Raeben wasn't that antidote. Bob Dylan wasn't that antidote. The only way I was going to heal what was broken inside of me was by giving the love I'd never received. Because that's the wound Herbert inflicted on me. The uncertainty that my parents would love me enough to take my side if I told them what he'd done to me.

I wasn't going to find the love I needed onstage. I didn't feel anything as Hedda any longer. A few weeks before the play opened at the Cherry Orchard Theater, I told Gordon it was best if someone else took the role. I went on acting for five or six years, mostly silent roles. Aunts and grandmothers. I still loved the theater. The moment when the audience goes silent before the curtain rises, that's always been holy to me. One night I was playing Bianca in a small production of *Othello*, and as I waited to enter the stage, I realized, *This isn't the only way for me to be in the theater. I can buy a ticket like everyone else.* From then on that's what I did.

"I'm sorry," I said.

"For what?" My mother smiled warmly.

I tried not to imagine the stranger directing my mother down the stairs with a knife, taking what he wanted from her body. I'd never believed in the death penalty but I was ready to inflict it. I wanted to find that man and crack his skull with a steel pipe. I tried to even my breathing. My anger could resolve nothing. It was love, not anger, by which my mother had chosen to live. I looked into her eyes, the woman I had always and never known, whose life had been shaped by suffering and strength I could never have appreciated. I wanted to hold her so completely that the young woman alone in the 78th Street apartment felt the love she had not received.

"Why am I sorry? Mom, that you were raped. That Ralph Summers sexually assaulted you. That your parents didn't protect you from Herbert Zuckerman. That you felt alone. That you've had to carry these experiences through your life. That all these things came between you and your dreams. You were right there, a few weeks from playing a title role at the Cherry Orchard Theater. If the world had been kinder to you, even just neutral, you would have had the life you wanted."

"That's what I'm telling you, Evan. It wasn't the life I wanted. If you feel that to have a full life you need to live as a writer, then you have to pursue that with all your heart and refuse to give up no matter what happens. And if you come to feel that's not the life you need? That's all right, too. For me, other things became more important than being an actress. I wanted to help people in a more intimate way than acting let me. I found that in holistic health. I wanted to be a mother. I was lucky to be yours."

"Mom, why didn't you ever tell me any of this? Why did we never talk about all these things that happened in your life?"

"There's a right time for everything, Evan. I'm telling you now."

I needed, my mother said, continuing her story, the realizations that acting and painting gave me. Stella, Raeben, Hedda, and Dylan helped me unearth the self-knowledge I needed to begin healing. For me, healing required more than acting. I needed to find the love my life was missing.

I met Ted Lore at a bar in the Village. He was a few years older than me, lived in Hoboken. He did sound design for bands. One of the most charming men I ever knew. He had this great verve for life, he never stopped moving: comedy clubs, concerts, he didn't love theater but he'd go with me. Ted was the first man who looked me in the eye and said he wanted to be with me as long as we lived. We were married at City Hall that winter. We'd known each other six weeks. He moved into the 78th Street apartment. Our relationship wasn't ideal, but he was willing to work through things. He started going to AA meetings.

We drove cross-country that summer for our honeymoon. Slept on the shores of Lake Michigan. Danced for an entire night in a Chicago jazz club. One night, in a motel in Iowa City, Ted choked me until I lost consciousness. I woke after he'd fallen asleep and slipped out of the motel. I can still feel myself tiptoeing to the door. Terrified that he'd wake violent. Terrified that he'd wake repentant, and I wouldn't have the strength to refuse his apology and leave. In the motel parking lot

Ted's pickup truck glared at me like it knew I'd done wrong. I couldn't have him driving through the city looking for me. I took a beer bottle from the garbage can, smashed it on the pavement, and stabbed the fractured bottle into the left rear wheel of Ted's truck. Then I ran. I was downtown before I realized I hadn't taken my wallet from the motel room. I'll never forget the bartender who gave me a quarter to call my mother. I must have been a sight. Sweat, bruises, dry blood on my face.

By the time my mother answered the phone I was crying so hard I could barely speak. My mother was silent a long time after I'd finished talking. Then she said, "You got yourself into this situation, you get yourself out."

I've never felt more alone in my life than in that phone booth. After she hung up I leaned against the glass wall and thought of walking back to the motel, lying beside Ted, letting him clean my bruises in the morning. He loved me. He would ask for my forgiveness, as he always did. I glanced at my reflection in the glass. Touched the bruises and blood on my face. I looked at myself and thought: *I am twenty-two. I am a rape survivor. I am a college dropout. I am a failed actress. I am a failed wife. I am worth something.*

It took me two days to hitchhike back to New York. Strangers gave me food and water. To survive by the kindness of strangers is a divine experience. I have never forgotten the faces of the people who drove and fed me those two days.

The first thing I did after I came back to New York was tell people what Ted Lore did to me. Women are taught to be ashamed of the things men do to them. I wasn't having that. I told Kenny. I told Denise. I told Alph. I said: "Ted Lore choked me in a motel room in Iowa City, so you won't be seeing him again." Kenny held me so tight. He came over with a Roche sisters record and we danced and cried, and he said, "This is a Ted Lore exorcism."

"I'm sorry," I said, trying to breathe away my anger. So this was the man whose name had been branded on her driver's license for forty years.

Me, too, my mother said. I hope your life is much less painful than mine. But these are the fires I came through. These are the events that made me who I am. Almost nothing in my life has gone according to plan. I didn't expect to live so much of my life on my own. I didn't expect to be alone in the woods with an infant. I didn't expect all those men to leave. No matter how difficult things have felt in my life, even in the moments I blamed myself, I have never relinquished the love I gave myself in that phone booth when I was twenty-two. I've learned what it means to take the pieces of the universe we're given, even the ones we don't want, burnish them with love, and return them in better condition than we received them. That's the reason we're here, isn't it? The best reason to be alive. The best reason to tell a story. To redeem what's broken in the world. It's what Hedda Gabler never learned.

None of this was an easy path. After I divorced Ted, I couldn't take the men's comments in the diner anymore. I found a secretarial job at a market research firm and eventually began consulting on market research itself. Worked eighty hours a week. Got promoted. Started my own firm. In five years I went from never having more than a hundred dollars in my bank account to taking cabs just for the feeling. I bought expensive clothes. I was taking vengeance on all the ways I had felt defenseless. It didn't take me long to learn that figuring out how to sell more tequila to men aged twenty-six to thirty-five wasn't helping anyone have a fuller life, let alone me. I had to struggle through my own blindness. I studied meditation and Kabbalah. Psychoanalysis, homeopathy, kinesiology. Nutrition, Reiki, essential oils. I didn't know how it would all come together. I was reaching in the darkness. Reaching for healing. Reaching for life. Reaching toward my own way of seeing.

That was when Dylan called. He was going through a difficult period, said he'd lost his sight again. Raeben was dead by then. I was in an unhappy marriage with Simon. I wanted to be borne back to that earlier time in my life. Dylan and I started seeing one another and it was like old times. It went on that way for years. It was wrong. I was married. He was married. It was a lonely period of my life. Dylan and Simon were more similar than either ever knew. Each completely devoted to their work. Being with both of them at the same time almost added up to half a man. I knew—

"Mom? It went on that way for years? You told me you saw him once. You told me—"

"Please listen to what I'm saying, Evan. Please."

She closed her eyes and inhaled a meditative breath.

"I knew," she said, "things had to change in my life. I had to move past Dylan. Past Simon, too. I had to find the love I'd always wanted. I remember thinking that this had to be the end of my first act. In the rest of my life, I told myself, I wanted three things, none of which I had at that time. A career that serves other people. A lifelong romantic partner. And to be a mother. Everything changed for me when you were born, Evan. You were the person I wanted to love. You made my life so much more joyful than I ever could have imagined."

She looked at me, and I remembered waking on childhood mornings to my mother standing in my bedroom doorway, saying, "Good morning, my sunshine boy," joyful in the life she had conjured from her suffering, at home in the refuge she had made for herself, with her son, and the animals she loved with all her heart, and the strangers who came to see her, my mother receiving their difficulties with the strength of her conviction that, as she had told me long before I could understand, we are each capable of healing, no matter what we have suffered. Her eyes held mine, and I saw as I never had before the majestic arc of her life.

"I wish I'd understood sooner. Everything you've gone through in life. I would have been so much more supportive of you."

"That wasn't your role," she smiled. "You were my child."

"I wouldn't have given all those men such a hard time if I understood everything you had gone through. How much you needed love."

"I don't regret anything in my life," she said, "so I hope you don't regret anything for me. I've had two of the three things I wanted in my life. My work and my child. That is two more deep sources of joy and meaning than many people ever get to experience. If I never find lasting romantic love, I'm at peace with that. I've tried in all the ways I know. I've had my heart broken many times. I still believe in love. I feel it in my heart. That each of us is capable of love. Maybe I just never had the right Yente, the matchmaker from *Fiddler on the Roof*—you know?"

"I'm sorry I made things harder for you," I said. "Do you remember that time I was sixteen, you were so excited about this new guy, and he came for dinner and made some dad joke, and I said, 'He's not as funny as the last one.' I was so proud that he never came back."

"If some man couldn't handle a little teenage recalcitrance," my mother laughed, "he wasn't relationship material."

"Then there was that time you introduced me to this balding guy who tried to sports-talk me. That bothered me because I'd just finished *A Tale of Love and Darkness* and wanted to be treated as an intellectual, not a basketball player. So I stared at his bald spot long enough to make him self-conscious, then said, 'Mom? I thought you said the balding guy couldn't hold a conversation?'"

"You were hurt by many men, Evan. I understood the times you felt too vulnerable to be open to a new relationship."

I thought of the trail of men who had come through our lives, the high hopes and angry departures, the trying heart of every man my mother loved, which, sooner or later, retreated into itself.

"I've always wondered," I said. "Is there a reason you were drawn to these damaged men? Roger, Luke, Ted Lore. They struggled just to have functional lives. You deserved so much better."

She inhaled, the sharp movement of her ribs visible through her sweatshirt.

"I've asked myself that for years," she said. "In the most difficult moments, I told myself love meant finding someone who needed everything I had to offer. I believed that we are all capable of transformation, and that I could help each of those men heal."

Her hazel eyes held mine and I felt a loving fury at her optimism.

"I wish I'd been more protective of us. Of myself. I'm sorry I put us through everything with Luke. I should have told him to leave the first time—"

"You're not responsible for anything Luke did."

"I know," she said. "Still, I let him into our lives knowing his history and his flaws."

We looked at one another, each acknowledging what the other had said. The IV silently dripped into her arm.

"Mom?"

"Evan?"

"The mother in your story doesn't seem at all like the grandmother I know. Bubbe was always so protective of me. I can't see her not intervening if she had even the slightest suspicion that a family friend was sexually abusing her daughter."

My mother nodded. There was hard-won understanding in her eyes.

"Nobody fails in this life by choice, Evan. My mother was sexually assaulted by a relative at the same age Herbert began assaulting me. The possibility that her daughter was abused by a man she trusted was too awful for her to consider. She saw what she could see."

She sighed, releasing memory into the room.

"That never meant she didn't love me. My mother was younger than you are now when I was born. The mistakes she made as my mother were never the totality of who she was. Later in my life, nobody was more supportive. When I was struggling on my own, she moved to Goshen to be near us. You and I both needed love, and she didn't hesitate to rearrange her life for us."

I thought of my grandmother reading *Charlie and the Chocolate Factory* to me those Friday nights in the pizzeria, grinning as she asked me why Augustus Gloop is such a schmuck. All her joy had been achieved against the violence she was subjected to as a girl.

"Repairing my relationship with my mother was one of the most healing experiences of my life," my mother said. "It was harder with my father. For years, he wouldn't talk to me about Herbert. He left the room any time I tried. The most he would ever say was, 'Herbert was a devoted friend to this family.' They remained close friends until Herbert passed, in the late eighties. My mother made sure Herbert and I never crossed paths. Why my father remained loyal to Herbert, I cannot and do not want to understand. My father came to me when he knew he didn't have much time. His apology was deeply transformative for me. For him, too. That's the Jewish theory of repentance, *teshuva*. Sincere apology can heal the person who suffered and transform the person responsible for suffering. Without my father's apology, I never would have been able to give you all he gave me. His love for theater, music, literature—there is so much of him in you, Evan."

I felt in that room with us the man I had never known. His memory was a debt and a blessing.

"I want you to understand this, Evan. Herbert Zuckerman wounded me in ways it took me years to understand. He decimated my sense of trust. He cut at my self-worth. His abuse left me with anxiety and depression. And you know what? I've taken that pain and spent decades helping other women recover from sexual violence. Listening to their stories. Making sure they know that their abusers never have the final word. That they will live full, loving lives despite what has happened to them."

I cried for all she had suffered and all she had redeemed. My mother, who had overcome so much she had never shared with me.

"I've spent my life healing," she said. "I still am. I broke certain cycles. And I worry about what I passed on to you. I know all those men who came and went bruised your faith in love. You were so young, and I let you get attached, and every time another man left I could see your heart break. I'm embarrassed that I believed in some of those men. But I want you to know that I'm not embarrassed that I believed in love."

"You don't have to apologize," I said. "I'm fine."

"I know love hasn't been easy for you," she said.

"I've had plenty of relationships with women. I guess I just don't believe in the kind of love you've always talked about. People never sound more foolish than when they think they're in love. 'Out of favor when I am in love,' that's Shakespeare."

My mother laughed tenderly.

"Evan, it's 'Out of *her* favor, *where* I am in love.' Romeo is speaking about the pain of unrequited love. It's actually quite romantic."

"So what, I misremembered the quote. It doesn't change that love is more an illusion than fact. You can read about the intellectual history of love as an idea, there was an excellent book by a Cambridge historian last year. The entire concept—"

"Evan, please . . ."

"—it's an important book, Mom. You can find ideas of romantic love in Greek philosophy, or medieval poetry, or *The Tale of Genji*. But the notion of romantic love as we know it comes from the early Renaissance. Western Europe was a highly rigid class society, and marriage was about affirming the social order. The rise of individualism as an ideology meant that people wanted emotional justification for marriage beyond what it's obviously about: procreation, continuing the social order. Love may be a story people want to believe, but it's not real in any ontological sense. If you study the history of the idea, you start to see love as—"

"Evan, you were seeing Laurene for years and I never met her. Not even a moment on the phone. We don't need a Cambridge historian to explain that."

"I wouldn't call it 'seeing.' We were both involved with other people."

"Camille, Christine, Mariam. Did I miss anyone?"

"Eight or nine others. You want their dates of birth and middle names?"

"I want to know what made you fall in love with each of them."

"I can't say I ever did."

We looked uncomfortably at one another. She wiped sweat from her forehead with a paper towel. A few strands of her hair clung to its moist surface.

"There's nothing as frightening as attachment," she nodded. "Nothing harder than loss. But nothing is holier than love."

"Mom. Can we talk honestly? I mean, where did love get you? What else could you have been in your life if you didn't spend all that time chasing love?"

"I had everything else I needed," she said. "But I understand what you're saying. I wasn't different when I was younger. I think of that line from *Pirkei Avot*, 'Ethics of the Fathers': 'You are not required to finish the work, neither are you free to desist from it.' I always wanted to model a loving relationship for you. I want you to know that just because I haven't had that in my life doesn't mean you can't find it in yours. None of us are complete until we learn to love another person with all our heart."

"I feel complete," I said. "Not perfect. But I'm comfortable enough with who I am."

"And who you are will change, Evan. That's what time does to all of us. You will face difficulty. You will need your own resilience. And you will need love. You've always been intelligent, but it's your heart that makes you special. Just don't forget that, all right? Don't turn your back on that part of who you are. Coming home when I needed you—"

"Anyone would have done that," I said.

"No," my mother smiled. "It's charming that you can't see that. Not every twenty-six-year-old would leave his own life because another person needed help. That's love, Evan. You've given it to me. One day you'll know how to give and receive love with someone else."

I imagined her alone in the house with her diagnosis as she began to lose weight and skin tone, convinced it was not time to call me. She had lived her life by self-reliance. She had made a life of her own in the city. She had made a life of her own in Goshen. She had raised me by herself. Only now could I see the courage it had taken for my mother to accept that I was willing to come home.

"Thank you," I said, "for letting me be here."

"It's always special having time with you, Evan. You might say it's my favorite thing in the world."

Her skin was gray beneath the fluorescent light. The crystal pouch of chemotherapy was nearly empty. She was exhausted and the drive home was going to be painful. We could dull her discomfort with the marijuana tincture and oxycodone. I would drive as slowly as possible. The most important fact was that the treatment was working. All her diligence—the BEMER, Huel, vibration plate, sauna, meditation, supplements, nutrition—was supporting her body through the worst of the chemotherapy. Once we returned home, she would have a week to rest before the next treatment. Our days would be different now that we were talking more honestly than ever before. There was so much more I wanted to know about the mother sitting across from me. We would sit on the hill and talk through the humid afternoons.

"Mom?"

"Evan?"

"You said leaving acting was the end of your first act. That makes raising me and building the health practice your second act. What do you want in your third act?"

"Oh, I'm done with predictions," she laughed. "Nothing in my life is how I expected it. If I've learned anything, it's to find the unexpected joy in the way things are. That's the third act."

"The unexpected," I said. "I keep thinking about that with the cancer. All those years of eating so well, exercising, striving to be as healthy as possible. And you end up with cancer anyway? It makes me feel that everything is arbitrary."

"Honey, it was the other way around. I did those things because I knew. My grandmother died of cancer. My mother had breast cancer when I was a teenager. When you were six, I tested positive for the BRCA gene. Women with that gene are fifty percent more likely to develop ovarian and breast cancer. Genes aren't destiny, but the odds were that I would go through this. My best chance at survival was always to keep myself as healthy as possible."

I remembered her sweating through her step-up workouts and jumping rope on the porch and cooking organic fish and locally grown vegetables. Tears welled behind my eyes. She had known that we would likely arrive here, in a hospital room like this, sooner or later.

"Mom, when you said women who have experienced trauma are more likely to develop cancer—is that part of how you think about this? That everything you've told me is part of why we're here?"

"There are two stories of every life," my mother smiled. "It's true that women who have suffered childhood abuse, sexual violence, and domestic violence are twice as likely to develop cancer. That's not some speculative theory. It's research from scientists at Harvard and the National Institutes of Health. I've thought about that. If those men are the reason I'm here. That's one story. But here's another story. Babies get cancer. Saints get cancer. Statistical probabilities are not destiny. All we can do is live the healthiest possible life. That's what I've tried to do. The rest is beyond my control, and perhaps my understanding."

"Why didn't you tell me this was always waiting for us?"

"Because you needed to live your life. You didn't need your choices to be shaped by something that might happen to me."

"All these years I've lived abroad, I could have been in New York."

"Resenting that the cancer I might or might not develop was preventing you from living your life? I wanted to watch you fly, Evan. I have found far more joy in seeing the life you've made for yourself than I would have in knowing you were staying close to home for my sake."

"Fly? I haven't done anything. I've spent years writing and have nothing to show for it."

"Exactly," she smiled. "You've spent years waking up every day and doing what you love most. It's all right if you haven't yet seen what you're here to see. You're still learning. You have time to become everything you will be."

"Mom, do we have to worry about how much time you have?"

"There's no way to know, honey. I don't know how much of your life I'll get to see. We live with that. We take every day we have. And we have good days ahead of us."

NIGHT

Thirteen

That night my mother was lifted by a second wind. In the garage she stood from the car by her own strength. Lucy was waiting on the dark landing, kissing my mother's hand as we came through the door. The three of us walked together into the dewy grass. Lucy squatted beneath my mother's favorite maple tree. Stars shone silver against dark sky. Trees swayed in the forest. In the morning the sun would rise over the mountains and we would walk the trails through the woods, picking ripened blackberries from their stems. We would sit on the hill and share the morning. In the last weeks, my mother had chosen to reveal more about her life before she was my mother than she ever had. Things would be different between us now. I could feel our friendship growing in the night.

"I'm so hungry," she said. "Let's eat."

"Want me to make you a burger?"

"Oh, enough of those damn things," she said. "I'm craving something sweet. Maybe an eggplant? Or a zucchini."

"Mom, have you ever had a craving for, like, apple pie?"

"Depends on where the apple is grown," she said, "and how much sugar has been added. I'm serious, Evan, don't laugh. Honestly, it's hard for me to imagine anything sweeter than a roasted eggplant. Or a cauliflower grown a few miles from here. Maybe a freshly picked strawberry?"

Lucy leapt onto the porch. We followed her through the sliding door. In the kitchen my mother withdrew one vegetable after another from the refrigerator. "Just look at these beets," she laughed, handing the beets to me over her shoulder, the roots thick with dirt. "And this cauliflower! Eggplant, cabbage, zucchini, asparagus. Let's have a feast!" She withdrew collards and kale and artichoke and squash and set the bundles on the counter. "And music, let's have music!" She wandered into the living room and looked through her records, withdrawing Patty Griffin, Ray Charles, George Gershwin, before settling on Miles Davis's *Sketches of Spain*.

She seemed more energetic than she had been in weeks. Her body was learning to withstand the chemotherapy. The cancer was receding. There were many nights like this ahead, my mother declaring her love for vegetables as Lucy scampered into the kitchen with her orange ball held proudly in her mouth. I snatched the toy from her teeth and tossed it across the living room. Lucy bounded after the ball, slipping across the wooden floorboards. "That's my toy!" I shouted, darting after her. Lucy dove for the ball, knocking it forward with her snout. It caromed off the sofa leg into my hand and she pawed it from my clutches.

My mother came into the doorway with a soaked broccoli head in hand, looked between Lucy and me, shook her head, and laughed.

We washed the vegetables in warm water. We cut cabbage and squash and beets. With stained maroon fingers we laid the thick slices in baking dishes lined with coconut oil.

"Should we spice all this? Or add soy sauce?"

She looked at me as if I had suggested roasting Lucy.

"Oh, I just want to taste each vegetable, you know? There's so much flavor in these vegetables, we don't need spices. This is going to be such a wonderful meal!"

There was joy in her voice I had not heard in weeks. She closed her eyes, inhaling the coconut oil rising through the artichoke and squash.

"Can you smell that?" she said. "Those beets? That eggplant? Ah, that's life!"

"Should we smoke?" I asked. "Seems like that kind of night."

"Not tonight," she said. "I don't want to be high. I just want to be here with you, Evan."

The coyote howled and Lucy barked and Miles Davis sketched Spain.

"Oh!" she suddenly exclaimed. "You know what we should make? Popcorn!"

"Giving up the health bit, Mom? You've kept up the act long enough."

She danced with Miles Davis to the pantry, withdrew a baggie of corn kernels, and said, "These are made from organic corn, certified non-GMO."

I handed her the stainless steel pan and she dashed in coconut oil and set the kernels on the stove.

"When you were a little boy," she smiled knowingly, "you used to stand in front of the stove and imitate the popcorn. I can still see you jumping up and down, shouting, 'I'm a popcorn, I'm a popcorn!'"

"You're making that up," I laughed.

"Careful, honey, I have a photo somewhere."

She crouched beneath the burner, until her butt nearly touched the floor, then leapt up like a jack-in-the-box, shouting, "I'm a popcorn!"

"Mom, you are crazy."

"Crazy for popcorn. Crazy for time with my son."

The kernels hissed beneath the stainless steel lid. She opened a drawer and withdrew one jar after another.

"Now, popcorn we can spice. How about cumin seed? Curry powder? And Himalayan pink salt. Let's get some healthy fats in there, too. Can you hand me the ghee? And coconut oil? Oh, that grapeseed oil has an especially nice flavor."

The eggplant lay gleaming on its browned back. Beets glowed blood red. Crisped collard and kale lay entangled in the baking tray. In the pan the bloomed popcorn was spiced and golden. We brought plates and silverware and a water jug to the den.

"All this dinner is missing," she said, "is poetry." She took an E. E. Cummings collection from the shelf and said, "Let us bless this meal."

"'O sweet spontaneous earth!'" she recited, standing as she spoke, Lucy sitting at rapt attention on her hind legs. "How often have the doting fingers of prurient philosophers pinched and poked thee! Has the naughty thumb of science prodded thy beauty! How often have religions taken thee upon their scraggy knees squeezing and buffeting thee that thou mightest conceive gods, but . . . '" my mother said with abrupt reverence, "'thou answerest them only with spring.'"

I could see in her expression the young actress on the stage of her choosing. We ate beets and broccoli and cauliflower and popcorn and every bite was divine.

"That's always been my favorite Cummings poem," she said. "I love how protective he is of nature. The way he scoffs at people who want nature to signify something more than itself. Can you think of another poem written so nearly from nature's point of view?"

"'Rains of summer join together,'" I said, "'how swift it is / my beloved river.'"

"Gosh, that's gorgeous. Bashō?"

"Mm-hmm."

"Let's hear another," she said, reaching for a handful of popcorn.

"'Winter morning / in a world of one color / the sound of wind.'"

"How beautiful," she said. "I've had those mornings in this house. Only snow and wind and silence. Standing at the window before all that wonder."

She sighed contentedly. I bit into the cauliflower, its flavor sweet on my tongue. I thought of the nights I stood at my bedroom window, wanting to be anywhere other than the farmhouse. I looked now at my mother and knew I was home. When she was healthy I would fly to London and collect my books and clothes from my flat, then return to New York and find whatever work I needed to pay rent in a dilapidated walk-up in the city, and I would write, and on Sunday mornings I could take the train to Goshen or my mother would drive into the city, and we would have brunch and walk the streets, talking about music, painting, Lucy, literature, tea. I had so much to learn from her. I had to transform myself as my mother had transformed herself. This was the end of my first act. After seven years, I was ready to leave behind the novel that I had written from resentment rather than love. It was time to begin the more difficult and worthy work of writing a book drawn from my mother's wisdom. To tell a story that burnished the broken pieces of the universe with love. That was the task that lay ahead.

My mother gathered more beet and zucchini onto her plate. It was summer, and the fireplace had been replaced by central heating, yet I could feel the magic of those flames in the hearth of my childhood. I felt wonder for all my mother had given me, the nights acting out plays of our own making. The genesis of everything I was trying to become was not my weathered Sartre paperback, or the Chagall painting in

Paris, or Marcel Proust's dreamlike prose, but rather the woman across from me, her eyes bright as she said, "Do you want more popcorn?"

I stood from the sofa, and, raising my hand to my brow to search the den for shore, I said, "Suppose I am a sailor in search of land on a clear night!"

"Suppose," my mother said, standing from the sofa as if twenty years had not passed since we had amused ourselves this way, "I am a silent tree in a white forest." She held her arms overhead and swayed like her favorite maple tree.

"Suppose I am snow falling on a winter night," I said, collapsing gracefully to the carpet.

"Suppose I am a mermaid in a vast ocean," she said, holding her breath and puffing her cheeks as she swam in butterfly strokes.

"Suppose I am a white-tailed fawn dashing through the high grass," I declared, taking a brazen leap across the den.

"Suppose," she said, "I am Hansel and Gretel leaving breadcrumbs along my path home." She tossed imaginary breadcrumbs across the carpet.

"Suppose," I replied, "I am an Arthurian knight in pursuit of love and justice and truth." I slashed the air with an imagined blade, and we went on this way, until Lucy fell asleep with her chin tucked on my mother's shins, and the coyote howled, and the freight train echoed through the valley, and the pine trees swayed over the farmhouse, and my mother's laughter quieted as she looked into my eyes and said, "I'm so proud of who you are, my sunshine boy. I love you with all my heart."

I WOKE THAT NIGHT to stars glimmering in the dark sky. Lying in bed, the room humid, my eyes traced the silhouette of mountain ridges. Another cry broke the silence. I hurried into her room. In the darkness, I could see her turning restlessly beneath the blankets, pleading incoherently, her voice fractured. The last wisps of her hair were gone. Moonlight shone on her smooth skull. She curled farther beneath the blankets, her body trembling, her eyes so rife with agony that my first thought was not of any human suffering but rather the Cruciatus Curse cast by dark wizards to torment their victims in *Harry Potter*. I reached for the bottle of marijuana tincture and the strip of oxycodone tablets on the nightstand.

"Evan," she murmured. I sat on the bed beside her and handed her the drugs. She dripped the tincture onto her tongue and swallowed the tablets. I touched her forehead and heat blazed my skin. She nodded to the bathroom and said, "Help me?" I reached my hands beneath her damp armpits. She winced as we lifted her upright and out of bed. We stood facing one another in the darkness, my hands holding either side of her rib cage and hers gripping my shoulders. Sweat seeped down her throat. She took a cautious step forward and I stepped backward. She glanced over my shoulder for anything on which we might trip. Through her damp shirt I could feel the bones of her spine left vulnerable by eroded muscle. Step by step we crossed the darkness. Her eyes in mine. Mine in hers. Our breaths calm. Her eyes trying to reason with the pain. Lucy leapt off the bed and trailed us into the bathroom, her concerned eyes on my mother.

We neared the toilet and I saw that its cover was down. Why hadn't I thought of that before I lifted her from bed? Every detail mattered. Every consideration reduced or inflamed her pain. Trying to hold her steady, I reached my foot under the toilet lid and guided it upward. The lid rose for a hopeful moment, then clattered down.

"Oh . . ." my mother moaned. She was no longer trembling. The pain seemed to be kept momentarily at bay. The marijuana and oxycodone were moving through her bloodstream, their relief imminent. I slipped my toes under the toilet lid and lifted again. We eased her onto the toilet before the lid fell. She exhaled, settling on the seat. I closed the door behind me.

In her bedroom the last strands of her auburn hair lay on the floor. I opened the closet and found the vacuum cleaner. I couldn't bear to imagine her hair vanishing into the mouth of the vacuum, lying in a garbage pail beneath banana peels, broccoli stalks, floss picks, until I carried it down the driveway, where on Thursday morning it would be collected by the disposal truck, which would bring it to a dump, where her hair would deteriorate beside old socks, candy wrappers, discarded self-help books, cardboard toilet paper rolls. How long had those strands of hair lived on her scalp? Had that hair traveled with her from Yorkville to Goshen? Through the years she studied psychoanalysis and meditation and Kabbalah, searching for her own way of seeing? That hair knew things about my mother that I never would. How could I vacuum it from the floor, as if nothing in life is holy? I returned the vacuum to the closet, reached for a broom, and swept the hair into a dustpan. I carried it downstairs into the kitchen. She called out to me. Maybe I could seal the hair in a plastic bag. In the dark kitchen I rifled through drawers for a baggie. Her voice called again. Why weren't there any zippered plastic bags? Her voice shouted louder. My mother was stranded on the toilet while I obsessed over her hair. We weren't going to reattach it to her scalp. When the chemotherapy was finished, new hair would replace what was now in the dustpan. That hair belonged with the broccoli stalks and old socks. It was honorably discharged.

She was panting on the toilet. Lucy knelt beside her.

"Can't walk back to bed," she said. "Bring pillow and blanket here?"

"I can help you to bed, Mom."

I couldn't bear the idea of her lying on the tile floor.

"Too much pain," she said. "Trust me, Evan."

I would do anything to help her avoid the excruciating pain that had left her turning beneath the covers, calling out to the night. In the closet I found pillows and blankets and made a nest on the bathroom floor. I knelt beside her, the tile cool on my skin. She leaned forward on the toilet seat, gradually setting her weight around my shoulders. I took her in my arms. It was startling how little she weighed. We turned slowly and I set her in the nest of blankets. Lucy curled beside her. I asked if there was anything I could bring her. Water, turmeric tea, a damp towel, cooked vegetables?

"No more chemo," she whispered, her eyes closed in anguish. "Nothing left to give . . ."

The words vanished into her panicked breaths. She was in too much pain to remember that just hours ago she had danced through the living room and read poetry aloud. In her mind the fact of the situation—the treatment was working—was overwhelmed by sheer discomfort. My responsibility was to help her see this.

"I know it's awful," I said. "I'm so sorry you're in this much pain. I don't know where you find the strength, Mom. But like you said, chemo is a cycle, right? Tonight we're at a low point. It always feels worst right after the treatment. Just think about how much more energy you'll have in a few days. Everything you're doing is working. The tumor is shrinking. You're almost through this."

She nodded, turning onto her side in the nest of blankets.

There was nothing more to do than comfort her as we waited for the marijuana and oxycodone to move through her bloodstream. I went into her bedroom for *Harry Potter* and read to her. In the darkness, on that bathroom floor, there was only my mother and me and Lucy. Everything of significance was on our side of the closed door.

She was able to sleep the remainder of the night in the nest of blankets without the return of the debilitating pain.

I helped her to bed at first light on Saturday morning. She asked for marijuana and dripped the tincture onto her tongue. She asked for oxycodone and swallowed two white tablets. I scrambled eggs and sautéed vegetables for breakfast. She shook her head at the plate of food. Lucy licked her face. Her skin sagged with dehydration. Beyond the window her favorite maple tree swayed in the summer sky.

"We'll walk out there soon," I said. "We'll walk the woods tomorrow."

She fell asleep as I read to her. I made her miso soup and she did not drink. I cooked her a grass-fed burger and she did not eat.

In the afternoon she asked for help to the toilet. We moved as we had the night before. Her hands on my shoulders. Mine on her sides. Her walking forward and me backward. Within a few minutes she called for me, too constipated to use the toilet and too weakened to walk back to bed. She lay in the blankets on the floor, taking pained breaths. She asked for her knitting and I brought her needles and magenta yarn.

"You," she whispered, lying on her side, propped on her elbow, looking at me, "were such a talented knitter. As a boy. You knit socks. Scarves. You never lost sight of what you were creating. I always admired that about you, Evan. You can create anything you want in life. You know that?"

She held the magenta knitting toward me. It was growing into a cap.

"Mom, you don't have to cover your head around me. I'm not afraid of my mother bald."

Her eyes were bright against ashen skin.

"Not for me," she said. "Babies need hats."

Breeze rustled against the window. Lucy nuzzled nearer to my mother in the blankets.

"Mom! Why are you talking like that? The chemotherapy is working. The tumor is almost gone."

I had to calm my voice. If my mother thought she was dying, it could only be because the pain was more extraordinary than any I could imagine. I had to remind her as gently as possible that more than eighty percent of the tumor was gone. Lucy kissed her hand. She understood that my mother needed comfort, love, affection. Lucy knew there was no purpose in seeking to convince my mother that the situation was other than how she perceived it. All that mattered was that she felt loved. She had been right about Lucy's wisdom. I had to follow her lead.

I sat beside her as she drifted in and out of sleep that evening. Plates of roasted vegetables and grass-fed burgers lay untouched on her bedside table. Dusk gathered at her window. It had been nearly a day since she had been able to eat or use the bathroom. I said, "We need to call Dr. Chen."

"Tomorrow morning," she said.

I went downstairs for her kombucha and returned to find her reading *Harry Potter*. She handed me the book, her finger holding a page toward the end, and nodded for me to read.

"'If there is one thing Lord Voldemort cannot understand,'" I read aloud, "'it is love. He didn't realize that love as powerful as your mother's love for you leaves its own mark. Not a scar, not a visible sign. But to have been loved so deeply, even though the person who loved us is gone, will protect us forever.'"

I read to her until she fell asleep.

Her cry woke me. The sky was black against the window. She was tossing beneath the blankets, her body shivering with pain. She turned in bed, suddenly aware of my presence, her eyes on mine, alarmed and outsized against her sunken cheeks. I reached for the vial of marijuana tincture on the bedside table and felt that it was nearly empty; she must have taken a week's dosage in the night. The strip of oxycodone tablets was empty on the nightstand. She looked at me with fear in her eyes I had never seen.

"The pain," she panted. "Honey, can't take . . . no more . . ."

I held her hand. Her fingers trembled in mine.

"Vermont," she rasped, "is the nearest state."

I rubbed her shoulder without any idea what she meant.

"Legal in Vermont," she whispered.

She nodded to her phone on the bedside table. Its blue light glowed in my hand. She had left open the web page of a medical clinic that explained its protocols for physician-assisted suicide. I set the phone down and sat beside her in bed and held my arms around her bony shoulders and caressed her bald head and she cried more completely than she had allowed herself in the last excruciating weeks. Her breaths were fragile and her palm warm in mine and her back curved against my chest, and I lay holding my mother, saying to her, "I wish I could take the pain away. I don't know where you find the strength, Mom. But you're not dying. The chemotherapy is working. The pain is speaking now. Chemo is a cycle. Tonight we're at the lowest point. The tumor is shrinking. You've overcome so much, Mom, and you're overcoming this. I know the pain is awful, let's sleep, all right? You'll feel better in the morning . . ."

She lay in my arms and Lucy curled beside her and the night mercifully carried the three of us to sleep.

Fourteen

Sunlight woke me. Beyond the window the sky was pale blue. The grass was growing wild, verdant green interspersed with patches of dandelion. Sparrows darted between trees abundant with foliage. Across the lawn fell the shadows of ferns and pines and maples rising skyward in the same orchestral breath. Mountain peaks folded into mountain peaks. My mother lay in my arms, facing away from me, as she had fallen asleep. Her bald head rested on my shoulder. Lucy lay beside her. On the rear of my mother's shoulder was a birthmark identical to the raspberry-colored mark on the rear of my shoulder. Within her body the immune and nervous systems weakened by chemotherapy had found needed reprieve in the night. Sleep, she had said so many times, is when the body heals. She had five nights before the next chemotherapy. She could rest and eat and regain strength. If she wasn't feeling well enough for the treatment on Friday, it could be postponed. The idea of Vermont had only been her pain speaking. I had to do everything I could, as compassionately as I could, to help her understand that. I pressed my lips to her scalp and she stirred awake.

"Good morning," she murmured, "my sunshine boy."

"How are you feeling, Mom?"

"Tincture?" she whispered.

"I'll get it now," I said. "Anything else?"

She was silent a moment.

"Evan?"

"Mom?"

"Stay with me."

We lay for a long time in that bed with her eyes closed, her head on my shoulder, our breaths interwoven.

In the kitchen I made coffee in the Moka pot. The steam rose from its silver lid, my anticipation gathering for the scalding black taste. I tilted the rich, dark liquid into a blue mug, inhaling the smell. I pocketed the marijuana tincture and walked upstairs with the coffee in one hand and a glass of cold water in the other hand. She reached out for the marijuana tincture but stared daunted at the glass of water. Her face seemed more shrunken than the night before, the dehydration further loosening the skin on her cheeks and neck.

"Can't," she said, nodding to the bathroom. So she was afraid to eat or drink because of the constipation. On her phone I typed *ovarian cancer constipation*. Lucy kissed her face.

"Mom? From what I'm reading, if you're in too much pain to eat or drink, the constipation could be serious. It's dangerous for you to risk losing weight. A hospital can give you nutrients and water through an IV while they figure out what's causing this bladder obstruction."

"Did you call the clinic?" she whispered.

"The clinic?" I had no idea what she meant.

"Vermont . . ." she said, her eyes unflinching in mine.

Nobody listed suicidal ideation as a side effect of chemotherapy, but my mother's waning desire to live was not different from the loss of her hair and muscle and skin tone. Those deprivations were temporary and so, too, was this. Under the duress of pain it was not possible for her to focus on anything else. Her body must feel as if there was no prospect of continuing to live. That was not her diagnosis. It was my obligation to remind her that the treatment was working. Not to argue. Not to yell. To remind her of this with the generous love Lucy expressed as she licked my mother's pale face.

"Mom?" I said, sitting beside her in bed. "The tumor is almost gone, right?"

"I can make it," she said, her eyes on mine, "to Vermont."

"Mom, I love you so much. I wish I could take away the pain. I know it's unbearable. But you're not dying. We need to get you medical attention for the constipation."

"Evan. Listen to me. Please. I'm asking you. Vermont . . ."

Her expression was pained and earnest. I walked into my room and called Dr. Chen. My mother would listen to her, if not to me. There was no answer. I left a voicemail asking her to call me as soon as possible. Sunlight shone on the hills beyond the window. I called the local hospital. A receptionist connected me to another receptionist. A cool female voice asked how she could be of assistance.

"If she's unable to eat or drink," the voice said, "the bladder obstruction needs attention. The last thing you want is the situation to go untreated and the pain to intensify."

"Thank you," I said. "We'll come now."

"We don't recommend driving to the facility in your personal vehicle. If you call an ambulance, the patient will have the necessary support if there is any medical emergency."

"Medical emergency?" It was a fifteen-minute drive.

"If there is any medical emergency, sir. The ambulance will also be able to take your mother directly into the emergency room and limit unnecessary movement."

I imagined my mother and me walking through the hospital parking lot as we had moved between the bathroom and bed, her hands on my shoulders, mine on her sides, her stepping forward as I stepped backward, each of us conscious of the anguish even the slightest misstep might cause her.

"Right," I said. "Who do I call for the ambulance?"

"Nine-one-one, sir."

It was like I had never lived in America. I thanked the hospital receptionist and dialed 911. A clipped male voice asked me to describe my emergency. He asked our address. He told me to remove any unnecessary furniture between the front door and the patient. Any animals should be locked in a separate room. The ambulance would arrive soon.

My mother lay in bed, looking longingly through the window at the swaying maple tree. I sat beside her in the tossed bedsheets. I told her that an ambulance was on its way. We would come home as soon as she was stabilized with water and nutrients. I would read to her as she fell asleep in her own bed tonight.

"Mom, I don't know what else to do . . ."

She looked into my eyes. She did not speak.

"I'm going to get everything ready," I said.

I packed medical marijuana, arnica, oxycodone, and *Harry Potter*. I ladled the miso soup into a thermos. I tried to focus on what else we needed. Objects were illusions. We needed patience and calm and to remain together.

In my bedroom I set out fresh food, water, and a blanket with my mother's smell. I went into her bedroom, where Lucy lay with her chin tucked over my mother's arm.

"Lucy, are you a dog?"

Lucy looked at me with concerned eyes. I reached for her and she curled nearer to my mother. I stroked Lucy's sleek fur, then slipped my arm beneath her belly and lifted her to my chest. My mother winced as she drew herself upright. She whispered for a long moment into Lucy's ear. My mother and Lucy gazed at one another, and I thought of the boy and sheep looking into each other's eyes in one of Chagall's better-known shtetl paintings, a devotional work to the bond between human and animal.

Lucy kissed my face as I carried her into my room. I set her on the blanket with my mother's smell, beside her bowls of food and water. I closed the door behind me, her eyes registering my betrayal.

The slam of a car door echoed in the driveway. I came into the humid afternoon to find two paramedics hauling a stretcher across the driveway. The paramedic nearer to me, a middle-aged woman with an athletic build and cropped hair, offered a hand and her name, Rory. She asked where the patient was. She asked if there was any unnecessary furniture or other obstacles between the front door and bedroom. She asked if all animals were locked in a separate room. She asked if the patient consented to be transferred to the hospital by ambulance.

"I'm her medical proxy," I said.

Rory nodded to the other paramedic, a man my age. I strode ahead of him, wanting to return to my mother's room before they arrived.

She lay beneath the blankets, her bald head now covered with the pale blue beanie. I sat beside her on the bed. She looked at me a long moment, then pressed her palm into the bed and grimaced herself into a sitting position. Her eyes looked clearly into mine. She said, "Evan, I don't want to go to the hospital."

"Mom, we need to get you medical—"

Eyes wild with fear, she shrieked, "I don't want to go!"

I hugged her. Her cheek warm against mine. Her arms around me.

"Mom," I whispered, "if we go to the hospital, we can reduce the pain. I don't know what else to do."

She stared desperately at me.

"Evan, I told you . . ."

I sifted through the disorienting thoughts of the morning. Had she told me an alternative? If there was any option beside the hospital I would walk downstairs and tell the paramedics we didn't need their help.

"What is it, Mom? What can we do?"

She looked at me with pleading disbelief.

"I can make it," she said, "to Vermont."

The door opened and my mother looked with quiet dread at the man carrying the stretcher. I whispered, "I'll be with you all the way."

She turned from me and stared stoically into the woods. A starling flew between pine trees. She pressed her palms into the bedsheets and with a sharp breath lifted herself to her feet. She walked slowly across the wooden floor with her own strength. She lay herself on the stretcher and closed her eyes. Rory fit a Velcro strap over her stomach. She nodded at the man my age, and they lifted the stretcher from the floor. My mother did not wince. I walked beside her as the paramedics carried the stretcher down the stairs, past the living room with its bay window looking onto the mountains, through the front doorway in which I had stood on the night I arrived home, stunned to see my mother emaciated by the illness she had concealed from me. The paramedics carried her slowly, practiced in descending stairs and pivoting around corners. The four of us came into the summer afternoon. Sunlight shone on the portion of her bald head left naked by her blue beanie. The paramedics carried her along the stone path, across the driveway to the rear door of the ambulance and lifted her inside. I climbed into the ambulance after her and knelt beside the stretcher. Sweat glistened on her sunken cheeks. Her eyes remained closed. Taking her hand, I said, "You're doing so well, Mom. We'll be at the hospital soon. We'll be home tonight."

Rory started the ambulance. She glanced over her shoulder and said to me, "We'll see you at Orange Regional."

"No, I'm coming with you."

"We can't do that, unfortunately," Rory said.

My mother's closed eyes revealed no reaction. It was as if in the moment she rose from bed she had transported herself beyond worldly events.

"This drive is going to be painful for her," I said. "Please let me stay with her."

"Not up to me," Rory said matter-of-factly.

My instinct was to ask who it was up to. But this was a matter of legal liability, a policy written at eight hundred dollars an hour, designed not to ease my mother's pain or my emotion but rather to insulate the hospital against liability. Arguing would only delay my mother's access to the nutrients, water, and medical attention she needed.

"Right," I said. "I'll follow you."

My mother's fingers tightened in mine. I kissed her forehead.

"See you so soon, Mom," I whispered to her.

She had hardly enough skin to cover her bones. It was going to be agony for her to endure the potholes and loose gravel on the back roads. Turning to Rory, I said: "When you put the hospital address into your

GPS, you're going to see two routes. At the end of our driveway, you can take a left, which will take you toward Route 17. Or you can take a right, which will take you toward Route 94. Your GPS is going to tell you to take the left because it's a few minutes faster. There's unpaved road on that route that will be extremely painful for my mother in her condition. Please take the second route. And drive slowly, please. OK?"

Moments later I was guiding my mother's Toyota Camry behind the ambulance. At the end of the gravel drive I looked over my shoulder at the farmhouse. We would be back tonight. My mother needed several hours of water and nutritional support via the IVs. She needed medicine for the constipation. I would read to her to pass the time. The ambulance tottered on the narrow road, and I tried not to imagine my mother enduring the pain of each bump and turn. We turned onto Craigville Road and I knew there was cell service. I called Linda and explained that my mother was on the way to the hospital, could she feed and walk Lucy? She said yes. The ambulance meandered past a field of hay bales. I called Dr. Chen's office and left a voicemail explaining that my mother was on her way to Orange Regional Medical Center and asking her to call as soon as possible. A Hasidic man trudged along the road, his *payos* moving with the breeze. I called Dr. Chen's cell phone and left the same message.

The hospital emerged on the hill, a gray citadel overlooking the highway. The ambulance turned into a private entrance, and a moment later I parked in the visitor lot and jogged into the emergency room. A boy clasped a bloody finger. An elderly man in overalls coughed. I gave my name to an attendant in scrubs behind the front desk. He made several calls, then gave me a room number and name tag. I jogged down unmarked hallways, past doctors in white coats, drawing nearer then farther from the number of my mother's room. A nurse with beaded hair led me up two flights of stairs and pointed to a room, then continued onward as I shouted thanks.

My mother lay on a medical bed, her eyes peacefully closed, still wearing the pale blue beanie.

"Evan," she murmured. I took her palm in mine.

"How are you feeling, Mom?"

"A little better," she said, "with marijuana tincture. Have it?"

She opened her chapped lips and I streamed the marijuana tincture onto her tongue.

"I'm going," she said, "to rest now."

"Is there anything I can bring you?"

"Just stay with me."

The door opened and a nurse entered. The slight wrinkles of her face and her silky white hair suggested she was in late middle age. In a tone intimating familiarity, she introduced herself as Cynthia and asked my mother how bad the pain was on a scale of one to ten. My mother held up seven fingers. Cynthia asked my mother where her pain was most intense, and she moved her hand over her lower abdomen.

"We need," Cynthia nodded, "a scan to see what's causing your bladder obstruction. In the meantime, we'll get you isotonic nutrition on an IV."

"Isotonic has higher sugar content," my mother said, her eyes suddenly alert. "Sugar feeds cancer cells. Hypotonic is better."

I wanted to cry and laugh and kiss her forehead. She was struggling through unfathomable pain, yet she was still herself, listening to every detail that concerned her health, insisting on the treatment she needed.

Cynthia agreed to the change. She turned to me and said, "By the way, the hospital hasn't approved medical marijuana on our facilities. You should hide that tincture from other staff."

"She's registered with New York State as a medical marijuana user," I insisted. "We bought this at a state-approved facility."

That was the way to challenge any bureaucracy, make your lies bold and certain.

"I understand," Cynthia said, "but—"

"Can we talk outside?" I said, wanting the freedom to argue as viciously as necessary outside my mother's earshot.

We walked into the hall. A man with one leg wheeled past us.

"Please," I said to Cynthia. "The tincture is the only thing that helps her pain. It's state approved."

"I understand," Cynthia nodded. "I work every day with terminal cancer patients. I know how much relief medical marijuana can give. I wish I could change the hospital rules."

Her word reverberated in the hallway, a fact from someone else's life mistakenly inserted into ours.

"She's not a terminal patient," I said.

Cynthia glanced into her manila folder. Her eyes appraised mine.

"Your mother's cancer," she said sympathetically, "is stage four. It metastasized a month ago. That's why her pain is unbearable."

"That's not right," I said. "She's not stage four. She's . . ."

I didn't know the stage of my mother's cancer. We had never discussed it.

"She's constipated," I said. "That's why she's in pain. She needs to eat, she needs—"

"That's part of it," Cynthia conceded. "But she's in this much pain because of how advanced the cancer is."

Two nurses rushed past me, and I thought of my mother gaunt and tired the day I came home, the gradual loss through the last weeks of her hair and weight, her eyes turning from mine when I asked what she wanted in the third act of her life, the nights she woke in too much pain to sleep, sweat glistening on her bald head as she pleaded with me to drive her to the euthanasia clinic in Vermont, and I understood that through every moment of physical anguish and emotional exhaustion, she had concealed from me the truth of this prolonged event, that her suffering had a destination to which I could not follow her.

She had known her diagnosis was terminal since the night she called me home. She had wanted to share with me all the time that remained to her.

"Do you need water?" Cynthia asked.

I could feel my palm pressed to the wall, holding myself upright.

"How much time," I asked, "does she have?"

"It's hard to say. Right now, the most important thing is getting her nutrition and water, and addressing her bladder obstruction. After that, you should talk to our hospice team. She might have as much as a month."

A month. Every moment now was precious. My mother was alone in her room. She hadn't wanted to come to the hospital. I needed to get her home as soon as possible. She could lie in her own bed with the view of the mountains and forest and the maple tree she loved. I would stay beside her. She would leave this world with all the love she had brought into it.

"How long," I asked, "will it take to give her the IV nutrition?"

"We can't know for certain," Cynthia said. "She'll need to stay at least the night."

"Do you have a cot for me?"

Cynthia nodded. I thanked her.

"We're going to conduct the bladder catheterization now, all right?" she said. "Dr. Kantorovich will speak with you about the results tomorrow morning. Come find me if you'd like to talk about anything."

At the hospital window I was surprised to find the sky dark. Dr. Chen had not returned my voicemails. I called Linda and explained that we had to stay the night, could she take Lucy home with her? She said yes. The fluorescent light shone against the darkness; the hall took on an otherworldly glow. Machines beeped. A hand touched my shoulder, Cynthia gesturing that I could return to my mother's room.

She was sleeping. Her bald head rested on a white pillow, her eyes closed. Two IVs were attached to her forearms. Her chest rose and fell with each breath. She had a month to live. The cancer had metastasized through her body. That was why muscle had fallen from her arms and torso and legs, leaving the bones that pressed now through the polyester sheet. She had known her diagnosis was terminal every moment of the last weeks. She had known that her life was ending in the hours she made dinner for me that first evening I returned home. She had chosen not to tell me. I tried to calm my breaths. We would talk once we were out of the hospital. She would explain why she had concealed this from me. I took her palm in mine and whispered that we were staying the night. I would sleep in her room. Linda was taking care of Lucy. Her fingers tightened in mine. I unfolded the cot and set it beside her bed. Lying in the darkness I tried to imagine the month to come. I would make her miso soup and cook her grass-fed burgers. We would smoke pot to ease her pain. We would read one another Ginsberg and Bashō and Hafez. We would laugh and cry and leave nothing unsaid. She would tell me how to survive her death. She would tell me how to take this broken piece of the universe and burnish it with love and return it in better condition than I received it. Drifting into sleep in the cot beside her, I tried to conjure my courage for the morning, when I would have to acknowledge to my mother that I knew what she had chosen not to tell me.

Fifteen

I woke on the cot beside her bed. My mother lay sleeping, her face less pale than the day before. The nutrients and water were working. The dehydration was receding. She was recovering. Chemotherapy is a cycle and we were at the lowest point. The first days after a treatment were always the worst. She struggled to eat and relied on the marijuana and oxycodone. With three or four days to recover after a treatment, she began to gain strength and stamina and feel more herself. The most important fact was that the treatment was working. We had to get her medicine for the constipation. By the end of the week she would be able to walk in the woods and practice yoga in the field.

She turned onto her side, and I remembered the singular fact that now governed our lives.

My mother had a month to live. There was no cycle. There would be no recovery.

Soon we would go home for the last time. I would cook for her. Lucy would kiss her pale face. She would tell me why she had concealed that she was dying.

I felt hunger pains. When was the last time I had eaten? My mother often described how the brain slows when underfed. Ahead were the most difficult conversations of our lives, and I hadn't eaten in nearly twenty-four hours. If I hurried I could find breakfast before she woke. I whispered that I would be right back, kissed her damp forehead, and left the room.

Wandering the hall, I tried to remember where I had passed a gift shop with snacks on my way to her room the day before. The corridors were painted a mild yellow that seemed designed to neutralize feeling. On the walls were landscape photographs of mountains, valleys, forests. There was something removed about these photographs. The images were digitally enhanced past recognition, so that the foliage and lakes did not appear as nature does in life but rather how the idea of nature appears to someone who rarely spends time within it, the way that genetically modified fruit may appear so ripened that it bears no relationship to how an apple looks on a tree or an orange grows within its grove. Staring at these photographs, nobody would know that outside the hospital were hills, gorges, lakes, and hiking trails widely considered the most magnificent for hundreds of miles, that people lived in this unknown fold of the Hudson Valley for walks beside the Wallkill River and the obsidian columns of the Black Dirt and the afternoon light over Schunemunk Mountain. The photographs had not been selected by anyone who lived here. They would have been thought up by a consulting firm tasked with making the hospital feel more cheerful. The photographer would have long ago stopped looking through the lens as an artist and begun doing so as a businessperson. The logic of the photographs, from their conception, sale, and arrangement on the walls, was not to bring out the discrete beauty of nature but instead to simulate the feeling of nature for as many people with as little effort as possible.

Everything in my mother's life had been arranged against this spirit of mass production. Her every choice marked the distinct person she was. From Bennington to Yorkville to Goshen, from theater to holistic health, the years in the woods with chickens, sheep, horse, dog, and boy, she had lived with integrity and imagination and the courage to follow her own heart far from a conventional life. She was that rarest thing, an individual. We had a month to celebrate her.

The gift store sold pocket icons and packaged candy: Jesus, Mary, Reese's, Hershey's. Snack bars in glossy wrapping read PROTEIN on the front and admitted on the back that the bar contained forty-eight grams of sugar. I imagined my mother laughing as I told her the sugar content on the bar. But the joke was on me: the bar was the closest thing the store had to food. I ate it in a few strides down the hall.

In her room she was sleeping with her lips ajar. I took her hand. When she woke I would have to acknowledge what I knew.

Mom, I want you to know that the nurse mentioned...

Mom, can we talk about something?

Mom, why the fuck didn't you tell me? How could you let me go through this without knowing what it was?

Her eyes fluttered open.

"Mom? How'd you sleep?"

"Evan," she said sleepily. "Sunshine boy..."

"Mom, can I get you anything? What do you need?"

"Just stay with me," she murmured.

We remained that way a long time, our fingers intertwined, nothing that I might bring myself to say as significant as the touch of her skin against mine.

Late that morning she pressed the help button and Cynthia came into the room. My mother gestured to the toilet. Cynthia said, "Of course, honey."

"I can help you, Mom. We've done it before, right?"

She nodded me to the door, her eyes refusing any explanation.

In the hallway I glanced through the window into our room. Cynthia gently lifted my mother upright in bed. She slid a bedpan beneath her, smiling warmly. I felt gratitude for the caring way she was tending to my mother. I turned from the window, giving my mother privacy. Sitting on the hallway floor I opened *Harry Potter*. I wanted to read every word of the seven novels and feel the loss and love and magic. A burly man in a white coat stood over me. He announced himself as Dr. Kantorovich and asked if this was June Klausner's room. I rose from the floor, trying to transform myself from a child with a book into the adult responsible for my mother. The doctor was balding, middle-aged, with a body that might once have belonged to a wrestler. His eyes searched mine as we shook hands.

"I reviewed the scans," he said in an eastern European accent, maybe Balkan. "Your mother has an acute obstructed bladder. Do you know the last time she passed stool?"

"Thirty-six hours ago," I said.

He nodded, as if this was what he expected.

"Is there medication for this?" I asked. "Or a procedure?"

Dr. Kantorovich's cedar eyes assessed me.

"In principle," he said, "we could operate. In her condition it wouldn't be advisable."

He let these words float between us, measuring their effect.

"Her bladder pain is excruciating," I said. "We need to do whatever will relieve it."

"Your mother's cancer," Dr. Kantorovich said quietly, "has metastasized through her body. That is what's causing her pain."

"So it's both," I said impatiently. "Why not operate? If it will reduce her pain."

Dr. Kantorovich's eyes moved slowly across my face. I wondered what portion of his time in America had been lived beneath the hospital's fluorescent lights.

"Please remind me your name," he asked. I told him.

"Evan, listen. Your mother weighs a hundred and five pounds. She has stage four cancer. To operate on her in this condition—it's not humane. Even if she could endure anesthesia, and surgery, the recovery period would be longer than it's reasonable to expect . . ."

Dr. Kantorovich concluded with an empathetic sigh.

"To expect what?"

"The recovery period is longer than her life expectancy," he said quietly.

"No, you have that wrong. She still has a month. Her tumor has shrunk by eighty-two percent. She's in pain because of the constipation. If you remove—"

Dr. Kantorovich's hand came to my shoulder. His eyes were bleary. I wondered how many patients he saw each day. It wasn't reasonable to expect him to remember each case. But this was no minor detail to get wrong. He couldn't make the most crucial medical decision of my mother's life with another patient's chart in mind.

"I don't know who you've spoken to," Dr. Kantorovich said. "Given the extent to which her cancer has metastasized, it's doubtful your mother will live more than a week."

Who were these spokespeople of death with their changing prophecies? We needed to resolve the bladder obstruction and get my mother home so that she could be in peace for the remaining month of her life.

"That can't be right," I said. "Her tumor has shrunk by eighty-two percent. Chemo is a cycle. We're at the worst point but . . ."

Dr. Kantorovich glanced into his manila folder.

"The tumor shrinkage is impressive," he agreed. "That's given her more time. It was extraordinarily brave of her to endure chemotherapy. She must have known it couldn't cure her. She's been past any hope of recovery for some time now. At this point, all we can do is try to manage her pain. Are you with me, Evan? Would you like a glass of water?"

Dr. Kantorovich was standing very near to me. How long had I been away from my mother? Would I hear the IV beeping if something went wrong? We still had six pages left in *Harry Potter*. And why had Dr. Chen not called back? Why had she become an oncologist if she wasn't going to pick up the phone when her patients were in need?

"—don't have to make any decisions now. I want you to consider three options. First, you can bring your mother home and arrange hospice care for her. Second, you can transfer her to a hospice facility. The nearest is the Kaplan Family Residence in Newburgh. Third, we can offer her palliative treatment here. If you take the third option, please understand that it's not a long-term approach. We would be talking about end-of-life pain mitigation strategies."

"Can you talk to me in normal fucking English?"

Dr. Kantorovich looked patiently at me.

"I appreciate this isn't easy," he said. "What I'm saying is that if your mother stays with us, a morphine drip would be key to our palliative approach. And in her condition she would only be able to withstand so much of the drug."

"You're talking about euthanasia?"

"Absolutely not," Dr. Kantorovich said sternly. "Physician-assisted suicide is illegal in New York."

"So what are we talking about?"

"You don't have to decide now," Dr. Kantorovich said. "But please consider these three options. You should know that, at some point, the hospital will want to know our plan of treatment. The unfortunate fact is that we rarely have enough beds for those who need them. Without a plan of treatment, it becomes difficult to justify keeping a patient in the hospital."

"Plan of treatment? You just said she couldn't be treated."

Dr. Kantorovich nodded as if we understood one another perfectly.

"Like I said, you don't have to decide today. I'm happy to talk more once you've had a chance to consider these options."

He clasped my shoulder and a moment later was gone. I walked down the stairs into the afternoon. A garden appeared between the hospital entrance and parking lot. I stared into a koi pond. My mother had a week to live. There would be no month of reading at her bedside. There would only be time for the last conversations. What we needed to say to one another had to happen as soon as possible. I needed to get her back to the house and find the best possible home hospice care. I wasn't going to subject her to Dr. Kantorovich's non-euthanasia. And she wasn't going to die in a hospice center with a hundred other sick and grieving people. The only choice was for her life to end in the place she had made her own.

She had known. She had asked me not to join her conversation with Dr. Chen after the surgery. She had let me believe that the shrinkage of the tumor meant the cancer was eroding when she knew it had already metastasized. She had been relieved by the reduction of the tumor not because it could save her life but rather because it prolonged the little time that remained to her. She had acted with such self-assurance, her decisions about her treatment seeming so precisely calculated and well-informed, that I had silently followed her lead. I had never asked difficult questions. That, I could now see, was what she had wanted.

In seven days she would no longer be here. I would be alone in the house.

It couldn't happen. I had no notion of how to endure this.

Staring at the ripples in the koi pond, I felt myself drawn back in memory to a summer day I was eight years old and my mother and I ran across the sand at Chincoteague, a woman with auburn hair and a child at her side. I splashed water at her and she laughed and gently splashed me in return, and we floated farther into the warm blue, her arms around me, her palm in my palm the moment before wind rippled the ocean surface and rain swept toward us and the waves were stronger than her trembling legs. She struggled against the water, back toward the safety of the shore, and sand slipped beneath us and waves towered above us, and I called helplessly for her as the storm stole me from her arms. A glimpse of hair across her face, her arms reaching blindly for me. She caught me around the belly and we were rising through the currents before another wave heaved us off-balance. Our legs collapsing as we grasped for each other. The waves drawing our bodies apart as she cried out to me over the deafening eruption of water against the shore. Bits of her body flashing like the pages of a flip-book. Her arm flailing above the water. Her eyes wild in a moment of reemergence. Her hands within reach if I could just fight through the seething water. There was a glimmer of light, then a wave that plunged me beneath all sight and sound and air.

I woke to sand and sunlight, coughing salt water, lying beside my mother. I never understood how she delivered us from that storm. It seemed an act as divine as any parting sea or burning bush. I asked her only once, that night, as she tucked me into bed.

All she said was, "I love you with all my heart, Evan."

Tension seized my chest. My mother was alive. She was not yet memory alone. How long had she been by herself in the windowless room? She didn't want to lie beneath that fluorescent light. She had said that nothing was as healing for her as nature. Every moment was one less she had to live. We had to get her to a room with a window, even if we were only in the hospital the rest of the day. I hurried through the halls, past nurses wheeling carts. At the intake desk the nurse with beaded hair, who had pointed me to my mother's room the day before, asked how she could help.

I spoke in an urgent tone.

There were rooms available, the nurse said. She couldn't guarantee it was covered by insurance. I thanked her and asked when we could move.

"I can't say when someone will be available for that," she said.

"Is the room open now?"

She looked gently at me. I was young, and alone, and could sense her measuring the practical extent of her sympathy. She reached for the phone, made a brief call, and wrote the room number on a note of paper that she tore from its pad.

My mother was asleep in the windowless room. She was struggling for the strength to speak. But she had formulated plans of her own and understood I had chosen not to follow her direction. Her silence since she had lifted herself out of bed and onto the stretcher was not lifelessness, but rather the stoicism required to endure excruciating pain.

Her fingers tightened in mine. I told her we were moving to a room with a view of the sky. She nodded. I wheeled her medical bed down the corridor, machines beeping behind closed doors. From behind the bed I could see sweat gathering in the wrinkles of her bald head left exposed by her beanie. There was barely enough room for the medical bed in the elevator. I squeezed against the wall and looked onto my mother's closed eyes. She was expressing no pain. She had retreated again into the stoic realm in which she had endured the ambulance ride. The elevator rose silently. It was impossible that my mother felt no pain but also implausible that she was sleeping through the agonizing movement. The only remaining possibility was that she was no longer breathing. I was not wheeling my mother toward the sunlight but rather her corpse.

I called to her. She did not respond. I listened for her breathing. I heard nothing.

There was no space in the elevator to navigate around the bed and come near enough to listen for her heartbeat. When was the last time my mother showed any sign of life? I hadn't checked her IVs before wheeling her out of the windowless room. What if they had stopped working while I was speaking with Dr. Kantorovich? The elevator continued its rise, indifferent to whether it carried one life or two. The doors opened and I rushed the medical bed into the hall and reached toward my mother. She exhaled sharply.

I kissed her bald head. There were two of us.

Our room was spacious, warm rays of sunlight glowing on the tile floor. Glass windows looked onto light blue sky. There was an en suite bathroom and plenty of room for my cot. Here was everything we needed for however many hours we remained in the hospital. I set my mother's medical bed in the sunlight at the center of the room. She murmured my name. I asked if she wanted the miso soup and she nodded. The IV nutrients and liquid were working. She was regaining her strength. Soon we would go home and she would lie in bed with her view of the forest, and we would leave nothing unsaid in the last days of her life. I offered her the soup, and she inhaled its smell, her lips closed. I tried to reconcile the pleasure she was taking from the smell of the soup with Dr. Kantorovich's prognosis. It seemed unfathomable that she had only days remaining to smell and see and touch. We had to acknowledge what we could no longer avoid.

There was nothing practical to discuss. If she had a week to live it should be in the comfort of our home rather than the sanitized anonymity of the hospital. Once she had absorbed enough nutrients and water through the IV we would call an ambulance.

I whispered, "We're going home, Mom. As soon as we can."

"Can't . . ." she rasped. "Stay here with me . . ."

Sunlight moved across her closed eyes, and I understood there would be no final drive home. The pain was too enormous for her to speak freely, let alone for her to be carried onto a stretcher, lifted into an ambulance, driven ten miles to the house, and carried to the final resting place I imagined, her bed with its view of her favorite maple tree. We had already taken her last voyage, from the windowless room to the sunlight in which she now lay. We would be here together, beneath this sky, until we no longer were.

Sixteen

On the third day I woke in the cot beside my mother's bed. She was asleep, her expression peaceful. Lying in the sparse sheet, I was reminded of the mornings of my childhood when my first conscious impression was of her smile. Sweat trickled now along her sunken cheeks. Her skin was sallow, its color reminding me of the drab gray used by Matisse to emphasize the listlessness of a slouching woman in one of his mid-career masterpieces. In the night her pale blue beanie had slipped from her head to her shoulder, where it lay confused, as if unsure what to conceal. I took the beanie and held my hand to her clammy forehead and felt a strange depth of gratitude for this moist touch, the stench of her sweat and beads of perspiration on her forehead. I dripped the marijuana tincture onto her tongue. She whispered, "Slept here? I did the same when you were in the hospital."

At her words I was in the hospital bed after my emergency appendicitis, six years old, my mother tracing the newly stapled scar ribboning my stomach. She had said that it would always be part of me.

She had always referred to the incident as the time my appendix was removed. I did not understand how evasive a description this was until I was changing one evening in the locker room at Oxford after a narrow loss in the intercollegiate basketball tournament, and the point guard on the opposing team, a medical student, asked about the scar that runs from my belly button across the right side of my abdomen to just above my hip. When I told him it was the remnant of appendicitis, he replied that a typical appendicitis scar is no more than an inch wide. A scar of this length, he said, coming closer to me, would only have been cut if the appendix had burst within me, causing internal blood loss so rapid that I would have died within an hour if not for immediate surgery. As I lay naked and sedated on the operating table, my bodily functions most likely had already begun to fail, my skin turning pale, even my blue eyes losing the pinkish hue of the conjunctivae, my pulse barely palpable.

My mother never told me how near I was to death. Only now, lying in the cot beside her medical bed, could I begin to understand the strength she had needed in those weeks. For not only did the appendicitis nearly end my life; it had also ended her engagement to Roger. From my hospital bed I had heard shouts in the night. Roger drunkenly berating my mother, blaming her for my near death, furiously insisting that her faith in holistic health was the reason the appendix went undiagnosed. The health professionals my mother had taken me to, whether holistic or conventional, all had the same diagnosis: it's a stomachache, nothing unusual for a healthy child, he's being dramatic but will feel fine if he simply rests. Hadn't Roger known how common misdiagnosis is for a ruptured appendix? He had no children of his own. He had never been responsible for another life. He had never felt the torment of medical decisions made in the dusk of partial information, as my mother had the nights she brought me to doctors, insisting I was in too much pain to only have a stomachache. Roger had broken his engagement to my mother because my near death was his first taste of the responsibilities of parenthood, and it was greater than he could bear. It was easier to blame the illness on my mother than to face the mortifying truth that all human bonds, all of life, is subject to the unpredictable instincts of illness and death, that a boy who one day runs through the woods, lost in his imagined stories, might the next day lie unconscious on a surgical table, enduring an operation that, if not performed immediately, will subtract him forever from the earth. I could still remember the last time I saw Roger, the night he came to the farmhouse to retrieve his last possessions, and as the door closed behind him, my mother knelt to my height and held me to her and said, as calmly as a human voice can speak, "Nothing is holier than love."

My fingers traced the scar that runs from my belly button to just above my right hip, the staple-like marking unaffected by all the years since the operation saved my life.

Sunlight shone through the glass window. I leaned nearer to my mother, so that even if she was too exhausted to open her eyes she could smell my presence, as she had inhaled the miso soup the night before.

"Good morning, Mom," I said.

Her fingers tensed in mine. I felt the miracle of this simplest fact: she could hear me. Language, that most transformative gift, was still ours to share. She had given me the words of books and plays and stories, and now I would return this language to her, not as stories from distant lands but rather of our own lives, the memories that were ours to share in these last days. Even if she could not speak we could live within words.

She opened her groggy eyes and glanced to the bathroom. She pressed the help button.

"Can I help you, Mom? We've done it before, right?"

She shook her head. A nurse came through the door, her gait and gaze exhausted.

"What do you need?" she asked.

"A bedpan," I said.

She returned with a metallic pan.

"Up you go," said the nurse, whose name tag read Barbara. She lifted my mother roughly and slid the bedpan beneath her. My mother winced, her eyes alarmed.

"Please!" I begged. "Slowly. Please."

"Sorry," Barbara said matter-of-factly.

My mother panted, propped on her side by a withered forearm. This nurse had acted as carelessly with her body as Cynthia had been tender. I was too stunned by her indifference to say anything meaningful. My mother shook her head, indicating that she couldn't use the bedpan.

"All right, then," Barbara said, lowering her into the bed. My mother looked as if she was holding back tears.

Barbara set the bedpan on the chair and left without looking at either of us. My mother took pained breaths. I brought the bedpan to her. Carefully she arched her back. The trickle of urine echoed slowly at first, then came as a pulsing stream. She winced, and the stream ceased, and I withdrew the bedpan from beneath her and walked to the toilet. I poured the urine into the toilet bowl, the fluid intermingling with the deodorized teal water on its way down the drain, and I remembered that I had not told my mother the implication of our decision to stay in the hospital. She did not know that if we stayed in this room the hospital staff would eventually insist on the morphine drip that would end her life. She had told me she did not have the strength for an ambulance. She didn't yet know the fate to which we were consigning her by remaining in the hospital. It was my responsibility to tell her. There was time to say everything we needed to one another. I had to understand why she had concealed the diagnosis from me. I was wounded. I would forgive her. We would leave nothing unsaid. Now was the moment. Freshly deodorized water surfaced in the toilet bowl, the putrid smell lingering in the room.

My mother lay with her eyes closed, inhaling short breaths. I came beside her and took her hand.

"Are you OK?" I said.

She nodded and squeezed my hand. I would have to ensure Barbara didn't return. Every moment of pain stole from my mother words she might speak or hear. We needed to speak. She needed all her strength for the conversation that lay ahead.

Mom, can we talk for a minute?

Mom, the doctor is saying . . .

Mom? I'll be with you every moment. I'll be here until the end.

I felt awful hunger. Besides the protein bar, I had eaten nothing since arriving to the hospital. I whispered that I would be back in a few minutes, and she squeezed my hand.

In the hall, figures in scrubs pushed medical carts. A nurse my age stood in the elevator. Her brown hair was drawn into an elegant bun and her dark eyes defied the despair of the hospital. I wanted to turn to her and say, "I am twenty-six, my mother is dying, I have never felt so helpless or alone." I needed the wisdom of this nurse. We could find a sofa in one of the lounges, and she would listen to me, and put her hand on my shoulder as I asked, "How do you endure this? How do you wake each morning and walk these halls of death and still smile as you are in this moment?" Tears welled in my eyes, and her arms came closer around me on the sofa in my mind. She glanced at me, not the nurse on the imagined sofa but the nurse in the elevator, and I was abruptly aware that I was dressed in the same sweatshirt and jeans I had worn through two nights on the cot and two days in which I had not so much as washed my face. I could feel oily accumulation on my skin, irritation beginning to show through my scraggly facial hair. The elevator opened and the nurse strode out. In the privacy of the elevator I could smell my sour odor.

The cafeteria offered stainless steel trays with artificial eggs and sausages. The refrigerator was lined with Diet Coke and ginger ale, rows of pure poison arranged by color scheme. There was no sign of embarrassment that the foods sold by the hospital were the sort that delivered artery-clogged, obese, heart-paused patients into its clutches. I wanted my mother's vegetables. I wanted to laugh with her as we cooked dinner one more night.

I piled my plate high with the artificial eggs, swiped my credit card, and wandered into the hall. I needed to call my grandmother. In her mind my mother and I were still at the house, enjoying summer days, her treatment progressing well. A fern rose from a clay pot on the hallway floor, presumably meant to brighten the dark meeting point of the corridors. The green leaves stretched toward the sky, and I felt the majestic swell of nature, the divine individualism of any living specimen that makes it different from all other living things. No matter how a plant, tree, person, or animal is curated, cut, or molded, it remains always its own organism, subject to the desires that mark it as different from all others that have ever lived and died. I glanced down the hall, saw nobody looking, and picked up the fern. There was no reason my mother had to have inhaled her last breath of nature.

She lay beneath her white sheets, eyes closed, exhaling a measured breath. Her hands were at her sides and her palms open to the sky. You can meditate, she had told me, from anywhere.

When she had completed her breathing exercise, I brought the fern beside her.

"Mom? Can you smell that?"

She breathed the fern's scent. Her palm was in mine. She could still smell and touch and hear.

In the afternoon there was a knock on the door. A woman with cropped blonde hair and a white blazer glanced at her clipboard. "Are you June Klausner?" she asked me.

I gestured to my mother.

"Right," said the woman. She seemed unperturbed that she had mistaken me for my mother. "I have a few questions for June Klausner."

My instinct was to protect my mother from whatever news this woman had come to deliver. I nodded for the woman to follow me through the door, and whispered to my mother that I would be back in a moment.

Nurses hustled down the hall. I turned to face the woman, whose name tag read Judy. She was middle-aged, with white skin drawn tight over narrow facial features and alert eyes that seemed used to managing checklists and subordinates. She said, "How are you?"

I missed England. Nobody there would ever ask that question to a person in my situation. I told Judy I was well.

"Have you had a chance to consider," she asked, "the options Dr. Kantorovich suggested?"

"We're staying in that room for now," I said. This was the only strategy, to play for time until my mother and I could discuss our options.

"Of course," Judy nodded. "In that case, we should discuss your mother's plan of treatment. Dr. Kantorovich's assessment is that there isn't anything that can be done for her medically, so—"

"She's still speaking," I said.

Judy nodded, pausing for just the right amount of time to indicate she was not dismissing my concerns.

"I understand," she said. "But Dr. Kantorovich estimates your mother would have to gain fifteen pounds to withstand the bladder operation.

With the cancer at her stage, that's not possible. The longer we delay a pain mitigation approach, the more your mother will suffer."

She had chosen her words carefully. *Delay, suffer, mother. Pain mitigation.* This was her job: to guide reluctant family members toward the most bewildering choice, to willfully end a life. Judy's jaw was rigid and her lips a thin line. She must have seen too many people die, witnessed too much grief and suffering, to feel the tragedy of each new death. It was no longer bearable to see the distinct person within each body. This was the reason the nurse named Barbara moved my mother so roughly as she maneuvered the bedpan beneath her. My mother's body was one among many that had to be adjusted to urinate. Every patient felt pain. Her discomfort was unbearable only to me, her death implausible only to me, for she was my mother. The experience I could already feel transforming me was to Judy an ordinary professional matter. Cynthia could still see the person within each body. Rather than harden her, witnessing suffering had made Cynthia sensitive to every human detail in the descent into death. The gentle way that Cynthia had held my mother as she peed into the bedpan was all I needed to know that Cynthia understood my mother's destination and wanted to make the journey more humane.

"As I said," I told Judy, "I won't let anything be rushed. Is that understood?"

My words hung naked between us. She was practiced in managing loved ones, knew how to apply empathy here and pressure there. But I was young, and alone, and she was concerned that I was not emotionally composed.

"Have you spoken," she said, "to your mother about end-of-life decisions? Do you know if she has any written instructions?"

We had never discussed the matter. How could we now? My mother had uttered only a few sentences since leaving the house. How could I decide on so final a solution without knowing definitively what my mother wanted?

"Evan? Did you hear what I said?"

"She stays alive no matter what," I said. "Understood?"

Judy's lips tightened.

"I want you to understand," she said, "what that means. Because if you like, I'll put that instruction on her chart. In that case, if your mother stops breathing, or her heart pauses, our staff will be legally bound to do everything possible to keep her alive. If they need to break her rib cage to insert a breathing device, they'll break her rib cage."

Judy paused, letting this image settle between us. She had given this speech before.

"The alternative," she went on, "would be for you to sign a do-not-resuscitate order. That doesn't permit us to take any steps to end your mother's life. But if her breathing or heartbeat stops, we won't revive her."

It was startling to me that the end of all consciousness, with its vastness, complexity, nuances, and unpredictability, could be described in such clinical terms.

We won't revive her.

There was no choice. I could stay by her bed as much as possible. Still, I needed to go to the cafeteria at least once a day, and there could be no certainty that in my absence her lungs would not pause, and the medical staff would not take measures with her body that my mother would neither want nor be able to prevent. I couldn't let her suffer such needless pain.

"I'll sign the DNR," I said. "But I don't want to hear anything more about morphine. Understood?"

Judy's alert eyes held mine, confirming our compromise. A moment later she returned with a clipboard and branded hospital pen. I took the pen in hand, and as my signature appeared on the page I was struck by how similar my handwriting was to my mother's. I thought of all the years of her handwritten notes, birthday cards on winter mornings, my name scrawled across a card propped on the bathroom sink, or atop a gift beside the Hanukkah candles, or a sentence on folded white paper telling me she was taking longer with a patient and would see me at dinnertime—*love, Mom*. How could I ever know she wanted the morphine? I couldn't decide alone. We would stay in the room as long as possible. With enough nutrients and water through the IV she would regain the strength to tell me what she wanted.

I handed the clipboard back to Judy and walked down the hall. My mother's phone buzzed in my jeans pocket.

"Dr. Chen," I said in a rushed voice. "I've been trying to reach you."

"You should have tried my office," she said.

There was no point telling her I had. All that mattered was whether she could prolong my mother's life. I explained the situation.

"It's all been so sudden," I concluded. "I thought your treatment eliminated eighty-two percent of the tumor?"

"It has," Dr. Chen agreed. "The cancer metastasized some time ago. Your mother knows there's only so much time the chemotherapy can give her. But with the way her treatment is progressing she should have more time."

The awful assumptions of the last days fell away. Dr. Kantorovich hadn't looked closely at her medical charts. Why had I trusted him? Why hadn't I been more persistent in finding Dr. Chen? I had stood by and done nothing as the hospital staff sought to end my mother's life.

"The doctors here want to put her on a morphine drip. How can I transfer her to you?"

"She's at the hospital?" Dr. Chen asked. "I'm just arriving."

"No, we're upstate. Orange Regional."

"She needs to get an ambulance here," she said. "I'll look at her right away."

"Thank you so much," I said. "Listen, she's in enormous pain. The drive here was excruciating. I don't think she can make it to the city. Can you come here?"

"I can't do that," Dr. Chen said.

"She can't physically make the journey. She's not going to live if she stays here."

"If she's here, I can help. I can't come to another facility and overrule their decisions. If you decide to come into the city, call me."

The line went dead. There was no way around it. My mother would have to find the strength for the ambulance journey to New York. It was her only chance at life. I hurried toward her room. She lay sleeping, her knee pressed at an angle through the polyester sheet. I slipped my palm into hers.

"Mom," I said. "I have good news."

Her fingers tightened in mine.

"Dr. Chen called us back. She says the chemo is working. It's a cycle, we're at the lowest point, but the treatment is working. We need to go see her now."

My mother's eyes remained closed. Tears ran along my face. I had been so close to letting her go. How would I ever have forgiven myself if I had let the medical staff end her life when she could still clench my fingers, feel my lips on her cheek, smell the fern? How had my thinking become so anxious and deformed that I had even considered ending her life? How could I have ever lived with myself if Dr. Chen had called after I started the morphine drip?

"I'm calling an ambulance," I told her. "We'll be with Dr. Chen in ninety minutes."

My mother's bloodshot eyes opened into mine. She looked as if she wanted to speak. She said nothing.

"Mom, we have to try. I know it's painful. I'll be with you."

Sweat dripped along her absinthe cheeks. She was going to die if I didn't call the ambulance. She murmured indistinctly.

"Mom, please. You can find the strength. I'll be with you in the ambulance this time. Dr. Chen can help. She can . . ."

With the slightest motion my mother shook her bald head.

"Mom, you don't understand. I didn't know how to tell you. If we stay here they're going to put you on a morphine drip. They're going to kill you. If you can get through the pain, if we can get you to Dr. Chen . . ."

She inhaled, gathering her strength. She gazed into my eyes. No words came. I took her phone into the hallway and dialed 911. Nurses hurried past me. A practiced male voice asked the nature of my emergency. I told him we needed an ambulance from Orange Regional to the city hospital. Was it possible to have extra cushions for a terminally ill cancer patient? And it was absolutely necessary that a medical proxy be permitted to stay with the patient in the ambulance. The dispatcher asked for my name and number, and Judy passed me in the hall, and I felt visceral hatred for this woman who had nearly taken my mother's life. I tried to breathe, to defuse the anger coursing through me. Judy vanished around the corner and I understood that my anger was not for her but rather myself. My resistance to the morphine drip was not that it would end my mother's life, but that it would make definitive what my choices had already left inevitable, that her life would not end on her terms. I had failed to listen to what she had asked of me. She had wanted to die in Vermont, where it would be immediate and painless. She had told me she was ready. She had not wanted to come to the hospital. She did not want to be transferred seventy-five miles to the city hospital. She wasn't moved by the promise that Dr. Chen could keep her alive because she no longer wanted to be alive.

How had I been so blind to her desires? She had used her last strength to plead with me to drive her to Vermont. She had not wanted to suffer her remaining days attached to beeping machines in the hospital. I had never considered her request to drive to Vermont. It was only her pain speaking, I had told myself. She didn't know what was best for her. I had become, without realizing it, one of the people who stood on the periphery of her life and insisted her ideas were unreasonable. I had valorized her individualism and been deaf to its expression.

I had convinced myself it was my obligation to encourage her through chemotherapy, to lift her spirits when they weakened, to remind her the treatment was working. The tumor was shrinking. She was surviving. There was life after the chemotherapy, no matter how painful the treatment was to endure. How many times had I repeated these words? Like all slogans, they concealed more than they revealed. The cancer had metastasized. She had known her diagnosis was terminal since she had called me home. Even if the tumor had shrunk by eighty-two percent, it was too late. She had endured the chemotherapy not because it could save her life but rather because it might give her more time with me. She hadn't told me. Perhaps she had believed there was something else to be done, that the BEMER, Huel, vibration plate, and infrared sauna might allow her to keep living despite the diagnosis. She must have gone on believing this until the chemotherapy overwhelmed her and she was left without the strength to announce, perhaps even to realize, that her struggle was over. By the time her optimism perished, mine was in full form. I had repeated the half-truths back to her. We had marched toward death, two people whose love for one another left us unable to confront the truth.

I stood in the doorway observing her labored breaths. There could be no more deception. Nearing her bedside, I rested my hand on her damp forehead. Her eyes were closed. I dripped the marijuana tincture toward her tongue, and my hand shook and the liquid ran along her chin. I wiped the tincture from her skin and felt myself nearing the precipice that would from now on shape my life. From the moment I left the hospital my life was going to be divided into the time my mother was alive and the time she was not. The first era contained everything I knew about the person I was: the farmhouse in Goshen, the chickens whose eggs we collected on those mornings we walked together up the hill, the days I lay in the sheep pen with my mouth open and a book held to the sky, the lonely teenage years in Goshen, the year I spent at the state university in western New York, the experience of arriving eager and naive at Oxford, the wandering years in Berlin, Jerusalem, and London, my non-relationships with the women I had not known how to love, the tireless writing by which I had tried and failed to make sense of my early life, the night my mother called to ask me to come home. I knew this variation of myself standing by the hospital window in the evening darkness. My mother knew him, too. But within me was another self. This person would emerge in time from the constellation of half-formed characteristics within me. He would marry, become a parent, succeed or fail at his chosen path, gain and lose weight, grow and banish facial hair, age and die. His thoughts would be different from mine. I looked at my mother's closed eyes, her skin loose above her sunken cheekbones, and understood that she would never meet this man. She was leaving my life.

BOY FROM THE NORTH COUNTRY

Of course I would always carry her within me. I would think of our memories together and tell stories about her to other people. I would think of her when I needed courage or comfort. I would live by the habits she taught me, those I knew came from her and those I did not. I would look at photographs of her. What existed within me would not be my mother, but memories of my mother. These memories would mutate with time, their details silently rearranged, or, more terrifyingly, vanish without warning from my mind. I would never know what I forgot. My memories would alter without permission, growing with time into sentiments and feelings attached to partial recollections. The vast compendium of my life with her, the stray events, half conversations, arguments, gifts, jokes, car rides, unfinished sentences, breakfasts, questions—with time all this would dissolve into a few canonical claims over my eroding memory. What remained might become the most precious feeling I carried within me, but that is what it would be, the remnant of feeling toward my mother rather than my mother herself. She was passing to a place I could not follow. I was going to be left behind, forever reaching toward the totality of her, the vastness of her personality, of any life, that supersedes the memory it leaves behind. Her contradictions, the variety and range of her facial expressions, the opinions she expressed in conversations I did not know I had forgotten—all this my mind was not, despite its most visceral desires, able to retain. I was helpless against my own design. I would remember her, but any memory risked deceiving myself. I would tell stories about her, but any story risked deceiving others. Is this how the whole human condition continues, one incomplete mutation at a time?

There was no alternative to memory and to story. The only way to live would be to tell. It was only through recollection that I would be able to recreate the intimacy I felt now, in these fleeting hours, when I could still press my hand to my mother's gaunt cheek, or place my fingers in hers, and feel myself involuntarily absorbed by the rush of memory conjured by the primordial touch of my skin against hers. For no matter how long I lived, or the distance I roamed from my origins, or the person I became, what could ever compare to the touch of my mother's skin, my first and most enduring impression of this world? The body from which I was born, and, like a memory, like a story, passed on imperfectly into the world.

Sweat shone on her forehead. I tried to grip the incomprehensible fact that all I would ever know about her thoughts and feelings she had already said to me. Her relationship to her parents, the names of her childhood friends, what she had learned and lost in her romantic relationships, her thoughts about flowers, tea, marriage, Ibsen, coconut oil, ladybugs—all that remained of this was what could be recalled. The thoughts she kept to herself, the parts of her that lived beyond what any two people know about one another: she was taking it all with her. There would be no archive of her thoughts, silent or spoken.

The same was true for what she knew of my life. All I would ever know of what she thought and observed about me had already been imparted. The age at which I learned to walk, the foods that as a toddler I loved or feared, the color of my first winter coat, my reaction the day she brought Bessie home to the farmhouse, the patterns in the friendships I made and lost, and in the romantic partners I chose—all this was blurred to me by either distance or proximity, by the fact that these were matters of my life rather than a life observed. Only she had witnessed my life in such detail.

When had she first called me her sunshine boy? She would never again say those words. I felt myself nearing that moment that divided the two looming eras of my life, and I knew that in the time ahead I would never become as meaningful a man, partner, parent, friend, or writer as I might have become with her guidance. How could a life lived only by my own best judgment ever equal a life in which I also had hers? I, too, would one day observe a human life through birth, infancy, adolescence, and adulthood. I would be condemned to do this without her wisdom. I would have to place the magenta cap she knit on the head of a child she never knew.

There was no choice other than to begin the morphine drip. She had told me every way she could. I would not sign the paperwork today. We would sleep together, in this room, one more night.

"I'm not ready," I called to the night.

My mother breathed slowly. I felt her eyes open and her voice saying to me, *Yes, you are. You have everything you need inside of you.*

"I'm not . . ." I kissed her forehead, begging her to wake. I hadn't signed the forms. With the IVs working she could still live through the week. We could talk one last time.

I'll always be with you, my mother said.

"Please don't . . ." I begged the night.

You have so many wonderful things waiting for you in this life, she told me. *You have such a life to live.*

"I don't want you to go," I cried.

There was so much in this life I did not expect, my mother said. *There was also joy.*

"I can't let go of you . . ."

You're not letting go. I'm here with you. Everything will always be as it was, only a little different.

Seventeen

On the fourth day I woke to sunlight. White clouds mingled in the expanse of sky, drawing nearer and farther from one another, infinite Pangeas of the sky. A cloud parted, and I remembered a summer night when I was eight and woke to the howl of the coyote, and saw the moon fiery in the black sky. Bessie lay asleep beside me, paws crossed. Tiptoeing into the hallway I saw my mother's door ajar and her bed empty. I wandered into the night, sweat trickling along the slight indent of my chest. I was a boy in the darkness. The coyote howled and a silhouette sat on the hill above the house. I went still with fear. My mother was alone as the coyote howled and roamed in the night.

Gathering my Arthurian courage, I charged up the hill, unafraid of any beast. I came panting to my mother's side, and in a rush told her she had nothing to fear, I would lead her down the hill into the safety of the house. A knowing smile flickered on her face. "You are brave, my sunshine boy," she said, "but we have no enemies in the night. For all their howling, the coyote will not harm us so long as we do not harm them. We are all admiring the same moon." She took me in her arms and we gazed at the orange light in the sky. I woke the following morning in my own bed, Bessie sleeping beside me, and I might have believed it all a dream had I not walked with my mother to the barn to collect our morning eggs and seen in the high grass the indent where two bodies had sat through the night.

Coughing echoed in the hospital room. My mother lay on a slight incline in bed, her eyes closed and green shirt stained by sweat. Tiny gray hairs rose like exclamation points from her scalp.

I looked at her lidded eyes and remembered that this was the day I would sign the forms to end her life. She was still breathing. She had spoken yesterday. Her palm was warm in mine. The IVs could keep her alive for an indefinite time. The hospital could not force me to sign the form. We could stay as long as we wanted.

She had been clear. She was ready.

Why had she not told me about the cancer when she was first diagnosed? We could have had more time together. We could have acknowledged that she was dying. We could have spoken about what we would each endure. If we'd had more days together, sipping the iced tea she made from the red clover that grew in our woods, watching her favorite films, cooking her favorite meals, sharing our best memories, then I could have accepted her decision to end her life in Vermont.

Why had we not done this? My mother had never even broached the possibility that I come home as soon as she was diagnosed. She had waited until the diagnosis was terminal. She had decided for me.

She stirred in bed. Her eyes did not open. I called to her. She did not respond. I took her palm in mine. Everything would have been more bearable if we had had more time together.

She inhaled another labored breath, and I understood that the summer I imagined was just that: an imagined alternative, a design for life in retrospect. Life is only experienced by forward movement. She could never have arranged the summer by which I convinced myself, a moment before, that I would have been able to come to terms with her death. No plan could have prepared me for what I felt now, for life is not as we imagine it but rather that image deformed by emotion, hope, dreams, the abrupt, accidental, and astonishing.

We had spent her last days together. We had watched her favorite films. We had cooked her favorite meals. No volume of time together could have prepared me for the end of her life.

Her lips fluttered. I didn't want to look at the clock.

A bleaker thought came. I remembered her saying the greatest wound inflicted by Herbert Zuckerman was the uncertainty of whether her parents loved her enough to take her side. I saw Ralph Summers's hand moving down her dress at Bennington, and Ted Lore gripping her neck in the motel room in Iowa City, and the rapist's knife pointed at her on 78th Street, and her divorce from Simon shortly after I was born, and Roger leaving her while she slept beside me in the hospital, and Luke shoving her to the floor that night I was fifteen. I thought of the surprise in her voice as she woke the second day at the hospital and saw me sleeping in the cot beside her, and I registered the unnerving possibility that she had never asked me for all she needed because it had never occurred to her that she could.

Why hadn't I come home of my own volition? I knew her well enough to guess that she might not ask. Why had I allowed those Sunday evening conversations to always drift toward my concerns—what I was writing, thinking, feeling? We talked about her clients, flower beds, Lucy, and latest date. Still my concerns had always been primary. Had I given her the love and security that had been so difficult for her to find? Had I ever broken the assumption that shaped her life, that others could be counted on only to disappoint? Had I made her feel that she could tell me the least comfortable of all facts, that she was dying?

I had understood myself as the conscientious son. That didn't square with all the facts. Perhaps I resembled something else: one of the countless men who floated wide-eyed toward my mother, one more in the long line of men who believed he loved her without truly understanding her, who took from her without ever pausing to give.

It was nearly ten in the morning. She was still breathing. She did not want to be. Whatever failures I was responsible for as her son, however I had given and not given what she needed from me, I had one last responsibility.

She lay peacefully in bed, eyes closed. "It's always special having time with you," she had said at her last chemotherapy session. "You might say it's my favorite thing in the world." She had chosen to avoid the unbearable pain of telling me she was leaving this world. She had decided that the last weeks we had together would not be shadowed by my struggle to accept what neither of us could change: that soon we would no longer see or speak to one another, that she would see no more of the son she had birthed, nurtured, and raised. She had chosen for us to live each day together, free from the truth of her impending death, for as long as we could.

That was the gift my ignorance had given her. Maybe it was not the choice I would have made. It had been hers.

I kissed her damp forehead.

In the fluorescent hallway several nurses sat behind the intake desk. Judy typed into a desktop computer. The look she gave me suggested she had consulted the legal department after our last conversation. I nodded resolutely. The hard lines of her face quieted and her eyes fell into understanding. From her desk she withdrew a clipboard and pen.

The words blurred on the page. I did not read them. We were past legal liabilities. The only reasons to delay were my own. They could not stand. I owed my mother this signature. The pen touched the white paper. I wrote the date, September 13, 2017. My hand trembled. From the moment I moved the pen across the page to form the letters of my name, this hand, which I would need to write, to remember, to recreate, would always be the hand that signed away my mother's life. I could not do it alone. I closed my eyes and felt her beside me. Her arms around my shoulders, her hand guiding mine, the way we invented stories by the fireplace when I was a child. The name—half mine, half hers—materialized on the page in the handwriting we shared.

In her room my mother breathed lightly. I took her palm in mine. I told her.

Her eyes opened. Love shone in her hazel eyes.

"Evan," she murmured. "Remember that you have. Everything. You need. Sunshine boy."

She breathed deeply, exhausted by the effort of speaking. Her tears streamed down my cheeks.

"Take care," she rasped, "of Lucy. Need each other."

The lids of her eyes closed. Her rib cage rose and fell. She inhaled another breath, gathering her strength.

"Evan . . . please don't blame. Anything that happened. Only love."

She was frailer than at any point in the last weeks, but she was still my mother, guiding me toward the understanding I would need to keep living.

"I'll be with you," I said. "I am here."

We remained that way a long time. Her hand in mine. Her rib cage rising and falling with each breath. Tears on my face and hers.

That evening I reached for *Harry Potter* and began to read aloud to her. She gently shook her head. There were only six pages of the book remaining. I wanted to read her the end of the story. She needed only to lie in bed and listen, as I lay falling asleep as she read to me so many childhood evenings. She no longer had the strength even for this. What mattered was not the symbolism of returning to her the story she gave me, but rather her comfort as she lay dying. Everything significant was in our touching hands. That was the purpose of the Harry Potter books, to convey the primacy of love. When I was a child, it had been the story of an ordinary boy who becomes a wizard. For my mother it must have always been the story of how a mother's love protected her son. That is the deep magic Harry is learning all along, not the skill of casting spells or flying a broomstick but rather the transformative power of love. In every encounter with darkness Harry relies not on magic but love: trust in his friends, the goodness of strangers, his mother's sacrificial protection.

I didn't know what time it was when Cynthia knocked on the door. We embraced, son and stranger, caretaker and executioner, two people who understood nothing and everything about one another.

Cynthia withdrew a vial of crystal liquid from her medical cart. She reached for the IV, and, as she replaced the liquid nutrition with the morphine, I thought of the figure in Jacques-Louis David's *The Death of Socrates* who, as he hands the goblet of hemlock to the condemned philosopher, turns away and clasps his hand over his eyes, unable to look at the man whose life he must end. Socrates does not flinch from the hemlock. He takes it in hand as he continues to speak, defiantly gesturing as his distraught disciples cry out, weep, beseech him to live, lean nearer for any word of parting wisdom. The four dialogues concerned with Socrates's death tell us that after his conviction in the Athenian court he is given the choice between exile or suicide. His disciples try desperately to persuade him not to end his life. He refuses their every argument. The soul, Socrates says, is immortal. He will live on through his teaching. This is why Jacques-Louis David paints Socrates gesturing skyward in his final hour.

The only figure in the painting who does not try to persuade Socrates against the hemlock sits at the foot of the bed. He faces away from his teacher, head bent and eyes closed in resignation. His ear is turned toward Socrates. For this is Plato, the student whose dialogues are the fullest living record of the life and thought of Socrates, as the philosopher himself wrote nothing of his own teaching. Near Plato's feet rest the scroll and ink pot by which he will record Socrates's death. Something else has always interested me about the Plato of this painting: Jacques-Louis David's choice to depict him as an elderly man. The crown of his head is balding, and his curls are gray. He bows his head and clasps his hand with resigned wisdom, whereas the younger disciples openly despair. Plato appears older even than Socrates, who is rendered with a finely muscled body, reddish beard, and energetic posture. Socrates was two generations older than Plato, who at the time of Socrates's death would have been between twenty-four and twenty-nine. Jacques-Louis David's portrait is not of an aged man but rather a wise one.

The crystal liquid began to flow from the IV into my mother's body. She lay with her eyes closed. Her hand clenched mine. She was leaving her body. She was leaving my life. The parts of myself that were incomplete were mine to finish now.

I saw ahead of me the final hours in which I would still be able to touch my mother's hand and cheek and forehead. The drug would travel through her bloodstream, gradually desensitizing her to smell and touch, the distance growing between the sensation we each experienced when our fingers touched, the probability that she might ever speak again dwindling into nothingness.

Cynthia nodded toward the hall. I did not want to leave my mother's side. Every moment was precious. Cynthia beckoned again, her hair white beneath the fluorescent light. I followed her. She closed the door behind me and glanced around cautiously.

"There's something you need to understand about the morphine," Cynthia said quietly. "Please don't repeat that I've shared this with you. Understood?"

I nodded, hardly conscious of my own body.

"Your mother," she said, "will be able to survive the initial dosage for some time. Technically this is pain management, because legally the hospital can't end her life. To increase her dosage, there needs to be a record of her medical proxy asking for more morphine. So that falls to you. It's best to say your mother is having trouble sleeping and needs more morphine. Not every nurse will understand. You will find those who do."

"But I already signed the document. I . . ."

"It's not how I would choose to arrange things," Cynthia said.

"How long will this take?" I pleaded. "How many times do I have to ask?"

"I can't say," Cynthia said. "It's never quick. You will know when the end is near. She will snore deeply, almost as if in a trance."

Cynthia rested her hand on my shoulder for the briefest moment and nodded sympathetically. She turned and walked down the hall. I still hadn't called my grandmother. I didn't want to say the words aloud. My grandmother's imagination was the last place where my mother was still well, happy to be home with Lucy and me.

In my mother's room the wall clock read 11:19, three minutes after

BOY FROM THE NORTH COUNTRY

Cynthia and I left the room. Every moment my mother remained alive was holy. But what was the significance of those holy moments in the infiniteness of time? My mother was born in December 1953, and I in January 1991. If I lived to the average life expectancy for a college-educated American male, I would survive until 2072. Of the one hundred and nineteen years one of us inhabited life, my mother and I would share only twenty-six, a mere fifth of our collective time. My mother breathed, her eyes closed and body resting. It did not matter how much longer she lived. I did not need more time to know what it meant to be her son.

My hand lay on her warm cheek. Soon her breathing would stop. I would leave the hospital and call cemeteries and make the arrangements for my mother's body to travel from this bed into the earth. I wanted to be able to touch her forehead as long as it was still moist. To observe the sweat on her neck. To wipe the dribble of saliva from her chin. To breathe her breaths. To be alive with her in the same room as long as possible.

Her breath quickened and her eyes fluttered open and I recognized the narcissism of my desire that she remain alive. I was hoping for her to live another tormented day while she had made clear since the last morning at the house that she no longer wanted to live.

I began to speak in a slow voice, describing my earliest memories, collecting kindling as she cut firewood on those winter afternoons, riding Misty through the forest, my mother reading to me by the fire. I described to her in all the detail I could conjure the plays we performed for one another in the living room and the stories she read aloud to me. I told her about the voices she used for the Sheriff of Nottingham and King Arthur. Did she remember those summer afternoons we drove the hills and saw two figures meandering over the valleys and she said,

"Now there are two people looking for a way to be alive"? And when it thundered I held Bessie beneath my bed. Where were you during those thunderstorms, Mom? You must have been closing the windows against the rain and herding our sheep and chickens into the barn. I sat beside her as the moon vanished from the sky, and I was no longer sure if she could hear me, and tears came down my cheeks as I said to her in the silence of the night, "Thank you for being my mother. Thank you for giving me your self . . ."

Late that night I stood to use the bathroom in the corner of our room. The door closed behind me, and she cried out. I crossed the darkness toward her. My hand came into hers.

"Don't leave," she murmured. "Can't do it without my child."

Eighteen

O n the fifth day I stood at the window as streaks of light fractured the dark sky. Birds sang, their melody reminding me of a song whose lyrics remained just beyond my grasp. Through my memory flew the birds who visited the farmhouse when I was a child. My eyes would rise from my book as I lay in the grass, following my mother's gaze as she exclaimed, "A blue jay!" or "Oh, a cardinal!" Called by the wonder in her voice, I would search the blue skies for the bird she described. "Where?" I might shout, looking over the mountains. She would stand behind me, a hand on my shoulder as she pointed toward the pine trees or rosebushes or lush lawn, saying, "Can you see her, Evan? Oh, now there are two blue jays!" And I would see two blue jays gliding through the spring morning.

My mother lay at a slight incline in the medical bed. Drool dripped on her chapped lips. She had not eaten in six days, and the bones of her neck and shoulders pressed outward through what little flesh remained. Beneath the sheet her legs were thin indents. She could not have weighed so little since she was a child. I stood beside her, my mind wandering to the photograph of the starved inmates lying in narrow bunks at Buchenwald, their ribs protruding and arms ghostly thin, the bewildered eyes of Elie Wiesel—the sole survivor of his family—at the center of the photograph. I dabbed a tissue at the saliva on my mother's chin.

Had she known that her body would decay like this, the stench of her sweat gathering in the room, her skin turned almost translucent over her shrunken facial bones? Is this how she imagined death, birds singing outside a hospital room as morphine slowed her heart?

She had known since I was a child that she had the BRCA gene, the genetic mutation that signals dramatically increased odds of suffering breast and ovarian cancer. Genes are the fundamentals of human life, but she had said they do not suggest a single fate. The specific way a gene manifests is shaped by human choice: our diet, exercise, and relationship to stress. She always believed her decisions could minimize her risk of cancer. If the disease came, she could use all she knew to survive. Her faith was optimism. With the right support, she had told me the first day we came home from her surgery, our bodies can heal from far more than we think.

She must have known that cancer is not randomly distributed. The BRCA gene appears in every demographic, but there is only one in which it is overrepresented: Ashkenazi Jews. One of every four hundred women in the United States has the BRCA gene. Among Ashkenazi Jews the number is one in forty. In men the disparity is even greater: one in one thousand American men have the BRCA gene, while in Ashkenazi Jews the number is one in sixty.

My mother never tried to explain this discrepancy. But she knew that childhood trauma, sexual violence, and domestic violence are linked to a higher risk of cancer. She had said we could not know. She had said that her choice was to live as healthy a life as she could. Still, I could not help but wonder. Was the mutation of my mother's BRCA gene from the possibility of cancer into cancer itself caused by her lineage of trauma? Had each sexual, physical, and emotional assault culminated in the mutation of cancer genes within her ovaries, leading her to the medical bed in which she now lay, the morphine nodding her to permanent sleep? Was my mother, who conjured the resilience to live through those men, now dying at sixty-three because of them?

She had said this was only one story. She had chosen to live by caring for herself in all the ways she could.

Her personal history might explain why the BRCA gene had been triggered, not why she had inherited it. That could only be explained by collective rather than personal history. Was the occurrence of the BRCA gene in Jewish bodies at thirteen times the general rate unrelated to the history of incineration, expulsion, exile, and enslavement from Pharaoh's Goshen to Auschwitz? Was the inexplicable frequency of the BRCA gene the historical consequence of Jewish experience, passed from generation to generation, like the prayers of the Siddur or the stories of the Haggadah?

What lived within my mother's body also lived within mine. The gene would not be satisfied only to take her life. It would do all it could to mutate within me and my children and the children of my children's children, a curse that, like a story, cannot be outrun. It was an illusion of time to see only my mother in the hospital bed. I was lying there with her. Beside us were all the generations to come.

I tried to slow my breathing. I was telling myself a story rather than reaching for a scientific explanation. But there was no scientific explanation.

I imagined my mother on the day the results came, an ordinary day of my childhood. She would have sat at her cherry desk in the sunroom, speaking on the phone to a doctor, or reviewing lab tests, confronted with the likelihood that hers would be an abbreviated life.

I wiped drool from her lips. Despite all she knew about her medical odds, she never would have permitted herself to imagine the end. She had struggled to remain alive as she knew best. She had never stopped believing there was another medical option. All her life she protected her body every way she could. It would have been unthinkable for her to accept that there was nothing left to do. In her holistic practice she often worked with patients who came to her after being told there was no treatment for their condition. How many Lyme patients had she been able to help through nutrition and supplements after they were told that nothing could be done besides heavy antibiotics?

She must have understood that, if death came, she would not choose its terms. It would be greater than her efforts. Sunlight gleamed on her bald head. The pretense of a well-ordered death is for the living rather than the dying. My mother was not Hedda Gabler, who insisted on the beauty of a spectacular death. She did not require epiphany. She had lived her life. She had been true to life and true to me. She was in unimaginable pain. She wanted to leave this world. Only I insisted on assigning meaning to the details of her death. I was still alive, and for the living, unlike the dead, everything is burdened with significance. The experience in which I found myself was not literature, with its structures, rhythms, and revelations, but rather life, in which nothing is well-ordered. My instinct was to demand meaning from this event. My obligation was to help my mother out of this world as she had helped me live within it.

I looked at the clock. I was supposed to have asked for more morphine every half hour. Since the drip began, the day before, I had not yet found the courage to ask for a single increase. I swayed into the hall. Nurses passed one another. The nearest was a middle-aged man in green scrubs whose name tag read Salvador. I asked him to increase the dosage. He blinked.

"How long has she been on her current dose?" he asked.

"Since last night."

"Well," Salvador said matter-of-factly, "let's give it more time to work."

Two female nurses glanced uncomfortably at me, their expression conveying that I had so boldly violated an unspoken code that it was not even worth explaining my mistake.

"I was told," I said, keeping my voice low, "that it's important my mother has an adequate dosage at all times. She's having trouble sleeping." I emphasized these last words, as Cynthia had instructed me.

"Like I said," Salvador replied, "you can check with us later in the day."

I stared dumbstruck. Was I going to have to plead for the medical staff to send more morphine into my mother's bloodstream, dulling her senses, depriving her heart of the will to beat and her lungs of the power to draw air? Was I going to be forced to make this decision again and again, the tormented choice eternally recurring beneath the harsh fluorescent light of the hospital hallway?

"Please!" I said. "She can't sleep . . ."

Cynthia stood at the far end of the hall, her white hair drawn into a ponytail, nodding to a male nurse my age. I hurried toward her and began to explain and the woman turned and was not Cynthia. "Sorry," I said, backing away. The fluorescent light was bright in my eyes. I walked down the hall toward the bathroom. Strangers stared at me. How loudly had I shouted for more morphine? I shut the bathroom door. My yellow stream of urine was thick and putrid, and my penis, which, like the rest of my body, I had not washed in five days, was dry and shriveled, its odor fetid. When was the last time I ingested anything other than the scrambled egg powder and machine coffee? My mother's last food had been miso soup. Was she hungry as she lay in bed? Or was she in too much pain to feel hunger? Hot water scalded my hands. Every moment was one less that I could hold her hand in mine. Once she was dead she would remain dead forever. My life would never be as it was. In the mirror my eyes were crusted with tears, wrinkles intermingled with shadow.

I had only one responsibility. She needed more morphine.

I threw open the bathroom door and charged into the hallway. The elevator let off two men my age in white lab coats, and as we nearly collided their eyes seized on me. The first stepped forward, palm held up, signaling to a wild animal that he meant no harm.

"Whoa there, buddy, are you lost?" he said.

"Where are your shoes, friend?" asked the second man.

Where were my shoes? I had no memory of taking off my sneakers, nor could I remember wearing them the last days. I was still dressed in the sweatshirt and jeans I had worn the morning we came to the hospital. My hands smelled faintly of urine. I saw myself as I must appear to the medical residents, which is what I assumed they were: a man who seemed to have neither slept nor showered in days, wandering the hospital without shoes. There was no time for any of the things that could go wrong if I didn't immediately dispel the notion that I was unwell.

"Thank you for asking," I said in an even voice. "I'm on my way to room 2223. Good luck with your rotation."

I drew meditative breaths as I walked to my mother's room. Opening the door, I heard a tearing nasal noise. She lay with her bald head tilted back, nodding rhythmically, her eyes closed. I came to her side and took her palm in mine. Her left eye twitched. The medical staff had told me nothing about the volume of morphine necessary to end her life. There was no way to know if she would live through the night. If she would survive a sixth day in the hospital, a ninth, twelfth, or fifteenth. I wasn't going to make it through the days to come if I didn't slow my breathing. I inhaled, as my mother had in the moments of her most immense pain. I closed my eyes and felt her beside me in the grass in her lotus pose.

Her phone buzzed on the nightstand. I said hello in a voice quiet enough not to wake her. A female voice introduced herself as Stephanie from Dr. Chen's office.

Right. They must be wondering why we never arrived.

"I just called Orange Regional," she said. "You didn't mention to Dr. Chen that your mother has an acute bladder obstruction. Unfortunately, Dr. Chen can't be of assistance."

The euphemism stung the silence. I glanced at my mother and she released another nasal snore. Her body odor was thick in the air. Had I not mentioned the bladder obstruction, or had Dr. Chen not listened carefully? It didn't matter. She had told her secretary to call and pronounce my mother dead. Dr. Chen had treated her for months and had not made the final call herself. The dying streamed into her office and the dead were no longer her concern. Dr. Chen had done all she could. But her responsibilities had always been to my mother's body rather than to my mother. This was the primary difference between conventional medicine and holistic health as my mother practiced it: she did not believe the mind, body, and soul could be neatly divided. She sat for hours in the sunroom with each person who came to see her, listening to their family histories and emotional vulnerabilities, believing that the fundamentals of health begin with the relationship to oneself. That routines that support well-being are more sustainable when rooted in self-love, while destructive habits—overeating, substance abuse—thrive on a damaged relationship to the self. She looked into the totality of each person, listening to their struggles, suggesting changes in nutrition and supplements and exercise, forcing nothing, working through each person's feeling within his or her body, a human treating other humans, believing always that each of us is designed to heal. I heard her saying that if something feels wrong, a new ache or pain, try to think through what might be causing it, consider nutrition and stress and posture. "I know my body well enough to understand when something is wrong," she had said about her cancer, which she had detected despite the infamous frequency with which ovarian cancer goes undiagnosed. She was never satisfied with one approach, which is why she had supplemented the conventional cancer treatment with the BEMER, Huel, infrared sauna, grass-fed burgers, meditation, vibration plate, medical marijuana, turmeric tea, and carefully selected nutrition. She was always reaching for another way to heal, trying alternate paths, like an artist determined to see. She had devoted herself every day to the health of each person who came to her, and as I stood at her bedside, listening to her nasal snore, I felt the holiness of this commitment.

I kissed her forehead. There had never been any possibility of taking the ambulance to the city to see Dr. Chen. I thanked the woman on the phone and hung up.

The sounds of the hospital corridor entered our room, snippets of conversation and beeping machines. I turned to see our door opening, and through it striding a robust man cloaked in the garments first worn by Hasidic Jews in eighteenth-century Poland. He wore no *payos*, and from this I understood he was Chabad, the Hasidic sect devoted to persuading other Jews to their ways. How many times in North London had an anxious teenage boy in the black hat of the Chabad stopped me on the street—"Excuse me, you are Jewish?"—and asked me to wrap tefillin or shake the lulav on Sukkot? I always gave the same response: "Yes, I am Jewish. No thank you, good shabbes." I never ceased to be amused by the expression on these boys' pimpled faces as they absorbed the unfamiliar contradictions of my response. Most of my Jewish friends demurred when approached by the Chabadniks, but I was never bothered to acknowledge what I am and wish the teenage emissaries a good day as they said to me, in the same tone with which the rabbi, closing the door behind him now, asked, "You are Jewish?"

I felt fury at his intrusion. We were not on the neutral public terrain of the streets, but rather the intimate space in which my mother's life was waning. He must feel so certain in the superiority and necessity of his official Judaism that he had entered without knocking to offer final blessings my mother had not asked to receive. Why did he think he had the right to enter our room: because he kept kosher, wore a yarmulke, was a pureblood? She didn't need him to make her a Jew. There was Judaism before the rabbis and there will be Judaism after the rabbis. He didn't want to pray with my mother as the distinct person she was. How could this be holy? To judge someone by nothing but blood? He was here not for her but himself. And what prayer did he want to say? The same he said each day, without distinct thought or intention. I wondered if he had ever heard the teaching of the Kotzker Rebbe, who said there is no greater scoundrel than he who prays today because he prayed yesterday. What did this rabbi care for Judaism beyond his tefillin and tzitzit? What did he know of what Jews had felt, thought, and written in the last two hundred years: Kafka, Proust, Oz, Peretz, Kushner, Gornick, Leonard Cohen, Singer, Potok, Dvora Baron, Sholem

Aleichem. Judaism is a story and he had stopped reading long ago. He had worn down the tablets and wasted the wine. Had he never heard the teaching of the Baal Shem Tov that all the laws and all the rituals can never be as holy as one open heart?

"We," I said to the rabbi, "are Jewish. Please close the door as you leave."

He looked longingly at my mother, as if I was denying him a fundamental right. Then he turned out of the door. After a moment I heard his voice echo down the hall: "You are Jewish?"

There was a knock at the door. A moment later Salvador entered, pity and concern in his expression.

"Cynthia told me to look for you," he said. "You can't ask for morphine like that in front of everyone. My shift is ending. Cynthia will be back tonight. I can't say there's anyone on shift now who understands these things."

Salvador increased the dosage and left the room. My mother's head nodded slightly. I sat beside her, reading *Harry Potter* aloud, the words gathered around us, rising from the floor, lying on the windowsill, sitting with the drool at the corners of her mouth, resting in the stains of the last socks my mother would ever wear.

These were my only obligations: to read to her, to wipe spittle from her lips, to ask for more of the drug that made her less able to know that I was there.

At twelve o'clock the nurse on call said, "Why don't we wait a little longer."

At one o'clock the nurse said, "Young man, I'd appreciate your patience."

At two o'clock the nurse said, "Please find me in the evening, as we discussed."

Through the day I repeated the same words: "Can we please increase the dosage? She's having trouble sleeping."

"Please remember this is a purely palliative procedure," Judy insisted. "It's never easy for family members. Maybe you should take a day at home?"

I stared at her, this pale woman with managerial eyes who believed people should die alone. The sky was black beyond the window. I returned to my mother's room. She was snoring peacefully, her arms still at her sides. The signs of her coming death had been apparent since the first night we sat together at the cedar table on the hill. A more practiced eye than mine would have seen. It had never occurred to me that my mother dying was even a possibility, because my mother was not supposed to die. I could understand her only as someone who was alive, because this was the sole way I had known her. It was the condition in which she was familiar to me, and therefore the only conceivable condition in which she could exist. Death was for other people. When I had heard of an acquaintance whose parent died, this fact felt so remote from my own life that it seemed neither a threat nor a possibility. Every person I met from this moment onward would only know my mother as someone who was dead, and only know me as someone with a dead mother. This fact would be as normalized to others as it would be jarring to me. For those who encountered my mother while she was dead, rather than while she was living, death would appear to be her natural condition, just as a refugee arriving weary and precarious to a foreign land is perceived as in his natural condition, when perhaps in the country from which he came he had a comfortable apartment, loving family, hot showers, devoted friends and colleagues, all taken from him by historical events over which he had neither control nor foresight. Like him, my mother had crossed the veil that separates those who understand their lives as under their own control, and those who understand that even the events most intimate to our lives are not subject to our own design. I could feel myself crossing that veil with her.

A bird flew by the window, a common starling with no unique markings. A lyric came to me, from the song I had struggled to remember that morning, a man lamenting in an anguished voice that the only thing to do was keep on keeping on like a bird that flew. I repeated the line to myself, trying to place its rhythm within all the lyrical fragments in my mind. I didn't want to be that bird. I didn't want to have to keep on keeping on. I didn't want to return to the world beyond the hospital window. I wiped spittle from my mother's chapped lips and another line in the song came to me, and I whispered aloud: "'The only thing I knew how to do was to keep on keeping on like a bird that flew, tangled up in blue.'"

The words lingered in the room and my mother's bald head jerked backward, and I understood that we were never going to finish the conversation about Dylan. There was so much she hadn't told me. She had not seen him just once, nine months before my birth, as she had said when I was a teenager. She had seen him for years before I was born. The story of a single encounter nine months before my birth was that, a story. Despite all my mother had told me about their relationship in the last weeks, I did not know the truth, not even close. Now she was taking it with her.

I stood trembling in the room.

In the faint reflection of the window I saw his hair on my scalp. She had never said I was his son. Surely she intended to leave me this ambiguity no more than she wanted to die without acknowledging the end of her life. I heard my mother saying that night in the car when I was fifteen, "What matters in life is whether people are there for you.

BOY FROM THE NORTH COUNTRY

When you suffer, when you thrive, who is there for you?" She had told me she wanted to live her own life, not be a footnote in Dylan's. I looked at my reflection and understood that my mother's refusal to discuss him was one prolonged act of protection, not against the answer but rather the question. Her desire had always been for me to become my own person in my own way.

I needed to have faith in her. I needed to trust that she had seen further than I could see.

Her palm was warm in mine, and we were in her sunroom on those childhood mornings, my mother asking me to feel within me the meaning of the words we repeated together.

I am loved. I am protected. I am free.

There were only hours left now in her life. Tonight, or in the morning, or the following night or the following morning, her lungs would stop breathing, her heart would cease to beat, the warmth would drain from her hands and forehead, and the sweat would no longer seep through the skin layered over her skull. She would no longer be ill and instead become a corpse. I would drive alone to the farmhouse. I could not fathom what waited for me. I did not know where I would live or who I would love. I wouldn't be flying back to London. It was time to create something new, to reach into the past, to draw on what came before me to make something worthwhile of my own life. It would be the most uncertain task I ever faced. I would only be able to endure what waited for me as my mother's son. I needed the courage of the twenty-year-old woman in the Yorkville apartment who, as she listened to Dylan sing a love song about his wife, understood that he did not love her and that she needed to achieve her own life. I needed the courage of the woman who made a life for herself in the woods with the joys of blackberries and bluebirds and a son dressed in home-knit sweaters. I needed the resilience of the woman who drew on her own suffering to help others heal. I needed the strength of the woman who refused to concede her life to cancer, who drew on all she knew to keep herself alive as long as possible, who had endured chemotherapy even after she knew it could not save her life, only because it would mean more time with me. I needed the sense of self of the woman who, at twenty-two, looked at her reflection and understood that she would heal only by giving the love she had never received.

It had been the purpose of her life. It was the reason she left Dylan, and the reason I had to leave him as well. He didn't love me. He didn't know me. He couldn't heal me.

My mother's love could.

She nodded another involuntary snore, and her bald head caught the overhead light, and I saw with startling sadness that she had spent her life in pursuit of lasting romantic love and had not found it. Now she never would.

I heard myself insisting to her that love is an illusion demanded by procreation. People never sound more foolish than when they are in love. I had told myself these views were reasonable, rooted in universal truth more than my personal experiences. I was fine. I bore no scars. My non-relationships were my choice, a responsible preference for freedom under mutually agreed circumstances. How had I convinced myself that there was no connection between all the men who came and went during my childhood, the trust given and broken, and my frightened heart? Beneath my arguments had always been the fear of a boy alone in the dark. I stood at my mother's bedside and shuddered at everything I had permitted myself to do under the cover of detached justification, my wordless escapes from Christine in Berlin and Mariam in Jerusalem and Laurene in London. I had recreated the patterns of male deception that wounded my mother's life and mine. Realization gathered on my unwashed face, as discomforting as the dried tears and dead cells that had accumulated on my skin in the five days since I'd showered.

My hand lay on my mother's shoulder. I needed to wake her. She didn't have to worry. She had lived her life in pursuit of love she never found, while at twenty-six I had not even begun to search. The uncompleted task fell to me. Nothing is holier than love. I saw that now.

She would never know. Her palm no longer responded to mine. My words could not reach her. Only my life could be an answer.

Nineteen

On the sixth day I woke to a tearing nasal noise. My mother's eyes were closed and greenish foam gathered around her mouth. With each snore her head jerked backward and more foam rose from her lips. Through the window the sky glimmered autumn blue. This was my mother's farewell, the last of all the sounds—exhilaration, pain, language—that would ever emerge from her body. There was no response to my fingers clenching hers. Color was leaving her, the skin on her face ashen. She snored again, a long nasal snort that made me want to turn and flee her body. How much longer was I supposed to stand in the shadow and sleep at the side of her death, imprinting on my memory these images when I wanted to remember her life, the mother who held me as she rode Misty, our horse, through the woods behind our house.

I didn't have the strength to ask for more morphine. Neither could I watch her die. I had promised I would stay with her until the end. How could I have known that it would require me to stand over her as death foamed at her mouth and turned her skin ashen and reduced the human being I loved most to a corpse?

She would never know if I left now. She had already departed. It was only her body in the bed. I could not know what trauma I was inflicting on myself by standing here as life slowly left her cooling palms and sallowing skin. It was time to leave.

Sun lit the greenish foam on her lips, and I thought of a memoir I had read the year before, written by a woman who was imprisoned with her brother and parents at Theresienstadt between the ages of twelve and fourteen. She recollected life at the Nazi concentration camp in immaculate detail: the intertwined fatalism and hope of the inmates, the social relations between captives and guards, the meager food rations, sleeping arrangements, hushed speculations about the fate of loved ones, weather conditions, curfews, silent prayers, family disagreements over who should eat the last bite of potato, memories of the comfortable life left behind, song lyrics, gossip, the polio epidemic that swept the camp, and the enduring attempts of her family to find hope in dehumanizing circumstances. The writer's mother perished at Theresienstadt, and her father was murdered at Auschwitz, and every uncle and aunt on either side of her family was killed by the German race theorists. Yet writing seventy-one years after her liberation, from the American city in which she had remade herself, married, and raised children, the writer confessed that she missed the concentration camp. For it was at Theresienstadt that she lived the last two years she would ever have with her father, mother, and brother. It was at Theresienstadt that she had the particular arguments with her parents that only a thirteen-year-old can provoke. It was at Theresienstadt that she smuggled bread from the kitchens, secretly celebrated her bat mitzvah, mocked the rigid facial expression of German guards, tended to her mother's swollen hands, laughed with her brother as he read aloud the poem he wrote for her fourteenth birthday. These experiences belonged to Theresienstadt, and she could no more disown her own memories than she could rewrite her life. She was the woman who survived those years.

My mother's palm was warm in mine. I would stay with her until it no longer was.

It was a little after ten in the morning. She needed another dose of morphine.

Her phone vibrated on the nightstand. On the screen I saw the photograph of my grandmother holding me to her chest, not long after she moved to Goshen to be nearer to us.

I felt overwhelmed by gratitude that my mother had concealed from me the difficulties between her and her mother. That she had welcomed her mother into my life. That she had never let the wound she suffered as her mother's daughter prevent my grandmother from loving me. That she had helped me with all those plane tickets to Key West. That my grandmother was here with us now, in the way she could be.

I had failed to call her in time. My mother and grandmother would never be able to say goodbye.

"Bubbe," I said, crying as I said her name.

"What's happening?" she asked anxiously. "I haven't heard from either of you."

I cried into the phone, trying to explain.

"Why couldn't she eat or drink?"

"What do you mean, morphine?"

"Wasn't the chemotherapy working?"

"How can there be no way to help her?"

I heard my own confusion compressed into my grandmother's questions. With each sentence her voice grew more helpless.

"I'm sorry . . ." I said. "I wanted to tell you. I . . ."

"You've done your best, Evan." She was crying and I was crying with her. "Have you said the Shema?"

"Bubbe, I don't know the words . . ."

"Yes, you do," she cried. "Say it with me."

"Shema Yisrael," my grandmother said, and I repeated after her. "Adonai Eloheinu, Adonai Echad. Baruch Shem k'vod m'alchuto l'olam va'ed."

She repeated the prayer in English: "Hear, O Israel, Adonai is our God, Adonai is One. Blessed is God's glorious Kingdom forever and ever."

We repeated the prayer three times in Hebrew and three times in English. My grandmother wept and her tears were on my cheeks.

She said, "Has it been painful for her?"

"No," I said. "There's been no pain."

"Thank God," she said. "Thank merciful God."

"Evan?"

"Yes?"

"Can I speak to her?"

My mother lay asleep, her eyes closed.

"Yes," I said. "She may not respond, but she can hear everything you say."

"Thank God," my grandmother cried.

"Here you are," I said. "I love you."

"I love you more," my grandmother said.

I turned on the speaker, lay the phone on my mother's chest, and left the room.

Judy typed into a desktop at the hallway console, her jaw taut. Cynthia spoke quietly with an elderly couple, her hand on the man's shoulder, the fluorescent light in her white hair. I looked between Judy and

Cynthia, and saw the two paths along which grief could lead me. My mother's death would transform me. I had no choice in this. But in the transformation that awaited I had choice. It would take all my strength to resist the way death had hardened Judy's heart, and instead find the grace in which grief draped Cynthia. Her immersion in suffering had taught her that nothing is as meaningful as kindness. I could feel each of these emotions within me, the bitter and tender each laying claim to who I would become. I felt burning anger at my mother's death. I could also see my mother in her lotus pose, saying, "Anger is a poison that harms the one who drinks it." I saw her with the chemo drip attached to her arm, saying, "You've always been intelligent, but it's your heart that makes you special, Evan." My purpose in the time ahead would be to redeem my grief as my mother had redeemed her suffering. To take this broken piece of the universe within me and burnish it with my mother's love. For it was only because she had redeemed her suffering that she had been able to love me so completely. I would learn to let her goodness grow within me. To let it shape my life. Standing in the hall outside her room, I could feel my anger dissolving into gratitude that I had been born her son.

I stayed by her side as light gave way to darkness. Her palm was warm in mine. I would always be her sunshine boy.

Twenty

On the seventh day sunlight woke me on the cot. I lay beneath the sheets, looking at the clouds moving across the blue sky, as I had looked onto the pine trees beyond my bedroom window on childhood mornings, unconcerned with time, unaware of anything more enticing in all of life than the swaying trees.

My mother lay with her eyelids peacefully closed. Her chapped lips were slightly open. Her body was still. The skin on her face was ashen. She had ceased snoring.

I rose from the cot and took her palm in mine. It was no longer warm. I kissed her forehead. She was not alive.

Through all the anguished hours, I had never imagined what I would do when the moment came. There was nothing in the room to suggest that my mother and I had inhabited it for seven days. I had worn the same clothes. I had never changed the sheets on my cot. The fern sat on the windowsill, my mother's pale blue beanie folded beside it. I took the beanie in my hand and looked at the closed door. I could not bring myself to cross into the world beyond our room.

I reached once more for her hand. For a long moment we remained that way, our bodies touching, as my life had begun and hers ended.

She was no longer within her body. She was memory now.

The fluorescent light shone in the hallway. I signed papers at the console, hardly aware of the movements of my body. Someone would call from the hospital to ask to which funeral home her body should be transferred. I descended alone in the elevator. I had not been outside for more than a few minutes in seven days. Summer warmth had given way to autumn chill. I found my mother's car in the parking lot and drove out of the hospital, along the winding back roads, past sloping farmland, hay bales and grazing cows. Beside the road walked a figure in a dark suit and fur hat, and I remembered sitting as a child in my mother's rusted station wagon and asking what the wandering man was looking for, and I heard her say, "A way to be alive." I neared the stooped Hasidic man walking alongside the road, and a second figure appeared beside him, and I heard myself say in the voice of my childhood, "Look, Mom, now there are two people searching for a way to be alive." My mother laughed, not the anguished laugh of the body so shrunken that even joy caused her pain, but the laughter of the young mother she had been, a woman alone on a country road with a son too young to understand the darkness from which this life had been improbably made.

I would always be driving these hills with her, searching for a way to be alive.

Peonies rose from the grass along the driveway. They were having their best year of the decade. I let myself into the house. Lucy came to me, a knowing sorrow in her eyes. I cradled her little body to my chest. We walked through the den into my mother's sunroom, its walls lined with remedies, supplements, books. I lay on the olive massage table, and sunlight came through the bay window, and tears fell from my eyes, and sobs shuddered my body, and Lucy's kisses were warm on my unwashed face, and I heard my mother saying, as she had so long ago, "No matter what has happened to us in life, Evan, we can always heal." My tears subsided, and began once more, and night came, and morning followed, and the mountains turned maroon with autumn, and I sat at my mother's cherry desk, and dusk fell, and as I began to write the coyote howled and the freight train echoed through the valley and the pine trees swayed over the farmhouse.

Acknowledgments

My greatest gratitude is for my mother. I never could have lived the years since her death without the love she left me. Her spirit and memory were in the room with me every hour I wrote. Lucy was there, too: she curled in my lap through the writing days and slept beside me through the nights. Lucy, my little one, my sweetest, thank you for the kisses.

I am grateful that I was able to write this book in the two living spaces in which the story takes place. My mother's home in Goshen was a healing sanctuary for her and has been for me. I am grateful that I have been able to live here; grateful for the trees and sunlight, the mountains and valley. My mother's apartment in Yorkville was passed between family members until the lease came to me not long before I began this book. I am grateful for the charms and mysteries of these rooms.

I am grateful to all those who have loved and encouraged me in the long road to a first book. Lily, in whose heart our mother's spirit lives on, and who is telling her own story in her own way. Granny and Gramps, whose love was complete; thank you for giving me more than I could ever express. Diana, Mark, and Josh, and all the Kirshes and Ralskes; thank you for being my family. Tom, my brother, my friend, thank you

ACKNOWLEDGMENTS

for your love. Altair Brandon-Salmon, for his most extraordinary friendship, without which I would not be myself. Elizabeth, for her love. David, who helped me into the forest and onto the path. Lorand, for the wisdom of his night runs, for helping me understand what it means to be myself. Oskar Eustis, for your love; for showing me that it is possible to grieve vulnerably while persevering fearlessly for life. Tom Powell, for years in the trenches; nobody laughed like us. Charlie Tyson and George Knaysi, my favorite flâneurs. Ruby Namdar, for his wisdom and whiskey. Chloe Zack, for her enduring friendship and eagle eye. Anne Germanacos, for her love and friendship; for welcoming me into the communities she nurtures. Bernard Schwartz, for hoops on the days the sentences weren't coming. Jen Viscardo and Jane Lesniak, for vital encouragement in a time of great need. Andrew Bacevich, for giving me a chance. Laura Nolan, for noticing my missing song. For generous notes on this book, I am grateful to Aminatta Forna, Tony Taccone, Charlie Tyson, Elizabeth Bryant, Dan Schifrin, Daniela Hernandez, Jon Frankel, Sandra Bark, Roberto Drilea, Ben Kaplan, Beverly Holtz, and Maisie Wiltshire-Gordon. For the gifts of friendship, sustenance, and encouragement, I thank Helge Peters, Ariel Swyer, Julia Harte, Danny Avraham, Steve and Torm Ross, Michael Ames, Bobby Puckett, Ruth Cooper, Kalypso Nicolaidis, Maria Semple, Adam Shatz, Menachem Kaiser, James Lasdun, Pia Davis, Michael Greenberg, Louise Steinman, Moriel Rothman-Zecher, Sid Mahanta, Laura Newmark, Tom Weiner, Leah Morse, Nishant Batsha, and Jason Francisco.

I am indebted to John Burnham Schwartz, who, in the tradition of the great editors of old, talked me into writing a far better book than I ever could have without him. In the world to come may every writer have an editor with John's gifts. Peter Steinberg and Yona Levin told me in our first conversation that the power of this book lay in the love between a

ACKNOWLEDGMENTS

mother and son. At a time when I had despaired that any book agent would see my story in this light, Peter and Yona restored my faith. For your heart and conviction you will always have my gratitude. Chris Beha first gave me the opportunity to tell my story in *Harper's Magazine*, which I have been reading with great pleasure since I was a teenager. Thanks to the *Harper's* softball team for eternal grit and occasional victories. Thanks to *The Night Editor* reading series, which invited me to share early pages. Thanks to the entire team at Penguin Random House, and especially to Helen Rouner for her patience, Shana Jones for her precision, Yuki Hirose for her thoroughness, and my publicity and marketing dream team, Christine Johnston and Jessie Stratton, for all their hard work bringing this story to readers.